Returning to the Lion's Den

A novel by
Marco Manfre

Also by Marco Manfre

The Outcast Prophet of Bensonhurst

Blue Blue Sea

From Darkness Into Light: The Biography of a Holocaust Survivor Family
(with Ronald Isaacson)

The Bomb Shelter Confession: A Detective Butler Mystery

To my discerning editor, judicious critic, best friend, and life partner,
my wife Claire

*Violence can only be concealed by a lie, and the lie can only be
maintained by violence. Any man who has once proclaimed violence as his
method is inevitably forced to take the lie as his principle.*

Alexander Solzhenitsyn

It's better to live one day as a lion than a hundred years as a lamb.

John Gotti

1

Entering the Lion's Den

The gut-wrenching recollections returned to Daniel over and over again.

Harrowing thoughts percolated through his frazzled brain as he lay awake for hours at night, yearning for sleep. When he finally succumbed, exhausted and distraught, gruesome images and sounds populated his scrambled, disjointed dreams. He suffered through those pounding, rough-edged nightmares: the heavy dull thud of a metal bar smashing into a skull; the man crumpling against him; bloody clots of dirt on the rusted blade of the shovel; sodden clumps of pebbly soil on the dead man's face, some of it falling into his slack, open mouth; the unpleasant sensation of cold sweat drizzling down Daniel's back as he struggled to dig the furtive grave on that oppressively muggy evening; the dirty black under his fingernails that lingered, even after he had scrubbed his hands raw, a stain, a mark of his transgression, a dead weight on his soul.

Later, after he had witnessed the double murder, knowing that he had been the intended target ... then, when he took the life of a friend, and after that, when he killed two other men, the original nightmares and alarming thoughts faded, only to be replaced by new ones that were even more horrifying.

When he awakened, shaking, calling out in terror in the early morning darkness, as he often did, Daniel's first thought was of the appalling bloodshed: he groggily recalled fragments of the carnage—never sure whether those images and sounds and feelings had been in his dreams or whether they were jagged splinters of memory of those ghastly acts of violence that were painfully and permanently embedded in his consciousness.

For years, those recollections and nightmare images melted away and then returned and then departed and returned in repeated waves.

And, even though he was not plagued with thoughts of those appalling incidents during his waking hours as long as he was occupied with the tasks of living, they were always there in the background, like a frighteningly powerful flock of shadowy birds of prey whose jagged claws dug into his back, holding him captive to his unwavering guilt.

Finally, with time, as the thoughts and dreams evolved into scars on his consciousness, they faded into the recesses of his mind and his very being and became inconsequential components of who he was. He transformed, becoming tough and exacting and accustomed to violence in the way that other people, over the course of years, adapt to the more routinely unpleasant aspects of their lives. But that part of the story comes after this.

1

*****

Ruth and Raymond Montello's only child, Daniel, was born on December 24, 1979. He had the best qualities of both of his parents: his father's steadfastness and capacity for hard work and his mother's high intellect and willingness to attempt to understand all aspects of a situation or point of view. He also had the capacity for boundless love that his parents exhibited on a daily basis to each other and to him.

He was also the beneficiary of his father's skepticism in reference to all that could not be proven to be true and dependable and accurate.

In addition, he had inherited the best physical traits of both Raymond and Ruth: his father's blue eyes and powerful physique, which developed without much effort on his part by the time he was 15 years old, and his mother's clear white skin and lush, dark curly hair.

But he had a serious weakness: he never felt sure of himself or of his place in the world; as a consequence of that, he tried too hard to please everyone and ingratiate himself with others in an attempt to fit in with them.

Daniel had been ritually circumcised as an eight-day-old and had attended Hebrew school twice a week for years until the time of his bar mitzvah, so he felt Jewish, but Angie, his father's mother, took him to church every so often and explained all about Church teachings, so he felt Catholic too. His mother did not object, as long as Angie did not ask to have the boy baptized or take part in any of the other sacraments. She wanted Daniel to embrace the cultural aspects and traditions of both of his parents. She assumed that her clever child would be able to compartmentalize the Catholic and the Jewish parts of his life, as she and Raymond had been able to do throughout their years together.

When Daniel asked what he was, Ruth explained to him that his religious upbringing and, therefore, his beliefs were Jewish *and* (*and*, not *but*) that his cultural heritage was Jewish and Italian Catholic. She told him that he was lucky to be able to celebrate Hanukah *and* Christmas and Passover *and* Easter and to feel comfortable in both synagogues and churches. However, that was not the case; on the occasions when he went, he felt uncomfortable and alien in both types of houses of worship, but his mother did not know that. She thought it was wonderful that Daniel was able to read and speak Hebrew and a bit of Yiddish and understand enough Italian to carry on simple conversations with his grandparents and with the Italians in their neighborhood.

Daniel *was* able to compartmentalize both of his cultural traditions, but *that* was the problem. He thought of those practices as lessons he had learned, just like formulas in geometry and the order of the planets in the solar system.

They were distinct bits of information that he stored away to be used at the appropriate times. He felt unlike the other boys, not that their religious backgrounds and ethnic group affiliations were very important to them. However, Daniel was always stumped and embarrassed when someone new asked, "What are you?" The first time he was asked, he answered, "I'm half and half," but that led to a blank look, so he explained, "My mom's Jewish and my dad's Italian" (meaning Catholic). That led to "But *what* are you?" After thinking for a few seconds, he replied, "I'm Jewish and Italian," to which the questioner said, "You can't be. You gotta be one or the other. It's like hot and cold. You can't be both."

He thought about saying, "I'm not too hot and not too cold," thinking about the porridge in *Goldilocks and the Three Bears*. He might have said "lukewarm," if he had known the word.

It's not that the other boys mistreated or ostracized him; they just thought of him as inhabiting a bleak, barren, lonely netherworld, images of which gave them the shivers because if Daniel got run over by a bus, as had happened to Gino Cavalla when he was nine years old, his soul would not be mystically and automatically beamed to either the Catholic or the Jewish version of heaven. They felt even sorrier for Daniel when, right after his bar mitzvah, which all of them had attended, he said that he did not believe in the afterlife.

A few other boys in Daniel's neighborhood in Bensonhurst were products of Italian Catholic-Jewish marriages, but each of them was one or the other in terms of religious faith: Catholic or Jewish.

He also felt different from the others because, even though he was tall and strong, he did not like violence; in fact, his stomach turned whenever he saw boys pushing each other or fighting. While the others cheered, he turned away and waited for the brawl to end. He could never understand what motivated the boys to become angry enough to punch, kick, and gouge each other. He was equally astonished each and every time the two combatants, a couple of days later, having made amends, acted like friends again.

One other characteristic marked him as unique: once he had made a friend, he could never turn on him. Other boys shifted their alliances on a whim; today's friend became tomorrow's enemy and any friend of that enemy was also an adversary. Of course, the opposite was also true: yesterday's enemy could easily become a comrade again. Daniel could not understand that. He wondered whether he would ever feel that he was part of the fabric of his neighborhood.

Then, on a chilly Friday in January, when he was 16 years old, Daniel was introduced to Mr. Morici. Daniel's closest friend, Dominic Savarino, and he were skimming through a copy of the *Daily News*, trying to decide which movie to attend that night. They were basing their decision on which one was most likely to appeal to girls; they had been told by some older boys that on Friday nights, the movies were a great place to pick up girls "who are ready to rock and roll." They were not sure that was true, but they felt they had nothing to lose.

Dominic told Daniel that they had to leave an hour early because he had to drop off a package for his father. When Daniel had asked, years before, what Dominic's father did for a living, Dominic had said, "He owns a trucking company." Then, with a sober expression on his face, he added, "He knows people who know people, and he is associated with them."

While Daniel thought he knew what that meant, he was not sure.

An hour before the movie was scheduled to begin, they walked to the Huntington Social Club on 86th Street. It was in a storefront with no windows. Inside, there was a large room with a well-stocked bar and tables and chairs; two smaller rooms were in the back, one of which was a fully-equipped kitchen. Four men were sitting at one of the tables sipping whiskey and playing cards.

Dominic walked to the table and waited for the hand to finish. Then a large pock-marked man with jet-black hair looked up at Dominic and said to the other men, "Look. It's the man with the muscle. You here lookin' for trouble?"

Daniel's stomach muscles tightened and his hands became icy cold.

"Yeah, Mr. Morici, I was born to be trouble," Dominic said, and then he sang a few lines of *Bad to the Bone*.

Mr. Morici said, "I love the way this kid does that." Then he reached up to Dominic's face and pulled the boy down to him; they embraced and kissed each other's cheeks. He asked, "So, Dom, how's your old man doing?"

"He's dyin', Mr. Morici. He's got a 102 temperature and he's been runnin' to the can every five minutes."

"That's too bad. It must be the bad clams he ate the other night."

"Either that or my mom's cooking," Dominic countered.

"Hey, don't you be saying nothing about your mom. Seriously, tell your old man I hope he feels better. You got something for me?"

Dominic removed a fat white envelope from an inside coat pocket and handed it to Mr. Morici, who opened a corner of the seal and looked inside before putting it in one of the pockets of his sport jacket.

"Thanks, kid. And who's this hiding behind your back like a puppy?"

"He's my best friend, Daniel Montello. Daniel, this is Mr. Morici."

Daniel moved toward Mr. Morici and extended his hand. Morici looked at Daniel's hand and said, "Sorry, kid. I never shake hands with people I don't know. It can lead to misunderstandings."

Daniel, embarrassed, withdrew his hand and smiled weakly. He had the sense that he was where he did not belong, but he was also excited to be in this slightly dangerous environment. He waited, nervous and energized, for Morici and Dominic to finish talking. Every so often, Morici looked at Daniel.

Finally, he asked, "Who's your father?"

"His name is Raymond Montello. He's a painter."

"Oh, you mean like an artist? Like Michelangelo?"

"No, sir. He's an industrial painter. He and his father work for a company that paints commercial buildings, bridges, tunnels ... that sort of thing. They also paint houses on the side. I help out sometimes during vacations and on weekends, but not much. They think I'm too young."

"You seem like a good boy. You stick close to your mom and dad. And stay in school. Otherwise, you can become a bum."

"Yes, sir," Daniel replied. "My parents tell me the same thing. My mother is a teacher."

"That's good. I have a lot of respect for teachers and cops and firemen and other city workers." The other men smiled when he said that.

Then the two boys left and walked to the theater.

*****

Dominic Savarino knew that he did not have to do well in school because his father had told him that he could "enter the family business" anytime he wanted. When Daniel asked Dominic how his mother felt about that, he said that she would never interfere in any decisions that his father made. Daniel wanted to ask a dozen other questions, but he held back.

The following summer, Daniel, who was now almost as big as his father, joined him and his grandfather, when they needed him, on painting jobs. A few of his friends had jobs lugging fruit and vegetable crates for the vendors at the farmers market on 86th Street, getting paid off the books. One evening, Matt Shapiro called Daniel to say that he had just gotten back from the hospital; he had fallen off his bicycle and broken his arm right before dinner. He asked Daniel whether he wanted to fill in for him at his job at Joe's Fresh Fruits for the rest of the summer. Happy to have something to do during the day and pleased at the chance to earn a regular salary, Daniel said yes. Matt explained that he had to be at work at 6 a.m., when the trucks from the farms arrived, and he had to stay until Joe told him to leave for the day.

"He pays me four bucks an hour, off the books." Matt said. "It's not a great job, but it's steady work. Anyway, I'm out of commission, so it's yours."

When Daniel arrived at the fruit stand at 5:45 the next morning, he told Joe what had happened to Matt. Joe, a short, rotund man with a perpetually flushed complexion, gave Daniel the once-over and then explained where to place the crates, how to open them and stack the fruit, and what to do with the empties.

At 2 p.m., Joe told Daniel that he would pay him at the end of the week, and said that he could go; then he asked, "Am I gonna see you tomorrow?"

Daniel assured the man that he would be there. He made a mental note of the fact that he had worked for eight hours. Matt had told him that Joe would sometimes "forget" how many hours he had worked during the week.

As he walked home, hot, achy, and tired, he met Dominic. Unlike Daniel, who was wearing a tee shirt, cut-off jeans, and a pair of old sneakers, Dominic was dressed well: a crisp, ironed sport shirt, sharply creased trousers, and new running shoes. Daniel explained that he had taken Matt's job.

"You know," Dominic said, "just yesterday, Mr. Morici was saying he could use another guy to run errands like I do. You interested?"

"I don't know. I just started this job."

"Listen, you're my friend, and, as a friend, let me tell you, there's better ways of spending your time that don't include luggin' crates of fruit and breakin' them up for the garbage and selling peaches to old ladies."

"I know. I'm worn out and I probably stink, but ... I don't know. What do you do exactly at your job at the club?"

"Nothing illegal, if that's what you're worried about. I just help clean up in the club; I pick up cigarettes or pizza for the guys; I answer the phone and I run other errands. I can get you that job in a second, and you'll make more money."

"Thanks, Dom. I don't know. It sounds better than what I do, but I already promised Joe I'd be there tomorrow."

Daniel was on time for work the next morning and the next and every other morning that summer. He worked as if he had a stake in the business. He did not like Joe because the man always tried to skim a few dollars from his weekly pay. However, one morning, when he saw Joe looking bruised and battered—one eye swollen shut, his cheeks and jaw as purple as an eggplant, and his lips twice their usual size—he could not help but reach out to the man. When he asked what had happened and how he felt, Joe painfully limped past Daniel and told him to do his job, saying, "Just do what you're told. I'm not paying you to ask about my health."

Daniel really had not needed to ask what had happened because he clearly

6

remembered the argument he had witnessed between Joe and a well-dressed young man the day before. Although he had not seen all of it, he had heard Joe declare, "I'm very happy with my current trash haulers. You're not going to scare me into using your guys at twice what I'm paying now."

That afternoon, right before Daniel left work, a truck from All-City Waste Management, not Joe's usual garbage collector, arrived to pick up the trash.

Dominic's words from a previous conversation came back to him: "You're being a sucker. Working for the guys at the club is a real opportunity."

Daniel's moral compass told him that working for the men at the club might not be the kind of opportunity he would like. So, while he labored six days a week for the rest of the summer, often being cheated in the process, his friend Dominic remained cool and comfortable working at the Huntington Social Club, earning much more money and dreaming of his opportunities.

*****

"Hey, kid, run down there and pick up a couple a pizzas and a meatball hero for us," Jimmy commanded.

"Sure."

"Plain ... nothing on the pie. Here's a few bucks. You keep the change."

"Thanks, Jimmy."

That's what Daniel did: he picked up pizza or calzone and sometimes sandwiches or cigarettes from the deli for the men. At first, he was perplexed because they always said "down there" or "up the block" instead of naming a store or restaurant. It was part of the shorthand language they used. Daniel knew not to ask, so he used his instincts to determine whether to go to Angelo's Pizzeria or Mike's Subs or whichever local establishment they meant.

Daniel thought about how quickly and dramatically his life had changed. Near the end of his senior year at high school, during dinner one night, his father had told him that the industrial painting firm at which he had worked for almost 20 years (and *his* father for more than 40 years) was shutting its doors. At the age of 42, Raymond Montello was out of work. Earlier that year, Raymond and his father had given up their house painting business because there were more painting contractors and less work in their neighborhood than ever before, so now he was not earning an income.

Daniel's mother, Ruth, told him not to worry, assuring him that they could survive on her teaching salary until his father found a job, although they needed a new car and they had to either come up with a substantial down payment on their apartment, which was going condo, or move within the next six months.

7

When Daniel declared that he would skip college and get a full-time job instead, both Raymond and Ruth looked horrified and began shouting at him. Raymond slammed his hand on the table and said, "No you won't!"

Then Ruth shushed Raymond and explained to Daniel that they both regretted his father's decision, years before, to drop out of college, saying, "We were stupid. I should have told him to stay in school and tough it out. He could have become a police officer; he's exactly the right type for that job and he would have had a good job with benefits and a nice pension."

Raymond looked wistful.

"I know, mom. You've told me." Then, looking at his father, he said, "I've never understood why you didn't just take the test to become a cop."

"I should've, but I was making decent money painting and helping your mother pay for college, and then we had other expenses, and then you were born ... Here's the lesson: you can never go wrong getting an education. So, we want you to go to college in the fall. I will find another job."

"I'll save my money from my summer camp job and give it to you."

"No. You hold onto it. If we need to borrow from you, we will," his mother said with a forced smile on her face.

"How much do you need for that down payment?"

"A lot. Don't worry about that. Enjoy your last weeks of school, and we'll just take things as they come," Ruth assured her son.

That same night, Daniel knocked on the door of the apartment in which Dominic Savarino lived. Dominic's mother told him that her son was at his job, so that is where Daniel went.

Since that first night, almost two years before, when Dominic had introduced him to Mike Morici, Daniel had been in the Huntington Social Club three more times: the yearly Christmas party two years running, which he attended the first time because Dominic had persuaded him that they would have a great time, and one Saturday night during the past school year when Dominic had asked Daniel to show up in his place because he would be at his grandmother's wake. That first Christmas party (and the second) had been wonderful and Daniel had felt welcomed there. The food from Federici's had been great, the music played by a local band was electrifying, and there was lots of silly behavior on the part of the normally humorless men who were regulars at the social club. Daniel had been entranced by the beautiful young women in low-cut, backless skin-tight dresses, all of whom were willing to dance dangerously close to him, an experience that was both intoxicatingly stimulating and discomforting. He had actually been relieved when the women left, at

8

different times during the course of the long evening, with the regular habitués of the club.

On that other night, when Daniel had reluctantly filled in for Dominic, he had started out feeling uncomfortable and apprehensive as he uncorked wine bottles, mixed simple cocktails which Dominic had explained how to make, poured drinks for the men, who were engaged in their typical high-stakes poker game, answered the phone, and picked up *cannolis* and milk for coffee from Ambrosino's Bakery down the street. After a while, however, once he had relaxed and become attuned to the lazy, masculine atmosphere, he enjoyed being there and felt proud of the fact that he had, in a small way, connected with the men. At 11 p.m., Mike Morici told Daniel to clean up, saying that he and Jimmy Tripelli and the four other men who were there that night were going down to Atlantic City for some action. Daniel wished he was going with them.

As he walked home, Daniel had felt exhilarated because he had violated clear boundaries and had not suffered any consequences. He had felt surprisingly at ease in that place. However, he also felt changed, as if he had lost his innocence and had jumped two steps toward adulthood. As he walked along the quiet streets toward his home that night, he had the sensation that he had touched ... had been in contact with an imperceptible ... something, an organism that would, little by little, cell by cell, transform him if he were to return to the Huntington Social Club. Therefore, after that night, he stayed away.

However, because he was sure that his parents' financial situation was more precarious than they said it was, he was now willingly walking to the club, hoping that, with Dominic's help, he would be able to work there.

"What are you doing here?" Jimmy Tripelli asked, giving Daniel the once-over as he lit a cigarette.

"I wanted to talk to Dominic, sir. I hope you don't mind."

"Oh, so you know Dominic, huh?"

"Yes, sir. He and I are friends. We've known each other for years."

"So you know our man Dominic over here?"

"Yes, sir. I do. We're friends."

Jimmy and all of the others always did that: asked questions whose answers they already knew. Daniel knew that Jimmy and the rest of the men in the club were compulsively observant. They noticed everything about everyone they saw, and they never forgot. Daniel assumed it was a survival strategy. He once said that to Dominic, who laughed and said that he had the wrong idea. Dominic said that Daniel should think of the club as the headquarters of a business enterprise, a family business.

9

Despite the fact that the men did think of it as a business, the family operation was organized roughly along the lines of a military organization. As such, all of the top men, Mike Morici, Robert Licardelli, Jimmy Tripelli, Tommy La Salle, George Salerno, Joe Galliano, and Antonio De Luca, whose father was the head of the family, were generally referred to as *captains*. At times, they were referred to as *caporegimes*. Each of them "owned" a territory within a part of Brooklyn and operated "businesses," such as gambling parlors, loan sharking operations, and protection arrangements, within his territory. People who wanted to operate businesses, legal or otherwise, in any of those territories had to receive the approval of the captain and kick up part of their income to that man.

Below the level of captain were the *soldiers*, sometimes referred to as *buttons* or *enforcers,* but more often just thought of as members of a particular captain's *crew*. They ran the day-to-day operations of the businesses owned by their captains for a weekly salary and they performed extra work for them on a contract basis. Some of the crew members had their own businesses as well, in which case they paid a portion of their weekly income to their captains.

Dozens of other men were, like Dominic's father, solely independent contractors who ran their legitimate businesses and paid part of their income, as commission, or more accurately, as tribute, to the captain who "owned" the territory in which the business was located. Unlike the other legitimate business owners in the area who were compelled to pay protection money to the family, the independent contractors were, in a minor way, connected to the family.

Of the captains, Michael Morici, who was sometimes referred to as *consigliere*, meaning counselor, was in the second highest position in the family hierarchy. He was also referred to as *underboss*. All of the captains gave a portion of their weekly earnings to him. He brought all of that money, minus his share, to the man at the top, the owner of the business, Carmine De Luca, who was generally referred to as the *boss*. De Luca rarely entered the social club.

Daniel knew that the men never used the traditional titles for their organization, *mafia* or *cosa nostra*, because it sounded too old world and too much like what it was, a criminal enterprise.

"So, you and our man here," Jimmy said, gesturing with his cigarette in the direction of Dominic, "are bosom buddies, right?"

"Yes sir ... a long time. We live in the same building on Bay Parkway."

"And your name is ... ?"

"Daniel Montello." He made sure to give his last name a lyrical Italian pronunciation. When people heard his given name, they sometimes assumed he was anything other than Italian.

"Okay, Daniel *Montello* ... " Jimmy gave the name even more of an expressive twist before he continued, "Go talk to our man Dominic, but don't take up a lotta his time. He's working."

Daniel smiled politely and exchanged some small talk with Dominic before he whispered, "I have to ask you something."

Dominic, who was washing glasses, shook his head and continued to work. After a few minutes, he told the men that he was going out for a smoke, to which Mike Morici asked, "Why outside?"

Dominic, realizing that it sounded suspicious, told them that Daniel wanted to ask him something private.

"Ooops," Jimmy cackled, "Sounds like he got a broad in trouble."

"Yeah," Dominic replied with a smile, "I think that's it. The jerk!"

Daniel smiled in an attempt to look embarrassed.

"Okay, Dom, but don't forget, we're expecting some high-level businessmen tonight. Don't go far. I don't wanna be sittin' here lookin' like a dick when these guys wanna order food."

"No, Jimmy. We'll be right outside the door."

"You got that hundred bucks I gave you. When I ask them what they wanna eat, I don't wanna have to ask you to pay attention. You write it down, and when I tell you to, you go out to whatever place in the neighborhood you need to go to get the food."

"Yes, Jimmy."

Outside, Daniel told Dominic that he needed a job; he explained about his father being unemployed. He asked about working at the social club.

"Well, it's only me right now. They fired every other guy I brought over to work for them. You sure you want this job now? You didn't want it before."

"Yes. The job I have lined up for the summer doesn't pay much. It's only a little better than working at Joe's fruit stand, which I did last summer. Besides, I'm not so sure there really is a job. The woman at the day camp said she'd try me out and see if she wants to keep me. I really need money to help my parents. They don't have enough for the down payment for the apartment; if they don't have it in six months or so we'll have to move. I don't know where we'll go."

Dominic said he would get him the job, but he told Daniel that he was not likely to earn enough in six months for the down payment.

"But you told me they're paying you $500 a week."

"Yeah, but that's because I do other work for them, especially Mike Morici." Then, after a few seconds of thought, Dominic said, "You know, the truth is, this could work for me too. I wanna do more of the other work ... outside work. I don't wanna clean up the club after these guys anymore. Maybe this will be my break. You go home. I'll take care of it. Talk to you tomorrow."

The next day, at school, Dominic told Daniel he had the job.

"Thank you, Dom. I appreciate it."

"Yeah, well, you know, it works for me too. Mike, he said I've been 100% reliable and since my dad is okay with it, once I graduate from school, they're gonna give me real work to do."

"Should I ask?"

Dominic smiled and explained that he did not know exactly what he would be doing, but he gave Daniel the possibilities, saying, "Mike'll put me in with one of his own operations. It could be numbers or card games or putting out some money on the street or girls or moving cigarettes or some other good kind of stuff, and ... before you start to get the shakes, don't worry—nobody ever gets hurt. As my father always says, these guys supply a need ... they wouldn't be in business if people didn't want what they sell. Ain't that right?"

"I guess so, but I thought you were going to work in your father's trucking business," Daniel replied.

"I will. He's connected to the family. He pays money to Mike Morici, who gives it to the big boss, Mr. De Luca. De Luca sends weekly payments to the real big guys, the ones who chartered his business, even though we don't see them and they don't see us, some men in the Gambino family."

"I understand. As long as I don't have to do any of that ... I just need the money. Besides my mom and dad needing it, I'm tired of being poor."

"I getcha. I don't need to tell you I'm gonna look like a jerk if you don't do a good job, but I know you won't let me down."

Once Daniel was sure that he really had the job at the social club, he had called Mrs. Davidsky to tell her that he would be unable to work at her day camp for the summer because he had accepted another job.

"I'm sorry to hear that," she had said. Then she added, "I'm glad you called me now, before camp starts. Some young people are very inconsiderate; they just don't show up. Thank you."

"You're welcome."

"What kind of job did you find so that you can't work for us?"

"Oh ... it's working in a store."

"Which one?" the woman asked.

"It's not around here ... It's in Manhattan ... it's a sporting goods store."

"Good luck to you, Daniel. You can learn a lot working a summer job."

At the end of his first day of work at the club, Daniel told his parents. His mother was upset because he had said he would be working at the day camp. His father, his face red and his eyes wide, said, "It's not really a social club; it's a hangout for *gavones*, low-lifes, you know, connected guys, mobsters."

"Did you know that, Daniel?" his mother asked.

"Yes, ma, but it's not like anything criminal happens there. The men are all nice ... mostly old, I mean older, like dad's age. They just play cards, eat pizza and sandwiches, and talk and laugh."

"Daniel, you gotta realize they also run their business out of that place," his father replied, sounding upset.

"But all I do is serve them drinks and buy food and clean up ... and, before I began working there, I had been there a few times. It's just a social club."

"You mean you've been there before? And ... you're telling me you don't see people with envelopes of cash or illegal doings there?" Raymond asked.

"No, I've never seen cash there, except for the money they give me to go buy food or cigarettes for them and what they put on the table when they play cards." Daniel felt that he was technically telling the truth. He assumed that the envelopes he had seen, including the one that Dominic had given to Mike Morici the first time he had been there, contained cash, but he could not be sure. Nevertheless, he felt sick because he was lying to his parents, something he never did, and because when his father had said "envelopes with cash," the reality of what he had gotten himself into smacked him in the face.

"Daniel, I'd like to meet these men. I just want to see what they're like before we agree to this," his mother said.

"No, ma. That's embarrassing. I'm almost 18. I've never done anything to disappoint you, have I? Besides, I've already begun to work there. I can't just walk out now. And, one more thing ... they pay me well, and we certainly can use the money now with dad out of work and you needing money for things."

His parents, looking embarrassed, told Daniel to wait for a minute while they talked over what to do.

"This is not a good idea," Raymond told Ruth once they had gone into their bedroom and closed the door.

"Does anything bad happen there?" Ruth asked.

"I don't know. I've never been there. Lou Savarino's trucking company is associated with that crowd. I don't know what he does exactly, but he's with them," Raymond explained.

"Is Daniel likely to get in trouble?"

"Probably not. I've seen cops joking outside with the men who hang out in that club. Sometimes the cops go in there, but it's not to arrest anybody. I just don't like him being with those people."

"Okay, so you tell him he can't work there," Ruth said.

Daniel, who had been thinking over his choices while his parents had been discussing the matter in their bedroom, surprised them by saying, "Please understand. This is something I want to do, I need to do, and I will do it, with or without your approval. That is that."

They were stunned, speechless. Before either one could even begin to reply, Daniel continued by saying, "Look. You two defied your parents by staying together, and you can't tell me you regret doing that. Right?"

They shook their heads in silent agreement. Then his mother said, "That was for love. What you're doing can be dangerous."

"You've always trusted me, and I've never let you down. You know that we need this money. Those kind of men are all over the neighborhood. You know that; they own a piece of almost every business in Bensonhurst. So what if I work in the club? I want to do this. The first time I see anything that makes me worry, I'll tell you ... in fact, I'll quit the job. How's that?"

After thinking for a moment, his mother said, "Don't do it."

"Sorry, ma. I'm doing it. You can't stop me. This is what I need to do. You have no reason to worry. I know what I'm doing."

Ruth remembered how Raymond had remained strong when her parents had objected to their relationship so many years ago. Then she said, "Promise us this: if you have even an inkling that there's any danger, you'll walk out. And you'll quit before you start college in the fall," she added.

"Maybe ... maybe not. If they want me to work there some nights and on weekends, I'm going to ... unless we suddenly become rich."

"I don't like it. Your father doesn't like it. Keep your promise to stay away from dangerous situations," his mother repeated.

"I will. I know how to take care of myself."

During the next few days, at Ruth's urging, Raymond, who was still unemployed, sat in the little diner across the street from the social club, nursing cups of coffee and observing who walked in and who walked out. Assuming he was a law enforcement agent whose job was to monitor the comings and goings of the club, the owner of the diner kept his distance from Raymond.

Now, weeks after that conversation with his parents, Daniel was walking the few blocks to Carmine De Luca's house on 83rd Street. Every so often, Jimmy Tripelli would tell Daniel to wait as he laboriously wrote in pencil on a legal pad, stopping every so often to lick the pencil point and think. When he finished writing his note, he always enclosed it in a plain white envelope, instructing Daniel to lick the gluey flap; then he would press it closed with his large hands and fold the envelope in half.

"This goes to Mr. De Luca. Put it in your pocket. Don't stop nowhere and don't let this note outta your sight. It's for Mr. D and only Mr. D. Nobody else sees it. *Capisce*?" Jimmy would always ask him.

"Yes, Jimmy. I understand," Daniel would reply. He had seen that Jimmy and the other men were always very careful about what they said when they used the telephone in the club or their cell phones.

As Daniel approached Carmine De Luca's massive three-story brick house, which was surrounded by a six-foot-high black wrought iron fence, he smiled because the only danger he had experienced so far at the club had been when he had brought back the wrong pizza. He was sure he had ordered a plain pizza, but when Jimmy had opened the box, he angrily exclaimed, "What the hell? I can't eat eggplant. It gives me gas!" The other men had laughed, and Daniel had run back to Angelo's for another pie.

One gate opened onto a wide stone walkway that led to the great front steps of the house; twelve feet or so to the right of that was a large double gate that opened onto the long, winding driveway that led to a matching brick garage with a highly varnished door.

Daniel had never been inside the house. He always hoped that when he delivered messages, he would be invited in, but Alphonse Caselli, sometimes referred to as Big Al, an imposing white-haired man with a dark face, after opening the door and scanning the street and sidewalk, would always take the note and mumble, "Wait here, will ya, kid?" Then he would run his eyes up and down the street again, move back into the house, and gently close the heavy oak door behind him.

Daniel tried to imagine what the house looked like inside. It was certainly big; there had to be at least a dozen rooms, not counting the basement, which he knew was fully furnished, because Jimmy and some of the other men from the club talked about the card games and whispered about the meetings they had down there. The windows, including the large bay to the left of the front door, were covered by drapes, so Daniel was never able to see inside.

Large, ornate cement pots overflowing with heavy greenery sat on either side of the door on the broad top step. A dozen ancient oak trees stood, like so many Praetorian guards, in the small perfectly manicured grassy areas on both sides of the walkway. A giant American flag on a tall white pole flapped and snapped proudly in the breeze.

Daniel liked standing there. He felt that he belonged, and he sensed that he drew a kind of dangerous power into his soul from the sturdy brick house that seemed to protect the neighborhood. In fact, even though there were occasional instances of burglary and of cars being stolen in other parts of Bensonhurst, the homes within the general vicinity of this house were protected by an unofficial Pax De Luca.

People driving by or walking along the sidewalk in front of the house knew not to stare; they would take a fast look and then hurry along. Daniel, imitating Big Al Caselli, always kept an eye on the walkers and the drivers of the cars that passed.

2

The Marshmallow Man

Dominic had been right: Daniel had not been able to earn enough money during those first few months to help his parents cover the down payment to buy their apartment. He asked Dominic to help him, but his friend spent his money faster than he earned it. Daniel's parents had gone to a bank, but since they owed so much on charge cards and had only Ruth's teacher salary coming in, they were denied the loan they requested. After a frantic couple of weeks of looking, they moved into a small basement unit a few blocks away.

Then Raymond found a low-paying job working for a local painting contractor; the owner of the company told Raymond that he would fire him if he ever got word that he was taking jobs on the side anywhere in Brooklyn.

That fall, Daniel scheduled all of his classes at Brooklyn College for mornings and afternoons, making sure to leave evenings and weekends free so that he could work at the social club. His mother and father, who suddenly looked older and very worried, periodically asked Daniel how things were going, but did not ask him to quit his job.

Now, during the times that he was at the club mixing and serving drinks and bringing back food, Dominic was often there. Although the older men treated Dominic like a novice, he fit right in. In that environment, he treated Daniel as the others did—as the kid who cleaned up—but outside of the confines of that strictly ordered setting with its unique customs and rules, Dominic was always a good friend. They still went to the movies together and played basketball on occasion, but Dominic spent most of his time, generally at night, working.

Daniel asked him what was new.

"Oh ... not much. Mike, he has me collecting from poker games and numbers parlors and for loan payments and, once in a while, I do some special jobs, but I can't talk about that, and you wouldn't wanna know."

Daniel smiled.

"What's so funny?" Dominic asked.

"It's just ... I'm sorry. I'm not trying to ... I'm sorry. It's just funny that you're collecting from poker games and, then, when you're in the club playing poker with the guys, you always lose your shirt."

"Oh, so you think it's funny?"

Daniel worried that he had injured Dominic's feelings. However, before he could apologize, Dominic said, "You're right; it is funny, but it ain't. I think those bastards use a system against me."

"I don't think so, Dom. I'm there before you walk in, and they don't seem to play any differently."

"I guess. Unlucky in cards ... lucky in love ... or, I mean, getting laid. Man, those clubs I been going to ... they are something else! The women. You oughta come with me some time."

"Time? Who has time? Between taking classes and studying and writing papers and working, I just barely have time to sleep," Daniel complained.

"So? Quit school. You can work a real job just like me. I'm pulling in close to two *g's* a week now ... and that's cash ... green cash. No taxes."

"No, Dom. Please don't ever ask that again. It's okay for you. I'm glad it's working out for you, although maybe you should start saving some money, and not spend it all on clubs and drinks and poker."

"I'll save when I'm old. Not now. Besides, I get a lotta stuff for free or at steep discounts. You know, like my car. I never told you. I said it was a steal, right?" He smiled with satisfaction as he said that.

Daniel shook his head. The car was a two-year-old black Cadillac Seville. Then he asked, "You didn't really steal it, did you?"

"Naw. If it was stolen, how could I register it and drive it around? I'm not stupid. It was given to me by a guy who couldn't pay what he owed. It's worth lots more than what he hadda pay, but it was all he had, so he gave it to me, papers and all, and I used my money to pay Mike what that guy owed."

"Did you tell that to Mike?"

"Naw ... I just gave him the $3,000 the guy owed outta my own money."

"But ... do you think that was a good idea? I mean ... Mike might have wanted the car or he might have wanted to sell it."

"The way I look at it, Mike had $3,000 comin' to him, and he got his money. I don't have to worry about you sayin' anything, do I?"

"Dom, you know me better than that. You're my friend, and besides that, I never want to say something that causes you or anyone else to ... get in trouble or hurt or worse."

"Okay ... I shouldn't have asked. I trust you, man."

"I just worry that you're going to catch it if he finds out."

Although it went against his principles, Daniel had begun to feel excited thinking about Dominic's way of life, and he found ways of justifying it. After all, in this case, he reasoned, if that man had borrowed money from a bank for the car and could not make his payments, it would have been repossessed. This was basically the same type of situation.

Then, even though Daniel felt he should not bring up the subject, he said, "You know. I've never seen a gun ... I mean on any of the men in the club."

Dominic smiled, and then he said, "'Course not! If you run your business the right way and don't violate any of the rules, nobody needs to pack a piece and nobody has to get hurt, although a few of the guys do."

"I'm glad to hear that. I promised my parents ... I'm a little embarrassed to say this, but I told them I would quit if I thought I was getting in too deep."

"You know, Danny, you're an anomaly. Hah. I bet you're surprised I know a word like that," Dominic asserted.

"No. I know you're a smart guy," Daniel said.

"Well, I was never a good student. I was always bored outta my skull in school, but I read a lot ... and I use the dictionary, so I know lotsa big words."

"Right. So, how am I an anomaly? I think I know what you're going to say, but go ahead."

"You, my old friend, are an anomaly, a stranger in a strange land, because you're not like the rest of us, but you're here anyway."

"Well, you didn't have to tell that to me. I know that, but the funny thing is I like working with Jimmy and Mr. Morici and the others. I think they're sharp guys in their own way. Sure of themselves. I actually sort of admire them," Daniel said with a shrug, not willing to admit to Dominic or to himself that he wished he was more like them.

"Well, wait until you meet Mr. De Luca. He's been to the club a coupla times. That man is something else, a real gentleman ... a Renaissance man. He speaks three or four Italian dialects and he knows about books and science and wines and all sorts of other stuff," Dominic stated with obvious pride.

After a few seconds, Daniel said, "I'd like to meet him one day."
*****

Daniel kept his job at the Huntington Social Club all the way through college. By the time he was in his final term, he was as much a fixture at the club as Jimmy Tripelli, Michael Morici, Lou Savarino (Dominic's father), and all of the other regulars. He also became acquainted with several established business people whose presence at the club at first surprised him. There was Marc Bernstein, the principal agent and owner of a local real estate agency; Todd O'Shea, a wealthy commercial property developer; Aaron Levinson, a city council member; and Ben Brickman, who was known as a political kingmaker. On occasion, men to whom he was not introduced were graciously ushered to the rooms at the back of the club, from which they emerged later on, smiling broadly as they walked out the door. One time, when one of those men had departed, Jimmy winked at Daniel and said, "It's good to have friends who work in law enforcement 'cause they can protect you from bad people."

Daniel delivered messages (never white envelopes with cash) to and from Carmine De Luca's house on many occasions. Much to his disappointment, he was never invited into the man's impressive, fortress-like home.

However, he did have an opportunity to see Carmine De Luca at the club one day. Dominic's description of him was accurate: De Luca was a tall, thin, elegantly dressed and well-groomed man with highly lacquered nails and exceedingly polished manners. He was healthy and youthful looking at 75, with a full head of thick silvery hair. When the man magisterially entered the club, all of the others, Mike Morici included, stood up, approached him, and then reached for his hands as if they wanted to kiss them, as they would for a prince of the Church or royalty. Daniel remained frozen behind the bar, not knowing whether he should leave his post to greet the great man. Before he could decide, Mike Morici led De Luca to the little room at the rear of the club, where they remained for close to an hour with the door closed.

As Carmine De Luca was being escorted to the door and to his limousine, which was parked right outside, he spotted Daniel. The man stared for a second and then smiled warmly as he painstakingly adjusted his hat and white silk scarf before walking out to the sidewalk.

Daniel chided himself for being overly impressed with the man. He reminded himself that Carmine De Luca, as the *capo* of the organization, was ultimately responsible for all of the wrongdoing committed by the men in the club, all of whom Daniel now thought of as friends.

He thanked his lucky stars that neither Jimmy nor Mr. Morici had ever asked him to do anything that would make him feel uncomfortable. At times, he felt guilty because, even though he performed only innocuous chores, he was, in that small way, enabling the men to be free to engage in loan sharking, protection schemes, illegal gambling enterprises, and other more serious crimes.

He continually made peace with his conflicted feelings by reminding himself that life is about balance. No one is all good all the time, although some are better than others, and no one is the embodiment of pure evil. He reasoned that his small role in the life of the club did not really matter; if he did not pick up after the men and run innocent little errands for them, someone else would, and he surely needed the money. Even though his tuition payments were low because he attended a city college, he would not have even that without the job. Of course, he could have worked somewhere else, but the hours and pay were good and, despite his occasional remorseful feelings, he liked being a part of the

Huntington Social Club and knowing the men who were the regulars. *Here I am*, he thought, *uneven ... out of balance with my surroundings and my life.*

*****

As Daniel entered his final year of college, he had not yet decided on a career. He had majored in English and thought about teaching at a college, but he did not want to borrow money to pursue a graduate degree, a requirement to land even a lecturer position. His English creative writing professors had told him that he had talent. Even though they referred to his writing as "lyrical" or "incisive" or "powerfully constructed," all of the stories that Daniel had written and submitted to literary magazines had been returned to him with polite rejection letters.

He decided that he needed professional career advice.

As he entered the college career counseling office, which was bathed in bright afternoon sunlight, he saw her. He caught his breath and suppressed a sigh. The bright, cheery-looking name tag on the diminutive receptionist sitting behind a desk read "Maria Reyes." Daniel, who was six feet tall, slumped down in the wooden chair in front of her so that they were eye to eye. He was so overcome with shyness that he was not able to form an intelligible sentence. The room was warm. Maria lightly dabbed at the coffee-brown skin of her forehead with a tissue. Then she pushed away a few strands of her glossy black hair which had tumbled down. She smiled brightly, her large dazzling eyes twinkling as she waited for Daniel to compose himself. Although she was not vain, she was well aware of the fact that she often had this effect on men.

Finally, she asked, "Would you like to set an appointment with Mrs. Goldman? She's the career counselor."

Daniel, pulling himself together, said yes, and waited as Maria checked the counselor's schedule. She asked Daniel a few questions about his major and how many credits he had completed, entering the information on a form. Then they chatted for a minute about teachers they knew and courses they had taken.

After she had scheduled an appointment for Daniel for later in the week, she asked whether there was anything else she could do for him.

Before Daniel could convince himself to politely say no and leave the office, he blurted out, "Would you consider going out for a cup of coffee or a movie or something with me at some time?" His heart was thumping so heavily that he was sure she could hear it. He immediately wished he had just thanked her and not said anything; after all, he reasoned, he should have waited until he had talked to her again later on in the week when he came in for his appointment or at some other time. This was not the way to ask out a girl.

21

He was about to apologize for his abrupt and completely inappropriate question when she looked at him gravely and said, "That sounds nice, but you should know I don't sleep around."

Daniel replied, "That's good. I don't either."

She laughed and then he laughed. Then they talked a while longer, until they were interrupted by another student. They arranged to meet that night at six for a quick bite to eat. Since Daniel did not have any more classes that day, he spent the next couple of hours sitting in the library trying to study; each time he pictured Maria's face and recalled her soft, honey-glazed voice, he smiled.

When he returned to the counselor's office, Maria was waiting in the hallway, already in her coat. She smiled warmly and said, "I'm glad you showed up. I was worried I had scared you off."

"Not a chance," he replied, pleased that she had said she was "glad."

He told her that he had to be at work in a couple of hours. When she asked him what he did, he told her it was a kind of waiter job at a private club. She asked where it was.

"It's in Bensonhurst, where I live," he answered.

"I know that neighborhood. I live in the ghetto."

"Oh. Where is that?"

"East Flatbush," she replied.

"Why do you call it a ghetto?"

"It's really not," she answered. "It's really a very nice neighborhood, but it's just that almost everyone who lives there is either black or Hispanic. You do know I'm Hispanic, don't you?"

"I assumed so. Does that matter? Does it matter to you that I'm not?"

"Of course not," she replied.

He went on to tell her about his mixed heritage.

"You call that mixed?" she laughed. "My mother is Cuban and Italian. Her father was Afro-Cuban and Taíno. Taíno is a native group, you know, what people call Indian or Native American. Her mother was born in a little mountain village in Calabria somewhere. My father is from the Philippines, so I'm not just mixed, I'm a mutt, or, as my mother says, a hybrid."

"Well, it's a great mix. You're ... you know, very pretty."

She smiled and put her arm through his as they walked down the hallway and out of the building. They went to a Chinese restaurant on Flatbush Avenue. As he helped Maria off with her jacket, he tried not to stare at her striking figure. They ate, talked, and then he said that he had to be at work soon.

When he offered to accompany her on her bus ride home, she told him that he would be late for his job if he did that, but said that he could walk her to the bus stop. As they stood at the busy stop, waiting, neither one seemed to be able to think of anything to say. They looked at each other a few times and smiled, and then, as they turned to each other again, their eyes locked. Daniel knew he was blushing; he thought that she might be blushing too, but because of her dark skin tone and the dim afternoon light, he was not sure. He wanted to put his arms around her and kiss her. Instead, he gently touched one of her smooth cheeks with the back of his hand. As he withdrew his hand, she reached up and grasped it. Before walking up the steps, she lightly kissed his cheek. He smelled vanilla and honey. Then she took a seat and smiled at Daniel through a window as the bus pulled out into the street.

*****

She told him that she had never had a boyfriend before; he told her that he had never been serious about a girl before her.

"What did you and Mrs. Goldman decide?" she asked.

"Oh. She was helpful. She said what I already knew: that a BA in English would look okay on a résumé for almost any job, but would not really help me, other than for a teaching position."

"So, what are you going to do?"

"I don't know. I should have thought about this earlier, but I never could focus on it ... the idea of a job. You were smart to major in something that leads to a career," he said.

"If you call library science a career path," she said with a smile.

"I told you ... I love libraries," he replied.

"There aren't a lot of people who can say that." Then she added, "It's funny what people like and don't like and how their lives end up so differently from what they might have expected."

"Oh? Like what?"

"You know. Think about people you know, older people. Are they living the lives they expected to live? How many of them hate their jobs, their marriages, the choices they've made. And the consequences. How many of them regret their ... I don't know ... their missed opportunities and how they've compromised? How many of them worry about their lives? Believe me, I know about that from the people around me."

Those words reverberated in Daniel's head. Regrets? Worries? Yes, he had a few. Lately, he had begun to feel uneasy as he walked home from the social club at night. He sometimes stopped dead in his tracks and turned around to see whether he was being followed, only to find that no one was there. Then

23

there was the fact that he had not seen Dominic in about a month. The day before, Jimmy Tripelli had called Daniel over and invited him to sit down at his table in the club. Daniel sipped the whiskey that Jimmy poured for him. He asked Daniel whether he had seen Dominic. Then they exchanged small talk.

"So, you're gonna graduate from college this year, huh?" Jimmy asked.

"Yes ... this June."

"Smart boy. I wish I had went to college, but I never had the brains. That's good for you. You gotta make good choices in life. Otherwise, they come back to bite you in the ass."

There it was again: choices and consequences.

"You know, there's lotsa opportunities for you here. Smart guy like you. You ever think about that? You know, moving up?"

"No. I like working here, but I have career plans," Daniel replied.

"Oh, yeah? Like what? You gonna be a lawyer maybe?"

"No. I'm going to be a teacher," Daniel replied, surprised that he had said out loud what he had considered to be only a possible fall-back job.

"Teacher, huh? Good career, but it don't pay much. You care about money, don't you?"

"Sure. I do, but I'm not money hungry, if that's what you mean."

"That's good. Everybody needs money, but they shouldn't chase after it so bad that they hurt themselves or their friends," Jimmy commented.

Then, during the ensuing silence, as Jimmy looked intently at him, Daniel began to perspire. He wished he was anyplace else. He began imagining that, at any moment, some other men would come through the front door and ... he did not know what they would do. It was not that anyone had threatened him or alluded to an imminent dangerous situation, but all of a sudden, all Daniel could think about was the lives of the men who frequented the club and the people they regularly harassed and hurt as part of their jobs.

Then, finishing his drink and slamming his glass down on the table, Jimmy said, "Well, I gotta make tracks. So, where did you say Dominic was?"

"I don't know, Jimmy. I told you ... I haven't seen him in a while ... in a few weeks. I used to see him here, and sometimes we'd go out together at night, but it's been a while."

"Yeah. His old man said he don't know where Dominic is. Like I said, people gotta make smart choices in life."

As he sat in his room that night, after making a quick phone call to Maria, Daniel thought about his life and his choices and their consequences. Then he thought about a story that he had written for one of his creative writing classes.

Even though his teacher had praised it, Daniel had not submitted it for publication because he wanted to work on it a bit more. He pulled it out of one of the drawers of his desk and made some changes. He knew it had potential, and it certainly was on a subject with which he was familiar. He read it again.

The Marshmallow Man
By Daniel Montello

This story may or may not be about a guy I know. It teaches a lesson about how luck can come and go.

Sammy Marshmallow had known it was only a matter of time before his early string of unbelievably good luck would run out or be broken. Or was it his neck that would be broken? He tried not to think about that because he had to concentrate. In two more days, Tony, who everybody called "Big Tone," was going to ask for this week's and last week's *takes*. Tone always collected the week's *take* from him on Friday; however, last Friday, Sammy had told Tone that he was sick ... sneezing and coughing and blowing his nose like there's no tomorrow; he knew *that* would keep Tone away. In fact, Tone had told him to spray the cash with Lysol, saying he would pick up the envelopes for both weeks this Friday, two days from now. Sammy would have this week's *take* on Friday—no problem—but there was no way for him to get his hands on the 30 *g's* ... 30 *big ones* that he had kept and lost from last week's *take*, especially not in two days. Where was he going to come up with $30,000?

As he slumped down on the plush leather seat of his black Cadillac Eldorado looking at the cars moving up and down Kings Highway, he tried to figure out what to do. It was almost 1 a.m. He drove home.

He had been so careful, always taking small amounts of cash from the envelopes given to him by the operators of the gambling parlors in his territory; he never lifted more than a *c-note* from each one because that amount would never be missed. After all, only he and the guys in charge of the gambling parlors knew how much was in the envelopes. Who would know that $100 was missing from each envelope?

It wasn't that he wanted to *eat alone*. Sammy was anything but greedy or selfish or disloyal. He had always been a stand-up guy; he had served Big Tone and the higher ups in the family for 20 years, always doing his job, always handing in all the *dough*, always keeping his mouth shut. But now, Rita, his wife and the mother of his three children, needed a big operation ... something to do with her bladder or her uterus or something like that. The doctor had said it would cost well over $40,000 total. Sammy did not have that kind of money and he did not have health insurance. His only health insurance over the years had been to do what he was told and mind his own business.

What's a man to do?

He thought he had figured it right. Once he had accumulated $1,000 in *c-notes*, he had gone to his good friend, Charlie the Book, and said that he needed lots of money for his wife's surgery. He told Charlie a cock-and-bull story about how he had raided his kids' college fund. In truth, Sammy had never saved enough money over the years for a college fund or for any other kind of fund. Somehow, despite the fact that he had earned in the area of $200,000 every year for the last decade or so, all of it in cash and none of it taxable, and a bit less for the 10 years before that, there was never an extra dime. Not one thin dime. He knew it was mostly his fault. He liked nice things: a new car every year, expensive suits, good food in fine restaurants, single malt whiskey, nice vacations with Rita and with Connie, his *goumada* ... What's a guy to do? He had needs. Of course, truth be told, Rita spent plenty; he gave her $3,000 cash at the start of every month, but she always needed more.

So, because he loved his wife and because a man who doesn't take care of his family is a *gavone* or *disgrazia* or worse, he approached Charlie. He had helped Charlie the Book out of plenty of scrapes over the years, some of them really bad, from the time they were altar boys together, and he had never asked Charlie for anything. Oh ... he asked for a little tip and credit now and then, but never anything big. This time, he told Charlie, he needed the real *low-down* because he had to score big. He figured that, with the right *info*, he could turn a few small bets into the $40,000 he needed.

Charlie was reluctant. It's not that he didn't want to help Sammy. In fact, he said he would lend a couple of thousand to him with no *vig* because of their friendship, but Sammy said that wouldn't work. A *coupla thou* was nowhere near what Sammy needed and, besides, how would he ever pay Charlie back? As it is, he would need every dime he won to pay for the doctor and the hospital. He laid it on the line: he told Charlie it was a matter of life and death.

"Can't you borrow from your boss?" Charlie had asked.

"Do you have shit for brains, you would ask me that?" Sammy had replied. "That would be like walking into quicksand, like Tarzan would always do in those old black and white movies you watch on the weekends, but I ain't no Tarzan. For one thing, in case you haven't noticed, I've put on a coupla pounds over the years, and, besides, this ain't a movie. All I need is a few big scores."

"How would that look, Sammy?" Charlie had asked. "Don't you think people would find out? Me and this book are accountable to the big man. He owns it. He finds out I'm helping you, I may as well jump off a bridge."

"Who's gonna tell? Me? You? I need those scores."

So, while Sammy stood behind him, polishing off a big bag of Kraft Jet-Puffed marshmallows, Charlie turned the pages in his ragged spiral notebook, studying the stats. When he realized that Sammy was looking over his shoulder, Charlie coughed hard, using that as an excuse to change position and lower the little book to his lap, where Sammy would not be able to see it.

Then Charlie wrote down on a sheet of paper *Syracuse* and the point spread. He told Sammy that it wasn't a sure thing, but it was a good bet, the best he could do. Sammy gave $500, half of what he had accumulated, to Charlie, and went home. When Syracuse won, Sammy called Charlie and told him to let it ride. After a few more bets, Sammy was up $8,500. Charlie advised Sammy to take his money and run, to which Sammy said, "No way. Let it ride."

"Listen," Charlie said, "this ain't no science. I don't know about any sure things, you know, rigged games or dives or anything like that. You could lose your little nest egg in less than a heartbeat."

Sammy, who had just torn open a new bag of marshmallows, reached in and grabbed a fistful. Then, while Charlie waited on the other end of the line, Sammy popped one into his mouth and chewed slowly. After he had chomped and swallowed a few more for strength and to help him concentrate, he told Charlie to let it all ride.

The next day, Sammy gave Charlie the $500 that he had kept in reserve, and told him to add it to the pot.

He kept telling himself that he should keep a little on the side for insurance, but because he kept winning, he threw caution to the wind. Not that he felt confident. He had plenty of *agita*, but what's a man to do?

Well, his good luck lasted and lasted. He had almost $20,000 now, and he began to feel shaky, so he told Charlie to put aside $15,000 and bet the other $5,000. He went to bed that night feeling good, knowing that he had to have a little balance and not risk all of his newly-won *moolah* on one bet.

Wouldn't you know it? That $5,000 hit so big, it more than doubled. He would have met his goal of $40,000 if he had let all the money ride. He ate two whole bags of marshmallows that night.

Talk about *agita*!

Well, can you guess what he did? Of course, he told Charlie to put the whole bundle on the next bet. Charlie advised him against this, but Sammy was sure it was the right move. Besides, Rita was scheduled for the surgery by that point, and he didn't want to stand there with his dick in his hand when it came time to pay the bill. Charlie told Sammy that, at the very least, he should spread his bet over a couple of games this time, so he made two bets of $13,500 each for Sammy. One paid off small time, but the other was a bust, so Sammy ended up with a little less than he had prior to that bet: $15,000 instead of the $27,000 he had before.

Charlie kept giving good advice to Sammy. He kept splitting Sammy's bets. Good thing. Sammy won on some and lost on others. Then, one Saturday, the roof fell in: all the bets went bust. Sammy was left with *zilch* just about when the first bills from the doctor and the anesthesiologist and the hospital were due to arrive in the mail.

Sammy had never been one of those guys who throws his bills in the trash. Besides the fact that he had always thought of himself as a good citizen, he knew that it wouldn't look good if debt collectors began calling his house or ringing his doorbell, so, last Friday, he took all of the envelopes for that week and brought them home. He counted out a bit over $30,000. Then he sat up and waited for Big Tone to call him. He looked at the clock. It was way past midnight when the phone rang.

"Yeah?" Sammy croaked when he picked up the phone.

"Where the hell are you?" Big Tone asked. He sounded more exasperated than angry.

"Who? Oh ... What time is it, Tone?"

"What time? It's You Kept Me Waiting Two Hours time! That's what time it is! Are you drunk or high or something?"

"Oh, geez. Oh, man. I'm ... Wait ... I gotta cough," and he did. Then he sneezed and sniffled and blew his nose right into the phone.

"Are you sick? Sounds like you're dyin' over there, Sam."

29

"Yeah, Tone. Sorry. I'm dripping sweat and puking my guts up and my nose is like a faucet." He coughed and choked a bit more.

"You got the envelopes? That's all I wanna know," Big Tone said. "I don't wanna have to go all over to collect now. I got a life too."

"I got it all, Tone. I'll get up and ... I'll ..." Then he sneezed again, like an atom bomb, right into the phone, and snorted a couple of times.

"No. You stay there. Take a coupla days to get over your cold or whatever you got. Then, after you shower real *real* good, open the envelopes like you always do to count the *take*, but this time, spray the cash with Lysol. Let it dry. Then put it in clean envelopes and give it to me next Friday with that week's envelopes. I can wait till then. I know I can trust you. *Capisce*?"

"You sure, Tone? I can get outta bed if you want."

"No. Stay in bed. You call Joey and tell him to cover for you."

"Thanks, Tone. I'll call Joey tomorrow."

After he hung up the phone, Sammy took a deep breath. Then he brushed his teeth and joined Rita in bed.

"Who was that?" she asked.

"It was Tone," he replied, closing his eyes and beginning to think about how he should bet the $30,000.

"Is everything okay? I heard you coughing and sneezing and choking," Rita said as she adjusted her hair curlers so that she could rest more comfortably on her pillow.

"Everything's copasetic. I musta caught something in my throat or I swallowed too hard."

Sammy waited until Monday to visit Charlie the Book. Charlie did not ask Sammy how he had come up with $30,000 and he did not ask why Sammy didn't just use that money to pay off at least part of the bill for the surgery. They talked a long time about how best to bet the money to make the $40,000 that Sammy needed and still have the

30

original $30,000 left, which Sammy had said he had to return. Again, Charlie did not ask.

Things went well on Monday, but not so good on Tuesday. By Wednesday night, the $30,000 had shrunk to just a bit over $18,000, so, as his sweaty fingers plucked handfuls of marshmallows from bag after bag of Jet-Puffed, Sammy and Charlie considered their options.

Finally, Charlie said, "That one; that's the way to go. If you put the 18 *thou* in and you win, you'll end up with about 60 *g's*, almost what you need for the surgery and to put back the $30,000 stake. I can lend you the difference. Don't you say no to me."

Sammy agreed. Then he sat quietly in Charlie's office and stared at the little television, waiting for the basketball game to begin.

Close to three hours later, the game was tied; it was a few minutes before midnight. Sammy had quickly polished off three more big bags of marshmallows and four beers, and now his stomach felt like the inside of a full-blast pizza oven.

At the final buzzer, with the last basket, Sammy's eyes bulged, his mouth fell open, and his heart dropped to his bloated midsection. His team had lost by two points. He looked at the unopened bag of Jet-Puffed on the couch next to him in Charlie's office. He picked it up, squeezed it until it popped, and then he threw it at the wall above Charlie's littered desk. It fell on Charlie's papers with a gooey plop.

Sammy sat. He was lost. Charlie felt awful. Neither one knew what to say. After a while, Sammy walked out. He sat in his Eldorado, thinking, looking at the traffic. Then he drove home. If you remember, that's how this little story begins.

Two days of sweating, of being sick passed. He couldn't wait for Friday so he could get it over with. But on Friday night, as he picked up the last of the envelopes, he wished it was Wednesday again or Monday or last month or before that, when his life had been humdrum and safe.

On his last collection stop of the night, as he walked past a poker table full of *swells* betting really big money, he thought about grabbing the kitty and running, but he didn't. That was low. Doing that was the modern-day equivalent of stealing horses in the Old West. Besides, at his age and with his extra weight, he wouldn't get 10 feet from the table before somebody would tackle him. And he couldn't bring himself to take from patrons of the family's business associates. And, besides, all the people there knew him. He'd have to *go south*, be *on the lam* for the rest of his miserable life.

Of course, he *could* do that. Send a message to Rita and one to Connie. No, not Connie. Rita, he could trust with his life, but not Connie. In fact, since he had been involved in this situation he had not spent any time with Connie or given her money or gifts. They had talked on the phone, but she knew it was over, although she didn't know why.

But, if he ran, how would he survive? How would Rita and the kids survive? They'd be better off if he was dead. Now, that was an idea, but how to do it? What's a man to do?

Then, as if God or some other mighty power had come to his rescue, a *Young Turk* jumped up from the table next to Sammy and pulled a gun; a shot rang out and half the people in the place screamed and ducked under tables and the other half ran for the exits. Then, as the *cugine*, whose first shot had missed everybody, took aim at a man next to him, two other guys from the table tackled him, causing all three men to stumble and fall against Sammy. All four of them tumbled to the floor. Before the bouncers could reach them, Sammy did what he never did: he reached over and punched the young guy and the two other guys over and over again. Then they all began to mix it up. By the time the bouncers had separated the men, Sammy's head was spinning, his lip was bleeding, one eye was blurry ... and he was overjoyed.

Sammy waited until the club bouncers had roughly

shoved all three of the other men out the door before he slowly stood up. The owner of the club, Bobby Quinones, helped Sammy to a stool at the bar and told the bartender to give him whatever he wanted. Then Bobby walked to the poker table to apologize to the few guests who were still there.

That was all the time Sammy needed to make his way to the men's room and pull the envelopes of cash with the night's collections from his inner pocket. He smiled with satisfaction as he weighed them in his hand because they were a lot heavier than usual. Then he opened the little window and pushed the envelopes out to the enclosed alleyway that he knew would be empty at this hour. He sighed with relief as he heard them plop. Then he ripped his shirt a bit more, punched his bleary eye and cut lip a few more times, and walked unsteadily back to the bar.

Sammy didn't want to wait too long. Just as Bobby walked back to him to make sure he was okay, Sammy frantically checked his pockets and patted his coat and then he bellowed, "Shit! They took my money! Those bastards ripped me off! I'm gonna fucking kill them!"

Bobby looked horrified. He opened Sammy's coat and helped him to check his pockets. Then, as Bobby scanned the room to find his bouncers, Sammy fell to the floor, dropping his untouched drink onto the ceramic floor tiles. The glass shattered. Some of the guests, already nervous, thinking the sound was another gunshot, began ducking for cover again. As Sammy lay there in the midst of the renewed pandemonium, he smiled to himself and dreamed of marshmallows.

The End

3

What a Trapped Rat Will Do

Daniel kept meaning to submit the story, but he was always too busy with school and working at the club and spending time with Maria. He decided to enroll in some education courses during his last term and take the licensing examination to teach school in New York City, figuring that he could attend graduate school at night. He hoped to earn his MA in English within a couple of years and then land a teaching position in a college. Maria had already secured a librarian position at Pratt Institute that she would begin in the middle of the summer, after she graduated from Brooklyn College.

He and Maria saw each other almost every day. He had met her parents, Sonia and Luis, and got along well with them. One evening, as he was walking from the bathroom in her family's apartment to rejoin Maria in her room, he thought he heard Sonia say to her husband, "Well, he's nice. Do you think they're serious about each other?"

When he told Maria, she laughed and said, "Mothers and fathers. They always worry about their children. Are we serious about each other?"

"I'm more than serious. In fact, I'm critical. Take me to the ER."

"Am I making you sick?" she asked with a wry smile.

"So sick I think I'd die without you."

"That sounds very bad. Well, I guess we'll have to stay together. I wouldn't want to be responsible for you dying before your time."

"I am dying. I'm dying to make love to you."

"I feel the same way. I've told you ... I lie in bed at night and dream of making love to you, but, you know, we agreed to wait. I couldn't possibly feel comfortable here and I definitely won't go to a hotel or anything."

"I know. That's fine," he replied.

"On another subject, I don't think your mother likes me."

"And I've told you they both love you. Yes, they were a bit surprised when I brought you home that first time, but it had to do with the fact that you were the first girl I've ever brought home. The first one I've ever cared about."

"You sure? You know I'm not sensitive about my color or my heritage."

"I'm sure. They have only me ... you know, an only child ... and they've always been all over me," he explained.

"Right, my big only-child man," she laughed. "Now, *my* mother used to complain that there were so many of us that she couldn't wait for us all to get married and move out."

"But she doesn't feel that way now."

"No. You know how she misses my brothers and sisters and her grandkids. All she talks about is those kids."

"I know. That's nice. Eleven grandchildren and one on the way. That *is* something," Daniel said. "I don't want a horde. I mean, I like kids and I want to be a father, but I think two is enough."

"Yeah. Well," Maria whispered, her eyes narrowing, "I've told you, I'm pretty sure I'm not going to want any. I've seen how my mother stayed home all those years and missed out on what she really wanted to do, like going to college. She talks about going now, but she won't ... and my sisters and brothers ... they struggle to make ends meet ... and there's no guarantee how your kids are going to turn out, but let's not talk about that ... at least not now."

On the bus ride home that night, he thought about a recent conversation with Jimmy. Daniel had said that he would work at the club during the summer, but that once he started a regular job in September he would have to cut his ties. Jimmy told him that the guys would give him $1,000 as a graduation present in June, and whenever he married his "little chippy," they would shower the couple with gifts. Daniel had never told the men at the club anything about Maria other than her name, and that was only when they had repeatedly asked whether he had a "steady squeeze."

He and Maria did not discuss his job. When he finally told her what he did, she made it clear that she thought he was crazy to be anywhere near "gangsters or other low-life types." She said there were gangs in her neighborhood; she could not understand how he could work in the club. After he had tried to explain to her, she shook her head and said more or less the same thing his mother had said: "I don't get it; if you have to work there, be careful."

Dominic was back in the picture now. He had not told Daniel where he had been during that month when he had not been around, and Daniel had never brought up the subject.

One evening, Daniel and Maria went to a nightclub with Dominic and his date, a stunning peroxide blonde in a micro miniskirt named Estelle. As Daniel and Maria traveled back to her house later that night, she asked him, "Is Dominic always like that?"

"Like what?" Daniel replied.

"I don't know. I thought he looked nervous, on edge; he seemed to be looking over his shoulder a lot, as if he was expecting trouble."

"Yeah. I noticed that. I didn't think you would. He's usually very good at covering up his feelings; he's always been able to do that, but not tonight."

Weeks later, Daniel realized that evening had been the beginning of all of *it*. In fact, that had been the moment when the beginning and middle of what was to become a very dangerous situation began rushing headlong to its catastrophic end ... the time when and the place in which a calamitous event that had been lying undetected had started evolving and developing the power to change and destroy lives. Later, after he had become entangled, Daniel wondered whether it is ever possible to intervene and take steps to prevent a disaster from occurring.

One Saturday afternoon at the end of August, Dominic called Daniel on his cell phone and asked, "You got some time for me, man?"

"Sure. What's up?" Daniel asked.

"Meet me ... you know where," Dominic said.

"You mean—"

"Right. You and I know where. How's about now?" Dominic asked.

"Okay. Be right there," Daniel replied, trying to sound unperturbed.

He walked quickly from his family's apartment to the building where he used to live, the one where Dominic had lived with his parents when he was younger. He entered the lobby, took the stairs to the basement, waited for a minute, and then walked out the door that led to the rear courtyard. After looking around to make sure he had not been followed, he walked across the courtyard to the narrow, trash-filled alleyway between two other buildings that faced the next street and out to the sidewalk on the other side. Then he turned right and entered the lobby of one of those buildings and walked the four flights of stairs to the roof, where Dominic waited for him.

"What took you so long?" Dominic asked.

"You've got to be kidding. I got here as fast as I could. And ... why all this cloak and dagger?"

"You weren't followed?"

"No. I did just as we used to when we were kids playing our spy games," Daniel replied, glancing at the door from which he had just emerged.

"Good. We gotta talk," Dominic said as he lit a cigarette.

Daniel waited, beginning to dread what he was about to hear.

"It's like this: remember when I was sort of missing a few months back? Well, I wasn't missing. Mr. D sent me to San Francisco to work with his brother. It's complicated. One day, he sends word I should go to his house. I'm excited 'cause I never been invited in there. While I'm in his house, he hands a plane ticket to me and tells me to go straight to the airport. He gives me a couple a hundred bucks and tells me to buy clothes in Frisco. He says I'll be picked up when I land. Funny thing, the whole time I'm in San Fran, I feel like a charity case, like his brother don't need me, like I'm a fifth wheel."

"That's strange. Are you all right?" Daniel asked.

"Yeah. I am. How's Maria?"

"She started her job this week," Daniel replied.

"Smart girl. You have a job yet?"

"No. Still waiting to hear. I should get a letter soon."

Daniel waited. He knew that Dominic would open up when he was ready. Finally, Dominic stubbed out his cigarette, peered over the edge of the roof for a few seconds, and said, "I need a little help."

"Okay," Daniel replied.

"It's like this: without telling you any more, you gotta be my eyes and ears. I gotta find a rat. All you gotta do is tell me who asks about me. That's all."

"I told you Jimmy was asking about you when you were missing back then," Daniel said. "Are you in trouble? Is somebody after you? Is that why you looked so nervous that night in the club?"

"No. I'm not nervous. Jimmy didn't say nothin' else, right? Just where's Dominic? He didn't ask you anything else?"

"Right."

"Okay. It's gonna be like this. I ain't disappearing this time, but I'm setting a trap. Somebody is gonna start askin' a lotta questions about me. It probably *will* be Jimmy. That's all I can say to you."

"Okay. And, if that happens, what should I do?" Daniel asked.

"Simple. You don't know nothing. Just watch and listen and then tell me. Like I said, I'm gonna be around ... just not at the club at not at Mr. D's house and not at my apartment. You can reach me at this number."

"But," Daniel said, taking the scrap of paper that Dominic handed to him and trying not to allow his anxiety to show, "I'm not going to put anybody in ... I mean I'm not setting up anyone to get hurt, am I?"

"Like I told you, Danny, this ain't the movies. Nobody's gonna get whacked, if that's what you mean. Mr. D has never called for that. It's just ... I'll tell you this much: somebody's been skimming money, a lot of money, but Mr. D don't know who for sure. In fact, that's why he sent me to San Francisco. It was to get me out of the money pipeline here. He had to make sure I wasn't the thief, so he sends me there, and I'm watched the whole time, and the money still goes missing ... a few thousand bucks each week. He tells me, when I get back, that he trusts me because he feels he's known me from the time I was a kid and because me and my dad are 100% loyal, but he hadda be sure."

37

"I don't feel good about this, Dom. I don't think I want to be part of it."

"All that's gonna happen is, when we find the thief, and it's probably Jimmy, he's gonna pay back what he took and then he gets fired and he don't work for another family because we blackball him all over the East Coast. Nobody's gonna get hurt, except in their pocketbook."

"Okay. If you're sure. I'll be your eyes and ears."

And so, a few evenings later, when Daniel saw that Jimmy had sent the two other men who had been in the club to Mr. D's house with a message, something that Daniel would normally have been asked to do, he was suspicious. He expected Jimmy to approach him, and, after smoking another cigarette, he did. Daniel was cleaning the stove and tidying up the kitchen in the rear of the club when Jimmy entered, filled a glass with water at the sink, and watched Daniel for a few seconds. Then he took a sip and said, "You know how I can get in touch with Dominic? I haven't seen him in a few days and the phone in his apartment just rings and his cell phone says his mailbox is full. When I call his father, he takes a message, but I don't hear from Dominic."

"I see him now and then, but not in a few days," Daniel replied.

"Okay. When you talk to him, give him this message: I gotta talk to him. It's very important."

"Sure, Jimmy. I will."

Daniel was on pins and needles for the rest of the evening. As he walked home, once he was sure that no one was following him, he called Dominic to report his conversation with Jimmy.

"Okay. I'll call him tomorrow."

"Be careful, Dom. I don't trust him," Daniel replied.

"Yeah. Well, I don't trust no one except my mom and dad and you, so you be careful too because I think this situation is gonna lead to blood."

"That's why I didn't want to be involved in ... I told you, Dom."

"Yeah. I know. It ain't gonna involve you ... It's just that I have this bad feeling about this. I think this is gonna be the end."

When Daniel arrived home, his mother excitedly informed him that she had opened his mail, and said that he had been appointed to a teaching position in Abraham Lincoln High School when the new term began the following week. He was too upset by his conversation with Jimmy and with what Dominic had said to complain to his mother about her having opened his mail. Then, as he read the letter, he realized that this period of his life was over. His appointment to a regular teaching position meant that he would finally be able to cut his ties to the Huntington Social Club. What had started out as a reliable part time job that paid well and did not involve dirty, heavy work had lately become a burden on Daniel's soul. He knew that he had been dishonest with himself each time he had attempted to justify what those men did. Yes, they provided services that people want and, yes, they acted like other men in his neighborhood, and not like gangsters, but he knew they came to the club to discuss business, hand over envelopes of illegally obtained cash, and talk about their dirty work. They never talked openly about what they did, but, from time to time, Daniel had overheard some of the men jokingly say things such as "he had it coming to him" and "he ain't no hard head no more" and other obvious allusions to how they spent their time when they were out of the club.

This letter meant that with the start of the school term in a few days he would be able to quit his job at the club, earn a decent income as a teacher, and enroll in graduate school. He figured that after two years or so of graduate school classes at night he might be able to land a lecturer position in English at some college somewhere, maybe an Ivy League institution.

He also decided that he had to put more effort into being published. The rejection letters from magazines and scholarly journals to which he had sent short stories, essays, and poetry had worn him down. He had felt so hopeless that he had not written anything new or submitted a story in months. Even though he had written 50 pages of a novel with the working title *Member of the Club*, the story of a *made-man* in the *mafia*, he had not looked at it in weeks.

The one constant source of joy in his life was Maria. During his gloomiest moments, when he pictured her lovely skin, beautiful eyes, and magnificent smile, he was filled with warmth. When they kissed good night, she always said, "I'll dream of you tonight and wake up feeling blessed tomorrow."

At the beginning of September, Maria moved from her parents' home to a sunny one-bedroom apartment on Ocean Avenue. There, away from the watchful eyes of her parents, she felt relaxed enough to invite Daniel to bed with her. She told him she was nervous; he said that he was too. They both longed for the comfort and warmth of their love for each other.

During that same September, Daniel began teaching, he bought a used Buick, and he enrolled in graduate school at Brooklyn College, attending classes two evenings a week.

Then, on a clear Tuesday morning with a brilliant blue sky during the second week of the term, as Daniel was about to begin a discussion of "Hamlet" with a freshman class, the World Trade Towers fell.

The horror and gloom of that calamitous day during which so many people had died in such a horrific manner and the lives of so many others had been viciously ripped apart deeply affected Daniel and Maria. Along with so many other people, they felt endangered, angry, empty, and desolate. However, despite their shared somber mood resulting from the horrific events of that day, their lovemaking remained explosively joyful, leaving them spent and blissful each time. Maria told Daniel that she was glad they were finally making love, saying that she thought about him all day long. Smiling, Daniel said that his days at work and his nights at school dragged because he so needed to be with her. When Maria said that she wanted him to move into the apartment, he packed his belongings and brought them there the next evening. He told her that he would stop working at the social club soon. He had unenthusiastically promised Jimmy that he would continue to work when he was available until they found someone to take his place.

A week later, a Friday, Jimmy cornered Daniel as he walked into the club, and said, "You know, your friend's kinda stupid. I'm tryin' to help him, but he don't show me no respect. He makes it impossible for me to reach him."

Daniel smiled in a weak attempt to conceal his anxiety. For the rest of the evening, he was sick to his stomach. Despite the fact that his mouth was dry, his fingers were icy, and his head hurt, he knew that now, more than any other time, he had to remain focused because he had to be Dominic's eyes and ears. He pushed aside his mounting sense of disgust regarding the lives of the men in the club and decided that he would absorb as much information as possible.

It was a busy night. By the time he left at a little after midnight, 14 men besides Jimmy Tripelli and Mike Morici had spent time there. Daniel had picked up bits of the usual chatter, nothing out of the ordinary, but as soon as he had locked the door, something that he did only when the men had left the club before he had finished cleaning up, he walked out into the evening heat, got into his car, and called Dominic.

"He said ... let me remember ... he said, 'Your friend is kind of stupid and he don't show me no respect,'" Daniel told Dominic.

"Well," said Dominic, "Jimmy's wrong on the first count, but right on the second. When we spoke the last time, he tried to tell me he knew I was lookin' into this thing for Mr. D, and he knows who the thief is."

"Really? How does he know?" Daniel asked.

"Now, who's stupid? He don't know. He was trying to smoke me out. After that conversation, I know *he's* the thieving bastard."

"I have to tell you, Dom, he sounded really fishy. I think you had better watch out for him," Daniel said.

"I'm gonna do more than that. Where you at right now?"

"I'm in my car. Ready to go to the apartment. Why?"

"My guess is he's watching you."

"No. I looked around before I called you," Daniel explained.

"Let me ask you this: Who left the club first, you or him?"

"Jimmy did. They all did. As we were walking out the door, Jimmy knocked over a whole bowl of pretzels. They scattered. Do you think he did it on purpose so he could get out of the place before me?"

"Maybe. And maybe he got into a car ... probably not his Caddy ... some other car, and he parked somewhere up the block from the club," Dominic said.

"To watch me?"

"Yeah. Maybe. Don't look around. Even if you see him or somebody else watchin' you, act like you don't. Just keep talkin' on your phone."

"Then what?" Daniel asked.

"I'm about 20 minutes away, so take a few minutes somewhere ... go for a slice of pizza or something. Then head to you-know-where."

"What? No. What are you going to do? I'm not going to do that. This is exactly what I don't want to be part of," Daniel said.

"Listen: I promise you nothin' bad is gonna happen."

"You don't know that, Dom."

"I promise you, and, at this point, with you makin' this here phone call, don't you think whoever is scoping you out figures you're talking to me? You'll actually be safer if you do what I say."

"I'm not worried about me. I can take care of myself. It's just ... I don't want to be part of this. Either you or Jimmy or somebody is going to get hurt. I wouldn't be able to live with that," Daniel explained.

"Oh? And what do you think is gonna happen if I don't get to the bottom of this? Somebody *is* gonna get hurt, maybe the wrong guy, maybe a few guys, and maybe you too."

"You know, Dom, I have to say this: you're my friend, but all of you guys, and this includes you, you set yourselves up for this kind of shit. I don't know why I ever—"

"Don't give me that crap! You begged me for this job. You musta made lotsa money all this time, more than you could've made doing another job."

"That's true, but I've never done a thing to put people in danger."

"No? How do you know what was in those messages you delivered to and from Mr. D? You don't know," Dominic whispered bitterly into the phone.

"Oh, God," Daniel moaned as he wiped sweat from his forehead.

"Don't play like you didn't know."

"I didn't. I mean—"

"And, another thing, every so often, I saw that you were a little bit excited being in that atmosphere, sorta like you wanted to be part of it, like you enjoyed being a gangster a little bit."

"Maybe, but I never saw or heard anything," Daniel stated. Then, after a few seconds, he whispered, "I guess you're right."

"Listen; don't worry about that or nothin' else. Just do like I say: hang up; don't act like you see anything. Then stop off for a slice or a drink or something, and then meet me ... 20 minutes."

Even though he had no appetite, Daniel walked to Angelo's and ordered a slice and a Coke. As he nibbled on the pizza and sipped the soda, he tried to understand how he had allowed himself to get in so deep. He made a firm commitment that he would not return to the club tomorrow or ever again. Then he wiped his mouth with a napkin, stood up, dumped the pizza and soda into the trash pail in the pizzeria, and walked out to the sidewalk. He looked around for a few seconds before getting into his car and heading toward his meeting with Dominic. He passed where his parents now lived and continued to the building where they used to live. After looking around again, he slowly entered the lobby and stayed put for a full minute, pretending that he was waiting for someone. He figured that if he was being followed, he had to give whoever it was time to see where he was going. He opened the door leading to the basement, walked down a few steps, and waited for a few seconds. He wiped his perspired hands on his pants; then he noisily walked back up, opened the door a few inches, and waited on the top step without emerging into or looking out to the lobby. Then he clomped down the steps to the blessed relief of the cool basement.

When he reached the dim, musty, narrow hallway that led to the boiler room, he imagined that he was passing through the gut of the beast that held him captive and that, soon, he would emerge into freedom.

He walked out into the rear courtyard and slowly made his way to the buildings opposite and then through the dark, litter-strewn alleyway to the sidewalk adjacent to the next street. Then he turned and entered the building. He climbed the stairway to the roof and stood there in the darkness. He was utterly alone. He moved to the edge, nervous, but enjoying the cool breeze. After waiting about 30 minutes, he decided to leave. As he exited the building and stood on the sidewalk, someone called to him from the darkness of the alley.

"It's me," Jimmy whispered.

Daniel looked around and then walked to Jimmy.

"What are you doing here, Jimmy?"

"What are *you* doing here?"

"I was visiting a friend who lives in this building."

"Oh, and would that be Dominic?"

"No. He doesn't live here."

"Okay, look ... I know you talk to him. I thought he'd be here with you."

"He's not. Look, Jimmy, it's late. I have to get home."

"Sure. I understand, but tell him this: it's to his benefit to talk to me, and not brush me off. Understand?"

"I'll tell him when I talk to him," Daniel said.

"You know," Jimmy said, "I used to think you were a civilian ... just a kid cleaning up, but now I'm thinking you're in this with Dominic."

Despite the sultry heat, Daniel suddenly felt chilled. "I don't know what you mean," he protested.

"Yeah. That's what they all say," Jimmy replied.

"Look, Jimmy, I don't know what you think. In fact, I don't care because I'm finished. I'm not coming in tomorrow or ever again."

"Now, how is that gonna look? Money's missing and you don't show up and maybe Dominic don't show up either"

"I'm going home, Jimmy. You're not going to try to stop me, are you? I've got six inches on you, and I can take care of myself. I don't want to fight with you, but don't get in my way."

"Oh, so you're a big guy. I oughta just let you go, and tell Mr. D what I been thinking ... that you and Dominic and maybe somebody else I have in mind have been skimming cash all this time."

"You're crazy!" Daniel declared. "I've never taken a dime from anybody in my whole life and I certainly wouldn't be stupid enough to take money from ... from ... people like you."

"People like us? You got your nerve, you little shit. You think because you go to college you're better than me. I oughta shoot you just for that."

And then, in an instant, Daniel felt pressure on one of his temples. He froze. He looked up at Jimmy's hand.

"Yeah, I should," Jimmy said as he lowered his hand, "but, you know what? I actually like you—"

Out of the corner of his eye, Daniel saw a shadow jump from the depths of the alleyway toward him and Jimmy. There was a quick, dark, blurry movement; he heard a *clang-thud*. Jimmy groaned and slumped against Daniel, who fell backwards onto the concrete alleyway, landing with a heavy, painful thump with Jimmy on top of him.

43

Daniel lay motionless for a few seconds, attempting to understand what had just happened. His head and back hurt; everything was spinning. His shirt was wet and slimy. As he looked up, he saw Dominic standing above him.

"You okay, man?" Dominic asked.

"Yeah. I guess."

After Daniel, with Dominic's help, gently rolled Jimmy off him, he sat up and held his head in an attempt to stop the spinning. He looked at Jimmy. In the dim light, Daniel saw that he was sprawled out, face up.

"Oh, God! I think he's dead. You killed him!"

"Quiet! No. He ain't dead. Just knocked out. Get up!" Dominic ordered in an angry whisper.

Daniel slowly got to his feet. He looked at Jimmy again. There wasn't a mark on him, but in the muted light of the alleyway, Daniel saw a splotch of blood spreading out from under his head onto the concrete. Then Daniel felt his shirt. It was wet and sticky. He frantically rubbed his hands on his pants. Dominic roughly shook Daniel and then he steadied him by grasping his shoulders.

"It's gonna be okay, Danny ... stay calm and, for God's sake, be quiet. If you make noise, some busybody's gonna come out and check."

"What happened?" Daniel asked.

"I clocked that bastard with a tire iron from my car. I dropped it over there. I better rub it down and take it with me. One sec."

After Dominic had wiped it down with a handkerchief, he asked, "Where's the gun? We better dump it."

"What? What gun?" Daniel asked.

"The gun he put to your head, which is why I clunked him."

"There was no gun, Dom. He put his finger there, as if ... as if he was ... Oh, God. He didn't have a gun. I looked up at his hand. He was pretending. Then he smiled and put his hand down."

Dominic looked down. Using his foot, he pushed aside paper bags and McDonald's boxes and bottles and other assorted garbage. Then, becoming angry, he kicked at the pile of refuse, scattering it across the alley. He pushed Daniel and looked down at the spot where he had been standing.

"I don't get it. I don't see the gun. It's gotta be here. Where can it be?"

"I told you," Daniel said in a choking whisper, "there was no gun. He put a finger to my head ... he made a kind of gun out of his hand; no gun."

"So you say," Dominic stated. "Here's what we're gonna do: I'm gonna back my car up to this here alleyway. We're gonna put Jimmy in the trunk and

44

take him to the hospital. You're gonna stand here and not say a word. If anybody comes along, you're gonna do whatever you have to do to keep that person from seeing Jimmy. You got that? After we get him in the trunk, I'll find the gun. I don't wanna leave any trace of this here incident. Understand?"

Daniel shook his head. He felt faint. Then he touched his shirt again and wiped his hands on his pants. His legs felt rubbery, so he leaned against the wall of one of the buildings. When he saw the car slowly mounting the curb in reverse and moving toward him, Daniel's first impulse was to tell Dominic that he was driving on the sidewalk; then he remembered. Dominic stopped the car a few inches from Daniel; he put it into park, popped the trunk, swung the door open, and stepped out. He scanned the empty sidewalk before walking to Daniel. Without saying a word, he lifted the trunk lid and forcefully turned Daniel toward Jimmy. As they lifted the man's motionless body from the ground, revealing a sickeningly large pool of blood on the concrete, Daniel felt weak. Blood dripped from Jimmy's head onto the ground and the rear bumper of the car as they carried him to the trunk.

When they placed Jimmy in the well of the trunk, his head turned to the side. Daniel felt sick when he saw the dark, wet spot at the back of the man's head. Dominic shut the trunk and searched the alley for the gun. After a few seconds, he angrily kicked at the garbage again. Then he scattered trash over the bloody spot and stormed back into the car and closed the door.

Daniel remained where he was.

"What the hell ya doin'? Let's get outta here," Dominic whispered through his open window.

Daniel walked to the sidewalk, past Dominic's car, and stood there for a few seconds. He felt dizzy. Then he began to walk back toward the alleyway.

"No! Get in. Now. In the car."

Daniel looked at Dominic and then into the alleyway.

"Get in now!"

After Daniel got in, Dominic drove toward the basement apartment where Daniel's parents lived, parking near the building.

"They got a shovel in their place?" Dominic asked.

"A shovel? I don't know. Why?"

"Because we need it."

"He's dead, right? You killed him."

"Hey, I saved your life. If he's not dead, I'll take good care of him. If he's dead, we gotta get rid of him."

"You didn't save my life," Daniel said.

45

"He had a gun and he was gonna cap you."

"The last thing he said was, 'I actually like you.'"

"And you believe that? He was gonna kill you."

"With his finger, Dom? There was no gun. I told you ... I looked. He made a gun out of his fingers, like we used to do when we were kids. Remember?"

"I know what I saw. He was gonna blow your brains out."

"You couldn't have seen his hand. You must have been far back in the alleyway because I didn't see you and Jimmy didn't see you. The way we were standing, you had to have been looking at Jimmy's back, so your view of his hand must have been blocked by him ... by his body. Yes, you saw him point to my head, but he wasn't going to hurt me. It was a make-believe gun."

"Yeah, well, it don't matter. He still mighta killed you some other way. You know what they say: guns don't kill people; people kill people."

"You're able to joke? You killed him. Oh, God!"

"Stop whining. We're gonna park here for a sec. It's a quiet street. You stay in the car. I'll check on Jimmy."

During the minute that Dominic was gone, Daniel prayed for the first time since ... he could not remember when. He wasn't sure how to pray. He felt like a hypocrite as he recited words of supplication to a God in whom he did not believe. Nonetheless, he was so absorbed in the process of attempting to reach out to a higher power and to a different plane of existence that he did not realize the car was rhythmically shaking. Then, in a moment of clarity, he stopped what he was doing, brought himself back to the here and now, and, after fumbling with the handle, clumsily pushed the car door open. He fell down to the sidewalk, scrambled back up, and lurched toward the rear of the car and the partially open trunk. Only Dominic's legs were visible; the rest of his body was in the trunk, covered by the lid as if he were being swallowed by a great beast. As Daniel grabbed Dominic around the middle and frantically tried to pull him from the trunk, he heard grunts and a gurgling, choking sound, a duet of one man's murderous exertions and the other man's frantic attempts to breathe.

Although Dominic repeatedly elbowed him in the chest, face, and abdomen, Daniel held on and finally managed to yank Dominic from the trunk. They fell to the street behind the car and punched and clawed at each other until Dominic landed a hard right on Daniel's nose, stunning him. Then they lay there on the street for a few seconds.

"We have to get up, Danny. If we stay here, someone's gonna see us. Get up now. Here, take my hand. Get up."

At first, Daniel said no and refused to move, but then he said, "Okay." He reached up and allowed Dominic to pull him up. Then, holding a shirt tail to his bloody nose, he watched Dominic shut the trunk. Dominic led him to the passenger side of the car, opened the door, pushed him in, and shut the door. Then Dominic got in the other side, put the car into gear, and drove.

"Listen, man. I did what I hadda do. It's not like our friend was gonna live anyway. I clocked him so hard with that tire iron before that he couldn't a made it. I just wanted to ease his way out. Better this way."

Dominic opened the glove box, pulled out a wad of tissues, and handed them to Daniel, who sank into his seat and held them to his nose.

"Now, we need that shovel. Your parents got one in their house?"

When Daniel did not reply, Dominic cursed under his breath, and then he said, "Okay. I know where we can get one."

Dominic turned the corner and drove back to the apartment house where he and Daniel used to live, where his parents still lived, and parked.

"I'm going in that basement. You stay here."

As soon as Dominic entered the building, Daniel released the trunk latch, opened his door, and walked to the rear of the car. Jimmy lay there, motionless, his eyes and mouth open. As Daniel bent down to check the man's pulse, he was overwhelmed with the odor of feces. He held his still bloody nose with one hand and placed his other one on Jimmy's neck. Nothing. Then he placed two fingers on Jimmy's wrist. Nothing. Daniel was suddenly overcome with a wave of nausea. He quickly pulled away from the fetid odor, painfully grazing the back of his already aching head against the sharp metal of the lock mechanism on the trunk lid. Then, turning, he retched. His nose began to gush again. He remained bent over, hoping to awaken from this appalling nightmare.

Dominic returned. He carefully placed a short-handled shovel on top of Jimmy, shut the trunk, and led Daniel back to the car. Daniel did not ask where they were going. He closed his eyes and sank lower into his seat. He hurt all over. He was hot. He felt wet from perspiration and blood.

Thirty minutes later, Dominic stopped the car and parked. Then he lit a cigarette and smoked. After another minute, he looked in the car's mirrors. Then he exited the car, telling Daniel to stay put.

A few seconds later, Dominic reached into the car and popped the trunk. Then he walked around the car and opened the door on Daniel's side.

"This is the place. Come on," he said as he pulled Daniel's arm.

"Where are we?" Daniel asked in a weary voice.

"It's a real good place. I checked it out. One of the guys told me about it.

47

Nobody's ever gonna look here. I don't think anybody's been here in years."

Dominic lit another cigarette and looked around. Then he pulled the trunk lid up, removed the shovel, and placed it on the street under the rear of the car. He reached in and grabbed Jimmy's shoulders. When Daniel did not move, Dominic said, "He's gone. It's almost over. You better help out because if I get caught, you burn too. It's time to worry about yourself, not this piece of shit."

Daniel moved as if he were in one of those dreams in which everything is in slow motion. He took hold of Jimmy's ankles and lifted as Dominic pulled his end of the body out of the trunk. Dominic motioned for Daniel to shut it. First, he tried doing that without letting go of Jimmy's legs, but he was not able to reach the lid, so he gently lowered his part of the body to the ground; Dominic held onto the upper part of Jimmy as Daniel shut the trunk. Then they carried the body to the sidewalk and down a few feet to a gate in a tall fence made of close-fitting wooden boards. After they entered the enclosed area, Dominic told Daniel to drop Jimmy's legs and shut the gate.

They walked slowly, Dominic backwards, Daniel facing Dominic, to a large pile of discarded building materials. After they lowered Jimmy to the ground, Dominic told Daniel that he was going back out to get the shovel. He was gone for several minutes. During that time alone with the body, Daniel kept his eyes closed. He knew that it was too late. He knew it was not a dream. He knew that he had descended into hell.

"Lucky, lucky," Dominic said when he returned. "Good thing I know a thing or two about a thing or two. I didn't barge out onto the sidewalk. I peeked through the fence and then I looked over it a bit. Wouldn't you know it? A cop car was comin' down the street. They woulda stopped me and come in here to investigate. I probably coulda outrun 'em, but I wouldn't a left you here."

When Daniel did not reply, Dominic handed the shovel to him and told him where to dig. Then Dominic took the shovel back and outlined on the ground the size and shape of the grave, saying, "It's hard dirt. Used to be a building here. Don't remember what. Burned down. Associates of Mr. D own the property. It should be good for a long time before anybody buys it or builds on it."

Then he handed the shovel back to Daniel and said that he would keep watch by the gate. Daniel began shaking.

"What are you, a baby? For God's sake, get a hold of yourself. You ain't dead. He is. He was a piece of shit thief. If I didn't kill him, somebody else would have. Stop being so scared."

"I'm not scared, Dom. I'm not worried about me or you. It's just ... I told you ... I never wanted to hurt anybody. Now I'm just as bad as you."

"We're all bad, Danny. All of us ... everybody. You think a man can go through life without hurting people? It can't be done."

"You're wrong, Dom. I've never hurt anybody before this."

"Well, you didn't hurt Jimmy. I did. I still say he was gonna kill you. I know I did the right thing."

"If it's the right thing, then how come we have to bury him? Why don't you tell Mr. D you found your man and you killed him? Tell me that."

"I said I did the *right* thing. I didn't say I did the *smart* thing. Jimmy was a *made-man*. I shoulda let him kill you, and then tell Mr. D, but I didn't."

"You shouldn't have hit him."

"Enough! We can rehash this tomorrow. Dig the hole, and be quiet about it. And hurry it up."

At first, Daniel felt weak and sick. Then, with each stab of the rusty shovel into the rocky, packed dirt, he felt angrier and hotter and more thirsty. He had not had anything to drink on this oppressively hot, humid evening, except for a few sips of that soda at Angelo's, for a couple of hours. He was sweating profusely. He wanted this night of hell to be over.

A few minutes later, Dominic took the shovel from Daniel and told him to keep watch by the wooden gate. Daniel dragged a broken plastic chair to the fence; the seat was cracked and stained. He sat for a few minutes. Then, as he looked over the gate to the sidewalk, he felt disgusted with himself and with how he had allowed his life to become derailed in this way. The sidewalk and the street were empty. He sat again. Jimmy had been married and had two grown daughters. Daniel wondered when they would realize that he would not be coming home. Would they think he had run off or had been hurt or hospitalized or arrested? Would they ever find out or imagine what had happened to him? Would they ever find his body and be able to have a funeral? Dominic seemed to believe that he and Daniel would be safe as long as Jimmy's body remained hidden. However, it stood to reason that, sooner or later, it would be found.

At that moment, sitting on that damaged chair in that God forsaken dump, Daniel resolved that when he got home he would confess to ... to whom? The police? De Luca? His throbbing head spun and he felt faint and nauseous again. He needed a drink of water; he was so tired that he had to concentrate on the sound of the shovel digging into the ground to stay awake.

Finally, Dominic walked over to Daniel and gestured with his head that it was time to complete the job. They each grasped a leg, dragged the body over the scrabbly ground, and pushed it into the poorly dug grave. It was too short;

Jimmy's head extended above the level of the ground. As Daniel pulled the legs and bent them at the knees, Dominic pushed Jimmy's head down with the blade of the shovel, smearing it with blood.

Daniel forced himself to look down. That was part of his punishment. Jimmy's eyes and mouth stood open. Moist dirt and gravel mixed with blood were on his face. Some of it had fallen into his open mouth. *At least*, Daniel thought, *we know he's dead, and not just unconscious. Or, do we?*

Without saying a word, Daniel slowly knelt down, leaned into the grave, and put an ear against Jimmy's mouth. He listened. He heard nothing. Then he stepped out of the grave and looked at Dominic.

Dominic, who still attended church regularly, recited the Twenty-third Psalm as he remembered it, getting as far as "Thou prepared a table for me with my enemies." He stopped and made the Sign of the Cross. Then he knelt down at the edge of the grave and, reaching down, took Jimmy's wallet and watch from the body. Then he asked Daniel whether he wanted to say anything.

Daniel looked at Dominic, then Jimmy's body, and said, "God forgive me ... forgive us, but I doubt that's going to happen."

As Dominic began shoveling dirt into the hole on top of Jimmy, the man's head moved to the side; Daniel's legs buckled for an instant. He started to call out to Dominic, but then he realized that it had moved because of the force of the dirt falling onto it. Daniel felt a mild sense of relief when Jimmy's face was no longer visible.

Then Dominic wiped off the shovel handle with his handkerchief and put it down on the ground.

"What are you doing?" Daniel asked. "It's ... he's not fully covered."

"I'm tired. You finish, if you want to."

Daniel picked up the shovel and completed the job.

They scattered cinder blocks, boards, and other debris over the gravesite. Then Dominic wiped the sweat from his forehead and hands with his now filthy handkerchief and began walking to the fence. Daniel followed. After peeking through the spaces and then over the fence, Dominic opened the gate and walked out, followed by Daniel; then he closed the gate behind him. He told Daniel to put the shovel in the trunk, saying he would dump it another time.

"I'm starved," Dominic said. "How about you?"

"No. I'm sick. Just take me back to my car," Daniel replied.

"Come on ... we'll pick up some food and sodas at McDonald's and we'll eat in the car. We don't look respectable enough to let anybody see us."

Dominic drove to a McDonald's that was a short distance away. When

50

they arrived at the drive-up window, Dominic told Daniel to turn his head away and pretend to sleep, saying, "The way you look, bloody nose and all, you'd scare the hell outta the girl."

They sat in the car in a deserted part of the parking lot, which was pretty active for that time of night. Dominic seemed to enjoy his food. Daniel did not eat, but he was dehydrated. When he finished slurping his giant soda, he was overcome with shame as he thought how Jimmy would never eat or drink or smile or walk again. He pictured Jimmy's family, and he felt sick to his stomach again. He checked his phone to see whether Maria had called. It was dead.

"Man, I didn't know you were so religious," Dominic said.

"I'm not."

"I heard you say, 'God forgive me.'"

"That just means that, if there is a God, we can't be forgiven for what we did. I don't spend much time thinking about God or an afterlife or things like that. You know. We've talked about this before."

"Well, Danny, I gotta tell you: you're headed straight for hell."

"You've got to be kidding. You live that life and you just killed a man and you think because you go to church and believe in God you're going to be forgiven? Give me a break."

"I will before you will. Look, you wanna go to a synagogue and pray, that's fine. That's good for you. Or, go to a church, but you gotta believe in something. Otherwise, you're like an animal ... you know, with no values. No offense, my man. Just the truth."

"And so, *my man*, you're telling me that I'm the animal even though you're the one who clubbed and choked a man to death? Is that it? I'm the jerk who got involved with you and your gangster friends, the worst fucking mistake of my life, but I haven't hurt anyone ... although I've helped you with this disgusting cover up and burial and all that ... and because I don't believe in God, I'm the animal ... not you ... me. Unbelievable!"

"Like I said, if you don't have religious values, you're like a skunk or a fox or a bulldog or some other animal. Sorry if you don't like it."

Daniel sucked the last few drops from his soda container; then he turned to the window, away from Dominic. He turned back a few seconds later when he heard Dominic snorting.

"You want some of this?" Dominic asked.

"God, no! Take me to my car. I need to get out of here."

Before Dominic dropped Daniel off down the street from his car, he said, "You can tell Maria and your mom and pop you were out with me. Say we got jumped. We fought them off. They'll believe that."

"Don't worry about what I say. I won't implicate you in this."

"I don't like that word. It sounds like you're gonna squeal."

"I don't know what I'm going to do," Daniel replied.

"You ain't gonna say nothing!" Dominic hissed at him. "If you do, *I* ain't the one who's gonna get in trouble. I know how to avoid situations. You'll end up in jail or Mr. D will take care of you. Think about your mom and pop and that sweet girl of yours. You'll make a lot of people very unhappy if you talk."

"Tell me this, Dom: what's going to happen tomorrow at the club when Jimmy doesn't show up?"

"I don't know. I *do* know that I'm not going to tell anybody that I spoke to him or saw him. You're going to say you said good night to Jimmy when he walked outta the club and you stayed behind to clean up."

"You don't need to worry about that. I'm not going back to that hellhole again ... tomorrow or any other time."

"Wrong! Listen, asshole, if you don't show up and Jimmy doesn't show, which, obviously, he won't, it won't take them geniuses two seconds to put two and two together and come up with some number that connects you to him. You ever think about that? Maybe you think Mike Morici and Mr. D, when they find out that Jimmy is no more and you just up and quit, are gonna say, 'Too bad he quit. He's a nice boy. We hope he has a nice life.'"

Daniel was silent for a few seconds. Then he asked, "What are they going to think when they see my bruised nose?"

"Here's what you do: you walk in there tomorrow with a smile on your puss, and when one of the guys remarks about your nose or how tired you look or any other such shit, you smile even bigger and say, 'You shoulda seen the other guy.' And if they ask for particulars, you give them a good story, again with a smile. If you wanna include me, that's fine ... just tell me now. And make it the same story you tell your mom and dad and your girl. The way people get caught in a lie is when they tell different lies to different people. Understand?"

Daniel said he understood.

"Good. Look ... this was kind of a ... what do they call it? A kinda baptism with fire. It's what happens in the real world. Speakin' of that, you know, you don't have to get a job as a teacher, struggling to make a few thousand bucks a year. I can get you in good. I'm pulling in 200 *grand* a year. That's tax-free. Before you say no, think about it. It's a good life. This thing that happened tonight, it hardly ever happens. I didn't expect it to happen."

"I know, Dom. It was my fault. I never should have listened to you about letting him follow me. I never should have gone to the roof."

"You have to start thinking like a man. A man says to himself, 'This is what I gotta do to survive and to take care of my family,' and he does what he has to do. If he don't do that, he ain't a real man. You know what he is?"

Daniel shook his head.

"A victim. He's a victim. Everybody can see it on his face and how he walks and how he talks. They say, 'Here comes, Daniel. He's a pushover. I can take from him and knock him down, and all he's gonna do is say, 'Thanks. I needed that.' That's you if you don't learn how to live like a man."

"Maybe you're right, but a real man shouldn't have to kill other men."

"Hey, like I said, Jimmy was a thief ... taking food from the family ... and he *was* gonna kill you. I'm telling you, there was a gun. You just didn't see it. And you wanna know why you didn't see it?"

"Why?"

"Because you didn't wanna see it. You blocked it out because you wanna believe the world and all its people are nice and they dance around and love each other, like in a musical. Well, that ain't real."

"And what happened tonight, is that real, Dom?"

"You're damned right It is. It's the law of the jungle: the fittest one survives, and all the weak ones, they die out."

"And you're the one who goes to church. Is that what Jesus taught, if you believe in those Bible stories?"

"Of course, I believe that and what they teach in church, but Jesus didn't live in this world, where it's dog eats dog. I'm tellin' you, I saved your life because that bastard was going to kill you."

"Why would he have wanted to kill me? That doesn't make sense."

"Sure it does. You ever see a trapped rat? It'll chew its way out of anything. Same with a man. He'll chew up whoever's in his way."

4
The Package Reappears

Daniel repeated the question, this time with a hint of sarcasm: "This one does not require any real thinking. Would someone, anyone, tell us why Hawthorne's book is called *The Scarlet Letter?*"

When that did not elicit a response from or even an involuntary movement on the part of any of the students, he told them to add that question to the assignment sheet that he had distributed earlier in the week, reminding them to return it to him on Friday to be graded.

When the bell rang at the end of the period, the last one of the week, he was sure that he was more relieved than the students.

One of the sophomores in this mostly freshman American literature class remained in her seat while the others made their way to the door. Then she hesitantly approached him.

"Mr. Montello, can I ask you something?"

He ignored her incorrect use of "can" and refrained from replying with the dog-eared line used by teachers throughout the ages. Instead, he smiled, attempting to look interested. She hesitated, looked down at her shoes, and sighed. As he waited for her to begin, he started packing his books and papers. She looked at him imploringly. Frizzy red hair, light freckles, green eyes, round, childlike face. She was dressed conservatively: white blouse, denim skirt, sensible shoes. He thought how that was not typical of most of the girls her age these days. He found it a refreshing change; most of them wore tight jeans and pullovers or dressed in a style that he thought of as "skimpy slutty haute couture."

"You want to tell me something. I want to hear, but you have to start talking first," he said.

Her lips moved, or did they quiver? She shook her head, apologized for wasting his time, and slipped out of the room. He shrugged, closed his briefcase, and followed her out the door, thinking, "Another day down, thank God."

Even though it was only the beginning of October of his first year of teaching, he doubted he would be able to make it to the end of the term. It wasn't that he disliked dealing with high school students. In truth, they made him smile, albeit in a weak, unenthusiastic way. His hours in the classroom, in meetings, at home preparing lessons and grading papers, and even his tedious, long evenings in his graduate school classes were reasonably agreeable times, but he was *always* so tired. Bone tired when his alarm went off in the morning;

so weary that showering, shaving, dressing, sipping a cup of coffee, and driving to work were exhausting, frustrating chores; too fatigued to play house with Maria after work and on weekends.

He had not told the true story of that night to her, but she knew something awful had happened. When she saw him late that evening, his nose was enflamed and raw, his lips were puffy, and his eyes looked like those of an old man glumly awaiting his final days. He had told her that he and Dominic had gotten into a fight with some other men. He knew by the look in her worried eyes that she suspected something much worse had occurred.

The next day, Saturday, when he stopped by the club to tell Mr. Morici that he would not be coming in that night or any other time, the man barely looked up from his drink. Daniel almost asked where Jimmy was because the awful events of the previous evening did not seem real to him.

"The new guy, Richie, can start working tonight," Daniel said. "He knows what to do."

Mike Morici told Daniel to get a clean glass from behind the bar. When he brought it to the table, Morici poured whiskey into it and told Daniel to drink, saying, "Looks like you need this." Daniel shook his head, declining the drink, but Morici insisted, so Daniel, still standing, picked up the glass and sipped. Morici, a derisive smile on his face, said, "Don't tell me ... the other guy looks worse. Right?"

Daniel nodded, finished the drink, and put the glass on the table. Morici looked at it. As Daniel walked out the door, he smiled ironically as he remembered that the men in the club had not given him the $1,000 graduation gift that Jimmy had promised.

Now, as he drove from his teaching job to the apartment, all he could think about was sleep. When he was not occupied with work, attending classes, or studying, he thought of that night ... of *it*. Those thoughts tore at his brain during the quiet times of the day. They flashed in and out of his consciousness as he lay in bed next to Maria, not touching her, not moving a muscle. He strenuously attempted to relax his aching, tired body and clear his mind, purge it, flush all thoughts from it, leave it devoid of activity so that he could fall asleep. And when he did slip into unconsciousness, he dreamed of that night, or else, when he awakened, he thought that he had. He was never sure because he always woke up in the middle of the night—the early morning dark—and was immediately consumed with thoughts of that night. Sometimes, he lay there, hoping, praying for sleep; other times, he crept out of bed and sat in the small living room in the dark. He tried not to awaken Maria. She needed her rest.

Besides that, if she knew he was awake, she would lead him back to bed, snuggle up against him, kiss him, and attempt to straddle him, to bring him to life. He did not want that because he knew he was no longer alive.

During their first weeks in the apartment, they had made love two or three times a day. After that dreadful night, Daniel always had to push thoughts of *it* from his mind and force himself to focus on Maria's lovely face and sumptuous hair and satiny skin to make himself ready. Then, as they kissed and grasped and shared their ardor for each other, Daniel was able to let go and allow himself to be transported to a place of exhilarating, sizzling ecstasy and comforting warmth. But when they finished, he always immediately felt guilty and empty and corrupt, as if he and Maria had made love on Jimmy's grave.

He never initiated their lovemaking anymore. Maria found it strange and upsetting. She was disappointed that, after that first rapturous period of fevered, joyous lovemaking, Daniel no longer wanted her. Then, assuming that, for some reason, he had become unsure of himself, she decided that she had enough desire and confidence for the both of them, so she took on the role of aggressor. Sometimes she was gentle and soft and sweet as she kissed Daniel and grasped him and guided him. At other times, she straddled him in a feverish, forceful embrace. He seemed to always need several minutes of encouragement before he was ready and able to participate in their lovemaking.

However, lately, no matter how much passion she exhibited, Daniel seemed to, at best, patiently lie there, as if he were waiting for it to be over.

"We have to talk about this," she said after Daniel had walked into the apartment, given her a halfhearted kiss, and collapsed on their bed.

He pulled off his shoes and turned over, ignoring her.

"I know something is seriously wrong. I don't think it's just 9/11. Even during those first few awful days, we were able to make love and you seemed to enjoy it. What's the matter?"

"I'm just very tired, Maria. I'll talk to you about it ... about things another time. Not now, please. I'm sorry. Just give me time to adjust."

"Adjust to what? Working? School? Me?"

"No. To ... things."

"It's either ... you don't really love me or you're not happy living with me. If either one is the case, please tell me. I love you, but I don't want you to feel trapped. That's not good for either of us."

"No. That's not it. I love you too and I'm fine ... I'm happy living here, as happy as I can be anywhere."

"As happy as you can be anywhere? Are you depressed? I mean clinically depressed? Do you want to speak to a psychologist? A psychiatrist?"

"No. It's nothing like that. I'm depressed ... yes, but it'll pass."

"When? It's been a couple of weeks now. I didn't expect you to move in and turn into a zombie."

"I'm sorry."

"No. Don't be sorry. I shouldn't give you a hard time. It's just that I love you so much and so look forward to seeing you ... and, as I told you, my mom was ... is very upset that I moved out and that we moved in together. She hasn't gotten over it yet. I don't want to think I made a mistake."

"You didn't. We didn't."

"So, if it's not me and you don't need to see a psychologist, then it must be what happened that night ... the fight, or was it something worse?"

"I need to sleep, Maria. I don't think I slept more than an hour last night. Can't we talk about this another time?"

"Sure. That's fine, but we do have to talk. Promise?"

"Yes. We'll talk ... just not today. Promise." Daniel closed his eyes and willed himself to sleep.

*****

He stood in front of the police station near his parents' house, watching people going in and out. He had said that he would drop by for a quick bite before his evening class. A police car drew up to the building. Two officers pulled a handcuffed boy from the back seat and led him up the steps to the building. Then Daniel walked back to his car and drove to his parents' house.

"Did you have a good day?" Maria asked when he walked into the apartment later that evening.

"Yes," he lied. He held Maria in his arms and kissed her with forced passion and counterfeit feeling.

"Oh, you seem to be better tonight. Good. Hungry?"

"No. I want to grade a few papers and then we can sit and talk for a while, if you want," he said.

"Sure. I'll just go back to my book. I'm really enjoying it. I'll tell you about it later. Let me know if you want anything."

He forced himself to concentrate on the essays that his students had written about *The Grapes of Wrath*. After he had completed his work, all he wanted to do was sleep, but he knew that was not an option. It was too early.

"So, how was your day?" he asked as he sat on the couch next to Maria.

She put down her book and told him about the new computer system they were installing in the library at Pratt to give students faster access to the book catalogue. He listened; he tried to understand what she was saying, but the waves of memory running through his head blocked out her voice.

"And ... since I knew you wouldn't be home until late, I went to Mitchell's apartment and we screwed for a couple of hours," she said.

When he realized that she was looking at him, he played back the mental recording of what she had just said, and smiled sheepishly.

"Okay, Daniel, that's it. What is going on in that head of yours?"

He did not know where to begin, but he had to try. He sat back on the couch and said, "Something happened that night."

"I know. I want you to tell me. Keeping it bottled up inside is killing you. You don't eat. You don't sleep. You're not here with me. You're going to destroy yourself. This thing is killing us."

"I know," he said. "I didn't want to worry you and I don't want you to hate me ... " he said, his words trailing off as his eyes began to tear.

"Daniel, no. Whatever happened will not make me stop loving you. I hope you know that I'm incapable of hating you."

"It involved somebody getting hurt ... killed."

She put her head down. He withdrew into himself. Then he told her the full story of what had happened that night.

"Where is this lot ... this place where you buried the body?"

"I don't want to tell you ... the more you know about it the more you could be hurt," he explained.

"Don't you trust me?" she asked.

"Of course. It's somewhere in East New York. I'm not sure where exactly. It's some run-down neighborhood."

"All of East New York is run down. Where did your wonderful friend Dominic dump the shovel?"

"I don't know. I guess in the bay somewhere. I don't know. Listen, no one is ever going to find out about what happened and I won't be in trouble ... at least not with the law or with Mr. De Luca. That's not the problem."

"You feel guilty."

"Yes. Of course I do. I called Dominic to tell him about Jimmy, instead of just going home. I saw him hit Jimmy. I helped him bury the body. I relive that night over and over again. It burns through my brain. Each time I think of it, I try to figure out what happened ... why it happened. I keep thinking that if I had not called him or if I had gone home or been stronger ... if I had done things differently—"

"It happened, Daniel. I knew ... Oh ... Never mind."

"I know what you want to say: 'I knew this would happen.' Right?"

"No. I didn't know, but you had to imagine that something like this would happen sooner or later. That's what those people do. You had to know it. I mean, if I did, how could you not?"

"I ... I wanted Dominic to find out about Jimmy. I didn't want anyone to get hurt, but I didn't want Jimmy to get away with what he was doing."

"What was he doing? He was stealing money from thieves ... from people who prey upon hard-working men and women."

"I know. I sort of ... I began to like being part of that life and I began to sort of think like those men."

"That's what happens. Remember when we first met and I said that I lived in a ghetto? Well, you've been in my neighborhood ... I mean where my parents live. It's not bad, but, if you're a teenage boy, sooner or later, one of the gangs is going to try to enlist you. All of my brothers said no. Only the smart, strong ones are able to do that."

"And I wasn't smart or strong."

"I don't know. Maybe you didn't realize what was happening. You have to figure that out. Now we have to deal with it. What are we going to do?"

"Maybe I should just go away ... let you go on with your life."

"My life is with you. I don't want to lose you, but if you want to move out, if you don't want to live with me, I won't hold it against you. If you stay, we have to confront this ... demon and find a way for you to get past it. I want to have a life with you," Maria said.

"I don't want to leave you. I want to go on with my life ... our life."

"Okay. What do we do?"

"I don't know. Maybe we can go away together ... to New England or something. Maybe that will help me," Daniel suggested.

"We can't do that. We both have jobs here. You're going to grad school. I'll be starting in the spring. We have this apartment. I have my family and you have your family. Running away isn't how you solve problems. You won't feel any better somewhere else."

"You're right."

"I understand how you feel, but, you know what? Jimmy was probably going to get killed at some point or another, and *you* didn't do it."

"But, if I—"

"If you hadn't been there, maybe it wouldn't have happened. If you hadn't walked into the career counseling office, we wouldn't have met."

"And maybe you would be better off than you are now."

59

They talked for the next couple of hours. By the time they got to bed, Daniel felt better than he had since before that night. Maria held him. After a while, he fell into a deep sleep. He awakened the next morning feeling more rested than he had in weeks.

"What do you say we go out to eat tonight?" he asked. "Something exotic like Thai or Ethiopian or something like that."

"Yes," she said with a smile as she walked out the door.

As he pulled up to the school and searched for a parking space, he saw what looked like Dominic's car double-parked in front of the building. Two minutes later, as Daniel walked to the entrance, Dominic called to him from his open car window, "Hey, man, you got a minute?"

"Just barely. I have to get to work."

"Oh, yeah. I see."

"What do you want?" Daniel asked from the sidewalk.

"You don't sound friendly. I got news for you. Come here for a sec."

"What?" Daniel asked through the open passenger side window.

"Come on this side. I don't wanna talk loud."

Daniel walked around to Dominic's side.

"Listen, Danny ... bad news. They found the package. Don't ask me how, but they found it. They're gonna come for you."

Daniel's legs felt weak and the morning's coffee shot up his throat with acidic fury. He stood there looking at Dominic, frozen to the street.

"Don't say nothin'. In fact, listen very carefully. I wouldn't be tellin' you this if they knew that I knew. In other words, they don't know. What I mean is I was in Mr. D's house last night. He invited me. Actually, I was leaving, but then I realized I left my jacket in Mr. D's study, where we were talking, so I go back to get it, but before I walk back into the room—I was in his big foyer ready to leave—I hear Joe Fish. You know him. In any case, they think I'm out the door. I hear Joe tellin' Mr. D how they got a tip from the cops about the package and how they dug it up and how they know it was you did it."

"I don't understand."

"Nothin' to understand. Somehow, the cops found the place ... you know, where the package is, and they dug it up or they told Mr. D and he had somebody dig it up. And, like I said, they think you did it."

"What should I do?"

"There's only one thing to do. Since I can't say nothin' to them about what happened ... how it wasn't really your fault and since I shouldn't even be tellin' you this and—like I said, if they knew I heard them, I wouldn't be tellin' you 'cause they wouldn't like that, but since they don't know, I'm safe to tell you—you gotta run. You should do it today. Don't wait until tomorrow."

"I can't. Where can I go?"

"Go to New Jersey ... to some woodsy place, and stay there for a few weeks or so. That's what I would do."

"No," Daniel said. "I'm not running and I'm not going to lose my job or Maria or anything."

"Really? And what do you think they are gonna do to you? Or ... to Maria or your mom and dad?"

"I'll go to them ... to Mr. D this afternoon."

"And tell him what, you asshole?"

"I'll say I met Jimmy and he punched me and I hit him."

"Why would he hit you? That story makes you sound very guilty."

"I am guilty."

"Yeah. Well, you see ... here's my worry. I'm worried that they are gonna do to you some things and you're gonna say that I had something to do with it."

"You did have *something* to do with it, but I won't mention you."

"Me? I wasn't even around that night. I was in AC playing the tables with a hot piece of ass that night."

"Sure, Dominic. Whatever. I won't implicate you."

"There's that word again. I don't like it. It sounds too much like *incarcerate*. Too much like *incinerate*."

"Don't worry, Dominic. I'm not going to *squeal*. You like that word better? I won't mention your name. You know why?"

"Okay. I'll bite. Why?"

"Because, one way or the other, you're going to end up in a shallow grave like Jimmy or a roadside ditch or a back alley. That's too bad for you, but it's the life you chose. Now, I'm going in to do my job."

*****

Strangely, Daniel felt better—not relaxed—but less upset than he had been since that night. He concluded that even though he was concerned by what Dominic had told him, he was relieved that the situation, his dilemma, was about to be resolved. But, he wondered, how did anyone find the grave and why would De Luca tie him to the killing ... the murder ... whatever it was? He *almost* remembered something that connected to that question, but he could not quite bring into focus that fragment of memory. In the way that, sometimes, a person cannot quite remember what he or she was going to say, this thought was almost, but not quite there in his consciousness. He was pretty sure it had something to do with the grave they had dug or the way they had dug it, but he could not call it to mind.

As he got into his car to drive home, he reached into his briefcase to retrieve his cell phone. He kept it on vibrate when he was at work and he checked it periodically, but had been too busy all day to do that. He saw four missed calls from a number he did not recognize. He decided he would call the number when he got home.

As he drove, he decided that Dominic was wrong about De Luca's people coming after him, because that just did not make any sense. However, he resolved that if they did approach him, he would remain calm and just tell his story. But, which story? He knew that he would have to admit that he had been there that night, but he could not ... would not say that he had hit Jimmy. He would say that Jimmy had approached him and asked what he knew about the money being taken. He would explain that he told Jimmy what he knew, which was nothing, at which point Jimmy hit him in the face and then drove off. He would say that he did not know what happened to Jimmy after that.

Dominic had to be wrong about what he thought he had overheard in Carmine De Luca's house. How would anybody have seen Jimmy being buried? He and Dominic had been in a dark, totally enclosed empty lot in a neighborhood with no high-rise buildings nearby. They had been below the sightline of anyone who might have been on the streets that night. Whoever might have seen Jimmy being carried or buried, if there really was someone, would also have seen Dominic. And, Daniel wondered, *Even if someone had witnessed that night's events, how would that person have been able to identify me?* It did not sound believable. Dominic had to be wrong. He had said that he was outside of the room where De Luca and Joe Fish were talking. He must have misunderstood what he heard. Dominic was crazy.

Dominic! Had *he* called one of the corrupt cops, one of the ones in the employ of Carmine De Luca? Had he told where to find Jimmy's body and had he implicated Daniel? *Implicated.* Daniel chuckled when he used that word as he attempted to solve the puzzle. But why would Dominic do that? Perhaps De Luca had suspected Dominic, and so he had blamed the crime on Daniel. But why would he then alert Daniel to the situation and tell him to run? Maybe Dominic knew that De Luca's people had been watching the two of them, and he figured that if Daniel ran, *he* would look guilty; Dominic probably figured that would take some of the pressure off him.

As Daniel was parking his car half a block down from the apartment building because he knew that at this hour of the day he was not likely to find a better spot, his phone rang. It was his mother: "Daniel, listen ... something happened. Listen carefully to me. Two men were waiting for me outside the house when I got home a few minutes ago. They asked for you. They said they owed you money ... a graduation gift."

Daniel was stunned and suddenly frightened.

"Does that make sense? Do they owe you money? A gift? They said it was a lot of money and they wanted to give it to you in cash. I didn't ask any questions. Do you think they were from that place where you used to work?"

"No. Nobody owes me money, although I wish they did," he said, attempting to sound happy and relaxed. "Did you tell them where I live now?"

"No. I didn't. It sounded like one of those scams. You know, where they say you won a prize, and all you have to do is pay the taxes or some other kind of thing so they can obtain your Social Security number."

"Right. That's probably what it was. Okay. I'll talk to you later."

This was more serious than he had thought. People were waiting for him so they could do ... what? Bring him to Carmine De Luca? Question him? Hurt him? He had been willing to talk to Mike Morici or Carmine De Luca, but he wanted to walk into a meeting, not be escorted in. Did they have the address of the apartment building and the apartment number where he lived with Maria? Probably not, but he decided not to go to the building. He was grateful that Maria would not be home for a couple of hours. He called her, suggesting that he pick her up at work at seven. Only Dominic knew at which school he worked, but, with the kind of contacts De Luca had, he would be able to find out.

From his car, he dialed the number of the missed calls.

"Hi, Daniel. How you doin'?" Daniel recognized the voice of Joe Fish.

"Hi. Is this ... Joe? Joe Fish?"

"Sure is. How are you, man?"

"I'm fine, Joe. What's happening?"

"I was hoping to see you."

"Oh. I'm sorry. I guess Mr. Morici didn't tell you. I don't work at the club anymore. I graduated from college and I have a teaching job now. I won't be going back there, because I'm very busy with my job and grad school."

"I know. Congratulations! That's why I'm calling. We owe you a graduation gift. We wanna give it to you. It's one thousand bucks. We wanna give you cash ... you know, kinda for how good a job you done all those years."

"Oh, you know, I thought Jimmy was joking when he said that to me a few weeks ago. You know, Joe, I don't feel right taking it, but thank you very much. You guys are so thoughtful."

"Don't be bashful, kid. It's good money. I wish somebody was handin' that kinda cash to me. I'd run to get it. You don't wanna offend us, do ya?"

"No, Joe. Don't b ... be offended, please. I mean, you guys were so good to me and ... you paid me well. I have a nice little nest egg. I would feel guilty ... I mean ... terrible taking that kind of money from you, but thanks anyway."

Daniel knew he had to cut the conversation short because his mouth was dry and he was so shaky that he was beginning to have trouble forming words.

"We *will* feel offended. Jimmy especially. He's the one that asked me to call you. Where are you? I'll come to you."

"Oh ... I'm on my way to Long Island. I have to visit someone there. Sorry, Joe. Is Jimmy there? Let me talk to him."

"No, Jimmy ain't with me. I'm in my car. You're going out to the island tonight? Don't you have work tomorrow?"

"Yes ... sure. I already told them I'm not going to be there ... that I was taking a long weekend. You understand."

"Oh, and you takin' that sweet little chocolate cupcake with you? What's her name? Maria? You lucky dog. I've seen her. Beautiful girl. What a sweet treat she must be."

Daniel suppressed a gasp.

"Daniel, you there?"

"Yes, Joe. I'm here. Listen, why don't I come around to the club on Monday afternoon? Let's say around 5 p.m. Would that work for you?"

"No, Daniel. It wouldn't. You know, you're being very rude. Didn't your mom, who I've had the pleasure of meeting, teach you to be polite and respond nicely to your elders, especially when they are going out of their way to give you a gift? I gotta say, you're embarrassing yourself."

"I'm really sorry, Joe, but I'm on my way to my aunt's place way out on the island. Maria is with me. I'll drop by Monday afternoon. I hope that's okay."

"Oh, your little beauty is with you? Let me say hello."

"Sorry, Joe ... she's asleep ... sleeping like a baby."

"Too bad. You know, I have to be in Queens tomorrow. Why don't I stay on the road and head out to your aunt's place? What's the address?"

"You know, Joe. I d ... don't know that address. Silly, huh? I just know how to get there. Listen ... the traffic's kind of heavy. I don't want to talk on the phone while I'm driving. I'll be there Monday at 5 p.m."

He ended the call. He opened the car windows and deeply inhaled the cool afternoon air. Then he closed his eyes and thought. He was not surprised that they knew where his parents lived; after all, he had lived there for years.

They had that phone number and his cell phone number, but how did they know what Maria looked like? The only times they could have seen her would have been when he had brought her to his parents' house, but that had not happened for a long time before that terrible night. And ... why would any of the men from the organization have been observing him back then? Then he had a sickening thought ... Dominic. Dominic again. But why?

He thought about calling Mike Morici, but he would just ask Daniel to come to the club. He considered calling Carmine De Luca's house to tell him his partially true version about what had happened that night, but he did not have the phone number, and it was unlisted.

He called Dominic. "Hey, Danny. How ya doin'?"

"I'm fine. I want to ask you—"

"Where you at? I'll meet you."

"No, Dom. What the hell is going on? This morning, you said—" He stopped talking when he heard the line go dead.

That meant that Dominic was worried that someone would hear their conversation and know that he had warned Daniel. Did that mean that Dominic really was looking out for him or did it add credence to what Daniel had begun to think, that Dominic wanted Daniel to run so that he would look guilty?

It was getting late. He had to decide what to do ... now. He went to his local branch of Chase, where he withdrew $2,000, roughly half of what he had on deposit. He left the couple of hundred dollars he had in his checking account. Then he called his mother to say that he would be going on a trip and would not be able to talk to her for a while, but that he was okay.

"This has to do with those gangsters, doesn't it? Did they hurt you?" she asked, her voice cracking with fear.

"No, mom. I'm fine. It's just best that I go away for a while. I'll get in touch with you. Don't call my cell phone. I'll get a new phone, and call you."

"Daniel, no. I'll call the police. They'll meet you. You'll be safe."

"No, ma. It doesn't work that way. At least one or two of them in the local precinct are on the payroll of those men ... and, before you tell me that you'll call police in some other precinct or something else like that, don't. They all talk to each other. I know what I'm doing. Trust me."

"Daniel, we trusted you. I don't know why I let you do this. Your father was the smart one. I gave in and convinced myself that you would be careful."

"It'll be fine. I promise ... I'll call you." He hung up and then he slammed his cell phone against his forehead over and over again.

5
Driving North

"You look awful. What happened to your head?"

"Oh, nothing. I bumped it. I'm fine."

"Daniel, what's the matter? Did somebody die?"

"No. It's just ... give me a sec."

"Tell me. You're scaring me. What happened?"

As they sat in Daniel's car in front of Pratt, he started telling Maria what had happened, but he was not able to focus. He thought about Jimmy and the bloody wound and the grave and the shovel.

Suddenly, he said, "Oh, no."

"What?" Maria asked.

"I think I know what happened. That night, Dominic didn't finish the ... I mean he didn't fully cover up ... you know. He put the shovel down. I picked it up and I finished the job. In fact, he wiped off the handle with a handkerchief before he put the shovel down on the ground. Then I picked it up. After I finished covering up ... Jimmy, I carried the shovel to the car ... to the trunk. He said he would dispose of it the next day. I never thought of asking him about it."

"What happened? Does somebody know about that night?"

"Yes. Somebody, probably Dominic, called one of the crooked cops who's on De Luca's payroll and told about the grave, but first, he must have gone back and put the shovel there. He must have worn gloves. The police probably did the fingerprints and they told De Luca the prints are mine."

"But how would they know they're your fingerprints?"

"I don't know. Well, when I got my teaching license, I had to fill out all sorts of papers and get fingerprinted. They must have access to those files."

"I don't know. That's kind of hard to believe."

Neither one spoke for a few seconds.

"What are we going to do, Daniel?"

"We have to go away ... out of the city ... out of the state. I'll write a long letter to De Luca. I'll explain everything. I'll implicate Dominic. He killed Jimmy. I think Dominic knew Jimmy wasn't going to hurt me. I think he planned on killing Jimmy before he got there, to the alley. Otherwise, why would he have taken a tire iron from the trunk of his car? He must be the one who told about me. He's hoping they'll be convinced I'm guilty and they'll kill me, but why? Why wouldn't he just leave things as they were? Why would he tell about Jimmy? I guess he worried that I'd talk about it because I felt guilty."

"I don't know, Daniel. I can't just go away. I just started working here. I don't think you should go away either. We could move to a new apartment."

"No. I don't think they know where we live, but they know where my parents live and they know about you ... at least, what you look like."

"What? How?"

"Dominic again. This guy, Joe Fish, he described you as a dark beauty or something like that. He's probably going off Dominic's description of you."

"I'm frightened."

"That's why we have to leave. Today. Now."

"I can't," she said and began to cry. "Daniel, if you leave your job now, without notice, you may never get a teaching job again, and then what will you do? Isn't there some other way?"

"No. I don't think so. I'm going to call my school tomorrow morning and tell the secretary and my department head that my grandmother in ... I don't know ... Arizona ... is ... dying or has Alzheimer's or something and I have to care for her. I'll take a leave of absence. I'm pretty sure I can do that."

Maria was silent.

"Please come with me," Daniel said.

"I love you and I want to be with you, but I can't just leave my job. I don't think I can just run away. Isn't there some other way?"

"I don't know. I think this is the best shot. I'll write the letter to De Luca. I'll stay away a few weeks. I'll get a cell phone that can't be traced. I'll put the new phone number in the letter."

"I'll never see you again."

"You will. I'll call back Joe Fish and tell him that I'm going away and that nobody knows where I'm going because I won't tell anyone."

"I'm not worried about me. I'll never see you again. I was so happy snuggling up to you at night. I thought we had a life. You *are* my life."

"Maria, listen: I can't stay here now. I'm radioactive. They're looking for me. If they pick me up or if I walk in there now, then, you're right—you never will see me again."

Maria insisted on going home alone, telling Daniel not to worry about her. As he watched her disappear down the stairs to the subway station, his heart sank and he felt defeated. He swore to himself that he would stay away for only as long as it would take to make his case to Carmine De Luca. Then, at the thought of what he was losing, he became enraged. He felt ready to kill someone, but who? Dominic? What good would that do?

He pulled out from his parking space and headed toward the Brooklyn-

Queens Expressway. Without thinking and without any plan, he drove over the Verrazano Bridge to Staten Island and then the Goethals Bridge to the New Jersey Turnpike. He headed north toward upstate New York.

Hours later, when hunger and exhaustion made continued driving impossible, he stopped at a diner on a country road in the middle of deep woods. Two men who looked like farmers were sitting at a table eating pie and drinking coffee. A skinny blonde was behind the counter. He used the toilet, washed his hands and face, and walked back out to the dining area.

"Counter or table or booth? Plenty of room," said the waitress.

He sat at a booth near the back. The waitress brought a menu to him and said that there were no more specials.

"That's fine," he said. "A big bowl of soup ... any kind ... and a burger special and coffee and a big glass of water. Please bring the water now."

"Sure. I guess you been driving a long time."

He gulped the water. Then he sucked on the ice cubes and crunched them in his mouth. While he waited for his Yankee bean soup to cool, he thought about a second conversation he had with Joe Fish while he had been driving.

"You got a lotta balls, kid. You lied to me before when you said you were goin' to Long Island, didn't you? Tell me straight."

"Sorry, Joe. It's not like you were being straight with me."

"Of course I was. I have your money right here. I wanna give it to you."

"No you don't, Joe. You want to talk to me about something else."

"Oh, yeah? What's that?"

"Look, Joe. I'm driving. I can't stay on the phone. I just wanted to tell you that I'm not going to be around for a while. My parents don't know where I'm going and Maria doesn't know. The truth is I don't know either."

"Tell me where you're going, kid. I'm sure you could use the money."

"I have to say this, Joe. I don't trust you. In fact, I don't trust anybody."

"How about your good friend Dominic? You trust him?"

"At this point, no. I don't. I've cut my ties with everyone. I told my mother that I would see her in a few months. I told my girlfriend that I'm radioactive and that I probably won't see her again."

"Okay, kid. You're doin' a dumb thing, but it's your skin. I'll call you tomorrow. Maybe we can come to an accommodation."

"Don't bother, Joe. I'm going to put the phone on the road now and then I'm going to run over it. I'll leave it on so you can hear the sound."

That is what he did. Now he was alone, away from his job, cut off from his family, Maria, and ... hopefully, from the men he used to admire.

*****

He slumped in his chilly car in a desolate corner of the diner parking lot, lost in depressing, dismal thoughts. He wondered how he could have fallen into such a deep and dangerous hole and how he could extricate himself and how he could protect his family and Maria. Was Dominic the one? Had Jimmy been the thief or had he been asking about Dominic because he believed that Dominic had been the one taking cash from the envelopes?

The grave ... the shovel. He fell into a restless sleep during which he dreamed of that awful night.

*****

Early morning sunlight streamed through his windshield. He awakened in a sweat. He was sore and he felt dirty. Then, remembering that he had to call his school to explain his absence, he searched for his cell phone before he remembered that it was miles back, crushed and dead on the road.

He entered the diner and used the phone hanging on the wall near the bathrooms. It was a difficult conversation because the school secretary wanted to know how many days he would be absent. When he told her that he would probably have to take off the entire term, she asked him to wait, put the call on hold, and transferred it to the head of the English department, Dr. Frankel, who complained, saying, "If we had known this we would never have hired you." Then he transferred the call back to the secretary, who explained which forms Daniel would have to download from the New York City Department of Education Web site to file for a leave. He thanked her and hung up. At this point, his job and all of the mundane aspects of his life had to take a back seat to his primary goal, which was to find a safe place in which to hide.

After he had used the toilet and washed up as well as he could in the little sink, he went to the same table at which he had sat the night before, and ordered breakfast. He asked the waitress, a different skinny blonde, where the nearest town was and whether it contained a library. After she thought for a while, she gave him directions to Oneonta, which she referred to as a "city." She said that it was only a couple of hours away by car.

By early afternoon, after many wrong turns and a fill up at a gas station, he found his way to a convenience store in Oneonta, where he bought a cell phone with pre-paid minutes and a box of business envelopes. Then he drove to the Huntington Memorial Library, where he printed out a Leave of Absence Without Pay form. He filled it out. Then he composed a letter to Carmine De Luca. He thought long and hard about what tone to use, eventually deciding that he had to sound secure and guilt-free.

Mr. De Luca:

Please understand that I was with Jimmy Tripelli one night back in August. He caught up with me in an alley between two apartment buildings on Bath Avenue near Bay Parkway. I had been visiting a friend. He asked me whether I knew where Dominic Savarino was. I told him I had seen Dominic earlier in the week but did not know where he was. He got angry and punched me in the nose. Then he drove off.

I do not know what happened to him after that. I know you want to talk to me. Joe Fish contacted me. I think you believe I am or was responsible for money of yours that went missing. Not only did I never take any money from you or anyone else, but I don't know a thing about it.

I am far from Brooklyn now and will remain away until I feel it is safe to return. Nobody knows where I am because I simply called my parents and my girlfriend and told them I was going away.

You will see the postmark on this envelope, but don't waste your time sending people up here. By the time you read this letter, I will be hundreds of miles away.

I would like to talk to you to straighten out this matter. If you are willing to promise that no harm will come to me, I will go to your house—nowhere else—to talk to you. I know you are an honorable man and a man of your word.

You may call me at the phone number that I have written on a separate sheet of paper that I've enclosed with this letter. I will dump this phone in exactly five days—that's enough time for you to read this note and call me. I would like to straighten out this matter. I want to return to my life.

Daniel Montello

He addressed an envelope and put the letter into it. Then he addressed one to the Department of Education and placed the completed form in that one. One of the librarians, a young woman, gave him directions to the local post office.

He wondered what Maria was doing at that moment; he hoped she was not too upset to work. He worried about his parents. He would call them from his new cell phone later in the day after he had figured out what he was going to do. He did not know what that would be.

At the post office, Daniel had a fright. As he handed a twenty-dollar bill to the clerk behind the counter, he saw a man who looked so much like Tommy La Salle that he thought about running out the door without his change. As he stood there, waiting for the clerk to complete the transaction, he told himself that, yes, he was in danger, but surely not here, in some little town in upstate New York. No one knew where he was. *He* just barely knew where he was. All that he knew for sure was that, one day after leaving home, he was miserable, lonely, and lost.

He stopped at a pizzeria just for the aroma. It was smoky and spicy and familiar. He slumped at a table far from the front window drinking coffee and reading a copy of the local paper. He had not slept well in his car in the diner parking lot. One of the men behind the counter told him there were a couple of hotels in town and a few motels on the outskirts, so he drove several miles out of town, stopping at a place called Sleepy Pines, a collection of tiny log cabins in the midst of a densely wooded lot a few hundred feet from the road.

He paid the manager, who had come out of his cabin when Daniel drove up, $50 in cash for a cabin. It smelled of pine and mildew and wood smoke. He locked the door, removed his shoes and jacket, and collapsed onto the bed. He seeded his mind with thoughts of Maria, hoping that they would blossom into sweet dreams of her that night.

When he awakened from a dreamless sleep, it was dark. He fumbled his way through the musty room and searched the walls by feel until he found a switch. One weak bulb in a fixture in the ceiling provided the only light. He shivered. There was no thermostat and no source of heat other than a stone fireplace. On the dusty mantel he found matches and a hand-written note:

To lite fireplace use these matches and balled up these news paper and pine cones for kindling plenty of wood once the fire gets going the wood is outside the door

Daniel followed the directions. Then he sat staring at the flames.

71

He knew that he had to make plans. For one thing, he had to buy clothes. All he had was what he had worn to work the day before.

Is that all it's been? One day?

He needed soap, shampoo, and other supplies. Later, as the fire was dying, he put on his jacket and shoes and walked out of the cabin to his car. The air smelled clean and damp and ... foreign. It was not just that he was in a new place ... it was that, to remain safe, he had to hide in the shadows.

He drove back toward Oneonta, stopping at a shopping center that he had spotted earlier that day. He bought clothing and toiletries. He removed his sport coat and put it in one of the bags. Then he put on the fall jacket he had just purchased. After placing the bags in the trunk of his car, he returned to the mall. He ate in the noisy food court, where, amidst families, groups of teenagers, and senior couples, he felt more alone than he had believed possible.

It was 9 p.m. He collected his thoughts, forced a smile, and called Maria.

"Oh, God. Where are you?"

"I can't say. I can say that I miss you so much it hurts."

"I miss you too. Are you okay?"

"Yes, I'm fine. I'm far from the city. I sent a letter to Carmine De Luca telling him that I'm willing to meet with him if he gives me his word that I'll be all right. I sent it today."

"Do you think you can trust him? I don't."

"I don't know. It's funny ... I should be frightened, but I'm not. I feel that I'm in control. I don't like being away from you and my job, but I feel strong."

"Your job! What are you going to do?"

"I downloaded a form for a leave without pay and I filled it out and mailed it. I'll worry about that another time."

"What address did you use?"

"My parents' house. That's the one on file for me. I never got around to changing it to your ... I mean our place."

"Our lovely life together didn't last long. Did it?"

"No, but we'll pick up where we left off ... once this is over."

"Have you spoken to your mom and dad?"

"I will. After I hang up with you."

"Your regular number didn't come up. Do you have a new phone?"

"Yes. I picked up one of those pre-paid things. You can reach me at this number for a couple of days. Then, after I speak to Mr. De Luca, I'll get rid of it and buy another one. I don't want them calling me. I want to keep them off balance until I settle this."

"You know, you don't have to call him *Mr.* De Luca, as if he's a person of great respect. He's a gangster."

"I know, but he is sort of impressive. In any case, once De Luca promises me safe passage, I'll talk to him and explain what happened, and it will be over. Please be patient."

"I can be patient, but I'm worried about you."

"I love you," he said.

"Forever," she replied.

His phone call to his mother was more difficult. Always the problem solver, she came up with a dozen ways of resolving his situation. He listened patiently, and then he said that he would think about what she had suggested. Then he spoke to his father, who, having a better grasp of the depth and seriousness of Daniel's circumstances, sounded more upset than his mother had.

It was much too early to return to the cramped confines of his little cabin, so he wandered through the shopping mall, eventually stopping in a Barnes and Noble, where he bought a copy of *The Return of the Native*.

Daniel slowly made his way back to the log cabin encampment through a driving rain. He was not used to traveling on unlit country roads at night in any kind of weather. More than once, he was startled by deer darting across the road.

The cabin was cold and damp, so he lit a fire. He was proud of the fact that he was able to do it quickly and efficiently. When the cabin had warmed up, he put away the clothing he had bought, with the exception of a sweatshirt and a pair of sweatpants, which he slipped into in place of his shirt and slacks. He put the toiletries in the bathroom and then he pulled the rough blanket from the bed, placed it on the floor in front of the hearth, and lay down.

He started reading. Halfway down page four, he realized he had lost track of the plot, so he started reading again from the beginning. After another ten minutes, he put the book down and attempted to clear his mind so that he would be able to focus. He thought of Maria and his parents and Dominic and Jimmy and that awful night. At that point, he knew he would not be able to read.

He thought about what Dominic had told him: *they* knew where Jimmy was buried and they believed Daniel was responsible. Assuming nobody had seen him and Dominic with Jimmy's body, which is what he believed to be the case, then Dominic was the only one who could have told them the location of the grave. Had he also implicated Daniel? How would he be able to convince the men in the De Luca organization that Daniel had killed and buried Jimmy? Why would he do that? Dominic had been afraid of being punished by De Luca because, instead of just collecting evidence to prove that Jimmy had been the thief, he had killed the man, a *made-man*, without permission. But why wouldn't he just have left the evidence of the crime buried in that shallow grave?

The only piece of information about which Daniel felt confident was that Dominic did not want any of them to know that he had warned Daniel. That was why he had hung up on Daniel yesterday. That might be one point in his favor. But the shovel. Why hadn't Dominic finished covering up the grave? Had he guessed that Daniel would pick up the shovel to finish the job and then be so damned stupid as to not wipe off his own fingerprints, even though Dominic had wiped his off earlier? Is that why he had told Daniel to put the shovel in the trunk of his car? The trunk ... there had been a big pool of Jimmy's blood in the well. If push came to shove, that bit of evidence might help Daniel to prove that Dominic was the killer, but he had surely washed away the blood by now.

Daniel felt tired again, but he wanted to think about this for a while longer. Even if they had the shovel, how would they be able to compare the prints on it to Daniel's? De Luca had a lot of pull and knew scores of influential people. Daniel wondered: Had De Luca been able to gain access to the files at the Department of Education and obtain a copy of his fingerprints? It was unlikely but possible.

Daniel was suddenly very thirsty. He put on his new sneakers and jacket and walked out of the cabin. The chilly early-fall air smelled of pines.

"Can I help you?" It was the manager.

"Hi. I was looking for a soda machine."

"Don't got one. You want a drink? I have a nice bottle in my cabin. About to crack it open."

"No thanks. I was hoping for a soda. You know, something sweet."

"Don't drink the stuff. Just black coffee, beer, and whiskey."

"Thanks. I appreciate the offer, but I'm not much of a drinker, especially when it comes to whiskey ... " Then a sickening thought flashed across his brain: whiskey ... Mike Morici had told Daniel to take a clean glass from the bar. Then he had poured whiskey into the glass without touching it, but Daniel had. When Daniel had finished sipping, he had placed the glass back on the table; Morici had stared at it without touching it.

Is Morici working with Dominic? Why? Were they the ones, and not Jimmy, who had been skimming cash? Did Dominic kill Jimmy because he feared the man was trying to collect evidence against him?

In the cabin, Daniel began to realize, as his eyes grew heavy and a curtain of leaden darkness began to envelop him, that no matter how many of the clues in this serious game he deciphered, he was going to be on the losing end.

6

The Woods Are Lovely, Dark, and Deep

Five days passed. Daniel had still not received a phone call from Carmine De Luca. He could not decide whether that was a good or a bad sign. Had the man decided not to call because he had bigger fish to fry? Perhaps he had figured out that Dominic and Mike Morici were the ones taking the money and that Daniel was an innocent bystander. Of course, it was possible that De Luca had not seen the letter. Maybe Daniel had addressed it incorrectly or Big Al Caselli, the doorman/bodyguard, had not given the note to him. Not wanting to lose his small advantage, Daniel decided that he had to wait, and not write again.

Each time he spoke to Maria or his parents, they sounded increasingly depressed and worried. He attempted to reassure them that he was playing his cards, the few that he had, the right way.

"Daniel, I'm going crazy. I can't work. I can't sleep. I want you home."

"I can't come home, Maria, not without a promise from De Luca."

"Then I want to see you. I have to see you. This weekend ... I'll come to you. Where are you?"

"I don't want to say."

"Do you think they have my phone tapped?"

"I don't know. I don't see how. They don't know anything about you except for your first name and how you look because that's all Dominic knows about you, but ... I just don't know for sure."

"Are you far away? Can you sneak back into the city? You could meet me somewhere ... anywhere."

"I'm afraid they might be watching you. As I said, I don't see how they could know about you, but I can't be sure. Be patient, please."

Even as he said that, Daniel was growing impatient. He felt constricted, as if he had been shoved into a box on a shelf and he was awaiting transport back to his life. He ate only when he was very hungry. He was bored and despondent and he was worried about money. He had spent much of the $2,000 that he had withdrawn from his bank account, money that he had saved up over the years to pay for graduate school. He had another $1,800 or so in his account, but he was reluctant to go to a branch of Chase to withdraw the rest because he feared that would allow De Luca's people to trace his whereabouts. For the same reason, he would not use his charge card or his checking account. He decided that, when he was ready to relocate, he would empty the account.

The thought upset him because doing that would mean that his life would never return to normal. He worried about bills that might be arriving at his parents' house; the only one he could think of was his one charge card. His car insurance was paid up for the year and his license and registration would not expire for months. He hoped to be home by then. He assumed letters would be arriving from the Department of Education, but he was not concerned about that.

He looked out the window of his cabin. It was a bleak, cold day. Deciding that he needed some exercise, he put on a second sweatshirt and his jacket and walked into the deep woods surrounding Sleepy Pines. After 45 minutes of walking, he heard the sound of a tree branch snapping. He stopped and looked behind him. Nothing. Silence. He thought of the final lines of his favorite Robert Frost poem: "The woods are lovely, dark, and deep, but I have promises to keep, and miles to go before I sleep, and miles to go before I sleep." He shuddered as he pictured the image.

The faint sound of gunshots echoed through the woods, making Daniel think that De Luca could easily arrange for his death here, in this desolate hunting paradise. As Daniel sat on a rocky outcropping, rain began to fall, almost instantly turning into a downpour. He pulled up his jacket collar and began trudging back toward the cabin, only to realize a few minutes later that he was lost. It all looked the same. He cursed himself for walking blindly and not keeping track of his direction. The heavy rain obscured his view of the sky; even if it had been a sunny day, he would still have gotten lost because he had not paid attention to the location of the sun. City dwellers notice only weather conditions and how light or dark it is outside. They do not take note of the sun's transit in the sky. He patted his pocket, and then remembered that he had left his phone in the cabin.

He frantically scanned his surroundings. Then, bending forward, he resumed walking. The rain beat down on his head, drenching his hair and dribbling down his forehead; although he pulled his collar up and held it closed with one hand, water trickled down his neck to his back. As he slogged through soggy spots, his sneakers and his socks became saturated. He stopped, looked around, shivered, and continued plodding through the gloomy, dank woods until he reached a spot where the undergrowth thinned out and opened onto a field. He struggled through thick gooey mud for another 20 minutes, eventually reaching a stone wall surrounding a farmhouse.

Not finding a gate, he scaled the wall and headed toward the house. Before he reached the front door, it opened. A scruffy-looking man with a long white beard stood there. Daniel told him that he was lost and asked how he could find his way back to Sleepy Pines. Without saying a word, the man disappeared for a few seconds, leaving Daniel on the doorstep. He returned, wearing a yellow rain slicker and hat and, after closing the door, brushed past Daniel and walked down the path from the house. Assuming the man did not want to bother with him, Daniel took a few steps and then looked around in an attempt to figure out which way to travel. Just then, the man pulled up in a battered pickup truck. He stared, not at Daniel, but straight ahead. When the man gunned the engine, Daniel approached the truck, pulled open the passenger side door, and climbed in.

As the man drove along bumpy, flooded roads, Daniel looked at the clutter in the truck: cigarette packages, beer bottles, newspapers, cans of motor oil, and crushed paper bags and wrappers of all sorts. The truck smelled of old food, but Daniel was so grateful to be out of the cold rain that he would have gratefully spent the night there. When they reached Sleepy Pines, the man stopped. Daniel thanked him, but the man did not reply. As soon as Daniel hit the ground, the truck puttered away.

Back in the cabin, Daniel checked his cell phone. No missed calls or messages. He dried his hair, started a fire, and hung his saturated clothes and jacket on a chair in front of the hearth. He placed his sodden sneakers as close to the grate as he felt was safe. Then he put on dry clothes. Tomorrow, he decided, he would buy heavier clothing, a hat, gloves, and a pair of waterproof boots. Then he added a compass to the list.

Later that night, Maria called him. She was frantic. "Some man called me a few minutes ago. He said his name is Joe and he's a friend of yours; he said he saw you and you were all right."

"What? No. I hope you didn't say anything."

"I listened. At first, I thought he was on the level, but then I asked him how he had gotten my phone number. He was very smooth. He sounded hurt, as if I had insulted him. He said something like, 'What do you think? Daniel and me are buddies. He gave me your number.' I think it was that Joe Fish guy."

"Sounds like it. Did you tell him anything?"

"I asked him where you were, but he didn't answer. He tried to get me to reveal something ... he kept beating around the bush, like he was hinting and he was hoping I would fill in the blanks."

"That's why they call him Joe Fish ... he fishes for information ... that and his name is actually Pesci, Italian for *fish*. When they need information, they call him and say, 'Go fish.'"

"He said he wanted to bring a package from you. He said he had my address on a piece of paper, but lost it. When I didn't say anything, he said how

Maria is such a nice name, like music playing, and he sang a line from *West Side Story*. Then he asked me my last name. How did he get my number?"

"Let me think," Daniel said. Then, after a few seconds, he continued: "They must have access to my old cell phone records. They probably called every number that I called on a regular basis."

"Oh, no."

"You're going to have to change your number. I think it's possible for them to find you. Hang up now and shut your phone. Get a new phone or just a new number tonight. Ask the person in the store what you have to do to be untraceable ... say you're trying to avoid an old boyfriend. Call me back as soon as you get it. I'll buy a new pre-paid phone now. As soon as I hear from you, I'll give you my new number and then I'll dump this one."

"Okay. I will. Bye."

Daniel understood that De Luca was not going to call him to arrange a meeting unless he stood firm and kept out of sight for as long as it would take. As much as he hated the thought, he had to come to terms with the reality of his situation. He would not be going home for a long time, if ever at all.

An hour later, while Daniel was in the mall, Maria called with her new telephone number. He gave her his new number. Then, after reassuring her that she would be safe, he turned off his old phone and dropped it into a trash can. Before returning to his cabin, he purchased winter clothing, waterproof boots, and a large knapsack. He counted his remaining cash, knowing that he would have to withdraw the rest soon, which would mean a move to ... he did not know where.

Back at the cabin, he wrote a short note to De Luca:

Mr. De Luca:

This is my second and last attempt to contact you. I'm surprised you didn't call me after my first letter. There's no point trying to contact my family or any of my friends because they don't know where I am. After I put this note in the mail, I will move again ... far away. If you want to meet me and end this nonsense, call the number that I have enclosed in this envelope.

I did not take your money and I do not know who did, although, at this point, I have my suspicions.

Daniel Montello

He addressed and stamped it and then he put it in his briefcase. He took out a folder of essays written by his students and threw them into the fireplace. Then he picked up *The Return of the Native*. Over the past couple of days, he had managed to regain focus. He read the last 50 pages and, since he had nothing else to do, he went to bed, falling into an uneasy sleep.

The next morning, he packed his belongings into the knapsack, paid the owner of the cabin what he owed, and drove into town, where he ate breakfast in a coffee shop. Then, after withdrawing all but $100 of his money from his bank account, mailing the letter, and filling up his gas tank, he headed west.

He drove for hours, with no destination in mind. As he approached Jamestown, in far western New York, his car began shimmying and shaking and making grinding sounds. After 20 uncomfortable minutes, during which he was sure he was going to break down on the remote two-lane road on which he was traveling, he came to a forlorn-looking service station. The proprietor, a tall gangly man with bright red hair, walked to the car as soon as Daniel brought it to a stop; he gestured for Daniel to pop the hood. Daniel assumed that he was about to be gouged, but he had no choice. The car was not drivable as it was.

After a quick examination of the engine, the man instructed Daniel to leave the motor running and exit the car; then he drove it onto one of the three lifts, all of which were unoccupied, and turned on the hydraulics. He scrutinized and probed the car's undercarriage, and then, shaking his head, he told Daniel that his struts were shot, his wheels were out of alignment, his ball joints were leaking lubricant, and all four tires needed replacement. When Daniel asked how much that would cost, the man walked into his office and, checking a large, moth-eaten catalogue, wrote some numbers on a scrap of paper.

"Two thousand one hundred and twenty-seven dollars."

Daniel's stomach fell. "Is it worth it? The car's kind of old."

"That's up to you. You can keep a car running as long as you want if you're willing to spend money on it."

"Okay. Right. How much for you to fix it enough for me to drive to the next big town? I'll dump it there."

"You sure you wanna do that? Sounds like you'd be throwing your money away," the man replied in an annoyed voice.

"I don't have that kind of money. Sorry."

"You can charge it."

"No. I don't have a charge card," Daniel replied.

"Hmm. Let me think," the man said as he scratched his stubbly chin. "Tell you what ... I can do the repairs, minus the tires, for $1,800. As I don't

79

have nothin' else to do, I can work on it now. The car will run okay, but you'll have to buy tires at some point soon."

"What about without the alignment? How much for that?"

"That would be $1,650."

"Sorry. That's still too much."

"What are you, a New York City Jew?" the man asked.

"Yeah. Something like that," Daniel replied, and decided not to add "A Jew who knows guys who could straighten you out in a minute."

As Daniel continued on his way, the car shook and lurched from side to side. He hoped he could make it to the next town before it died. It was just another part of his old life that he would have to abandon.

The car seemed to sigh with relief when Daniel shut it down in the parking lot of a motel on the outskirts of Jamestown. He irrationally hoped a night's rest would do the car some good. After he had booked a room, he called Maria's cell phone. She asked him when he would be able to come home.

"I'm so sorry, Maria. Be patient. I think this will be over soon."

"It will never be over. I don't know why I asked you when you'd be able to come back. You'll never be safe here again."

"They haven't contacted you again, have they?" he asked.

"No. I'm fine, but we'll never have a life, will we?"

"Yes. We will. If I have to spill my guts to the police and we have to run away to some other country, we will."

"I can't do that. I have parents and sisters and brothers and nieces and nephews and a good job. I can't just give up all of that."

"No. Of course. You're right," Daniel agreed. "I'll straighten this out this week one way or the other."

"Be careful. Don't do anything dangerous."

"I won't. I can't believe how I got myself in so deep. I was just trying to earn money and I ... I guess I began to think it was all okay ... I mean what they do and how they live ... I fit in and I thought I wouldn't be touched by what they did, but now we're both suffering the consequences of ... my blindness."

"You didn't know."

"I did know. I think I realized that I could get too involved. I sort of liked the thrill of being with those guys. Oh, I don't know."

After he hung up his phone, he ate at a little roadside restaurant within walking distance of the motel. Then he returned to his room and watched the news on television until his eyes began to close. Maria was there, and then she wasn't ... it was Jimmy or Dominic or. ...

80

He woke up in a cold sweat in the dark room, grateful to have been rescued from the horror that he had just seen and felt. It had been the old dream, but with a few nasty new twists: Jimmy's dead body was in an open shallow grave in the basement of the apartment building where Daniel had lived. Daniel was alone, covered in blood. He was holding the bloody shovel with what looked like a hunk of Jimmy's scalp adhering to its rusty blade.

Two days later, the phone call came in.

"Daniel, this is Carmine De Luca. I am sorry I did not call you sooner, but I never received the first letter you referred to in your note to me."

"You don't have to apologize, Mr. De Luca. I just want this misunderstanding to be over."

"Of course. Such a shame. I will not ask you where you are. I know you will not want to reveal that. How shall we resolve this problem?"

"I would like to meet you, just you; someplace where I would feel safe."

"Of course. You do not need to worry, Daniel. I am a businessman. I am not an angry man. Would you like to come to my house?"

"No."

"But what's wrong with my house? I thought you wanted to come here."

So, he did see my first letter.

"No, Mr. De Luca. I'm far from Brooklyn and my car is in bad shape. I would like you to meet me where I am ... in a public place ... you alone."

"That is not how I do business, especially with someone like you. If you come here, I will guarantee your safe passage," De Luca replied.

"You are a man of honor, so I know you are speaking the truth, but I will not return to the city until I know this is over and I am safe. If you are unwilling to meet me where I am, then I will make no further attempts to contact you."

"Why should I care?"

"Let me ask you this, Mr. De Luca: during the period of time that I have been *in the wind*, has your problem ... the problem of your money being stolen, has that ended?"

"I do not know what you mean. No money of mine is missing."

"Oh. Then I guess I was wrong. I thought that was the issue ... or at least the beginning of it. If someone is still taking your money, I think I know who it is. And, if you are willing to meet me, alone, I will tell you exactly what happened to Jimmy Tripelli ... how he died and who did it."

"Why should I believe you? You are making it obvious that you do not trust me. Maybe you want to harm me."

"Mr. De Luca, I am not one of you ... I did not choose to live your kind of

81

life. I foolishly thought I could work with your people and not be affected by their life ... that I would not be tainted by it. I want to return to my girlfriend and my family and my teaching job and my life. I don't want to hurt anyone."

"You know, young man, I do not usually agree to this sort of thing, but I will make an exception in your case. Where shall we meet and when?"

"I'm in Jamestown. It's in far western New York State."

"Is that near Niagara Falls?"

"No. It's about 200 miles south." Then, after consulting a map he had picked up from a rack in the motel office, Daniel said, "Meet me in the public library in Jamestown. It's on West 5th Street, between Washington and Cherry. When is a good time for you?"

"None of this is convenient for me. I will call you back in an hour."

"Why?" Daniel asked.

"I must arrange this trip with my driver."

Daniel sat still, breathing deeply, attempting to quiet his racing heart. He did not know whether meeting this man was a good idea, but he felt he had no other choice. *My life hangs in the balance of this meeting with a gangster*, he thought. Then, as he walked to the parking lot, he began to plan. He turned the key in the ignition of his car, praying that it would start. It did. He put the car into gear, hoping that it had healed itself during its two-day rest and that it would no longer shake and groan, but, as he drove, it sounded and felt worse than before.

After traveling a few blocks, he pulled to a curb and consulted the Jamestown map again. Then he drove a few more blocks and pulled into the parking lot of the library. He walked into the building and introduced himself to the librarian, Mrs. Marshall, and the woman who was stationed at the check-out desk, Ms. Flynn. When he asked how he could go about taking out a library card, they told him that he had to present proof of residency in Chautauqua County. He smiled and said that he would do that in a couple of days. He told them that he was an English teacher and explained that he had specialized in nineteenth century literature. He told them that his girlfriend was a librarian in Brooklyn. After a few more minutes of cordial and what he hoped had been memorable conversation, he left the building. He scanned the parking lot. Then he walked to the sidewalk and followed it to the corner, turned up that street, and walked all the way around the block and back to where he had started. Then he returned to his car and sat.

An hour later, De Luca called, saying he would meet Daniel in the library in Jamestown in two days at 4 p.m.

*****

On the day of the arranged meeting, Daniel spent time in the library. He made sure to talk to Mrs. Marshall and Ms. Flynn again so that, later, when he would say hello to them in the presence of De Luca, it would be obvious that they knew him. Then he left the library. If he had not been so overwrought, he would have had a difficult time keeping his eyes open because he had hardly slept since the phone call two days before.

At 3 p.m., he parked his car in the lot and walked into the library again; he sat at a table near the librarian's desk, thumbing through magazines. At a little after 4 p.m., Big Al Caselli walked in and spotted Daniel. Then he walked out and returned a minute later with Carmine De Luca. Big Al stayed near the door. As De Luca approached his table, Daniel stood up and looked at the man. Then, although his hands were cold and clammy, he extended them to greet De Luca. The older man held Daniel's hand for what seemed to be an excessively long time, all the while looking at him, although he seemed to be staring right through Daniel. It was as if he were somewhere else. Then he focused, released Daniel's hand, and sat; Daniel sat across from him.

"You know," De Luca began, "we could have met in a pleasant restaurant, and not in this God forsaken place. I had to fly out of LaGuardia and then lease a car here. Back in the city, I would have bought a nice meal for you."

"That's a very kind offer, Mr. De Luca, but I feel more comfortable here. Everybody knows me."

Attempting to mask his annoyance with a rigid smile, De Luca said, "Have it your way. What do you have to tell me?"

"First, I never stole any of your money or money from anyone else in my life. I worked in the club as a bartender, messenger, and clean up person. I never saw any cash except for what Jimmy or Mike Morici or the other men gave me to buy food. I was never in a position to take any money, and I never did."

"I know that. Go on."

"You know that? Then why have I had to hide out for the past month?" His already throbbing head began to make him feel dizzy.

"That was your decision. Joe Fish wanted to talk to you. You chose to run away from what would have been a congenial conversation."

"He did not sound congenial on the phone."

"He called to ask you about a situation. You know which one."

"Jimmy. Right?"

"Go on."

Daniel told the story. When he explained that Dominic had hit Jimmy on the head, he added, "but Dominic said he did that to protect me."

Carmine De Luca sat in silence for a moment, digesting the information, before he said, "Go on."

"Then Dominic and I put Jimmy in the trunk and we buried him at a construction site. End of story."

"That's it?"

"Yes."

"There must be more to this story. First, how did Dominic know that Jimmy was following you?"

"He asked me how it was I left the club after all the others, and I told him that Jimmy knocked over a bowl of pretzels as we were all leaving, and I stayed behind to clean up. Then I locked up. Dominic said Jimmy did that on purpose."

"What did Dominic hit Jimmy with?"

"A tire iron ... from his car."

"Jimmy ... he died from the blow to the head?"

Daniel thought long and hard before he reluctantly said, "No. I don't think so. I was in the car. Dominic got out. I felt the car shake ... I got out ... I saw Dominic reaching into the trunk. I think he was choking Jimmy. I'm not sure."

"And you didn't do anything?"

"I did. I pulled Dominic from the trunk. We both fell down. He punched me on my nose."

"I see."

"Why did you run when Joe Fish called you?"

Fighting the excruciating pain that was blazing through his head, Daniel explained, "That morning, Dominic caught me as I was about to walk into the school where I work ... where I worked, and told me that he had overheard Joe Fish telling you that Jimmy's body had been found and that I had killed him."

De Luca remained silent for a minute. Then, as he stood up, he said, "You can go home, young man. You are off the hook."

As Daniel walked De Luca to the door, he made sure to introduce him to Mrs. Marshall and Ms. Flynn, both of whom smiled. Mrs. Marshall said, "Have a nice afternoon, Daniel."

He smiled as he watched Carmine De Luca and Al Caselli get into a black Oldsmobile, exit the parking lot, and drive in the direction of the local airport. He waited another 10 minutes before getting into his car and driving back toward the motel. He felt relaxed and warm and relieved. He knew he had handled the meeting well. Two people were witnesses to his having been with

Carmine De Luca. The women had probably never heard of him, but they would be able to describe him and, perhaps, remember the name. On top of that, De Luca had said that Daniel's long nightmare was over. As he pulled to the side of the road to call Maria, he could not help but notice the gleaming Cadillac with two men in the front seat that slowly passed by because it was not a typical kind of car for Jamestown, New York. However, when it did not reappear, he convinced himself to forget about it.

Daniel told Maria how the conversation had gone. When she said that he should return home as soon as possible he told her he wanted to wait one more day. Then he called his parents and, without giving details, he explained that something bad had happened during the summer and that Dominic had implicated him. When he told them about his meeting with De Luca, his mother said, "Thank God." His father said that now Daniel had to watch out for Dominic because he might be in trouble with De Luca.

Shortly after Daniel reached the outskirts of town and entered the country road that led to the motel, he saw, in his rear view mirror, a car behind him. When Daniel attempted to accelerate, his car lurched and bucked and cried out in mechanical agony more than usual, so he slowed down. The car following him slowed. Daniel's hands instantly became sweaty and cold. He scanned the shadowy, desolate road ahead and the woods on both sides of him. He remembered that, a short distance ahead, there was a dirt driveway. Alternately looking at the road ahead and the headlights of the car in his rearview mirror, he proceeded slowly until, spotting the driveway, he turned into it and accelerated. The car wobbled and jumped and coughed on the rutted tree-lined lane. He did not see the other car in his rearview mirror, but he continued on the curving driveway until he reached a farmhouse, where he parked next to a blue pickup truck and an old Mercury sedan. He walked to the front door and, his heart thumping loudly, he knocked.

A short, heavy middle-aged woman dressed in a housecoat answered the door. He told her that he had engine trouble and asked whether he could use her phone to call for a tow truck. First, she shook her head no; then she said that he should wait on the doorstep. She closed the door. Daniel looked behind him. Nothing. A man wearing overalls opened the door. Daniel repeated his request.

"What seems to be the trouble with your car?"

"It just about broke down, sir," Daniel nervously explained.

Closing the door, the man said, "Well, I got my flashlight. Let me take a look and listen. I'll see if I can get you going."

"It happens when I drive," Daniel said. "I don't think you're going to be able to tell by checking the engine. I'd like to use your phone to call for help."

"Let's check it anyway. Maybe I can get you on your way. Not likely you are going to get a tow truck out here so fast, and my wife don't like strangers staying over. She's kinda funny that way."

Daniel turned again to look at the now dark driveway. He felt he would be safe in the farmhouse. He started the engine. The man listened and probed.

"I don't see much and it don't sound bad," the man said.

"I know. You have to hear it when I drive."

Daniel looked at the curving driveway again. He could not see all the way to the road because of the twists and turns of the lane.

"Okay. Drive a few feet. I'll listen," the man said.

Daniel did as the man requested. Then he stopped and backed up to where the man was standing. He turned to the dirt lane again. No one was there.

"Sounds like struts and ball joints," the farmer said.

"Yes. That's what the guy at the garage a few miles out of town said."

"Then you should have gotten it fixed. I'm sorry, but you can't stay here. You'll have to be on your way. Do you live nearby?"

"Oh. Not far. I guess it'll be okay. I'll leave now. Thank you."

As his car rocked and shimmied along the long, curving dirt driveway toward the road, Daniel convinced himself that no one had been following him, that he was simply being overly wary. He was also exhausted.

It flashed for only a second. A few feet to his right, as his car negotiated a twist in the driveway, the glare of his headlights reflected off what appeared to be eyeglasses ... and a face at the edge of the dense woods. Up ahead, near the entrance to the driveway, he spotted a car parked on the road. He stopped and looked and waited. Then he removed his foot from the brake pedal and gently pressed the accelerator, inching forward. As he approached the end of the drive, his headlights revealed the side of the Cadillac that had been behind him earlier. It was blocking the exit to the road.

Daniel threw the car into reverse and, turning his head, he quickly began retracing his route toward the farmhouse backwards. As the car bounced and swerved over the rutted driveway, it skimmed and brushed against the undergrowth on both sides. Then the rear end smacked into a small tree on one side, coming to a head-jarring halt; Daniel immediately put the car into drive, moved forward a few feet, and started back toward the farmhouse, again in reverse. He saw a man wearing glasses standing in the driveway. He was holding a gun, blocking the way. Daniel stopped, looked ahead, knowing that the Cadillac was parked up there. Then, looking behind him, he quickly backed

86

up toward the man, who jumped aside. Daniel maneuvered the vehicle along the last few feet of the driveway and broke into the clearing in front of the house. He quickly spun the car around and braked; it slid sideways on the pebbly ground, the driver's side slamming into the front end of the pickup truck that was parked out front. Daniel, who had not been belted in, lurched violently to the side and then forward, smashing his mouth against the steering wheel.

He sat up, his hands to his mouth, tasting blood. Big spotlights on the front of the farmhouse turned on, bathing Daniel in light. Since his door was crushed against the truck, he could not exit the car that way, so he painfully slid over to the passenger side and reached for the door handle. His heart stopped as a man wearing metal frame glasses suddenly appeared and reached for the outside handle. As Daniel locked the car from the inside, he saw the man raise a pistol and point it at the window. Daniel scrunched down on the seat and covered his head as gunshots rang in his ears and chunks of jagged glass rained down on him.

He screamed and held his body closer to the car seat as more gunshots rang out, followed by one eardrum-shattering blast. Then silence. Remaining flattened on the seat for a few more seconds, Daniel wondered whether he had been shot. As he slowly, cautiously sat up, carefully peering through the space where the car window had been, he saw nothing.

He warily opened the door and looked around. Next to the car, the man with the glasses lay on the ground. Blood was seeping from raw flesh on his neck and from gaping wounds on his chest. The pistol was on the ground next to him. The farmer was kneeling a few feet from the car, his shirtfront covered in blood, a shotgun on the ground next to him. Then he fell forward.

At that point which, even though it took only seconds, seemed to last for agonizing minutes, the farmer's wife ran down the steps to her husband, howling in anguish. Daniel exited the car and stood on shaky legs; then he fell to his knees next to the wailing woman. He turned the farmer over; the man's eyes were open, staring lifelessly. The woman screamed and repeatedly hit her chest.

Daniel turned to the harsh sound of a car scrabbling along the curving driveway and then breaking into the clearing. Standing, he grabbed the woman by her shoulders and attempted to pull her up. She swung hard, knocking Daniel down, next to the man with the glasses. As Daniel looked at her holding her husband's head in her lap, the Cadillac screeched to an abrupt, dusty stop. A large man in a black sweat suit jumped out of the car, fell to one knee, and fired a pistol in the direction of Daniel and the woman. Daniel ducked. The woman screamed and held her chest, blood seeping from between her fingers as she fell forward onto her husband. Daniel rolled under his car and then quickly turned his body and scrambled under the nearby pickup truck. He saw the feet of the man in the sweat suit running toward him. He lurched into a partially filled drainage ditch next to the truck and scuttled into the front yard of the house. Two more gunshots! Daniel got to his feet and, keeping his head down, he dashed to the house, made a quick right to the side, and darted into the backyard, where he ran behind an old red tractor, crashing into a metal box and scattering tools and pebbles over the ground.

As he looked out from behind the tractor, Daniel saw the man run into the yard, which was also brightly lit with spotlights mounted on the back wall of the house, and stand there, about 30 feet away, looking around. Daniel held his breath. He did not know whether the man had heard the sound of the tool box. Daniel felt trapped. If he stayed put, the man would find him. If he tried to run, he would be cut down. He peered at the man through a space beneath the seat of the big machine. The man walked toward the tractor. Then he bent down to look under it. Daniel crouched behind one of the large tires. The man moved off and searched the yard; he looked in a tool shed, tugged on the locked doors of a walk-out basement, peered into the thick, impenetrable woods behind the house, and scanned the nearby field. Then he opened the back door of the house. Daniel used every atom of psychic energy that he possessed in an attempt to convince the man to check the house. After looking around, the man walked into the house and closed the door. Daniel's heart skipped a beat. A few seconds later, as he stared at the door from behind the tractor, Daniel slowly began to stand. Then, still hidden by the tractor, he froze as he saw the curtains in a rear window move ever so slightly. Daniel slowly lowered his body and pressed against the big tractor tire.

The next few minutes crawled. Daniel was torn. This was his best chance to escape, but if the man was behind the thin curtains looking out the window, he would see Daniel as soon as he moved. Daniel looked behind him. The woods were thick and brambly; he knew he would not get far, so he waited.

The man emerged from the house, checked his gun, and scanned the yard again. Then he began walking to the tractor. Daniel gently pulled a long, heavy wrench from the tool box; with his other hand, he picked up a handful of pebbles from the ground. As the man was about to come around the tractor, Daniel slipped to the other side, flung the pebbles toward the house, and crouched down. The man quickly moved away from the tractor and toward the clicking sound of the pebbles hitting the house. Daniel leaped up and slammed the wrench down on the man, only managing to graze the back of his head. The man groaned, put a hand to his head, and quickly turned toward Daniel, who plowed into him. They fell to the ground, Daniel on top, the gun falling from the man's hand. Daniel hit him across the forehead with the wrench. The man punched Daniel's face and attempted to turn over and reach for the gun, but Daniel, who was facing it, got to it first. The man grabbed Daniel's shirt. Daniel smacked the man in the face with the wrench and got to his feet in one swift movement.

He shoved the wrench into a pocket. He had never held a gun, but he had seen enough television shows and movies to fake it. He stood several feet away, pointing the gun at the man's midsection. It was a semi-automatic. Daniel saw that the safety was off. He kept his finger to the side of the trigger. When the man attempted to stand, Daniel kicked him in the leg.

His mouth was so dry and he felt so shaky that he decided not to talk, knowing that his panic would come through. Instead, he gritted his teeth and, moving closer to the man, he stretched out his arms, bringing the gun in line with the man's crotch.

"Okay ... take it easy. Don't hurt me ... don't shoot. I ain't gonna hurt you. You're in control. I can see that. Please don't shoot me," the man pleaded.

Feeling more confident, Daniel said in a husky voice, "If you move or talk, I'll fucking kill you. I really want to shoot your nuts off. Don't you move!"

The man froze.

"Slowly turn over onto your stomach and lie flat ... Now!"

The man did as he was told.

"Stretch your arms out! Now you're going to answer some questions. Then I'm going to decide what to do with you. Understand?"

The man shook his head in agreement.

"Did Carmine De Luca send you to get me?"

"I don't know who ... I got a phone call. A guy met me ... gave me cash to come up here and wait at that library for you. That's all I know."

"What did he look like?"

"Short ... messy ... old ... it was dark. You don't check people out with these kind of contract jobs. It's not personal."

"How did you know what I look like?"

"I was told to look for a black 1995 Buick Century and I was told what you look like ... there was a picture too."

"What kind of picture?"

"A photo ... a photograph of you and some other guys at a table ... some kind of party."

"Show me the picture."

"The other guy ... my buddy Ronnie got it."

"Where did you come from?"

"The city ... Queens."

"Don't move. I have to think about what to do with you. I should just shoot you now, but I won't. Let me think. Okay ... you're going to slowly reach for your wallet, your cell phone, and your keys and throw them on the ground. Do it now! Remember, if I don't like how you do this, I'll shut you down, and I'll enjoy doing it."

The man slowly reached for his wallet, phone, and keys, and tossed them a few feet away. Daniel, pulling back from the man while still pointing the gun at him, kicked the belongings a few feet further away. Then he carefully bent down, picked up the things, and put them in one of his pockets.

He wanted to pull the trigger ... hurt the man ... rip the flesh from the back of his head, but he knew he did not really want to kill him—that would haunt him more than Jimmy's death did. But he was filled with blazing anger. He tried to figure out what to do. He could not take a chance. Daniel knew that if he left the man on the ground, he would be able to get up and follow him ... and now, it was not just business; the man might hunt Daniel down because it was personal.

He told the man to slowly stand and walk to the front of the house. Daniel followed. Then he told the man to lie down on the ground again. Daniel opened his car door, swept shards of glass from the passenger seat to the ground, and reached in, turning his head to keep an eye on the man. When he turned the key, the engine did not start. He pulled the key out of the ignition and eased himself out of the car. Then he opened the trunk and looked inside. He shivered, thinking of Jimmy and the blood on that night.

"Okay. Stand up ... slowly. Now come here. In the trunk," Daniel said.

"No, man. I ain't doin' that. If you're gonna shoot me, do it now, while I'm standing ... not in there."

"I'm not going to shoot you ... unless you don't cooperate. I'm not one of you. Why did you have to shoot the woman?"

"She was a witness. I had to do it."

"You're a piece of shit, but I won't shoot you. I just want enough time to get away. Get in the trunk."

"I ain't doing it ... and, you know what, I don't think you're gonna shoot me. In fact, I don't think you even know how to shoot a gun."

"You're an idiot. Why do you think De Luca hired you? I killed one of his men, Jimmy Tripelli. One in the side of his head. When I said I'm not one of you, that means I don't kill people for money. What I did to Jimmy was for survival. I'll do the same to you if I have to. It's your choice."

"I'm scared of small spaces."

"Look: you see that latch. It's a trunk release. It's there in case little kids get stuck in a trunk. It's also for schmucks like you. I'm taking your Caddy. You wait until you hear the car start up and drive off. Then you can get out and go back to Queens and be grateful you're alive."

After the man had climbed into the trunk, Daniel ordered him to turn over onto his stomach. Then, still pointing the gun at the man, Daniel smashed the wrench into the plastic trunk release over and over again, shattering it. After he slammed the trunk closed, Daniel gasped and then he sighed with relief. He threw the wrench into the drainage ditch; then, with his foot, he nudged the body of the other man, the one with the glasses. He was dead. Daniel checked the man's pockets, pulling out his wallet. He examined the farmer and his wife. Their wide-open unseeing eyes and slack mouths made him feel sick.

He ran to the Cadillac, opened the door, put the gun and the two wallets into the glove box, started the engine, and sped out of the yard to the curving driveway and onto the road. He made sure to notice the address of the house and the name on the mailbox. He drove to the motel and parked far from his room. With the gun in a pocket and the wallets in his hand, Daniel walked to his room.

Once he had locked the door, Daniel collapsed on the bed. He was overwhelmed with the same sense of dread and anxiety that he had felt on the night of Jimmy's death. No—this was a deeper, more harrowing feeling of revulsion and terror. Then, telling himself that he could take the time to decompress later, he opened the wallets and pulled out the two driver's licenses. He dialed 911 from the man's cell phone to report the shootings at 901 Willow Way. Using an unnaturally deep, throaty voice, he said, "Three people are dead, including one of the shooters, a man named Ronnie Leventhal; the other shooter, a man named Manny Friedman, is in the trunk of a car parked on the property."

He did not give his name and did not explain how he knew about what had happened at the farm.

Only after he had hung up did he realize the blunder he had made.

91

7

Prior Justice

When Daniel viewed the local news on the black and white television in his motel room that night, he could not help but feel simultaneously removed from and embedded within the images that he saw on the screen. First, there was the nightmare videotape again: one plane and then the second slicing through those buildings ... and the orange-black flames and the sickening collapse of the towers. His eyes welled with tears and his hands involuntarily clenched. Then, a few minutes later, there was a video of the road, the curving lane, the farmhouse, three bodies covered with sheets, two next to each other and one a few feet away. And there was his Buick with the trunk open.

The reporter said that John and Emma Van Eyck of 901 Willow Way, lifelong residents of the area, had been shot dead, most likely victims of a botched robbery; an unidentified man, apparently one of the robbers, had been killed by a shotgun blast, probably from the weapon found next to John Van Eyck's body. The police said that a pickup truck registered to the Van Eycks had been found on the premises. A Buick Century with New York plates whose side windows had been shot out was found at the scene. Police said they were checking with the New York State Department of Motor Vehicles to contact the owner of the car whose registration was found in the glove box.

There was no mention of the other car, the Mercury, or of a man having been found in the trunk of the Buick.

Daniel had not used his real name when he registered at the motel and he had not used his charge card since he had left Brooklyn, but he had introduced himself to the two women in the library, so he had to leave. He hurriedly packed his belongings, paid what he owed to the motel manager, and drove off in the Cadillac. It was a little after 11 p.m. He did not know where to go.

After Daniel had traveled a few miles from the motel, he stopped on the side of the road to call Maria to say that she might, just might hear a news story about him, although he doubted that New York City news stations would carry it. He did not tell her what happened, saying that he would explain another time. She was frantic, telling him that she did not think she could take much more of this. "I can't eat. I don't sleep well. I can't concentrate on my work. And I miss you so much it hurts. When am I going to be able to see you?"

"I miss you too, but you can't be with me now. Let me go. I'll call you back tomorrow. We'll talk then."

He called his parents, awakening them, to warn them not to believe what they might see on the news and saying that the police might call them to ask his whereabouts. His mother cried; his father told him to be careful.

Daniel traveled southwest, stopping at a motel in New Castle, Pennsylvania at 4 a.m. He used the charge card of the dead man, Ronnie Leventhal. He figured he would be able to use the charge cards of the two men for another day or two. He also had close to $900 that had been in their wallets.

Although he suffered through disturbing, alarming dreams, awakening over and over again in a sweat with the sound of screams—his screams—in his head, he stayed in bed until 11 a.m. Then he showered, put on clean clothes, and walked to a nearby luncheonette. None of the newspapers that he skimmed through had stories about the shootings back in Jamestown. Several articles covered the continuing, desperate appeals from families of victims of the World Trade Center attacks who were asking for information about missing loved ones and the heart-rending stories of others hoping that at least the remains of family members who died that day would be found.

As Daniel entered the parking lot to return to his motel room, he saw two police cars parked near the Cadillac. A police officer was searching it. The door to his room was open. He froze; then he slowly turned around and walked back to the sidewalk, speeding up once he had passed out of view of the parking lot. He asked a woman carrying groceries for directions to the bus station.

At the terminal, after scanning a map on the wall next to the clerk's booth, he purchased a ticket to Morgantown, West Virginia. He could not decide whether he was more upset that the police had almost caught him and had taken his belongings, including the gun that had been used to kill Emma Van Eyck, or disappointed that they had missed him. He was that tired.

His phone rang.

"Daniel, is this you?"

"Who's this?"

"You don't know me. I work for somebody you know."

"Oh, you mean Carmine De Luca."

There was silence on the other end of the line. Then the unidentified man said, "We don't need no names ... and I don't know no Carmine."

"Whatever. What do you want?"

"I was watching the news. They show your picture. It seems you're really in the soup now. I feel kinda sorry for you. I wanna help you come home and straighten out this here problem you have. What do you say?"

Daniel swallowed hard before saying, "Why should I trust you? I thought I had an agreement, but two men tried to kill me."

"I don't know nothin' about that. Listen—"

Daniel hung up and turned off his phone.

Everyone knew. The motel clerk must have seen his photograph on the television news, probably the one from his driver's license, which surely came up when the authorities searched the registration record of the Buick. Now that the police had gone into his room they had the gun that had been used to kill Mrs. Van Eyck. He had not thought of wiping off his fingerprints. He turned on his phone and called Maria. It went to voice mail.

Shortly before the bus was about to depart, his phone rang. This time it was Carmine De Luca.

"Daniel, I heard about what happened to you. I want you to know that I am looking into it. I had no idea."

"You're full of shit, Mr. De Luca," Daniel replied.

After a few seconds of hesitation, De Luca said, "I will excuse that comment. Of course you're upset. How could you not be? It's a shame. As I said, I will get to the bottom of this, and I will make sure that whoever did this thing is punished. In the meantime, why don't you come home? I'm sure your parents want to see you. I will take care of everything. You will be safe."

"Tell me this: I asked you before: is someone still stealing your money?"

"I still do not know what you mean by that. What I do know is that now you are in more trouble than before. If you do not make peace with me, you will never be able to come home. If you show your face or use your name anywhere, you will be put in jail and you will die there. I will be in touch."

After Daniel hung up, he called Maria again. He left a message for her: "I want you to know that I will love you forever, but I don't think we'll see each other again for a long time. I don't know how I'll live without you, but there's no use kidding ourselves: I'm lost. Maybe you should forget about me."

Then he turned off the phone and boarded the bus to West Virginia.

He woke up with a backache as the bus pulled into Morgantown. His first thought when he reached the sidewalk outside the bus terminal was to ask for directions to the police station. It was time to end this wretched, pointless journey. Then he decided it would be best for all concerned if he were dead.

A cool river breeze carrying the scent of—he could not quite place it, but it was appealing—wafted over him. He smiled at the thought that the need to satisfy his hunger was more compelling than what had been, only a few seconds earlier, the desire to give up his freedom or end his life. Choosing food over a jail cell or an early trip to the grave, Daniel walked in the direction of the smell, to a barbeque restaurant called Patty's Place, where he ate spare ribs, roasted potatoes, and biscuits with gravy. He felt stronger and more optimistic when he walked out into the sunshine.

Daniel decided that Morgantown was the kind of place in which, sooner or later, he would be recognized. He needed to hide out in a more rural, more isolated hamlet, a place where people did not watch television news programs, all of which were probably broadcasting his photograph over and over again. A local paper that he skimmed through showed his picture under the headline "Brooklyn Man Wanted in Double Homicide in Rural New York Town."

He walked to University Avenue and followed it south along the banks of the Monongahela River until it intersected with Route 73. He stayed on the right side of the road; each time he heard a car or truck coming up from behind him, after making sure it was not a police car, he put out his thumb. The first dozen vehicles passed him by. Then, as the temperature dropped, a truck labeled Shorty's Landscaping stopped for him.

"Where you headed, boy?" the driver, a squat, heavyset man in his sixties with a full white beard asked him.

"Anywhere. Just looking for a place to stay the night," Daniel answered in what he hoped was a casual, country twang

The driver told him to hop in. They traveled in silence for a while. Then the man, who introduced himself as Shorty McCaffery, asked Daniel his name.

"It's Fr ... Frank Williams." He made a point of not looking at the man.

"And where you from, Frank Williams."

"Oh ... from Long Island originally, but that was a long time ago. I've been traveling for the past couple of years."

"Really? On yer own?"

"Sure. Why not?" Daniel replied, taking a quick glance at the man.

"Oh. No reason. You know, you have the look about you of a wanted man," Shorty stated with the hint of a smile.

"No! Not unless you count my girlfriend, who was driving me crazy."

"Girlfriend or wife?"

"Well, she might as well have been my wife," Daniel replied.

"Travelin' kinda light ... Did you lose your gear?"

Thinking quickly, Daniel said, "Yeah. Some kids ran off with it in the bus station back in Morgantown."

"Must be them college jerks. Everything's a joke to them. The smarter they and their mommies and daddies think they are, the dumber they act."

"No doubt," Daniel replied with a smile.

"You got any money?" Shorty asked.

95

Immediately sensing danger, Daniel replied in a dejected voice, "No. Not much. Just enough for a room and a meal, and then I'll be tapped out."

"You want a job?"

"What kind? Doing what?"

"Didn't expect you'd be so particular, considerin' how to don't have one now and no prospects," Shorty said.

"You're right. If you're offering a job, I'll take it as long as it's not near a big town," Daniel answered.

"Yeah. I thought you'd say somethin' like that."

Two hours later, Shorty turned onto a narrow country lane which led to a clearing in the midst of woods holding a collection of ramshackle trailers. He pulled up to a large blue one with a canopy out front.

"This one's mine. You can come on in for a bite to eat. Then you can pick a trailer for yourself, but not that one," Shorty said, pointing to a small yellow one. "Clay lives in it. He's real mean. You wouldn't want to stay there. In fact, steer clear of him if you smell alcohol on his breath ... and most other times too. I would've fired him years ago, except he's my wife's friend from when they was kids."

Daniel followed Shorty into his trailer. It was large and roomy and very clean. A slim, attractive woman in her forties with long black hair was cooking something that smelled astonishingly good.

Daniel started to correct Shorty when he introduced him to his wife, Lola, as "Frank." He had begun to say, "Daniel," but got only as far as "Dan ... " To cover up his momentary slip, he turned away from them and coughed and cleared his throat. Shorty smiled and then pointed to one end of the trailer, saying, "That's where you'll find the accommodations."

After Daniel had washed up, Shorty steered him to a place at the table. His mouth watered as Lola brought over a large crock of steaming stew. When she lifted the glass cover, Daniel breathed in billows of pungent, aromatic vapor. He ate slowly to conceal just how hungry he was. Shorty and Lola scooped up large spoonfuls of the stew and noisily chewed and swallowed. They tore off huge hunks of homemade sourdough bread which they used to sop up gravy.

As Lola washed the dishes, Shorty and Daniel walked through the little settlement. Daniel shivered.

"Ain't used to the mountain cold, huh?" Shorty asked.

"No, but I'll be fine."

Shorty explained that he owned the dozen trailers, the vehicles and equipment, the land on which they were parked, and the surrounding 100 acres, explaining that the property had been in his family since colonial times. "Used to rent out the trailers, but now I let my boys live in 'em ... mostly white guys, but some Mexican kids too ... good workers. We do landscaping for the county and for families in big houses in the next hollow during the good weather; we cut and deliver firewood and do snowplowing in the winter. None of it don't pay much, but it's a livin' and it's legal."

Daniel, who was so cold that his teeth were chattering, wished Shorty would stop talking and let him pick a trailer. Finally, Shorty said good night, telling Daniel that he should be at his trailer by 8 the next morning for work. As Shorty walked back to his place, Daniel looked at the other trailers. After a few seconds, encouraged by the cold to decide quickly, he walked to a brightly lit one, and knocked on the door.

"Come on in," called a gravelly-sounding voice.

Three men were sitting around a television watching an old movie which was barely discernible because of the static and jumpy images caused by poor reception. Beer cans, dirty dishes, pots, and clothing littered every surface and much of the floor. The air smelled of body odor and rancid food.

"Now, who might you be?" asked the gravelly voiced man.

Daniel told the man his made-up name and said that he had just been hired. Neither of the other men looked up from the television.

"Okay. Make yourself at home. This here's Zeke, he's Toby, and I'm Russ. There's a free bed over there in the back. Just throw the stuff on it onto the floor. Give us ten bucks for food and beer, and we'll be all set."

Daniel handed a ten-dollar bill to Russ. He declined the beer that Zeke held out to him, saying he was too tired to drink. That set off a round of raucous laughter and head shaking. Once he had removed the mountain of clothing from the bed, Daniel saw a filthy, ragged blanket that was held together with strips of duct tape and, below that, a stained sheet. There was no pillow.

"Is there a washing machine here?" he asked.

"No. Why?" Russ asked.

"I wanted to wash this stuff. It's kinda dirty."

"Yeah, well, we didn't know you was comin' into town. Otherwise, we would've told the maid to wash and iron for you."

That led to several comments from the men about what else the maid could do for them and how they knew how they were going to spend their money on Saturday night when they were in town.

"It's okay. I've slept on worse," Daniel said.

He sat on the bed and turned on his phone, but was unable to use it because there was no reception. He held it up. That did not work. He stepped out of the trailer and held the phone high above him. Still no reception. As he put it in his pocket, he remembered that he had left the charger in the motel room that the police had searched. He pulled the phone out of his pocket and turned it off. Then he looked up at the clear, cold, dark sky with its countless gleaming pinpricks of light. He hoped ... he needed to believe that Maria was looking up at the sky at that moment.

"I guess there's no cell phone reception here."

"Too many mountains. We're deep in the boondocks, man," said Russ.

Daniel got out of bed at seven the next morning when the other men began stirring. He was awake ... had been for hours. Besides his recurring nightmares and disturbing thoughts about Jimmy and the blood-stained shovel, now he repeatedly heard the gunshots and pictured Mr. and Mrs. Van Eyck and their ragged, bloody wounds. He had also worried about bed bugs and, each time he had heard a noise during the night, he braced himself, thinking that one of the other men was coming to rob or attack him.

There was running water in the bathroom sink, but no soap, and the towels smelled like wet dog. The walls and floor of the little shower were coated with green and black mold and the toilet bowl was unspeakably, repulsively filthy. He washed up at the sink as well as he could. When he looked in the cracked mirror above it, he hardly recognized himself. Since he did not have a razor, he could not shave; he decided that he would grow a beard.

He dug a chipped, dirty cup from the pile of unwashed dishes in the kitchen sink, scrubbed it with his fingers because the sponge that had probably been yellow at one time was black with filth, and drank the coffee that one of the men had brewed; he ate a couple of oatmeal cookies from an open package. Then he followed the others to Shorty's trailer. There were about two dozen men, mostly white, a few Hispanics, and one black man. After Shorty had assigned the day's work to the other men, he motioned to Daniel to follow him.

"This here wood has to be split," Shorty said, pointing to an enormous mountain of logs. "You ever cut firewood before?"

"Yes, sir."

"You got a pair of gloves?"

"No. I don't."

"Okay. Borrow mine. On Saturday night, when you and the other boys go into town, make sure you buy what you need ... clothes, food, whatever. By the way, I pay cash ... no taxes ... $5.00 an hour. Okay with you?"

"Yes. That's fine."

"I thought you'd like that. You can stop for lunch, a half hour, and you can knock off at 5 p.m. I'll be back by then. You can take little breaks, if you need 'em, but not too many and not for long. Lola keeps an eye on things when I'm not around, and she's meaner than I'll ever be. I want all this cut down to size. This is a try-out. I expect you'll be a good worker. If not, I can hire some more Mexicans. Those boys sure do know how to work."

"I won't disappoint you, sir."

"Call me Shorty, not sir. I ain't no gentleman."

"Okay, Shorty. I have a question. Is there anywhere I can get cell phone reception or find a computer to send an email?"

"Fancy, fancy. Nope. Not for miles and miles, but there's a couple of phone booths and a post office in town, if you know about those old fashioned ways of communicating."

"That's fine. Thank you, Shorty."

He realized that mailing a letter from whatever town they were near might not be a safe thing to do, but, he thought, nothing he had done since that night with Dominic had been safe or smart.

At noon, his hands burning and his back breaking, Daniel stopped splitting wood. In his entire life, he had never used his body, machine-like, as he had during the past four hours or so. As he stretched, he felt chilled, so he picked up his jacket and put it on his sweat-soaked body. He picked up the old orange juice bottle that he had repeatedly filled with water during the time that he had worked, and walked to the trailer.

The little refrigerator contained only beer, a half stick of butter, and an open package of white bread. In one of the cabinets above the sink he found boxes of cold cereal and cans of Campbell's soup and Dinty Moore Beef Stew. There was no milk for cereal and no clean pots in which to cook soup or stew on the small stove, so he opened a can of stew and, after scrubbing a spoon as well as he could with his fingers, he ate directly from it. He drank more water. Then he lay down on the bed to rest for a moment.

He was awakened by a voice yelling, "You in here? Ain't you supposed to be working on that pile of firewood?"

Daniel sat up in bed. Lola, her hands on her hips, was staring at him.

"Oh. Sorry. I conked out. I'll get right to it."

He had slept for over an hour. That meant he had to work more quickly now than he had in the morning to complete the job. Of course, he did not need this job. He felt for his wallet. He knew he had enough cash, but what he would not have if he quit would be a safe place to hide. He wanted to wait a while before moving on, at least until the story of the shootings in Jamestown had become old news. For all he knew, police everywhere, even in whatever little town was nearby, were circulating his photograph. That thought made his blood run cold and his heart beat furiously in his chest.

He split logs. His hands and shoulders and back vibrated with jagged spears of unremitting pain. Each time he stopped to catch his breath, he felt that he would not be able to drag another log to the chopping block, but he managed to do it over and over again. With each lift of the axe, every muscle, from those in his neck down to his calves, cried out in distress. Each time he brought the axe down on the wood, he groaned in agony as pain radiated and vibrated through his body. Then he heard a truck coming up the road to the settlement. For a second, he thought it was the sound of the black Cadillac scrabbling up the curving driveway to the Van Eyck farmhouse; he had a flashback of the man in the sweat suit jumping out, positioning himself, and shooting Mrs. Van Eyck.

It was one of Shorty's trucks. A tall black man with close-cropped hair stepped out and stretched his back. He began unloading bags of peat moss. Daniel walked over to the man and offered to help.

"Well," said the man, "I know you are new to this place."

"Yes. Today's my first day."

"Here's my advice: walk down this road and keep walking and never look back. Young man like you can do better."

"This is just a temporary stop," Daniel explained.

"Yeah. Ain't it? We're all cut from the same cloth ... all the men here." Then, looking Daniel up and down, the man continued, "Except for you. I think you're different from the rest of us."

"How can you tell?"

"Well, for one thing, you offered to help me. Nobody here does a lick more than he needs to do and none of them help each other." Then, after a few seconds of thought, the man said, "You have a different look about you ... like you were city-bred. Am I right?"

"Well ... "

"That's okay. I didn't mean to pry. Name's Prior. Prior Justice. Yeah, my folks had a good time giving me that name."

"I'm Frank Williams. I like your name, Mr. Justice."

"Now, you don't have to be so formal. Prior is all you have to call me."

Once Daniel had finished helping Prior unload the truck and haul the peat moss to a nearby shed, he returned to his gargantuan task; he knew he would not be able to complete it before Shorty was due back in the compound.

Prior, who had gone into one of the trailers for a few minutes, returned. He gestured for Daniel to give the axe to him. He held it for a second, as if he were weighing it; then he set up a piece of wood on the chopping block, brought the axe up, and with one fast, smooth stroke, split it in half as if he were slicing through an overripe melon. He did that three more times.

Handing the axe back to Daniel, he asked, "Did you see how I did that?"

"I saw you, but I don't know what you did that made it seem so easy."

"It ain't so easy. Nothing in life is easy except for getting in trouble. It's all in the mind and the shoulders. I can finish this pile for you in 20 minutes, but you wouldn't want me to do that. Would you?"

"No, sir ... no, Prior. I appreciate your help, but it's my job."

"No. That's not the reason. Listen, Frank ... answer this question: Why did you help me with those bags of peat moss?"

"I guess I just think people should help each other out, and, to be honest, I needed a break from this job."

"Okay, so it comes down to attitude. You have the right attitude—and you're honest, which very few men are—but your shoulders are not working for you. They are working against you. Watch my shoulders, not the axe."

Prior set up and sliced through six more thick logs in seconds, something that would have taken Daniel three or four minutes. He watched the man's shoulders. He could not explain what he saw, but he thought he could feel in his own shoulders what the man was doing. When Daniel brought the axe down on the next log, he moved his shoulders as Prior had. The axe blade sliced through the wood swiftly and smoothly. He split the next few logs quickly and with less effort than it had taken before. Prior watched Daniel for a minute, and then he walked back to his trailer.

When they returned from work two hours later, the three men who shared the trailer with Daniel sat on the couch eating large subs and gulping beer. Once Daniel, who had completed his task on time, understood that the men had not bought any food for him, he washed a spoon and a pot using his hands; he was too tired and hungry to care whether or not they were actually clean. Then he poured chicken noodle soup into the pot and heated it on the stove. Not wanting to wash a bowl, he ate the soup directly from the pot. Then he washed the pot and spoon and left them on the side of the sink to dry.

"Ain't you forgot something, boy?" Toby asked.

"No. What?"

"Don't he talk like a city boy from up north? A real Yankee, ain't you? You think your New York City ways are better'n ours?"

101

Daniel was not in the mood to be bullied, so he asked, "What is it you think I forgot, country boy?"

The other two laughed, but Toby said, "Country, and proud of it. Are you some kind of Yankee that thinks he's better than us?"

"Look, I'm tired, Toby. Either tell me what you think I forgot or leave me alone. Either one is fine with me."

"Well, besides the fact that you forgot your manners, it looks like you're about to walk away from that pile of dirty dishes in the sink."

"In case you didn't notice, I washed the spoon and pot I used. That's all. I'm not going to wash what you guys left in the sink."

"That's the rule, boy. If you take from the sink, you gotta wash what's in the sink. Either that, or you can sleep outside in the cold tonight."

Daniel looked at the other two, both of whom smiled and shook their heads in agreement, so he turned to the sink to wash. Then he turned back and said, "How the hell do you expect me to wash a sink full of dishes when there's no soap and that sponge looks like you used it to wipe up dog shit?"

"That's for you to figure out," Russ said.

"Disgusting. You guys live like pigs."

"You callin' us pigs, you shit-faced Yankee?" Zeke, asked, standing up.

Daniel felt strong. He thought about how he had used his shoulders to split the remaining logs with speed and agility; he wished he was holding the axe now ... or the pistol ... or the wrench he had used to subdue the man in the sweat suit. Instead, he walked to his bed, picked up his jacket, and headed for the door to the trailer.

"If you leave, you ain't comin' back ... and you ain't gettin' your ten dollars back," Toby sneered.

"Screw you," Daniel hissed as he walked out into the dark compound.

After feeling good for a few seconds, Daniel realized that he had just put himself in a very bad situation. The late October night was bitterly cold. He could not just knock on another trailer door because all of the workers had seen him with the three men that morning when they reported to Shorty's trailer. They would want to know why he had moved out, so he knocked on Shorty's trailer and told him what had happened.

"I'm not complaining. I just don't know where to go," he explained.

"Go back to the trailer. You have to accept their ways. You're the newcomer. They shouldn't have to bend to your whims," Shorty said.

"I can't go back. They live like pigs and there's no food or soap or anything clean in there."

"Then you're gonna have to sleep in the cold tonight. Sorry, boy. I don't interfere in this sort of thing."

Daniel curled up on top of the bags of peat moss that he had helped Prior to load into the shed. It was bone-chillingly cold, but he was so fatigued that he did not feel it; he slept through the night in a deep, exhausted sleep.

Sunlight hit Daniel's face, awakening him. Squinting, he saw Prior at the open shed door. Daniel looked at his watch. It was 6 a.m. Prior sadly shook his head and then he invited Daniel to warm up in his trailer.

As Daniel, huddled in his jacket, sat by the electric heater, Prior poured a cup of hot coffee for him. Then he put two slices of whole wheat bread in a toaster, broke two eggs into a frying pan, and put out a place setting at his little wooden table. Daniel looked around: nothing was out of place; the sink was empty and sparkling clean; the trailer smelled fresh.

He wolfed down the food, almost as grateful for the cleanliness of the plate, cup, and silverware as he was for the warm nourishment. Prior even had napkins. When Daniel finished eating, as he petted Shadow, Prior's black terrier, he told the man what had happened at the other trailer. Then he described the filthy conditions. Prior shook his head knowingly.

"Now, what you going to do, Frank?"

"I won't go back there, especially after seeing how nice one of these trailers can be."

Neither one said anything. Then Daniel asked why Prior had been at the shed so early in the morning.

"Oh, I'm an early riser. I get to bed early, usually around 9 p.m., right after I read my Bible. I get up early so I can get a jump on my work."

"Oh, and I interrupted you. I'll help you. We can go out right now. I want to repay you for your kindness."

"The only repayment is for you to offer me a kindness when I'm in trouble, which is sure to happen one day."

"Of course," Daniel said. He wanted to add that the only reason he was there, in that trailer deep in the wilderness of West Virginia, was because he had been trying to help someone who he had thought was a good friend ... someone who turned out not to be a friend at all.

"Now, just stay here until it's time to report to Shorty. I'll do my job."

"One more thing, Prior ... I hate to ask, but I really need a shower. In that other place—"

"Sure. Go right ahead. Plenty of soap and shampoo and clean towels. Just don't go and take any of my clean undershorts," Prior added with a smile.

As the hot water coursed over his aching body and the sweet-scented soap washed away several days worth of grime, Daniel sighed with pleasure. When he finished drying his body, he used the towel to wipe down every surface in the little shower until it gleamed. Then he shook out the towel and hung it over the shower rod to dry. Putting on his dirty clothes, he imagined how nice it would be to slip into clean underwear, socks, and outer clothes.

He looked around, hoping he would find some chore that he could do for Prior, but the place was perfect. When Prior returned, Daniel offered to pay for the food he had eaten. Prior looked hurt.

"I'm sorry. I'm just so grateful ... not just for the food and the shower, but for the fact that you've made me feel welcome."

"No money. I make more than what I need, and you are welcome. Allow me tell you a little secret ... you're the first man, other than Shorty, who has ever been in this trailer."

"Well, from what I've seen, you're lucky. I don't know them all, but the three in that other trailer are pieces of shit and the others who I've seen just a couple of times don't look much better."

"I don't like that kind of language, especially when you're talking about men, Frank. I don't abide it."

"Sorry, Prior. Why has nobody else ever been in here?"

"Can't you guess?"

"Oh. Well, that's their loss."

"Say, you want me to ask Shorty for you to work with me today?"

"Oh, yes. That would be great."

"I think you can see that I'm a hard worker. I don't fool around on the job or drink or curse. And I expect you to be honest with me."

"I understand."

"And, if you want, you can move your gear to the other bedroom. You see how clean I keep the trailer. I expect you to follow my rules. It ain't paradise, but it's better than a lot of places I've hung my hat over the years."

Daniel sighed with relief. He believed that if he stayed with Prior, he would be able to tolerate working and living in this mountain wilderness for a while, at least until he decided on his next move.

*****

At 6 p.m. on Saturday night, all of the men piled into Shorty's trucks or their own cars to travel to the hamlet of Perkinsville. Its *WELCOME* sign proudly proclaimed that the town had a population of 785, three churches, a post office, a movie theater, and three restaurants. It did not mention its half dozen bars, all of which offered high-stakes poker games, loan sharking services, and exceedingly friendly hostesses.

Daniel's first stop, when he saw that his cell phone still did not pick up a signal, was for change at a Laundromat. He also picked up a copy of the local paper, which was the only one there. He breathed a sigh of relief when he saw that it did not carry his photograph or stories about the double murder. Then he walked to a phone booth on a corner near three of the bars, and called Maria.

"Oh, God, Daniel. Are you okay? Are you safe? Why didn't you call?"

"I'm fine. No cell phone service or phones where I work. How are you?"

"I'm going crazy. I worry about you all the time. The local news had stories about you for three straight nights after the Ground Zero news. Not so much now, but you're still in the paper. They say you murdered a couple, used stolen credit cards, and lots of other—"

"It's all untrue. Some men tried to kill me or capture me ... I don't know which. One of them was killed by the man, the farmer. I was hiding in my car, so I didn't see. Then another guy showed up and tried to shoot me, but I got away ... he killed the woman—"

"Stop! This is too much. I want you home. You'll be safer here."

"No, Maria. Not yet. If I come home, De Luca's men or the police will pick me up. I *won't* be safe and you wouldn't be either. I have to stay where I am. Just give me a little more time to figure out my next move."

"Then I'll come to you. I'll do what you said ... I'll quit my job and I'll find one where you are."

"There are no jobs here ... I'm really out in the country; far from the city."

"What are you doing?"

"A job ... manual labor, but it's good. I made a good friend. It's peaceful and very pretty here."

"You're making it sound like you're happy there. I can't believe it."

"No. No. I miss you so much it hurts, but I have to do something. I can't just hide out in motel rooms all day. I've had it rough, but I'm okay now."

"This is making me crazy, Daniel. I don't know how much longer I can function like this. Please do whatever you have to ... you have to come home."

"Maybe you should do what I said in my last voicemail. Maybe you should forget about me—"

"No! Don't leave messages like that. Just come home."

"I will ... as soon as I can. I don't want to stay on the phone. I don't see how De Luca could trace your phone since you have a new one and he doesn't know your last name, but I don't want to take a chance. I'll call you again soon, and I'll figure out how to get home to you."

He called his parents, providing them with the same information that he had given to Maria. His mother said that the police had questioned her about where he was. She had said that she did not know. Then she tearfully read from a list of solutions to his problem that she had written down. When she was done, Daniel said that he would think about her suggestions. His father sounded like a defeated old man. As he was saying good-bye to his father, he heard, in the background, the sound of his mother crying.

After Daniel hung up the phone, he returned to the Laundromat, where Prior was making a wash. They went to a restaurant called Rita's Country Cooking, which Prior said was the best place around for miles. Daniel was the only white person there. Prior ordered for the both of them: barbequed short ribs, fried cabbage and bacon, candied yams, and skillet cornbread. They followed that up with praline pecan cake and peach ice cream and coffee. They ate in silence. Daniel stopped eating just before he made himself sick.

"What's this town like?" Daniel asked.

"Oh, it's okay ... pretty much like any other place in this poor part of this very poor state," Prior replied. "I've been working for Shorty for only a year. My people are from South Carolina. Now, that is a whole different world."

"Aren't things better now?"

"Oh, yes. I don't mean the color problem. As far as that goes, there's places down south—West Virginia is not the Deep South, in case you didn't know—where black and white people get on better than in most other parts of this country, even New York or Chicago."

"I've heard that. Then what did you mean?"

"Oh, I guess I mean the way of life and ideas. There are whole counties in the Deep South where people live like right after the Civil War ... no electricity or running water or sewer systems and certainly no new ideas. Do you know, in some of those places, evolution is still a forbidden topic and the local preacher is the only authority? Now, I've got nothing against preachers, but people have to be free to think and to adapt to the world."

"Is that why you left South Carolina?"

"No. I didn't exactly leave. I got drafted ... served in Vietnam ... ended up in California ... then I just drifted across the country."

"You were in Vietnam? You're not old enough."

"How old you think I am?"

"If I hadn't heard you say that, I would have guessed 40, at most."

"Ha. Let me think ... 40 years ago, I was in high school. I'm 55."

"I hope I look as good as you when I'm ... if I make it to your age."

"Okay. Is that my opening? Is this when I ask you what kind of trouble you're in, or should I keep my questions to myself?"

"That obvious, huh?"

"As clear as the worry lines on your face; in addition, I don't believe you don't have a driver's license."

"Yeah. I had to tell that to Shorty. I can't take a chance driving, in case I'm ever pulled over for speeding or anything like that."

"So, your name is really not Frank Williams, is it?"

"No, but I'd rather not tell you my real name. And, for your sake, as well as for my own, I'd rather not talk about it."

"That's okay. I don't need to know, but understand this: if you don't do what you have to do to settle your issue, whatever it may be, you will ruin your life. Little sores today grow into bigger ones as time goes on, and they eventually turn into cancer ... and you know how bad cancer is."

They returned to the Laundromat to pick up Prior's clothes; then they walked to a clothing store that stayed open late on Saturday nights when all of the work crews in the area came to town. Daniel bought underwear, shirts, pants, work boots, a heavy coat, and other clothing to get him through the upcoming winter in the mountains. He also bought another backpack.

"That's going to add up to a lot of money, you know," Prior said.

"I have it," Daniel replied, adding, "You don't have to worry. I didn't steal it. Well, that's not totally correct. Some of it came from a couple of scoundrels ... gangsters. I'll tell you about that some other time."

Then they walked to a grocery store to buy food and other supplies for the week. Daniel insisted on paying for all of it because he had eaten Prior's food for the past few days.

After they had locked their belongings in the truck, Prior asked Daniel whether he wanted to go to a movie.

"I would go, if that's what you would like."

"No. I just thought you might want to do that," Prior said.

"What I would like, actually, is to buy some books."

"What kind of books?"

"You know ... good books. Literature. Before I got caught up in this part of my life, I was an English teacher."

"I am impressed, but, sorry, no bookstore, and this little metropolis does not have a library. Locals read only the Bible and not many of the workmen who come to town are readers, unless you count comic books and girlie magazines."

"That's okay. I'll manage."

As Prior started the truck, Daniel asked whether they should wait for the men who had traveled to town with them.

"You want to wait here until the sun comes up tomorrow morning?"

"Oh. No," Daniel said.

"Some of them won't be ready to come back even then. They'll be asleep in some girl's bed or in some alley ... and one or two might not make it back until Monday morning, after they call Shorty and ask him to pick them up."

"But, won't they be pissed at you ... at us?"

"They already don't like us ... the Mexican boys, they're okay, but the others ... they hate me because they think their skin tones make them better than me and they hate you because they know you're better than them."

On the drive back to the encampment, Daniel and Prior discussed books they had read: *Crime and Punishment, Invisible Man, Absalom Absalom, Their Eyes Were Watching God, Beloved, The Great Gatsby.*

Once they had put away their groceries, Daniel showered and was finally able to change into clean clothes. Prior was out, walking Shadow. When Daniel came out of the bathroom, he saw a large cardboard box on his bed; it was filled with books: *The Complete Works of Mark Twain, Cry the Beloved Country, Ulysses, The Complete Shakespeare, The Autobiography of Malcolm X,* and dozens more, some of which he had never read. He pulled out a copy of *On the Road,* thinking it an appropriate choice.

8

Home for Christmas

On the afternoon of the Friday before Christmas, which was on Tuesday that year, Shorty told the men that they could take off to visit their families. He wanted them back no later than the evening of Wednesday December 26. A few men said they would not be returning because there was not enough work for them, to which Shorty did not object since he did not need more than a dozen men for snowplowing and salting roads and driveways until spring. He said that he was driving down to Mississippi to visit his mother. Lola was staying behind to keep an eye on things and in case people came along to buy the few firs, pines, and spruces they had left for Christmas.

Prior told Daniel that he wanted to visit his sister and her family in South Carolina, but since he did not have a ride to the nearest bus station, which was miles away, in Fayetteville, he would not be going anywhere. Daniel said that they should take one of Shorty's trucks; he would drive Prior to Fayetteville, take the truck back, and pick him up on Wednesday. He also said that he would take care of Shadow while Prior was gone.

"I can't let you drive. Like you said, what if a police officer stops you?"

"I'll drive slowly. No one will bother me. It wouldn't be like driving for a job, with leaves or wood or equipment in the truck, which is more likely to attract the attention of the police. I'm sure I'll be fine."

"I don't know. Don't you want to visit your people?"

"I do ... Christmas Eve is my birthday, but I can't."

"Your birthday. How old are you going to be?"

"Twenty-two."

"Why can't you go home? What's your trouble that keeps you living here, away from your family?"

"Maybe when you get back, I'll tell you."

"You know, your situation, your hurt's eating at me. Making up with loved ones and settling problems ain't easy. Getting in trouble, now that's real easy, like fallin' off a log. I know. I got myself in trouble when I was just a little older than you. My life became hell. My wife, who I needed like the air I breathe, told me to settle it. I didn't know how. She took our little son and moved in with her mother, telling me she would wait there for me to straighten out my life. Women don't have but so much patience with men and their problems. They want security. Well, years passed. She moved on ... I don't know where. I haven't seen my son in more than 30 years. I don't know if either

109

one of them is alive or gone on to the other world. Ah ... if I only knew then what I know now ... "

After a moment's hesitation, Daniel said, "I'll tell you this much: my problem is more complicated than just a situation involving me. There are people, a lot of them, who I have to keep away from."

"I know that. I know you're on the run; I'm not asking who you're running from, but I'll tell you this very important thing ... you have to know how to talk to people. The ones who you love and trust, you have to open up to them. Don't keep them in the dark; if they love you, they'll be there for you and they will understand. Now, the ones who mean to do you harm, you have to talk to them like you love 'em more than you love yourself. But—and this part is very important—you have to always keep your fists balled up and be ready to strike."

"I understand. I'll think about what you said."

"At least, you should call your family."

"I spoke to them from that phone booth last week. They understand, but I'll call them again, after I drive you to the bus."

"Do they really? Do they understand?"

At that, Daniel's eyes filled with tears. How *could* Maria understand? His imprudent decisions had led to the series of appalling events that ripped him from her, from his parents, his job, his life. At times, he became so infuriated and disgusted with himself that he thought about bashing his head into a wall, a tree, the sharp metal corner of one of the trailers, but he did not want to end his life in that way. At other times, he fantasized about getting hold of a gun, like the one he had taken from the man in the sweat suit, and going back to Brooklyn and knocking on Carmine De Luca's door and drilling bloody holes into everyone in the house until he and the big man were the only ones left. Then he would take his time; he would tell De Luca how much misery he had caused and how wrong he had been, and then Daniel would shoot the man in the gut. He hoped that what he had read about that kind of bullet wound being the most painful and causing the slowest, most agonizing, most demeaning death was true. He wiped his tears, snorted, and said, "Even if I thought I could visit them, how would we get to the bus station? No one is going to drive us and we can't leave Shorty's truck in Fayetteville for five days. How would we work that? Besides, what would you do with Shadow?"

"I'd take him with me. I've done that before. Hid him in a basket. He's a good boy. Never makes a peep. It's only a five-hour trip to Greenville."

"No. Leave Shadow with me. I'll drive you to Fayetteville and I'll pick you up Wednesday night. It would be my pleasure."

"No. I won't let you. It's too risky for you. Besides, you should go home. Go home today, tonight ... don't waste your life out here. Take it from me: there are solutions for every problem, but you're not going to find any here. Get out of this place, and find your solution."

Daniel became excited, in fact, elated as he thought about seeing Maria and his parents, but then, reminding himself that the risk was too great, he brought himself back to reality. But, if he did not go home now, when would he be able to do so? When would it be safe to return to his life? What *was* the solution to his problem? Was there a solution? If so, Prior was right: he was not likely to find it here in this wooded hiding place.

Daniel and Prior had a quiet dinner in the trailer, after which they both turned in, worn out from their week's hard labor.

The next morning, Saturday, with no work and nothing to do, Daniel was bored. He missed the physical exertion, so he put on a sweater, his heavy coat, boots, gloves, and a stocking cap and ventured out into the frosty air. He was used to performing heavy work in all kinds of weather conditions; in fact, he had learned to enjoy it. He marveled at how adaptable he was. He had evolved from a neatly-dressed college educated city boy who had never spent any time in the woods to a country roughneck. He felt that he had gained a few pounds; he knew that he was considerably stronger and more physically durable than he had been only a few weeks before.

He began to jog along the woody snow-covered perimeter of the compound. It was deserted. All of the cars belonging to the workers, except for the one belonging to Clay, the man Shorty had said was his wife's friend from childhood, were gone. He thought again about going home for Christmas; then he pushed that notion from his mind.

As he approached Shorty's trailer on his third pass around the compound, a curtain in one of the windows fluttered and Lola's scowling face appeared. Daniel, not sure what kind of mood she was in, did not wave hello; he just continued to jog.

He returned to Prior's trailer, poured a cup of coffee, and brought it to his room, where he sat in a corner near the electric heater and tried to read, but could not concentrate. When he had finished his coffee, he walked to Prior's room at the other end of the trailer. Through the partially open door, he saw that Prior was still asleep. The fine curly points of Daniel's newly-grown beard caught on the top edge of his sweater, as they always did. He looked at himself in the bathroom mirror and then he pulled a pair of scissors from a drawer and roughly trimmed his beard. Then he shaved until his skin was smooth.

111

He walked to the door of the trailer and onto the front step. All was still and silent. Just then, the door to Shorty's trailer opened; Clay emerged, looked around, and stepped down to the ground. As he walked to his car, he spotted Daniel; he turned his face away, got into his car, and started the engine. Daniel stepped back into the trailer, closed the door, and looked at Clay through a small window near the door. As Clay waited for the car to warm up, he smoked a cigarette, occasionally looking in the direction of Prior's trailer. Then he trudged back to Shorty's trailer and talked to Lola in the doorway for a few seconds before returning to his car and driving out of the compound.

Later that day, when Daniel was walking Shadow, Lola approached him. "Hi. When you headin' home for Christmas?" she asked with a smile plastered on her face in a counterfeit attempt to sound bright and cheery.

"I don't think I can get home right now."

"That's a cryin' shame. Why the hell not?" she asked.

"It's a long story. I wouldn't want to bore you with it."

"That kind of answer means there's a woman involved. Right?"

"That's part of it, but it's kind of complicated."

"Ain't it, though? That's kind of the definition of life: a complicated, disappointin' series of events until they lay you in your grave."

"You're right. Hearing someone else say that makes me feel better."

"Oh, sure. Misery loves company, love," Lola said.

Daniel loosened his grip on Shadow's leash. The little dog did what Daniel had hoped it would: it pulled him a few steps from Lola. However, she caught up with him. Neither one said anything for a while.

"You know, Shorty ain't my husband," she explained.

"Oh. I didn't know. He's a nice guy."

"Well, he can be nice. He's a lot older than me; you know that."

He wanted to say, "Look, Lola, I don't care who goes in or out of your trailer when Shorty's not around. Just leave me out of it." Instead, he just looked at her and shook his head.

"Well, you know, if you ever want to stop by for a drink when Shorty's not around, just knock. I'm like kind of a mother to the boys."

"That's mighty generous of you, but I mostly keep to myself." Little by little, he had begun to pick up the phrasing and twang of the men around him.

"Now, why is that? Strong, good looking young buck like you. Don't you partake in the pleasures of life, such as getting a snootful and socializing in town with the girls on Saturday nights?"

"No. Prior and I go in to have a bite to eat; we do some shopping, use the

Laundromat ... that sort of thing."

"You don't spend time with the rest of the boys? Why?"

"I don't get on with them. It has to do with a run-in I had with Russ and his boys when I first got here. They don't like me 'cause I'm a Yankee."

"But you get on with that colored man. Why is that?"

"He's a very nice man."

"I know. Kinda funny ... a good looking young guy and an old colored man. Kind of a suspicious relationship."

Daniel, aware of the trap she was setting, said, "Not really. He doesn't bother me and I don't bother him. As I said, Lola, I stay to myself and I let others live. I don't want to bother anybody and I don't want to be bothered."

"That's good. You know, Shorty trusts me completely. That's why he leaves me in charge when he goes away. I make sure the men are doin' their jobs. I make sure all the rules are being followed. Take that dog, for instance. Shorty don't like the men to keep pets; he says they mess up the place. I guess he's held off on tellin' the colored man to get rid of that there dog."

"He's a good dog, Lola, and we clean up after him. In fact, Prior's trailer is very clean ..., just as neat and clean as yours."

"Whoa! What you tryin' to pull? You ain't never been in my trailer."

Surprised by her reaction, Daniel reminded her of his first night in the compound, when Shorty had brought him home for dinner.

"Oh, yeah. That is correct. I misremembered."

She turned away. Then she turned back to Daniel. He waited.

"Just keep our conversation in mind. I can be real mean if I'm crossed." Looking down at Prior's dog, she said, "Shorty does everything I tell him to do. Of course, on the other hand, I can be sweet as sugar and warm and cozy too. You come visit me if you ever need counseling or comforting. Like I said, I'm like a mother to the boys. Shorty knows that."

Daniel looked down at Shadow, who was patiently waiting to resume his walk. He zipped his coat further up his neck and allowed the dog to lead him to the deep, snow-covered woods.

When he returned to the compound, Daniel looked at Shorty's trailer. Parked next to it were four trucks, three of which were fitted with snowplows. After he dropped off Shadow at Prior's trailer, he walked to Shorty's place and knocked on the door.

"Here for some counseling so soon?" Lola asked.

An hour later, Daniel and Prior, with Shadow in a covered basket, were sitting next to Lola in a truck as she drove them to Fayetteville. Even though she had agreed with a smile, Daniel knew she was not pleased to be doing this.

When Lola dropped them off at the bus station 90 minutes later, she said she would have a bite to eat in the coffee shop across the street while they bought their tickets. After they had done that, they told her that they would be back in town at 5 p.m. on the day after Christmas.

Daniel called Maria from the bus station to tell her that he was coming home. Her unreserved shrieks of happiness vibrated through the phone, and he felt cheerful for the first time since his nightmare had begun.

Daniel would take a bus with Prior to Greenville, South Carolina, at which point he would board another one to the Port Authority Bus Terminal in Manhattan; then he would take the subway to Maria, arriving at the apartment at around midnight. He called his parents to say that he and Maria would figure out a safe way for them all to get together.

On the trip to Greenville, Daniel opened up to Prior. He revealed his real name. He described his insecurities as a child, his mixed background, and what his neighborhood in Brooklyn was like. Then he explained why he had decided to work at the social club and how he had been simultaneously repelled by and drawn to the men who frequented it and how they earned their living; he sighed and then he whispered as he recounted the story of Jimmy's death and burial, concluding by saying, "I had to run; other things have happened since then, but I don't want to talk about that now."

Prior sat quietly for the next few minutes. Daniel feared that the man was angry with him, and then he saw that Prior had fallen asleep. He wondered how much of his story Prior had heard. Eventually, as daylight faded into a cold inky blackness, Daniel fell into a peaceful sleep.

When they exited the bus in Greenville, Daniel said that he appreciated the offer, but could not go home with Prior. As it was, he would not reach New York until the early hours of the morning.

Before they parted company, Prior said, "I've put a great deal of hard thought into what you told me on the bus. You are in the middle of a thorny and precarious situation. I don't know how you should go about solving your problem, but think about this: when a boy is confronted by bullies in a schoolyard or a man is tormented by other men, he better face them head-on and knock out their teeth and be ready to kill them, if he must. If he doesn't do that, he will end up being their lackey and their slave. Nobody wants that. Be careful, Daniel. God speed."

Daniel believed that since none of De Luca's men had gone to the apartment, he would be safe there. However, he would have to be very careful when it came to visiting his parents or meeting them somewhere because he had to assume their house was under surveillance by De Luca's men or by the police or both. He took comfort in the fact that he had been gone for months and that, according to Maria, he was no longer in the news.

As the bus approached New York via the New Jersey Turnpike, Daniel became so energized that he found it difficult to remain seated. At Port Authority, he ran from the bus to the subway. He was elated to be sitting in a rocking subway car and was thrilled by the grinding, squealing sound of the wheels screeching along the tracks. He burst from the train at Avenue J and rushed up the grimy, littered staircase to the quiet, dark street. It was 1:35 on Sunday morning. As he walked along the sidewalk to Ocean Avenue, which was also quiet, but not traffic-free at that early hour, he could not believe that he was home. His heart was jumping out of his chest at the realization that, within a few minutes, he would be holding Maria in his arms. As he approached the building, he decided that, no matter the danger, he would remain here. He hoped Prior would understand.

Daniel pushed open the lobby door of the apartment building and entered. As he reached the staircase, he heard the lobby door open again. He took the stairs two at a time. When he reached the first landing, he felt himself being roughly pushed to a wall; his face smacked against the cold, painted surface. He grunted and tried to turn around, but he could not move ... somebody held him against the wall; a foul-tasting cloth was shoved into his mouth, and then he was in darkness as some kind of rough fabric bag was pulled down over his head ... heavy hands yanked his knapsack from his back, held his shoulders, pulled his arms behind him, and wrapped what felt like tape around his wrists. Then he was brutally pulled down the stairs. He tried to call out, only to choke on saliva; he attempted to use his feet as brakes, but the strong hands pulled him. He felt the cold air. He heard the beep of a car being unlocked; the hands were thrusting him into it. Using every bit of strength that he could muster, he held his body as rigid as he was able, but the hands shoved him in; then he felt hands grabbing his legs and heaving him further into the car. Car doors slammed shut; he heard the engine start and then he felt the car moving rapidly along the street.

A while later, hands roughly pulled him out and dragged him over sand. A freezing wet gust of air wafted under the cloth bag to his face; he heard the sound of waves. He knew the feel of the wind and the sound of the surf were to be his last living sensations. He was terrified; he was angry. He felt that if he could see, he would be able to demolish the men who held him ... tear them to pieces. That was all he wanted; at that moment, he did not fear death. He wanted

115

to hurt these men who were deciding when and how his life would end.

He was pushed down onto the sand. He heard mumbled talk. Then the bag was pulled from his face and he was brutally turned over. He saw three men. He did not recognize them. One of them pulled the cloth from his mouth; then, using a flashlight, the man looked at what appeared to be a photograph. The other men looked at it too. Then the first man shined the flashlight directly at Daniel's face.

"Good thing," one of the men said. "Would of been a shame to take out the wrong guy so close to Christmas."

The others shook their heads in silent assent. Then the first man said to Daniel, "Look, we don't know who you are or what you did, but these are your last seconds on earth. If you wanna say a prayer, do it now. It won't hurt when I whack you ... I promise."

Daniel closed his eyes and held back tears. He shook violently; his pants felt cold and wet. He gave up. He wanted it to be over. Then he thought of Maria. He prepared to force himself up and lunge at the men.

Then one of the men said, "Look ... some guys over there. Do it fast ... Then we gotta take *them* out too."

"No. They're coming this way. I think they're cops."

The men ran. Daniel turned his head. Through his tears, he saw a group of men in overcoats running along the beach after the first group. He arched his back and struggled to free his hands, only managing to hurt his already bruised wrists. He gave up again, this time, ready to be arrested.

Two men pulled Daniel up; they quickly cut off the tape and, keeping his arms behind his back, locked his wrists in handcuffs. After frisking him and taking his wallet and phone, they led him to a car, pushed him into the back seat, and drove to midtown Manhattan, where the car stopped in front of an office building. They whisked him through the lobby and to an elevator that brought them to the 15th floor, where they ushered him into a large office that contained only a small steel table and three straight-backed chairs. One of the men removed the handcuffs and Daniel's coat. Then he pushed Daniel down onto one of the chairs that he had placed in front of the table. He pulled Daniel's arms forward and handcuffed him to a paint-chipped steel ring attached to the top of the table. Then the men left.

Daniel sat for what seemed to be hours. Everything outside of the floor-to-ceiling windows was dark. He did not know what time it was. Somewhere, in the chaos of that early morning, he had lost his wristwatch. He was cold and achy. He wanted to talk to the men ... to confess everything ... say how he had killed Jimmy ... no; he had not killed Jimmy. He was drained and confused.

As the sun began to come up, two men in suits walked into the room. One was a tall, heavy white man with close-cropped dark hair who seemed to be in his fifties. The other was younger, probably about forty, a broadly-built African-American man with a shaved head. Looking tired and disgusted, the men stared at Daniel for a long time; then they began thumbing through a green file folder that was labeled *Daniel Montello* and giving each other knowing looks.

Finally, the black man spoke: "I'm Special Agent Reginald Harris and this is Special Agent Robert Canciello. We have not read you your rights because you have not yet been arrested."

The other man, Canciello, said, "We're tired. It's Sunday. We're giving up our time with our families to do you a solid. You're going to have only one chance to help yourself. Do you understand?"

"Yes. I guess so. Listen ... I really have to use the bathroom."

After giving his partner a look, Canciello said, "Smells like you already pissed on yourself."

"I know. I really have to go. Then I'll agree to anything you want."

Canciello uncuffed Daniel and led him to a bathroom. He watched Daniel from behind. Back in the office, Harris said, "We won't cuff you again. Just sit and don't move. Here's a cup of coffee."

Daniel sipped the strong, hot coffee. He was burning with anger. These cops or FBI agents or whoever they were thought nothing of depriving him of his rights. He wanted to punch them, tear their heads off. He felt strong and infuriated; he was not afraid of getting hurt, but he knew that attacking them would eliminate any chance he might have of seeing Maria and his parents.

Harris spoke: "We're going to make this simple so we can settle it quickly and get home to our families."

"You're in a world of trouble, Daniel," Canciello said. "We're your ticket to redemption ... or we can be your trip to hell. It's up to you."

Daniel shook his head in agreement.

"Long story short, *they* have you for at least two felony homicides and credit card fraud. They can probably add at least a dozen more charges to that."

Canciello waited, staring at Daniel. Then he reviewed the folder again.

"Anything you want to say?" Harris asked.

"I'm tired of running. I'll tell you everything that happened to me."

"Now, that's the right attitude. We're listening," Harris said.

As Daniel told his full story to the men, he thought about how he was providing them with more information than he had given to Prior and to Maria

117

and his mother and father. As he spoke, the men wrote in notebooks; neither one interrupted him. Once Daniel had finished talking, he felt completely sapped of energy. The men continued to write for another couple of minutes.

"What you have just told us could be true. Of course, it could also be a pack of lies. Can you prove any of it?" Harris asked.

Daniel thought for a while before he said, "Well ... Dominic could verify what happened to Jimmy Tripelli, but he won't. As I said, he's got to be the one who told De Luca about me and where Jimmy's body is ... was buried. I told you how he made sure I used the shovel after he wiped off his prints and how I stupidly put it in the trunk of his car."

"Yes. You told us that," said Harris.

"As far as Mr. and Mrs. Van Eyck goes, one man—I forget his name—was killed by Mr. Van Eyck, I guess. His body was laying there next to my car. The other one, the guy who killed Mrs. Van Eyck for no reason, the one I locked in the trunk of my car, if you find him, I'm sure *he* won't talk."

"That's what happens when you hook up with gangsters," proclaimed Canciello in a holier-than-thou tone of voice.

"I know. I told you ... I blame myself for everything. Do I need a lawyer? Can I call my girlfriend and my parents? They expected to see me today."

"Calling a lawyer's up to you. I told you you're not under arrest. We're FBI. We don't care about the death of a mobster or two old folks in upstate New York. We can turn you over to the New York City police or call the authorities in Chautauqua County or the ATF or any of a dozen other law enforcement agencies. They would love to prosecute you. If you want that, then you can call a lawyer or your girlfriend or wife or whoever the hell you want. That would be fine with us. Then we'd be able to go home," said Canciello.

"If you don't want me, why did you pick me up? Why were you there on the beach last night ... this morning, whenever it was?"

"All in due time. First, you have to decide whether you want to work with us or you want us to turn you over to be prosecuted," said Harris.

"If that's my choice, I'll do what you want. I can't imagine what that is. I have to tell you: I was nothing more than a clean-up guy in their social club. I never saw or did anything other than what I told you."

"That may or may not be true. As we said, we don't care," said Harris.

"Okay. What do I have to do?"

After reviewing the file again, Harris said that their target was Carmine De Luca and his operations. The FBI had been listening in on phone conversations at De Luca's house and the social club for years and observing and photographing who walked in and out. None of that surveillance had provided them with information that could lead to the arrest or prosecution of any of the top members of the family. They had followed many low-ranking members and associates for even more years. They knew the kinds of crimes in which those men engaged, but they could not prove De Luca's involvement.

Then Canciello interrupted his partner to say, "You remember that line in *The Godfather*, where they talk about buffers? One of the members of the family says, 'Yeah, a buffer. The family had a lot of buffers.' He's talking to a committee in Congress."

Harris scowled at Canciello before resuming: "We watched you for a long time. We didn't know your connection to the family. We assumed you were a kind of junior associate, but we weren't sure. One of the things we want from you is help with our hierarchy sketch of the De Luca crime family."

"I told you, I was just a kind of busboy. I don't know all of the members of the family ... just the ones who went to the club," Daniel wearily explained.

"Be that as it may," Harris continued, "you can help us. Our problem has always been getting audio surveillance of the club."

Harris stopped talking. As Daniel waited for him to continue, he felt the walls of the room closing in on him.

"You expect me to do that? If I even showed up there, they'd kill me."

"I would square it with them. I'm on good terms with one of their soldiers. Aren't you curious to know how those men knew where you were going to be last night? Don't you wonder how they knew that?"

"Yes."

"Well, I have been feeding *intel* to someone in their organization."

"You told them I'd be visiting Maria? You told them who she is?"

"No. I just told this one man where to wait for you and when."

"How did you know?"

"We've kept tabs on you. We didn't know where you were exactly, but we monitored phone calls to Maria Reyes and to your parents. We had seen you with her plenty of times and we knew where she lived, so we got her cell phone carrier to provide us with her number, and we monitored it."

"You put Maria in danger."

"No. De Luca's men don't know her. Besides, they *do* know where your parents live, and they haven't hurt them," Harris said. "Look, Daniel, you got yourself into this. You're in deep shit. We didn't do that to you. You and Canciello and me, we don't matter in the big scheme of things. It's very important for us to cut off the head of this snake, not just catch a dozen worms who run gambling parlors or loan sharking operations. This is much bigger. This man, this De Luca, has ordered hits on dozens of people over the years, not all of them criminals. He runs narcotics and guns and he doesn't care who buys them. We've stopped shipments of weapons going to known terrorist groups, at least one of which may have come from De Luca's people, but we have not been able to connect it to him or to his captains or to the people above him in the Gambino family to whom De Luca pays tribute. As Harris said, there are buffers, layers of people. De Luca and the captains in the family generally steer clear of direct contact with the dirty work. They don't talk about business over the phone. We need to connect the dots and prove it in court. In this time of national emergency, we have to put this bastard De Luca behind bars."

Daniel's head swam; he was overwhelmed, dizzy with thoughts of how he had admired and enjoyed the company of men who sold arms to terrorists, maybe to the people who had attacked America on that blue-sky Tuesday morning in September. He put his head down and squeezed his hands together.

"I don't understand. Even if they don't hurt me ... even if they believe what you tell whoever you tell and they believe I didn't do anything to them ... not stealing and not killing Jimmy, why would they want me around? I left them to start teaching school. I told them I was leaving that job for good."

"But now you're in trouble. When they welcome you, and they will, you will tell them that you're out of work, that you can't get another teacher job because you ran out, that you owe money, and you don't know what to do."

"But they're going to know I was talking to cops or the FBI."

"Right. We want them to know that. You're going to tell that to them at the beginning, just as I'm going to tell my man that you did not cooperate at all and that we moved your files to the police in upstate New York for prosecution. He'll tell them, and that will let you in the front door. There's nothing they love more than a man who defies the police or the Feds."

"And then I'll go on trial for a double murder I didn't commit?"

"No. We're just going to *say* we turned you over to the authorities up there. We'll smooth it over with those upstate hicks and we'll create a phony paper trail for De Luca's people to see so they'll believe there wasn't enough evidence to charge you with any crimes."

"And then I waltz back into the social club? Assuming they don't just kill me to make sure I'm not a threat to them, what would I have to do?"

"We'll lay all of that out for you once you sign some legal documents. Once you do that, you're ours, and I do mean ours ... for as long as we need you. In exchange for signing that you will help us, that you will help out your country, we'll recommend to our superiors that all charges against you are dropped. All federal charges will disappear in an instant—or, more exactly, they will be kept in a sealed folder for us to reinstate if you don't do as we ask for as long as we ask. Our superiors in the Justice Department will put pressure on all the other law enforcement people who want a piece of you to leave you alone. They'll fold because we will tell them that we need you as a witness for a matter of national security."

"That sounds fine, but what's going to happen when I contact De Luca's people? What makes you think they won't kill me just for the heck of it?"

"We can't rule that out, but it might happen anyway. Do you think you're going to be able to remain in hiding for the rest of your life?"

Daniel shook his head, and then he said, "I want this to be over. I want to be with Maria. I want to see my parents and the rest of my family."

"You will, but not for a while. Once you sign the papers, I'll contact my guy on the inside, one of De Luca's men," explained Canciello. "He thinks I'm dirty. He believes he has something over me ... the details don't matter. He pays me for the information I give him, all of which makes him look good. I'll tell him that we have you and that we know what you did and what you didn't do. He'll be able to guarantee your safety, we think. As I said, we can't be sure, but this is your best bet—actually, it's your only option, and we have to get you in right away. They know we have you ... the longer we keep you the worse it will be for you because they will be sure you flipped."

Daniel closed his eyes and thought for a full minute. Then he looked directly at Harris and Canciello and said, "Okay. I'll do it."

"One more thing," said Canciello. "We knew about Jimmy Tripelli. We knew about him before you told us; they talked about him over the phone a lot. We think somebody *dropped a dime* on you. You think it was Dominic Savarino. You may be right. We're not sure. You say Morici probably got your fingerprints from that whiskey glass and got someone to compare them to the ones on the shovel. That makes sense; we know De Luca pays off some of the local cops. They or somebody else may have run the prints for him, but we don't know that for sure."

When Daniel didn't say anything, Canciello said, "Here's something we need you to explain: Is it possible that Jimmy Tripelli was not the one skimming money? Perhaps it was ... or is Dominic Savarino. Maybe he wanted to lure Tripelli to that rooftop to murder him because he knew that Tripelli suspected him. What do you think? Does that make sense?"

"I don't know. Dominic's a snake, but ... " He stopped talking and sighed.

"Take it easy," Canciello said. "Take your time."

"I told you, he said ... Dominic said that when he disappeared a few months ago it was because De Luca had sent him to San Francisco, probably so the big man would be able to see whether the money was still being stolen, and it was, so Dominic was allowed to come back and De Luca assigned him to find the thief. That's what he said. I don't know if it's true."

"We believe money was still being taken when Savarino was on the West Coast. Savarino probably had or has a partner, possibly Michael Morici; he's probably the one who kept taking the money. We do know that Savarino has a serious ... very serious gambling and coke habit. He needs continuous infusions of cash, and we know of at least one other member of the family with other addictions ... Michael Morici. So, there it is: Savarino and Morici. They may have conspired to kill Tripelli because they were or are in the skimming together and they were worried that Tripelli suspected one or both of them."

"I guess that's possible. So, money is still going missing?"

"From what we have been able to gather, yes. A few thousand a week."

"So," Daniel asked, "if it was or is Dominic or Morici or both of them, why didn't they just stop taking the money once Jimmy was dead? That would have been the perfect time because it would have made Jimmy seem guilty. They had probably stolen a bundle by that time."

"I imagine that may have been their plan, but, as I said," Canciello explained, "they're both addicts; Dominic Savarino plays high-stakes poker almost every night and snorts cocaine like it's oxygen and Morici is hooked on pills. They need the cash. They never have enough."

"Okay. You know, I really don't care who was or is the thief. I just want to get back to my life. I don't understand how you're going to make it right with De Luca's men so I can return to them and not be murdered."

Canciello told Daniel that he would inform his man in De Luca's family that Daniel had not cooperated or provided any information to the FBI, so they were sending him upstate, where he would be interrogated in reference to the double murder. Canciello would make it sound as if the FBI was so infuriated with Daniel for not being cooperative that they hoped he would burn. At the same time, Canciello would tell the man that he was sure Daniel had never taken any money from the family's operations and had not killed Jimmy Tripelli. The man would give the information to Carmine De Luca, who would see Daniel as a stand-up guy who refused to snitch and who had not stolen from him. Then Daniel would be able to make contact with the family again.

"I guess that sounds good," Daniel said.

Canciello explained that Daniel would not be able to call anyone until the FBI had finalized the details of his cooperation agreement and had shuffled his file to the proper people. Once they had done that and had left a bogus paper trail to make it seem as if he had been questioned by the police in Jamestown and then, to the disappointment of the FBI, been released for insufficient evidence, Daniel would be able to walk the streets again.

"Okay, so they'll believe I didn't cooperate with you, and the murder charges didn't stick, but why will your man believe you when you tell him I didn't kill Tripelli or steal the money? After I spoke to De Luca in that library in Jamestown and he told me I was off the hook, two men tried to murder me."

Harris explained, "We don't think that was De Luca's doing. There's obviously some disarray and dissension in the family. The son, Antonio, is unhappy that he is still just a captain. He's a loose cannon. He may have ordered the hit on you. It's also possible that Morici did. We believe that Morici is De Luca's *consigliere*. If that's the case, he knows everything the old man does. In fact, at this point, he really runs the day-today operations. Isn't that correct?"

"Yes. He's the one who's out there. De Luca stays home. But you still haven't explained how you'll convince your man that I'm not the thief they've been looking for and I didn't kill Jimmy to protect myself."

"You're going to have to trust us on this, Daniel," Harris said. "The man believes everything Canciello tells him; when he feeds information to this guy, it's always accurate. This guy is going to want to bring this *info* to De Luca so it looks like he's valuable to the family."

"I see. Tell me this: if you knew I was coming into the city ... to Brooklyn, and you wanted to pick me up, why did you tip off De Luca's people? Why not just pick me up on the sidewalk?"

Harris explained: "It comes down to reinforcing Canciello's credibility and showing that he doesn't care about your safety. It's also about letting the bad guys see that we're after you too. If we had just picked you up, Canciello's man might have thought you actually had turned yourself in, and that would have destroyed your credibility. When Canciello gave the information to the guy, he told him that they would be able to snatch you without interference because the Bureau did not believe you were actually coming back to the city. He said that the guys monitoring your phone calls had dropped the ball. That happens all the time. Of course, now he's going to have to apologize to his guy, and say he doesn't know what happened. It's actually better that way. It's more believable. Let me tell you, on a daily basis, there are dozens of screw-ups and miscommunications in the Bureau. Canciello's guy will believe that."

"You have to trust us, Daniel," said Canciello. "We're going to trust you now. We have to shuffle some papers and speak to our superiors. Take a nap. You can't call your girl or your parents. If this is going to work, if we're going to nail De Luca and get you back to your life, it's going to take time. You can't call anyone. When we return, the next part of your life will begin."

As the men reached the door, Daniel asked, "What happened to the men who were going to kill me?"

"We have them," Harris answered. "They're contract killers. They don't know or won't say who hired them. Doesn't matter. We have them on enough charges so they'll spend years in the slammer."

Then Daniel asked Canciello, "By the way, who's your man on the inside? I may have heard of him."

"Oh, you know him. He's a bottom-dweller who's known as Joe Fish."

After the men left the room, the enormity of his new situation began to oppress Daniel like a ponderous, dark weight. Then he thought about his choices: *Refuse to sign their agreement ... they'd arrest me or hand me over to the police here or upstate. Sign their paper ... they won't arrest me. That means going back into the lion's den; those guys might kill me. If they do, I hope it's quick. If they accept me, which I doubt, what would I be doing for the FBI? How deep would I have to go? How long would I have to be there?*

He thought about how one bad decision had brought him to this terrible point, this cold, shadowy hellhole, how it had brought him, a few months back, to that alleyway and to Jimmy's death. If Canciello and Harris were right, then Daniel had helped to set up Jimmy to be murdered so that Dominic, and possibly Morici, could continue to steal. He wondered how such people are able to conduct their activities from year to year, decade to decade, and live openly in society, thinking, *They aren't lowlife purse snatchers or burglars. They dress well, drive expensive cars, live in beautiful homes, and are part of the community. Everybody knows who they are and what they do, even the police, but nothing ever happens to them.* In all the time that Daniel had worked in the social club, he had not heard of any of the men being arrested. A few of them had been arrested when they were younger, before they had become associated with De Luca's operation, mostly for petty crimes; a couple had served time in jail. But, once they were affiliated with De Luca's family, they were immune. Why was that?

Oh, sure, the FBI was trying to gather evidence that could be used to arrest and prosecute Carmine De Luca and the captains in his organization, but was that likely to happen? And now, they expected Daniel to work with them on the inside to help them obtain evidence. What if Joe Fish were to pretend to believe Canciello and then, instead of clearing the way for Daniel, what if he were to give him the so-called *kiss of death*? What if he and Dominic and Morici were all part of the skimming operation? Dominic, he could believe; he knew about the gambling and the coke. Morici ... Daniel had not seen signs of a drug habit, but, of course, Morici was not the kind of man who Daniel had ever felt comfortable looking at and studying. Joe Fish ... he had always struck Daniel as a reliable member of the family, but, who knew? Maybe he was over his head with a house mortgage or fancy cars or women or ... who knew what? None of those men and none of the others could be trusted, and now Daniel was supposed to return to them and ... and what? Ask for a job? Doing what? Would they believe him or would they cut his throat?

His head hurt. He was exhausted. The FBI men had not handcuffed him, so he walked to the door of the office and looked into the hallway. It was silent and empty. Then he remembered that it was Sunday. He wondered what Maria was thinking. Maybe she had heard the scuffling on the staircase; maybe she had called out or screamed. Daniel tried to remember whether he had heard cries or a woman's voice as those men dragged him down the stairs to the car. That cloth bag over his head had muffled his hearing. Besides, he had steeled himself, had tightened every muscle in his body in anticipation of a beating or worse and had not paid attention to the sounds around him. They had pulled his backpack from him. If they had left it on the staircase, Maria may have found it. Of course, she would not have known that the clothing and shaving supplies in it were his. Then he remembered something solid hitting him on the back right after the men had thrown him into the back seat of the car. It was probably his backpack.

The hallway was empty. He needed to use the bathroom again. Thinking it silly to wait for permission and becoming increasingly irritated with how he was being treated, Daniel walked out of the office. He used the toilet and washed his hands and face. Then, as he ran his fingers through his hair, sand rained down on the sink, so he scooped water into his cupped hands and sloshed it onto his head over and over again. He rapidly ran his fingers through his hair again. He shook his head and then he dried his hair and face and hands with paper towels.

Back in the office, he looked through one of the floor-to-ceiling windows at the mostly deserted early-morning street below, thinking that if the men did not return soon, he would find a telephone and call Maria. He was hungry; he had not eaten in ... he had to think ... not since the bus had left him off in Greenville, at least 12 hours ago. He sat and waited. Then he got up and paced.

Then, without thinking, he put on his coat. His wallet was gone, but he refused to feel hopeless. Prior had taught him how to use his shoulders and his mind to split mountains of firewood, how to pick up and carry heavy loads, and how to make other types of arduous animal-like work seem easy. Daniel felt strong; he decided he would use his strength to extricate himself from this abysmal situation. If he had used his inner control at the beginning, none of this would have happened. He walked to the elevator, trying to figure out where he would go without money. He could call Maria from a telephone booth, reversing the charges. But what good would that do? Of course, she could take the subway to where he was and bring money so that they could go home together. Home? Where? Would that put her in danger? He knew that he had to shield her; maybe it would be best to leave her in the dark and allow her to move on with her life.

As he walked away from the elevator, hungry, weary, and confused, he saw, through an open doorway to an office, his backpack. The FBI had probably taken it from the car in which Daniel had been brought to the beach. His clothes were in the backpack, along with his wallet, but not his phone. Shoving the wallet into his pocket, he rushed to the elevator, hit the button, and then, thinking better of it, he walked quickly to the nearby staircase door and hurried down 15 flights of stairs to the lobby. It was deserted. He ran to the doors and out to the street, where a clock read 8:35. He was at the intersection of 46th Street and Park Avenue. He walked quickly along the early-morning street. Before he could decide what to do, he had to eat. He went to a luncheonette, where he ordered scrambled eggs, potatoes, toast, and coffee. He forced himself to eat slowly, not because he was concerned about manners, but because he wanted to maintain control. He sat for a while, drinking a second cup of coffee. Then he counted his money; it was all there.

Choices: back to West Virginia without telling Maria ... go to Maria and figure out what to do ... go to my parents, but their house is surely being watched. I won't endanger my parents.

He walked out of the luncheonette and headed west and then north on Fifth Avenue until he reached Saint Patrick's Cathedral, from which hundreds of people, smiling and glowing with pre-Christmas cheer, were emerging. As the churchgoers descended the grand stone steps to the street, Daniel was overwhelmed with sadness as he thought about his parents, who were surely looking forward to seeing him; it grieved him to think about how much pain he had caused them and how disappointed and worried they would be when he would not show up. He pictured Maria lying awake all night, wondering, worrying about him. She would spend Christmas with her parents and the rest of

126

her family without him, sick to her stomach, unable to eat or join in the festivities, maybe wishing she had never met him.

Daniel knew that he could not go home again ... at least not until the charges against him were dropped and De Luca had been convinced that he had not stolen money and had not killed Jimmy Tripelli. He remembered what Prior had said about confronting bullies and not acting like a lackey or a slave. Daniel understood that he had to face De Luca and his men. He would never be free until he had done that. He decided that he had to sign that agreement with the government and do what Canciello and Harris had in mind for him.

When Daniel walked back into the bare office, the two men were seated at the little table. Harris nodded to him. Canciello asked whether he had enjoyed his breakfast. Then, after telling Daniel to sit, Canciello pushed a pile of papers toward him and held out a pen. He explained each of the papers before asking Daniel to read and sign it. One was a confidential informant agreement; another was an affidavit that contained Daniel's earlier testimony about Jimmy Tripelli's death and burial and the murder of Mr. and Mrs. Van Eyck; two papers indicated that as long as Daniel cooperated with the FBI and did not commit any felonies *other than those committed in conjunction with his role as a federal informant*, all criminal charges against him would be vacated. A couple of others had to do with waiving Daniel's right to legal representation. By the time Harris got to the last papers, Daniel had stopped listening. He simply waited for Harris to finish talking, and then he signed his name. The two agents signed and dated each of the papers as witnesses.

When they had finished, Harris told Daniel to pick up his backpack. As they descended to the lobby in the elevator, he reminded Daniel that any violation of the terms of those agreements, including contacting anyone before they said he could, would lead to his immediate arrest. He drove Daniel to the Chelsea Savoy Hotel on West 23rd Street, where he handed cash to the valet and asked the man to watch his car. They walked through the lobby to the ornate elevator and up to the fourth floor. He ushered Daniel into a small, clean room, explaining that the government used it all the time and nobody would know he was there as long as he kept his head down.

"Stay in your room ... it'll be just for a few days ... long enough for us to create papers to make it seem as if you were questioned in upstate New York for the murders. When you want food, call the concierge desk. They'll go out and get you whatever you want. It's all covered. De Luca's men can't know you're here. They can't know we've put you up in a hotel. They have to think we've put you in the system because you won't cooperate with us. Mob guys rarely

127

come to this part of the city, especially around Christmas, so you'll be safe. I'll be here early on Wednesday morning, the day after Christmas. At that point, I'll explain everything to you. The next day or so, you'll be able to return to Brooklyn and your family. Don't worry. You'll know exactly what you will have to do. You'll be well trained. I'll keep the room key. Here's some cash."

"I don't need your money. I have mine," Daniel said.

"I know. We counted it. But you're a government employee now. Think of this cash as part of your salary."

"You knew I might run out, didn't you? That's why you left my wallet in that other office."

"We hoped you would. The way we figure it, if you're too timid to make a break for it, you'll never survive among those vipers, and if you didn't return, then we can't trust you. My money was on you getting a bite to eat and then returning to sign the papers."

"What if I hadn't returned?"

"Oh, we would have picked you up and shipped you upstate."

"You mean one of your men was following me?"

"Yeah. He was probably sitting right next to you, eating ham and eggs and hating your guts for keeping him out on a Sunday morning."

*****

Daniel fell into a deep, anxious sleep in which he dreamed that he was tied up and locked in a refrigerator in the back of a truck whose rocking eventually propelled him through the cargo doors and onto a muddy road.

He awakened in a sweat; the clock on the night table read 4:45. He was not sure whether it was afternoon or early morning. When he looked through the window, he saw hundreds of people on the sidewalks and dozens of cars, buses, and taxis. Too much activity for 4:45 a.m.

Despite what Harris had said, Daniel had to get out of the room. He jammed toilet paper in the space in the strike plate of the door jam and gently closed the door, deciding not to ask for a duplicate room key at the desk. He wandered the frigid streets, eventually stopping at a small Chinese restaurant below street level on Eighth Avenue. It was brightly lit with colorful Christmas lights. He smiled, thinking about how, some years, when his mother did not want to cook a big meal for the entire family, he and his parents and his Grandma Miriam had gone to the movies and then to a local Chinese restaurant for what they called "Jewish Christmas." They always spent Christmas Eve or part of Christmas day with his father's parents. His heart became heavy and his stomach turned sour as he thought about how he had disappointed all of them …

and how his actions had forced them to have to deal with so much grief.

On the way back to the hotel, he bought newspapers, magazines, candy, and a bottle of soda at a newspaper stand. A large middle-aged man in a long overcoat and fedora thumbing through a copy of *Esquire* turned to glance at Daniel before putting down the magazine and picking up another one. Daniel paid and quickly walked down the street, past the hotel, and south on Seventh Avenue. He ducked into the entranceway of a bookstore that was, along with most of the other businesses on that street, closed for the day. He waited. When the man did not appear, Daniel continued down Seventh Avenue and turned onto 22nd Street to Eighth Avenue. He waited for a minute; then he continued back to 23rd Street to the hotel. He looked around before going back in.

He stayed in his room that night and all day Monday and Tuesday, which was Christmas day, reading, watching television, and sleeping. Each time he picked up the phone, he remembered the agreements he had signed; he thought of the terror he had felt when those hands had grabbed him and dragged him, hooded and gagged, to a car and then down to the sand of a beach to be murdered. He could not put Maria or his parents in danger. He thought it odd that De Luca's men had approached his mother only once, at the beginning, when they had asked for his whereabouts, saying they owed money to him. Why hadn't they threatened his parents or hurt them or held them hostage? He was grateful, but he could not understand it. Perhaps they had decided to wait, figuring Daniel would show up sooner or later. Maybe someone on the block, perhaps a neighbor, was being paid to be on the lookout for him.

*****

He awakened early from a fitful sleep on Wednesday. The clock read 6:00. He did not know what time Harris was going to arrive. He called down to the concierge for breakfast and *The New York Times*. He showered, shaved, and dressed in the only clothes he had: jeans, a sweater, and heavy work boots.

After he had eaten, he skimmed through the newspaper, looking up at the door each time he heard a sound coming from the hallway. He came across a small article in the Metropolitan section of the paper about the apprehension of "Daniel Montello of Brooklyn who is wanted in connection with the murder of a farm couple outside of Jamestown, New York." It stated that "the man has connections to the De Luca crime family," going on to say that he had been transported to Chautauqua County for questioning. Special Agent Robert Canciello of the FBI was quoted as saying, "We hope they can make a good case against him. He's one of those tough guys who swears a sacred oath to be loyal to his crime family. He was not the least bit cooperative when we questioned him. That's all the information we have at this time."

Daniel wondered whether an article about him would also appear in the *Daily News* and the *Post*. De Luca's people were not *New York Times* readers. He hoped his parents and Maria would not see the article, but he knew they would. Neither one ever missed a copy of *The Times*.

By 9:30, Daniel was frantic. He had read the entire paper; he could not concentrate on television. He wanted to be out ... to be on the street ... to go home, but he waited. As it had been for so long, his life was in the hands of others.

At 11:00, he heard footsteps in the hall, and then his door opened. Harris said, "Sorry for the delay. I'll give you the bad news first: I spoke to the Chautauqua County district attorney this morning; she won't play ball with us. She wants to interview you. Oh ... I see you have the paper. I guess you saw the article. Looks like we jumped the gun. She's coming into work today just to interview you. She's some kind of hard head. We're going to go up with you. Don't be concerned. It's just a pain in the ass formality. We won't release you into their custody."

Daniel's stomach lurched. He closed his eyes and made himself rigid until the feeling passed. Then he sat on the bed. "I thought you said you would be able to straighten this out. Why is this happening?"

"We don't usually have this kind of trouble. This woman is insisting that she can't go along with us. She demands we surrender you to her for questioning. We'll bring you there, but we won't surrender you. Worst gets to worst, we'll hold you as a material witness in a federal matter having to do with homeland security, but I doubt we'll have to do that."

"You're sure of that?"

"Pretty sure."

"What's the good news?"

"Nobody else wants you ... just this one D.A."

Daniel groaned. Then Harris told him to get his coat, saying they were going to LaGuardia for a flight to upstate New York.

A couple of hours later, Daniel, accompanied by Canciello and Harris, walked into the offices of the Chautauqua County district attorney. A lawyer, Bruce Barrett, was waiting for them. A burly police officer walked Daniel and Barrett to an interrogation room. Canciello and Harris stayed behind. A few minutes later, a petite blonde in her mid-forties breezed in and introduced herself to Daniel as District Attorney Marjorie Fleming. She directed a cold smile at Barrett. She spent a couple of minutes reviewing a file and then she told

Daniel that she would be turning on a video camera. She explained that he was not under arrest and that she would be asking him questions about the murder of John and Emma Van Eyck of 901 Willow Way, Jamestown, New York.

She asked Daniel to explain what had happened to Mr. and Mrs. Van Eyck. He briefly told what had happened at the farm that day. On the flight to the Jamestown area, Harris and Canciello had told Daniel what to say and what not to say, including not implicating himself in anything having to do with De Luca or his family.

"So, you don't know why those two men were after you or why they tried to kill you or why they shot the Van Eycks in cold blood?"

"Before Mr. Montello answers, Marjorie, I would like to state for the record that I am representing him."

"I can see that, Bruce. Who retained you?"

"A relative of Mr. Montello's. I will permit my client to speak to you about the double homicide, but that is all. No other matters are pertinent."

Fleming looked coldly at Barrett. Then, after reviewing her files, she repeated her question: "Why were those men after you and why did they try to kill you? Why did they shoot the Van Eycks?"

"I don't know whether they were after me. I was there because I had car trouble. I stopped to ask for help. I don't know why they shot the people."

"The dead man found at the scene was later identified as Ronnie Leventhal. Did you know him or why he was after you?"

"No, and as I said, I don't know that he was after me."

"The other man ... Did you know him?"

"No."

"The police in New Castle, Pennsylvania found two wallets and driver's licenses belonging to Ronnie Leventhal and a man named Manny Friedman in a motel in that municipality and a cell phone. Do you know anything about that?"

"I was in New Castle, but I don't know anything about that."

"I see. What if I told you the motel manager has testified that the room in which the wallets were found was the one he had rented to you?"

"I rented a room in that town, but I never saw any wallets."

"There was also a gun, a Glock."

Daniel was silent. Harris and Canciello had coached him to do that in reference to the gun.

"Whose gun was that?" Fleming asked.

"I don't know."

"What about the black Cadillac in the parking lot?"

131

"I had driven it to New Castle."

"Is it your car?"

"No. I took it to escape the shooting scene. After one of the men killed the farmer and was shot dead and the other man killed the woman, I ran away and hid. Then, when I had a chance, I took the Cadillac and drove away from there as fast as I could. The car belonged to one of the men ... I think the one who killed the woman."

"We could hold you on auto theft charges," the district attorney said.

"Did the owner of the vehicle file a complaint?" Barrett asked.

Fleming scowled. Then she smiled and said, "No. We have not yet located Mr. Friedman, but I'm sure he will file a complaint when we find him."

The room was silent for a minute; then Fleming continued: "I have to tell you, Daniel ... Mr. Montello ... because I don't play it fast and loose, as some law enforcement people do, that we did not find any usable prints on the wallets or Glock, so we cannot tie you to them. But, I have to ask, how did they end up in your room in the motel in New Castle, Pennsylvania?"

"I don't know. I was out of the room for a while. I don't know what happened while I was away."

"Why didn't you return to the room?"

"I had no reason to stay. Nothing of any real value was there."

"That is odd. You left your clothes there."

"It wasn't much. I wanted to catch a bus out of town."

"I see. Now, the manager of the motel has also testified that you paid by charge card ... the charge card of Ronnie Leventhal. Is that true?"

"No, ma'am," Daniel replied, becoming uncomfortable and very nervous until he thought about the strength in his shoulders and how he had to be in control of the situation.

"Well, he says you used that card. At the very least, we could hold you on credit card theft."

"Marjorie," Barrett said, "I have here a sworn affidavit signed by Charles Barton, the manager of the Triple Star Motel in New Castle, Pennsylvania, in which he states that Daniel Montello paid for two nights in cash, $163.45. No credit card. Cash."

"Let me see that," Fleming angrily demanded.

After she had reviewed the document, she gritted her teeth and said that she would personally interview Charles Barton and check the motel receipts.

"Another question, Mr. Montello. ... " Her voice trailed off as she accented the final vowel sound of his name. She studied the file again.

"Are you almost through, Marjorie?" Barrett asked. "I am supposed to meet the mayor for drinks, and I must get ready."

Fleming dead-stared Barrett before asking, "Did you meet with a man named Carmine De Luca in the library in Jamestown a short while before the shootings at the farm?"

"Yes, I did."

"Why?"

"Is Mr. Montello's personal conversation with someone from his old neighborhood in Brooklyn pertinent to the murder?"

"We'll see. Why did you meet him?"

"Daniel, you do not have to answer that question," Barrett said.

"No. It's okay. I was in the library reading a magazine, and Mr. De Luca walked in, so I said hello to him."

"Anything else?" Fleming asked.

"Just a personal conversation," Daniel said.

"What was the nature of your personal conversation?"

"Oh, the usual man talk: football, sex, food ... that kind of thing."

"Do you know that Carmine De Luca is a member of organized crime right in your neighborhood?"

"I've heard people say that. They say that about a lot of Italian people."

"So, you've—"

"Enough, Marjorie. My client's conversation with a man from his neighborhood who may or may not have ties to organized crime has no bearing on the matter at hand—the murders at the farm. Are you through?"

"No ... one second ... ah, yes ... Shortly after the shootings, a 911 call was made to the police. Did you make that call?"

"No. I did not. I drove south as fast as I could to get away from there."

"Oh? And, tell me again ... why did you stop at the Van Eyck farm?"

"As I said, I had car trouble."

"You mean when you crashed into Mr. Van Eyck's pickup truck?"

"That happened later. After he had examined my car and told me what he thought was wrong, I began driving out, but the car was shimmying and making such terrible noises I was sure I was going to break down, so I backed up to the farm and lost control, and smashed into his truck. I was going to pay for the damage, but then one of the men ran into the clearing and began shooting."

"Is that when the Van Eycks were shot?"

"I don't know. When I heard the gunshots and saw the man shooting, I ducked down. I didn't get out until the shooting stopped. I think Mr. Van Eyck shot the man and then the man shot him ... or it could have been the other way around. As I said, I didn't get out of my car until the shooting stopped."

"A window of your car was shot out. There are bullet holes in one of the doors. Who was shooting at you? Were you shooting at someone there?"

"I don't know who shot at the car. When the man came into the clearing and started shooting, I ducked down and closed my eyes. I didn't shoot anyone. I've never shot a gun in my life. That's all I know."

"Why were you there?"

"I told you ... to ask for help with—"

"No!" Fleming shouted. Then calming herself, she continued: "I mean why were you in Jamestown?"

"I left my teaching job ... I was having trouble ... I'm embarrassed to say, but it was too much for me, so I told them I needed to take a leave of absence. I was confused about my next stop, so I just got in my car and traveled. I've always wanted to see this part of the state."

"Really?"

"Okay, Marjorie. We've given you plenty of time. You have not established any grounds for holding my client. We're leaving. I have an appointment. Have a good day."

Daniel and Barrett stood up, but before they could walk out the door, Fleming said, "Wait, Barrett. There's more going on here than meets the eye. For instance, why was Mr. Montello picked up by the FBI?"

"I really don't know. In fact, I was told that they're no longer interested in him and they hoped you could put a case together, but, of course, you can't."

9

Back in the Lion's Den

As Daniel and Barrett walked from the interrogation room, Canciello asked, "Rough, huh?" Daniel shook his head. He sat in the back of the car; the agents talked to Barrett on the sidewalk for a few minutes before shaking hands and parting company.

On the ride back to the airport, Canciello said, "Mr. Barrett says you were great. You didn't give her a hook to hang her case on. And, just as important, you did not implicate De Luca in any way. Good for you! Barrett's going to email the transcript to us when he gets a copy. I'll use that when I talk to Joe Fish. It's ironclad proof that you're not a rat. He'll eat it up."

"I've never been so sick in my life," Daniel said. "I think it was worse than when those guys were trying to kill me. All I could think of was ending up in jail in that crappy place."

"You're fine. She doesn't have a case," Canciello said.

"I know I should feel better now, but I don't like lying, especially to a district attorney. I mean, I could be prosecuted for that, right?"

Harris said. "You lied because if you didn't you'd be prosecuted for killing two people, which you say you didn't do. We want to protect you because we're more interested in putting De Luca and his captains in jail than prosecuting you."

Daniel was silent for a while. Then he asked, "What happened with that motel manager, Charlie something or other? What made him change his story?"

"Lucky for you, Charlie Barton has a long criminal history. A few open cases. We gave him options. He chose the right one," Harris explained.

"You mean you strong-armed him?"

"As I said, we gave him options."

"And Barrett? Where did he come from?"

"Bruce is one of ours ... a top-notch criminal attorney," Canciello said.

"Who hired him? He said a relative had retained him. Who even knew I was being questioned? Who's paying him?"

"Your Uncle Sam is covering his fee."

On the plane ride back to the city, Harris explained that Daniel would have to stay in the hotel for one or two more days. Before he could go home, Canciello had to sit down with Joe Fish to explain what had happened to Daniel; he wanted to be able to give to Joe Fish a copy of the transcript of the interrogation conducted by the district attorney in Jamestown and a copy of a phony transcript of Daniel refusing to cooperate with the FBI after he had been picked up at the beach. He said that all of that information, along with what Canciello would say, should be enough to convince Joe Fish that Daniel was not a threat to De Luca, and could be trusted.

Daniel asked whether he could call Maria and his parents.

"Yes," Harris said, "but not until we have a training session. I want to make sure you know what to say. You don't want to slip, and say something to your family that may get back to the mob. You did well with that DA, but in their own way, mob guys are smarter and more difficult to fool than college-educated attorneys. Before you speak to any of those *wiseguys*, you have to feel sure of yourself and know your story by heart. We're going to have to spend a little time working on that. Luckily, the only part of your story you have to change is your dealings with us ... in other words, how you didn't tell us anything. Everything else that happened before and after, like your meeting with Fleming, is fine. You can talk about those things as they happened. But, as I said, we'll practice for a while first."

The next day, Thursday, at around 4 p.m., Canciello knocked on Daniel's hotel door. "It worked like a charm. Joe Fish practically wet himself when I put the transcript of your interview with the DA and the phony one with the FBI into his hands. He said he had read a news article about you. He broke my balls about how you didn't cooperate with us. I pretended to be really pissed. Of course, I told him I didn't believe what you said about the murders upstate, but, as the transcript shows, there's no evidence to tie you to them."

"Okay. Now what?"

"Now we go over your story and how you're going to act with those guys when you meet up with them."

Daniel spent the next hour reviewing with Canciello what he would say about his interrogation by the FBI and how he would approach De Luca's organization. By the time they finished, he felt sure of himself and very anxious to return to Maria and his family.

"Joe Fish asked me where you are," Canciello said.

"I guess that's not surprising."

"No; it's not. I think he thinks you're some kind of mob hero. He wants to be the one to bring you back. Everything this guy, Joe Fish, does is to burnish his image with the family. He's not fully Italian, so he can't become a *made-man*, so he tries to be everywhere and do everything for De Luca."

"But you can't tell him where I am because you don't know. Right?"

"Right. I told him we left you at the airport in upstate New York. I said I don't know where you are, but I think you're planning on going home."

"When *can* I go home?"

"Tomorrow. That should be enough time. Here. Take this card; it's Barrett's, your attorney. It has my cell phone number and Harris's and our direct line at our office on it. Take this cell phone; keep it hidden in your house and make sure it's turned off when you're not speaking to us. Call one of us from this phone twice each week, or more if you have a problem. Our numbers are in it too. Don't ever call us from another phone or when anyone else is around. If anybody sees the business card, tell them you have to stay in touch with your lawyer because he's still finishing up some details about your case. Once you're sure you've memorized the phone numbers, destroy the card. Never call the FBI main office or the police. You don't know who's on De Luca's payroll or trying to curry favor with him. Only call our direct numbers."

"I understand."

"One more thing ... even though this is the modern version of the old *mafia*, it still operates according to the feudal system. What I mean is everybody below the level of the *boss*, or *don*, owes allegiance to him and they all give part of what they earn to him. In return, he protects them on the basis of his stature and his contacts. If and when you speak to De Luca, remember that he is like a lord of the manor, like a baron on a feudal estate. Show respect to him."

"I understand. May I call my girlfriend and my parents now?"

"Sure. Remember to call us. We have an important job to do together."

As soon as Canciello left the room, Daniel called Maria.

"Oh, my God! I thought you were dead. Where are you? Are you okay?"

"I'm fine. It's finally over. The FBI tried to connect me to Jimmy's death and to De Luca, but I denied everything."

"Should you be talking about this? Where are you? Are you coming home? Tell me you finally are ... I've been a wreck. Oh, I'm sorry—"

"Don't be sorry. Don't ever be sorry. This has all been my fault. I'm so glad to be talking to you. It's all going to be all right now."

"Thank God. We missed being together for your birthday and Christmas."

"I know. I'll make it up to you. I'm nearby. I'll be home tomorrow. And don't worry about what I say. Nobody can hurt me now."

"What about those charges? Those murders?"

"I spoke to the DA in upstate New York. There are no charges. I didn't do anything wrong. They don't have a case."

"And ... those people?"

"No ... that's fine. Turns out, one of them got hold of the transcript of the interrogation with the DA and with the FBI, and they know I didn't do anything to hurt them, so I'm off the hook."

"How do you know that?" Maria asked.

"Oh ... one of the police officers or agents or somebody ... a nice guy ... he found out and he told me. Don't worry. It's all good."

They talked for a while about all of the normal parts of Maria's life ... her job, the apartment, her family. He was not able to contribute to that because nothing in his life had been normal for months, but he enjoyed listening. Then he told her that he wanted to call his parents. He spoke to his mother for a few minutes, promising that he would be home soon. She cried. His father refused to talk to him. He told his mother that he understood.

*****

From his first few minutes with Maria, Daniel knew that something was wrong. The air between them when they embraced, which had always sizzled, now seemed to be tepid. It wasn't that she was indifferent toward him; no, she smiled brightly and returned his kisses as he held her, but she responded to his months of pent-up desire with what seemed to be sisterly affection. He understood; she needed time and reassurance, so they sat at the kitchen table and talked. He filled in the details of his months away. He told her where he had gone and what he had seen and how much, even during his most frightening ordeals, he had thought of her. She smiled and reached across the table to hold his hand. He talked about his meeting with De Luca in the library in Jamestown and the men who followed him and the gruesome murders of the Van Eycks. With a bit of pride, Daniel explained how he had pushed aside his terror and overcome the man in the sweat suit, locking him in the trunk of his car. She cried when he told her about the depths of his despair during that long, lonely period of time when he had felt isolated and had wished to die. She looked sad when he said that he had been able to persevere only because he knew that if he survived he would be able to return to her.

Then he told her about his time in the scruffy, hilly woodlands of West Virginia and about Prior, his friend. Her face drained of its lovely rich color as he talked about the men who had abducted him and how, as he lay on the sand of that windy, deserted beach during what he believed were going to be his last seconds of life, he had thought of her.

Then, feeling guilty and uncomfortable, he fed her the fictional version of his interrogation by the FBI, saying with what he hoped sounded like pride, that they had called him "a hard-nosed mobster." When she asked him why he had not told the truth about Jimmy and Dominic and the mob, he explained that if he had, he would not be sitting with her. Then he told her about his interrogation by the district attorney in Jamestown and how a lawyer had been there. In answer to her question, he said he guessed the state had called in the lawyer because he could not afford to pay for one. He said that was the end of his old story and that he was ready to start on the next chapter of his life with her.

She made tea. He drank his quickly. She made a grilled cheese sandwich for him. He wolfed it down. As she brought another sandwich to him, he wrapped his arms around her waist and pulled her down onto his lap. She giggled, kissed his cheek, and extricated herself.

She sat across from him, delicately sipping her tea as he devoured his second sandwich. He tried to understand what she felt. Men have different needs from women. He was hungry for her, but she needed time. After all, he had abandoned her. She had waited. That was enough. Now *he* would wait.

He knew that, at some time soon, he would have to return to those men, walk back into the lion's den. He would have to see Mike Morici and Dominic, the ones who had set in motion a plan whose goal had been to end his life. Since he had told Carmine De Luca that Dominic had killed Jimmy Tripelli, if the man had believed him, it was possible that Dominic's standing with the family had deteriorated. He might even be in danger or dead. Daniel knew that he would probably have to talk to Joe Fish, who might, despite what Canciello had said, be skeptical. You never knew with these guys. Sometimes, their smiles and glad-handing were more menacing than their angry stares.

Agent Canciello had told him, "Just look as if you had been through the mill, which is true, of course, and a little angry and a little desperate. Let them pick up on your cues. These guys are like a wolf pack: they'll check you out and sniff your ass over and over again until they sense that you're not an intruder, not a danger to them. Their first instinct is always survival. They're going to want to welcome you because you're young and smart and you've made it through hell. They're going to want to like you because you defied the FBI and that hick town DA, if they believe those stories, and even because you handled that contract killer, Manny Friedman. Don't dwell on any of it. In their world, real men don't talk about their exploits; they let other people talk for them."

When Daniel had asked what the men in the club would want him to do, Canciello had said, "I don't know, but I doubt they're going to send you away. At worst, you're an unknown quantity, and they're going to want to keep you near. At best, they're going to see you as a top draft choice or Rookie of the Year. Just don't push. In fact, if they make an offer to you, shake your head like you don't know. Don't act too hungry, but remember: you don't have a job, you owe money, and you have a girlfriend who likes nice things."

When Daniel had begun to look nervous and uneasy, Canciello had told him that the first few minutes with De Luca's men would be challenging. He said that, even though Mike Morici probably was or still is in league with Dominic and might still want Daniel dead, he would not dare to act on that, saying, "Unless he can prove that you're a *plant*, he won't be able to give a reason for wanting to hurt you. We've created a good story, a believable one; it will be up to you to act the part of a man who has been injured and needs the protection of the family."

Each time Daniel pictured what it would be like when he confronted the men in the social club, his hands and feet became instantly cold and his stomach constricted, but he wanted to follow through with the plan. He wanted to hurt them all, the entire nest of vipers. He wanted to stop them from terrorizing people and stealing and he wanted them to suffer for how they had damaged his life and tried to kill him. Besides, he had to do it: the government owned him.

Just a bit more than three months since that beautiful September day that had turned so ghastly, a morning when so many people had been incinerated at their desks or in airplanes, Daniel was going to attempt to rekindle a relationship with men who were selling deadly weapons to terrorists. Other men and women Daniel's age had run to enlist because they knew that their country was in danger. They were not sure they understood who the enemy was, but they wanted to protect the homeland from further attacks. Daniel felt guilty that during much of those first three months of fear, heartache, and sadness, he had been running for his life and not taking part in the great national mourning. He felt he had an obligation to help destroy De Luca's criminal family, but he was also frightened for himself and for those he loved.

Each time he thought about applying for a teaching position or another job and steering clear of the Huntington Social Club, Agent Harris's words echoed in his head: "We're in this together, Daniel ... in case you think you're going to be able to run away from your agreement, don't. It would take us less than five minutes to reinstate all of the charges against you, and Canciello and I would make it our life's work to apprehend you and make sure you spend the rest of your days in a maximum security prison."

Daniel and Maria visited his parents that night. His mother clung to him for a full five minutes. He held her tightly and kissed the top of her head. Although it became uncomfortable, he did not attempt to break free because he understood that she needed to fill an aching, empty spot in her soul and replenish her depleted stores of hope. Then he approached his father, who looked older and more worn out than Daniel remembered him. This time, it was Daniel who grasped and clasped and would not let go until the man softened and embraced his son tightly and wept against his chest.

When they returned to their apartment later that night, Daniel felt chilled and drained. He noticed that when he told Maria he needed to get to sleep, she seemed relieved. They lay in bed, holding each other close; then she shifted, moved her body away, but continued holding his hand. As he stroked the top of her head and the smooth skin of her face, his constant companions—his flashbacks of Jimmy in his grave and bloody images of the Van Eycks—began filling his head. He moved closer to Maria, wrapping his arms around her and inhaling her scent. As he took comfort in the feel of her body, he was able to flush those rasping thoughts from his mind. Eventually, he fell into a deep, dreamless sleep.

When he awakened on Saturday morning he was alone in bed. He heard the sound of the coffee machine in the little kitchen. Again, he reminded himself that she needed time to get used to him.

They spent Saturday shopping. He bought a cell phone; he had shut off and hidden at the back of a closet the one given to him by the FBI. They took a long walk, after which they sat on the couch in the apartment, reading. That night, they visited friends, none of whom asked where Daniel had been for the past few months. On Sunday night, Maria asked Daniel what he planned to do.

"I guess I'll look into how to get my job back." As he said that, he felt bad because he was lying to her. "If I can't rescind the leave for the next term, I'll look for another job. Don't worry. I still have a couple of thousand. In fact, I'll redeposit that money tomorrow."

"You don't plan on buying a car, do you?"

"No. Not yet. I'll call the insurance company tomorrow and tell them about the accident up in Jamestown. Then again, maybe I shouldn't. I'd need a police report, and I don't think I should open up that can of worms."

"No. Don't. They wouldn't pay you much for the car anyway."

The next morning, Daniel stayed in bed for an hour after Maria had left for work. Even though it was New Year's Eve day, she was in the middle of a major restructuring project and wanted to work on it for a couple of hours.

Daniel showered, shaved, and dressed; he put on a clean shirt, slacks, and black shoes. Even though Maria had left fresh coffee in an insulated carafe, he decided to go out to eat. He slipped into a black leather jacket that he had bought that weekend, locked the apartment door, and walked to a local luncheonette. He ate a leisurely breakfast and read *The Times*. Then, checking his watch, he walked to the bus stop. A bus came along almost immediately. A few minutes later, he descended to the street and walked to the Huntington Social Club. Suppressing his anxiety, he walked to the door of the club. It was locked. Since he wanted to ... had to walk into the club looking and acting confident, he knew he should not stand outside, as if he was a penitent waiting for a confessional box to become available. He strode off down the street, wondering where he could wait without being seen by any of the men who would be headed for the club that day, finally deciding on the library. Even though they were not stupid men, none of them were readers.

After a few minutes of searching, he picked out a book entitled *Mafia Dynasty: The Rise and Fall of the Gambino Crime Family*. Daniel wanted to learn about the now-weakened Gambino family, which was linked to De Luca's organization.

At 1:30, he stood up, stretched, and put the book back on the shelf, figuring he would borrow it another time.

He went to the library bathroom, where he washed his hands and checked himself in the mirror. Then he walked to the Huntington Social Club. He opened the door and stood there for a few seconds. Mike Morici looked up. If he was surprised to see Daniel, he did not show it. Sitting next to him was Tommy La Salle, one of the captains. He did not look up from his copy of the *Daily News*.

"Hi, Mike," Daniel said.

"Well, look who it is," Mike said with a smile. "Sit down and have a cup of coffee with us, will ya?"

As Daniel sat, Mike motioned to a young dark-haired man behind the bar. The man put a cup of coffee in front of Daniel.

Mike said, "We were just about to have lunch. Stay; break bread with us." He handed a fifty-dollar bill to the young man and told him to go.

"What should I get, Mr. Morici?" the young man asked.

"I gotta tell you everything? We have an honored guest. Get something nice, Dino. Make sure it's enough in case any of the other guys show up."

"Well, I'll never know unless I drink it. Right?" Daniel said, holding up his coffee cup and smiling.

"Never know what?" Tommy La Salle asked.

"I'll never know whether that kid, Dino, put something in it," Daniel said before he took a sip.

Neither Mike nor Tommy smiled. Then Mike said, "So, I hear you've had some adventures the past couple of months, huh?"

"I wouldn't call it that, Mike. Let's just say I got to see some interesting parts of the country and I learned who my friends are."

"Oh. Is that what happened? We all wondered," Mike said.

Daniel smiled and sipped his coffee. They exchanged small talk for a while. Mike fumed about "the rag-head bastards who did a job on us on 9/11."

Tommy said, "I wish those shits had came to Brooklyn so I could pop 'em one by one right between their slanty eyes."

Daniel sipped his coffee and looked at the two men, attempting to figure out their next move and how he should react. After a long, awkward silence, which Daniel enjoyed because the two men appeared to be more uncomfortable than he was, Dino returned with a cardboard box filled with food. The smell was intoxicating. It smelled like ... home.

"Bring it to the back, Dino, and set it up nice," Mike said. "We'll eat back there, like gentlemen. I hope you're hungry, Daniel."

"Oh, yeah. I am. You know ... one of the things about being on the run is you never have time to relax and enjoy a meal," Daniel said, smiling again.

When Dino emerged from the back to say that the food was on the table, Mike, Tommy, and Daniel stood up and walked to the little kitchen. Mike appeared to be flustered, as if he had expected Daniel to have slunk into the club and gone out of his way to win the good graces of the men there. In fact, Daniel thought, Mike had probably hoped he would have steered clear of the club altogether. Mike certainly would not have expected Daniel to look so self-possessed and act so at ease. The fact that Mike had not called anyone to announce that Daniel was there meant that he and De Luca had probably discussed how to handle the situation. Then Daniel began to wonder whether Mike's instructions to Dino about getting "something nice" had been a signal.

He began to feel anxious when Mike closed the door to the little room. Mike approached Daniel, who, without being asked, held his arms above his head. Tommy patted him down, reached into his pockets, pulled out his wallet, checked it, and put it back. He flipped open Daniel's phone and scanned his messages, saying, "New phone." He wrote the number on a scrap of paper. Then, nodding at Mike, Tommy sat down. Daniel sat, attempting to look happy and relaxed.

Swallowing his anxiety, Daniel said, "Nice spread, guys."

There were platters of salad, lasagna, meatballs, and veal cutlets and two loaves of warm Sicilian bread.

"Where's the wine?" Mike asked.

Tommy looked at Daniel. Then Mike told him that Daniel was their guest. Tommy got up and opened a cabinet. He came back to the table with two bottles of red wine and a corkscrew.

"So, Tommy, I guess you figure Daniel and me are gonna drink from the bottles, huh? If that's the case, there's no wine for you."

Tommy sneered at Mike. Then he stood up, grabbed three wine glasses from a cabinet, and brought them to the table. Although he was not hungry, Daniel ate a bit of each of the foods. When Mike offered more to him, Daniel declined, saying that while he had been on the run he had learned to eat less and enjoy his food more.

Patting his bulging midsection, Mike said, "That's the trouble with you young guys—you're always tryin' new things. Now, take me: I know how to enjoy a good meal, a nice glass of wine, and a piece of ass."

Daniel smiled and sipped his wine.

Then Mike said, "Okay, Danny, we have business to discuss."

Daniel attempted to sound confident. He thought about Prior and the hidden strength that the man had taught him to draw from his shoulders and his convictions. He sipped his wine, put the glass down, looked Mike in the eyes, and said, "Jimmy asked me over and over again where Dominic was. He hinted that there was some issue. I didn't know what. Before I go any further, maybe I should be telling this to Mr. De Luca. This concerns big problems."

"You got your fuckin' nerve, tellin' me who should and who should not hear your story! You're lucky I don't wring your skinny neck right now!"

Daniel wanted to smack himself in the head for that mistake. Now Mike had the upper hand. He knew he had to find a way to regain his position of strength. Then he said, "You know, while I was on the run, Mr. De Luca came up to where I was so we could talk about the issues. We had a nice one-on-one."

Looking annoyed, Mike said, "Yeah. I knew about that."

Daniel told the story as he had been coached. It was all true, except for his actual dealings with the FBI. When he finished, he was wet with perspiration. He hid his shaky hands on his lap. He knew that Mike was taking that in; he had to act. In an angry voice, he growled, "So, Mike, do you call that an adventure? I don't. I'd call it a lot of other things, but I don't want to spoil this nice lunch."

Mike sat back in his chair. Tommy played with his fork. Sensing his advantage, Daniel leaned all the way forward and said, "I couldn't help but notice you didn't seem surprised to see me when I walked in here. How is that? Did one of your friends in law enforcement tip you off that I was coming?"

"If anybody's working with the cops, it's probably you," Mike spit out.

"Well, if that's what you believe, why am I still here?"

"You've become pretty nervy, haven't you?" Tommy said.

"Yeah," Daniel said, reminding himself to use at least a little street talk. "That's what happens when people you thought you could trust turn on you ... you learn how to survive. That's the feeling you get when you bash in the skull of a hit man and you take his gun. You learn to feel strong, like nobody can touch you. And, one more thing, when you come that close to being killed, which, besides that time, as you well know, happened on the beach just a few nights ago, you learn not to give a flying fuck. Nobody can hurt me because I came so close to death twice in the past few weeks, it's like I'm dead already."

"Well, ain't you brave?" Mike snarled.

"No. It's not being brave. It's being pissed. No. That's not really it ... not the right word ... it's too gentle. It's being enraged, red with anger and waiting for some explanations. That's what it is."

"Who knows if anything you just said is true?" Mike asked.

"Well, it's a Mexican standoff, isn't it? I know I've been wronged and my life's been knocked off its tracks and you wonder if I'm tellin' the truth. Hah! Now, don't that beat all?" Daniel said as he pounded on the table.

"Calm down. Don't start saying things you're gonna regret."

"I regret a lot, Mike ... like, I had to run out on my job and now I can't get it back and I don't have any money and, after being *in the wind* for so long, my girl and me are like two strangers."

Mike seemed to soften. Then he said, "We'll talk this over with the big man to see what he says about it. But, one thing: if you talk to him, be polite. He ain't gonna wanna take no lip from you or nobody else."

Daniel smiled, remembering how, when De Luca had called him shortly after the first attempt on his life, he had told the big man that he was full of shit. He looked at Mike and Tommy. They were surprised that he was smiling.

"One more thing, Mike ... How did you guys know when I was coming home? Kinda interesting that three goons were waiting, ready to pick me up and whack me on the beach. Who are you working with that you were able to get that kind of information? Somebody in the police or the FBI, maybe?"

"Watch your mouth, Danny boy. We'll call you in a day or two ... we'll let you know what Mr. D decides to do."

Although his stomach was in knots and his head was throbbing, as Daniel walked out of the Huntington Social Club and onto the bright, cold sidewalk, he felt good. Not only had he played his part in this little scenario well, but, despite his anxieties, he had enjoyed doing it. He began to think that this new connection to the De Luca family might not be so bad after all.

10
Letting Bygones Be Bygones

Daniel was grunting his way through his last set of sit-ups as Maria walked in the door. She asked how he was.

"Fine. You ended up working just about a full day."

"I had to. Besides my project, I spent time filling out an application for a new position: assistant director. I don't have enough experience, but it never hurts to apply. Besides, no one's going to look at it now. I just wanted to fill it out before I lost my nerve. So, what did you do?"

"I sat in the library and read and cleaned the apartment and I exercised."

"Oh. What about your job ... your leave?"

"Couldn't find anyone at the Education Department. After all, it's holiday week. I won't be able to find out for another week or so."

"You seem kind of chipper. I'm glad. I'm glad you're back."

He stood up and embraced her. She held him tightly.

"I'm going to wash up ... kind of sweaty. I'm sure you can tell," he said.

"I don't mind," she said.

"Really?"

"Yes, really. Let me run to the bathroom. Wait for me in the bedroom."

Her words instantly aroused him. He congratulated himself for being patient. Of course, she needed time. For men, sex is the thing, the be-all and end-all. Women see it differently; they need the comfort and security of a solid relationship, a kind of nest, before they are ready for love making. He had been gone so long, during which time she had held in her feelings. She had worked hard to be strong, to convince herself that he would return to her. Now she needed to believe the new situation, feel in her heart that he *was* back and that he would be staying; she had to do that before she could let down her guard and open herself up to him again. He understood that. In truth, his feelings were not that much different. He had never felt ready before he met Maria because, even though his animal instincts had been aroused on more than one occasion when he had been with other girls, he wanted a relationship first. As he undressed and slipped under the covers, he thought of how different he was from the men at the social club, all of whom talked about the many women they had bedded in so many different places and at so many different times ... and most of them were married. Daniel remembered when Dominic had referred to him as an "anomaly." He had said, "You, my old friend, are an anomaly, a stranger in a strange land, because you are not like the rest of us, but you're here anyway ... "

146

That, Daniel decided, would be his ace in the hole. He would act like them, dress like them, walk like them, laugh like them, but since he was not like them at all, he would be able to rise above them and find a way to gather the evidence that the FBI needed to destroy Carmine De Luca's crime family.

He trembled with anticipation as he waited for Maria to join him. Being here, being with her was his reward for those frightening months on the run, when he had been isolated, with only his memories of home sustaining him and with loneliness as his only companion. He was sure that now that he was back, everything would work out well—a few weeks with De Luca's men, during which time he would do what he had to do—then he would make his exit and find a regular job, at which point he and Maria would plan their future. Of course, he did not know what he would be doing for De Luca's family. He was surprised that he was so eager to immerse himself in that shadowy, dangerous world. Despite the attempts on his life, or maybe because he had survived them, he no longer worried about connecting himself to those people. Recollections of the spicy tomato-saucy aroma and homey flavor of the food that he had shared in the back room with Mike and Tommy returned to him in pleasing waves, not because he had enjoyed it—he had not been hungry—but because it reminded him of familiar places and happy times in his life. In a way, he envied those men who lived as they wanted and never seemed to worry about consequences.

"I'll be right there," Maria called from the bathroom.

He kicked back the covers and stared at the ceiling. Then he stretched his arms and legs; he put his hands behind his head and waited.

"Very nice," she said with a laugh as she walked into the room. "You are quite a specimen of virile manhood."

"I sho' did many a hard day's work out in them hills," he said in a silly attempt to sound like an Appalachian native.

"Well, it paid off. You look bigger and stronger," she said as she began to unhurriedly remove her clothes and drop them to the floor.

"Oh, Maria, you are so beautiful. I can't begin to tell you how much I needed you all that time."

"Only during that time? What about now?"

"I think you can see how much I want you now."

As Maria slithered onto the bed, Daniel gently but firmly grasped her arms and pulled her on top of him. He did not just kiss her; he devoured her. She responded to him with equal ardor. Just as they were at the height of their passion, Daniel's cell phone rang. They were startled for a second; then they resumed their feverish lovemaking. After a few rings, the phone grew silent.

Shortly after that, first Maria, then Daniel moaned and sighed.

They lay side by side. After a few silent minutes, Daniel sat up, reached down to his clothes, and pulled the phone from his pocket.

"Who has your number so fast?" Maria asked.

After checking his missed calls and seeing that there was a voicemail for him, Daniel said, "Oh ... it's just the carrier testing the phone. I had some trouble with it earlier. No big deal."

"Good. Come back here."

"You know I will always love you," Daniel said.

"You sound so dark and mysterious."

"*You* are dark and mysterious and sultry and beautiful and smart and more wonderful than I deserve," he said.

"That's true," she said with a smile. "I'm starved. Let's eat. Let's go somewhere. Then we can get back to bed early and cuddle again. That's how I want to spend New Year's Eve. As long as we're together, I'm happy."

"Me too. Cuddling is nice, but I want more than that."

"And you will get it, my he-man," she said with a laugh.

As Maria dressed, Daniel listened to his voicemail message. His face darkened. Then he dressed. While Maria was in the bathroom putting on fresh make up, he dialed his phone.

Gritting his teeth, he said, "Dominic, it's Daniel."

"How you doin', my man?"

"I'm doing just fine. How are you these days?"

"Everything's copasetic. When you get back in town?"

"A few days ago, but you know that."

"Yeah, sure. Mike, he gave me your new phone number. He said you look good ... like you filled out."

"As Mike said, I had a lot of adventures."

"Yeah, well, I'm just glad that's all water over the bridge."

Daniel smiled, but did not correct him. He did not talk either; since Dominic had called him, he obviously wanted something.

"Say, Danny, old pal, you wanna get together tonight ... hit some bars ... a kinda welcome home and New Year's Eve party?"

"Oh, man," Daniel said, attempting to sound disappointed, "I can't. Maria and I are going out for a fast bite, and then we're going to stay in."

"Come on, man. Bring her along. It'll be nice."

"Sorry. I just got back. I have to take care of her."

"What're you gonna do tomorrow?"

"Tomorrow? I don't know, Dom. Probably visit my parents and her parents. We haven't made plans. I need time to adjust, you know."

"Sounds like you're going back to your old boring life. You gonna be a teacher again? I thought for sure you wouldn't wanna get stuck in a classroom with high school punks for the next 30 years."

"Don't know. I don't have anything else cooking for me. What am I going to do? I'm not even sure I can get another teaching job; I owe big time."

"Come on. Mike, he gave me your number because he wants for us to have a kinda informal *sit-down* ... you know, to see what we can do to make up to you for the ... misunderstanding."

"I don't know," Daniel said as he became keyed up by the thought that they wanted him in. He had assumed that, if they wanted him at all, it would have taken a few meetings. Of course, he realized, Dominic might be lying.

"What's there to know? Let me lay it on the line. I'm still a nobody, but I'm sorta a somebody, if you get my drift. When my employers ask me to do something, I try to comply. You don't wanna make me look bad, do you?"

Daniel said, "No. Of course not, but, as I said, I told her we'd go out."

"How's this? Go out with your girl. Then drop her off, and we'll talk in my car. Tell me where and when."

"I don't like talking business in cars. Since I was on the run, I like to be in buildings, you know, safe places. Why don't we get together on Wednesday? You pick the place." Daniel wanted to be agreeable, but he did not want to sound too interested because that might cause Dominic to sense that Daniel had his own reasons for being willing to meet him.

"Okay. You know, my work day starts at noon and I usually have things to do 'til way past midnight. I'll call you tomorrow, and we'll talk it over."

When Maria emerged from the bathroom, she looked questioningly at him. He knew she had heard him on the phone; he did not know what to tell her.

"Who was that?" she asked.

"Oh ... just Dom ... you know, Dominic," he said, making a sour face.

"You're meeting *him*? Why?"

"No. I don't know. Maybe ... I'll think about it. It's a long story. I can't explain right now. Let's go out."

"No!" she said, stamping one high-heeled shoe on the floor.

"Don't get sore," he said.

"*Sore*? Now you're talking like them?"

"It's complicated."

"Well, Daniel, you said I was smart; I *can* understand complicated things.

149

Tell me why you would meet that son of a bitch who ... did what he did and then tried to blame you. If it weren't for him, you wouldn't have had to run, you would have your teaching job, and—"

"I know. I know better than you what harm he caused me."

"Right," she said, scowling, her hands on her hips.

After a few seconds of silence, Daniel asked, "What?"

"What? You don't know what? Sure, you were the one on the run, but don't you have any sense of what I went through? What your mom and dad went through? How I thought I'd never see you again?"

"I know. I'm sorry. It just happened."

"No. It did not *just happen*. You let it happen by working in that dirty hole with those rats, even after I told you what could happen to you. I think you actually liked being there, no matter how much you said you didn't."

"I didn't. At least, I usually didn't. I admit I liked the atmosphere sometimes, but I never thought anything bad would happen to me or you."

"And now, after all you've been through and all I've been through, when I'm first feeling safe with you again, you're going to meet that bastard? I don't get it. Do you want to walk back into that snake pit?"

"No, but despite what happened, Dominic is an old friend. I think he feels bad and wants to make it up to me."

"He's a low-life gangster murderer!" she shouted. Then, in a whisper, she asked, "Don't you think you might be risking what you and I finally have again? Don't you think you should call him back and say you can't make it?"

After a few seconds of thought, Daniel said, "Yes. Of course. You're right. I won't meet him."

"Call him back and tell him."

"No. I don't want to get into it with him on the phone. We didn't make any solid plans," Daniel explained.

"Okay. I'm sorry I got so upset. I just saw that whole scary situation starting all over again. You know, one of the things that upset me was, if something had happened to you while you were away, I might never have found out. I mean, losing you ... knowing that you were hurt or dead would just about have ended my life, but not even knowing ... waiting for you and not knowing might have been even worse. I don't know whether I explained that right."

"I understand. One of the things I thought about when I was in danger was you ... what would happen to you and how sad you would be."

"Nobody should ever die alone. I hope we die together—a long long time from now—holding hands while we're in our rocking chairs."

"Now, that's a picture. Get your coat. Let's go out. I'm starved."

They ate in a local place. Shortly before they left, Daniel dashed to the bathroom, telling Maria that he did not think he could wait until they were home. He called Dominic and arranged to meet him on Wednesday. He asked Dominic not to call, saying that he had promised Maria he would keep his phone turned off the next day, January 1, 2002.

*****

Shortly before noon on Wednesday, as Daniel was preparing to leave the apartment, he used the special cell phone to call Agent Harris to tell him about his lunch with Mike Morici and Tommy La Salle and to say that he was on his way to meet Dominic Savarino at Tommasino's in Bensonhurst. Before he hung up, Daniel said, "I don't know how this is going to turn out, but I have a good feeling about today. I think they want to keep me close. You know the old saying about keeping your friends close and your enemies closer." When Harris did not respond, Daniel said, "It doesn't look good that I go to these meetings with these guys by bus. I need a car. Can that be arranged?"

"How would you explain that to them? They know your car was totaled up in Jamestown. You tell them you owe money. How would you get a car?"

"That's how they live: they buy whatever they want, whether or not they have the money for it. I should be doing the same thing."

"Sorry. There's no money for that. Look, once this gets going, we can increase your weekly pay."

"What weekly pay?" Daniel asked.

"You're on the payroll ... $400 a week. Of course, you have to come to our office in midtown to pick it up in cash. We don't want to leave a paper trail. What we usually recommend is to come in once a month. Easier that way."

"Okay," Daniel said, even though he was disappointed.

"Call me if something significant occurs in your conversation with Savarino or if you have other information for us," Harris said.

Daniel made sure to be a few minutes late. He timed it perfectly. Dominic had been waiting long enough to be uncomfortable, but not enough to be annoyed. He got up from the table at which he had been drinking red wine, and greeted Daniel warmly. Daniel returned the hug and cheek kiss.

"You're lookin' good ... like you've been working out," Dominic said.

"Yeah. I did a lot of manual labor while I was away."

"Well, somebody has to work," Dominic said with a wink.

"So it seems."

"Come on, look at the menu. Let's order," Dominic said.

Dominic ordered Zuppa di Pesce and linguine. Daniel told the waiter he wanted red snapper filet with vegetables, no pasta.

"What's the matter? You're away from Brooklyn in the boondocks, and you don't want pasta no more?"

"No. I'm just not that hungry right now. Nice place. I don't think I've ever eaten here," Daniel said.

"No? I'm here all the time. Here or some other place. I eat all my meals in restaurants. I go home just to sleep or to get laid ... speakin' of which, how's that little piece of dark meat you got?"

"She's great, Dom, but don't talk about her that way." Then, becoming angry, he said, "She isn't a piece of meat or a piece of ass. She's my girl. She's very special to me. *Capisce?*"

"Don't get so touchy. I know she's special. I didn't mean nothing. No offense, man. I just don't feel that way about any girl."

"I'm not offended. I just want to avoid any confusion."

They sipped their wine in silence, and then Dominic said, "You know, you coulda ordered anything you wanted here. They don't charge me in any of these places. I just leave a nice tip for the waiter. His name is Vincent. I got a car for him once."

At the word "car" Daniel's ears perked up.

"Before the food comes, let's straighten out something," Dominic said.

Daniel waited.

"Look ... I know you didn't want to be involved in that thing with our friend ... you know, that night in the alley. I also know you think I *dropped a dime* on you, but it's not true. I never did that. In fact, if you remember, I'm the one that told you to depart before they *dropped a hammer* on you."

"I know, Dom. I know you're my buddy."

"That's right, and don't you never forget it."

"So, what are you doing these days?"

Leaning close to Daniel, Dominic said, "A little of everything. In fact, I'm moving up quick. I'm not ... you know, a *made-man*, but maybe sometime soon. I'm a good earner for the family. I got my hand in a lot of pots."

"Good for you. I'm happy for you. Are you taking care of your health?"

"What do ya mean by that?"

"I know you were snorting the last time I saw you," Daniel whispered.

"Yeah. Look ... I don't do that no more, so don't go and tell anybody that I do. That could be a real career killer for me."

"Sure, Dom. I understand."

"Speakin' of which, things are changing very fast. The big man, you know, he's smart and he's a man of respect, but he's old ... very old school. His oldest son, Antonio—everybody except for his old man calls him Tony—he's been waiting to take over to present a new business model. I don't mean any kind of betrayal, you know, but when Tony takes over, it's gonna be a time where everybody makes a lot of money. The old man, he should retire to Miami or Vegas or someplace where it's warm all year."

Daniel shook his head in silence.

"Okay, let's cut to the chase: I think they're gonna ask you do you wanna work with them. Don't be quick to say no. There's lotsa ways of makin' money that don't involve gettin' your hands dirty."

"If they offer, I'll listen," Daniel said.

"Good. So, we're gonna let bygones be bygones and we are gonna be buddies again? That would be good for both of us."

"Dom, we never stopped being buddies. It's just that because of what happened that night ... what you did, what you made me do, I had to run and hide, so the only way we could've been buddies would have been long distance."

At that, Dominic shook his head in agreement. Then he asked Daniel if there was anything he could do for him.

"Nothing I can think of right now. How's that car of yours?"

"I got rid of that one. I got a new one, a Benz. I'll show it to you later. What're you drivin' these days ... that same old Buick?"

"No. It met an untimely end. No car right now."

"Man, you gotta have wheels. How much money do you got?"

"A couple thousand ... that's it."

"That may be enough for a down payment. This guy I know, Ralphie, he owes me a big favor. I can get you a cream puff from him. He'll take your *two thou*, and you can give him the rest as you earn it. How does that sound?"

"Sounds good, Dom."

"Good. Here's our food. *Buon appetito.*"

"*Buon appetito,*" Daniel replied.

*****

Daniel drove his new car, a one-year-old silver Buick Park Avenue, to Pratt. He called Maria to tell her that he was waiting outside for her.

"I'll be out soon. It's so boring here on days with no students."

While he waited, he tried to figure out what Dominic had wanted. From the time they had met in the restaurant earlier that day, Daniel had wrestled with

153

this question. He wondered whether Dominic was setting him up for a fall.

Maria came out, looked around, and walked past the car. Daniel opened his door and called her name. They kissed hello, and he ushered her into the car.

"So? Does this mean you have a job?" she asked.

"Well, one is pending, but not yet. Do you like it?"

"You said you were going to wait. How did you get it?"

"I bought it through a friend ... very good terms. Let's go home."

"A friend. Who's the friend?"

"Oh, you don't know him. It's somebody I knew when I was younger. We ran into each other today, and he told me he owns a used car business. Next thing I knew, he showed this one to me, and it's mine."

"How much was it?"

"It was a lot, but it has only 13,000 miles. He's letting me pay it off when I can. I only had to give him $2,000 down. I took it out of my bank account and gave the cash to him."

"Who's the friend?"

"As I said, you don't know him. His name is Kenny Goldsmith. We went to high school together. He wanted to help me."

On the way home, Maria did not initiate any conversation; she replied to Daniel's comments with one-word answers. In the apartment, Daniel skimmed through a magazine. Then he went to the bedroom, where he found Maria on the bed looking through a book. Her back was to him. As he walked over, he heard her sob. Her eyes were red, tears were dripping down her face onto his open high school yearbook. She looked up at him and pointed to the page.

"There's no Kenny Goldsmith," she sobbed.

"Oh. He must have been absent that day."

"I looked in the section labeled *Camera Shy*. His name isn't there."

"I don't know. Maybe I knew him in middle school. I'm not sure."

"What are you doing? I know you're lying to me. What is going on now? Did you meet Dominic? Is that what you did? Did he steal the car for you?"

"Of course not!"

"Of course not, he didn't steal the car for you or of course not, you didn't meet him? Which is it? Please tell me the truth?"

He looked down, and then he said, "Okay, Maria. I'll tell you the truth. Yes, I did meet Dominic. It was just a lunch. He felt bad for what happened to me, so he hooked me up with a guy he knows. Ralph something or other. I gave him $2,000, and I can pay him as I get the money. That's it."

"I don't believe it! You met him after we agreed you wouldn't. You *did* lie to me. I'm so upset."

"No. I didn't lie to you. I had to change my way of thinking. I can't burn all of my bridges. I have to stay on the good side of these people ... and I felt I should see what Dominic wanted. You know, he could be a friend or he could be my worst enemy."

"With those people, you never see what they want. You see what they want you to see ... what they want you to believe."

"You don't understand. It's a man thing ... a male thing. It's a totally male world. It operates differently from the way women might think. A lot goes without saying. We ... I mean we men ... we understand each other."

"Oh. Did you understand what Dominic was doing that night when he set you up to bring Jimmy what's his name to him to be murdered?"

"No. I didn't expect that, but, you know what? They're never going to get the better of me again. I know how to handle them. In fact, I am not only smarter than they are ... I'm stronger than they are."

"And why does that matter? You're not going to see those people again. Right? I mean today's lunch was the end of your connection to them. Right?"

"There are things I can't tell you ... for your own protection. You have to trust me. I may have to deal with them a little longer, but don't worry. I'm smart and I'm strong and I'm in a position to do some good."

"I don't know what that means. *Do some good.* Are you going to work for the government or the police or something?"

"No. Of course not, but I may maintain some contact with some of De Luca's men. As I said, you have to trust me. You know I can handle myself."

"Can you? I'm not sure and I'm not sure I really know you. I thought I did, but now I'm not sure. I should have quit my job and run off with you. That way, you wouldn't have to 'maintain some contact' with those bastards."

"I'm glad you didn't. A life on the run is not a life for you."

"And, Daniel, a life where you work with those gangsters is not good for either of us. If you stay with them, mark my words, you'll end up dead or in jail or I'll go crazy and jump off a roof or end up dead all alone."

He approached her. She backed away, saying, "Not now. I don't need comforting and you don't need loving right now. You have to think about what you have and what we can have and what you want out of life. You can't play both ends of the game and think it's not going to affect us. I'm tired. I'm going to bed. Please sleep on the couch tonight."

11
The Basement Senate

A little before midnight, Daniel's phone rang. He had not been asleep, so he answered it on the first ring. It was Tommy La Salle asking Daniel to come to Carmine De Luca's house. Daniel looked in the direction of the bedroom before he said that he would be there in 20 minutes.

After he hung up, he used the other phone to call Agent Canciello to tell him where he was going. Daniel asked whether he might be walking into a trap.

"No, not if you're going to De Luca's house. If they wanted to meet you at some desolate spot, then yes. This is unexpected, but I think it's a good thing. Keep your eyes and ears open, but don't ask any questions."

As he drove to De Luca's house, Daniel thought about what Maria had said. Then he thought about what Prior had said to him about his wife moving out years before when Prior had been in trouble ... about how women need security. For the one hundredth time since he had returned to Maria, he wrestled with his choices. He wondered how he would be able to maintain ties of any sort with De Luca's people and manage to keep Maria with him. He knew that if he walked away, the FBI would reinstate the criminal charges against him.

He parked in front of De Luca's house and walked to the imposing front door. He was tense, but energized. Right now, he decided, he had to concentrate on the *sit-down* and how to walk out of there alive. He imagined that Canciello was right, but maybe he did not know about bloody murders that had occurred in Carmine De Luca's fine brick home.

As Alphonse Caselli opened the door, Daniel wondered whether he lived in the house with De Luca. Caselli gave Daniel a hard look and then he flicked up his head. Daniel lifted his arms above him and spread his legs. Caselli's method of frisking was faster but more thorough than the way that Tommy La Salle had done it. When he was satisfied that Daniel was *clean*, Al led him to the finished basement, where Carmine De Luca and his son Antonio, Mike Morici, Tommy La Salle, and Eddie McPhee were seated around a card table playing poker. Sitting on a couch talking were Robert Licardelli, George Salerno, and Joe Galliano. They all looked at Daniel. Only De Luca smiled and said "*Buona sera.*" Daniel returned the greeting. Then, knowing that he had to act with confidence, Daniel approached De Luca and held out his hand. After hesitating a second, De Luca grasped Daniel's hand and shook it.

After a look from De Luca, Tommy La Salle pointed to a folding chair in a corner of the room. Daniel brought it to the table, but there was no room. De

Luca nudged Mike Morici, who was seated next to him; Morici made just enough room for Daniel to squeeze the chair in.

Without looking up from his cards, De Luca said, "Daniel, sit for a while. We are almost through. Observe how we play. You can learn a lot about a man by how he plays cards and how he treats his friends."

The dozen or so times that Daniel had played poker with his friends had taught him that there is much more to the game than just having the winning hand. He watched the action on the table, trying not to look at the cards held by De Luca and Morici. Each hand involved much betting and very little conversation. None of the men displayed any emotion, whether he won or lost.

After about 45 minutes, during which time Daniel's eyes never left the table, Carmine De Luca announced that the game was over by saying, "I thank you gentlemen for giving an old man a few hours of entertainment."

As the other men stood up, De Luca picked up his cell phone, dialed, and said, "Now, Al," and hung up.

Daniel, who had gotten up with the other men, froze. He grasped the table with both hands; then he moved back and, keeping his arms down, formed tight, hard fists. If they were going to kill him, he was ready to swing first.

He heard the door to the basement open and saw Al Caselli slowly and laboriously clomping down the carpeted steps, carrying a large tray overflowing with food.

"Go on, boys, wash your hands," De Luca said as Al placed a platter of sandwiches on a table a few feet away from the men.

All of the men, Daniel included, walked to the two little washrooms in the basement to wash their hands. After they had done that, they sat but did not touch the food. Once De Luca had emerged from the bathroom and sat at the head of the table, he said, "*Mangi.*"

The men loaded their plates—Daniel saw that they were good china pieces—with Italian cold cut sandwiches and side dishes. Al brought over pitchers of foamy beer from a keg. As the men ate, they talked, laughed, and joked with each other. De Luca smiled at them as if they were all his sons.

Daniel forced himself to eat while he listened to the conversation, most of which was about the card game and some woman named Rosanna. A few of the men told ribald jokes, none of which seemed to appeal to De Luca. Then De Luca pushed his plate away, sat up straight, and began explaining the history of the senate of ancient Rome. He told the men that the word "senate" was derived from the Latin word "senex," meaning "old man." Then, looking around the table, he asked, "Do you understand what that means?"

157

First, no one spoke, then Tommy La Salle said, "Yeah. It means they were all old farts makin' up the rules of the country."

Eddie McPhee laughed; then, when he saw the scowl on De Luca's face, he stopped and pretended that he had been coughing.

"No! *Sciocchi* ... imbeciles. Have you no understanding of the past? I would like someone to provide an intelligent answer."

No one moved. Then, Daniel sat up and looked at De Luca.

"Yes?" De Luca said.

"No ... I was just sitting up to listen—"

"Don't be shy. Go on. Speak."

"I think it must mean that the Roman senate was an assembly of wise men, an assembly of elders, men of great experience."

De Luca turned to Daniel and then he looked at each of the other men in turn. Then he turned back to Daniel, and whispered, "*Bravo.*"

The room was quiet as the men finished their food. Daniel could not eat another bite. De Luca stared at Daniel and mumbled to himself. Then Eddie McPhee raised his glass of beer and said, "I think we should toast to the memory of Jimmy Tripelli, our good friend and honored captain, who suffered an untimely and ... and unhappy ending."

The other men looked at De Luca, who was still mumbling to himself. Finally, he lifted his glass an inch from the table, at which point the other men, Daniel included, raised their glasses and said, "To Jimmy."

Shortly after that, De Luca stood up, tapped Eddie McPhee on the shoulder, and whispered in his ear. Eddie listened; then he shook his head in agreement, and walked up the stairs. A few seconds later, Daniel heard the front door to the house close. Al Caselli slowly made his way down the stairs and approached the table; he looked at De Luca, who nodded. Big Al put the glasses, plates, silverware, and pitchers in the sink behind the bar. Then he put the platters with their few remaining sandwiches and the bowls of side dishes in the refrigerator near the bar. After he had wiped the table clean, De Luca asked him to leave, saying the cleaning woman would wash everything tomorrow. Big Al slowly clomped his way up the steps.

Then De Luca told the men they had a bit of business to conduct. All eyes were on him. After clearing his throat, he said, "A few minutes ago, we toasted Jimmy Tripelli, may he rest in peace," at which point all of the men except for Daniel made the Sign of the Cross. De Luca seemed to be lost in thought for a minute or so. The only sound was the hum of the refrigerator.

"Yes, poor Jimmy," De Luca continued. "So unfortunate. Such a loyal friend ... or is it lying-thieving bastard Jimmy? I don't know. Maybe you men can help me." Again, he looked at each man in turn. A couple of the men coughed. Mike Morici belched, and then excused himself; he looked nervous, as if he needed to use the bathroom. Then Daniel remembered what Agent Canciello had said about Morici's addiction to pills.

"Gentlemen," De Luca said, "I am an old man ... maybe I am not as smart as I was when I was younger ... maybe I am a little slower, but one fact is undeniable: this family, my family either prospers or falls, depending on whether we work together or we cut each other's balls off. That brings up the Roman senate, which our young friend here described as ... How did you put it?"

"An assembly of elders."

"Yes. Well, we are the elders of this family. I sent Eddie McPhee on an errand and told him to go home after that. Too bad he's half Irish ... too much drinking in that race; otherwise, he could have moved up in our organization and become a captain. Well, we are the elders of the family. There are too few of our kind of people left throughout the city and the rest of the country. So many good men gone, some incarcerated, so many important families are like paper tigers now. Then, there are those who rat out their families. My stomach turns when I think of the shame that men we know, like Sammy Gravano, have brought on their families. I knew him years ago, right in this neighborhood. It makes my heart heavy. He should burn in the lowest depths of hell!"

All of the men mumbled agreement with that.

"But, even lower than that ... lower than a sewer rat, is the one who takes food out of the mouths of the men in his family. Not just because it's thievery, not just because it takes resources from those to whom they belong, but because of ... Do you know what other great harm it causes when somebody steals from the family? Do you, my wise senate of elders?"

No one spoke. Most of them looked at De Luca. One or two kept their heads down. Daniel felt uncomfortably warm.

"Well," De Luca asked. "Nobody? You, young man, Daniel, would you answer my question? You're young, but I think you understand."

"I'm not sure I know anything. I respect you, Don De Luca, but I am not of your world. You know I do not have the experience."

Smiling, De Luca said, "He talks like he's in a gangster movie, like he's saying, 'Don Corleone.' Nobody has called me Don De Luca in years."

All of the other men laughed.

"But," De Luca continued, "it's a fine tradition. *This thing of ours* ... it may not be the way it was back in the old days in Sicily and in other parts of the south of Italy; however, we must preserve the traditions and we must be accountable, so I ask you again: What other great harm is caused by a man taking food out of the mouths of members of his family? Tell me. One of you must know. I insist that you think about this."

Again, no one spoke. De Luca looked at Daniel. "You know, don't you? You are reluctant to speak. Don't be. These men know a great deal and I trust them, but you have certain gifts. Tell us. Answer my question. What great harm is caused by a man who steals from the family?"

"Don De Luca," Daniel said. Then, before continuing, he cleared his throat. "If I understand your question, then I think that a man who steals from the family, besides taking what is not his and depriving the family of those resources, causes disorder and mistrust, which can lead to grave consequences."

De Luca scowled. The other men, seeing the big man's displeasure, started to grumble and smirk. But then, Carmine De Luca, the chief elder of his family's senate of elders, smiled and shook his head in agreement. Then he asked Daniel to go upstairs for a few minutes.

When Big Al began walking him to the door of the house, Daniel said that Mr. De Luca had asked him to wait. Al pointed to the living room. It was large and lush and heavily decorated, with ponderous drapes and sturdy, cushioned furniture. Daniel sat on a gold plush easy chair that could have held three men his size. Big Al sat near him.

"Do you live here?" Daniel asked.

"I might as well. I have a small house in Dyker Heights. It's only ten minutes away, but I'm here fourteen hours most days. I'm here at 7 a.m. and I don't usually leave before nine. Today's a marathon. My wife understands."

"I'm sure it's tough."

"No. I wouldn't say that. I love the old man. He's like a father. I'm proud to be his right-hand man. He takes good care of me too."

Then Daniel said, "Mr. D sent Eddie McPhee home. He can't be part of ... I mean a *made-man* because he's only half Italian, right?"

"Yeah. That's the unwritten rule, although it's changing. You know, with so many Jews and Irish and others coming in, it ain't only Italians no more. In fact, at the beginning, it was only Sicilians and others from the south of Italy."

"My mother's Jewish." Then, remembering that he had to try not to sound so much like an outsider, Daniel continued, "I was brought up Italian, but sort of like a Jew too ... you know ... the best of both worlds, so to speak."

"Yeah. I hear ya. My wife's half Jewish and half Italian."

"That's Brooklyn for you," Daniel said.

"Yeah. I hear your girlfriend's a *moulignon*."

Daniel stiffened at the epithet, a corruption of the Italian word for eggplant that he had often heard people use to refer to black people. Squelching his anger and convincing himself that Big Al did not know any better, Daniel said, "She's great. Absolutely gorgeous, smart, a hard worker, and one hundred percent loyal to me."

"Yeah, some colored girls are sweet."

"Actually, she's part Italian, part African, part Native American, and part Filipino. All of it makes one great girl." Then thinking that since he wanted to appear honest and tough and not out to infiltrate the family, he said, "But Al, don't call her a name again. I don't like it. Show some respect."

"Okay. Sure. I didn't mean nothin' by it."

"I know. Forget it."

"You wanna watch TV?" Big Al asked.

"No. If it's all the same to you, I'll close my eyes, but you can watch TV. It won't bother me. After all I've been through, nothing bothers me."

"Yeah. That was somethin' ... I mean ... I don't know what happened, but that was some crappy little town up there when me and Mr. D met you in that library. How'd you find that place?"

"Oh, there's lots of places a man can hide when he has to, even though, considering I didn't do anything wrong, I shouldn't have had to run."

*****

Al nudged him awake and said, "They want you. Good luck."

Daniel stood up, stretched, and then he walked down to the basement. It was 2:15 a.m. The room smelled of cigar smoke. The men were still sitting around the big table. Tommy La Salle pointed to the chair at which Daniel had sat during the meal. As Daniel sat, he looked at Carmine De Luca, who seemed to be staring into space, thinking.

Finally, De Luca said, "We have talked, Daniel. By the way, I'm curious: why did your parents name you Daniel?"

"My mother likes names from the Bible."

"Ah. Daniel, as in the one who was cast into the lion's den. He survived, just as you survived your exile when we misjudged you. Even though I do not believe Bible stories to be true, they teach many important lessons. One of them is that only the strong and those of great determination survive. Of course, having a good education is important too. You know, my mother, God rest her saintly soul, wanted me to be an *insegnante*, a teacher, but Original Sin pulled me in this direction, and that is how I came to be who I am."

161

De Luca sipped what looked like brandy. None of the men spoke. Daniel refrained from saying that he was, or had been, a teacher because De Luca knew that. De Luca knew everything ... except who was stealing from the family.

"Of course, the real sinners in society are the politicians and the CEOs of corporations and the bankers. Do you think we are sinners, Daniel?"

Daniel swallowed hard and then cleared his throat before he spoke: "I believe your family is a business enterprise that performs many valuable services for the community, even if some people won't admit it."

"True," said De Luca, "but I see you answered my question in the way that politicians do: you did not answer it. Are we sinners?"

"Yes."

At those words, the already quiet room seemed to take on another, deeper, gloomier layer of silence.

Then De Luca said, "Continue. If you are a thoughtful man, there must be more to your answer than that."

"There is." After a few seconds of thought, Daniel said, "Your business enterprise is no better or worse than a bank, a legal gambling establishment, an insurance company, or any other business, but, sometimes, the way in which it conducts its affairs is sinful, if you believe in sin."

"Do you believe in sin, Daniel?"

"As the priests and ministers and rabbis explain it, no."

"But you believe that people commit sins?" De Luca asked.

"I used the word 'sinful' to remain consistent with your question. A better word would be 'wicked' or 'harmful.' Sometimes the family conducts its business in ways that hurt innocent people."

Some of the men grumbled. De Luca looked interested. Then he said, "It's late. I cannot keep these kinds of hours anymore. I will ask you gentlemen to leave. Tommy, stay for a minute."

*****

Daniel was on the couch when Maria left for work the next morning. He had not slept at all. Besides his usual vivid recollections of all of the violence that he had witnessed, he could not help but wonder what De Luca and Tommy La Salle had spoken about after he had left. In addition, his heart ached because of the way his relationship with Maria had soured and because he was disappointing her. He hated lying to Maria, but he was concerned that telling her the truth would endanger her. Of course, if he did not tell her that he was cooperating with the government, she would think he wanted to be a part of the De Luca family. He did not understand why he had been invited to De Luca's house. Had it been to be judged? Possibly. If that was the case, he believed he had done well. He had spoken intelligently and honestly to the big man, who seemed to appreciate what he had said. He had tried to connect with Al Caselli on his level and to act as if he was comfortable there. Daniel thought that De Luca believed his explanation about what had happened to Jimmy Tripelli. The man could not possibly believe that Daniel knew anything about the missing money. That was another thing. After all of his denials, De Luca had made it clear that someone *was* stealing money from the family. What about Dominic? His name had not come up. Could De Luca believe what Daniel had told him and still believe that Dominic was someone to be trusted? It was confusing, as was Daniel's entire life.

He called Agent Harris to report on the *sit-down*, if that is what it had been; at this point, he was not sure. When Daniel finished talking about who had been present and what had been discussed, Harris said, "Good. Play it cool. Show you're interested, but don't lay it on too thick." Then, to Daniel's surprise, Harris asked about his relationship with Maria.

"It's bad. She knows I saw Dominic and she's upset that he helped me buy a car. I didn't talk to her this morning. I slept on the couch, but she probably heard me go out during the night and come back very late. She's a smart girl. She probably knows where I went ... unless she thinks I went out to see another woman. That would be even worse."

"For this to work, *if* it works, you're going to have to break Maria's heart. You cannot, let me repeat, cannot ever tell her what you're doing. Do you understand me? Do you understand how much of a disaster that would be?"

"What *am* I doing? Tell me again."

"First, you're attempting to find your way into the De Luca crime family so you can collect information to bring them down. We were not bullshitting you about the weapons going to terrorists. We stopped shipments, but we can't prove they came from De Luca. We have to shut him down. Our country is at war, and you are a soldier in that war."

"That makes me feel good. That's a reason to risk my life and my relationship with Maria, but I have to tell you, I feel like I'm still on the run, as if this is not my real life and I can't wait to get back to it."

"You will. Look ... maybe you'll collect some usable information within a month or two. Then you can go back to your life, if that's possible."

"This is going to sound funny, but I sort of, when I'm with them, I sort of want to be part of that world and I want them to like me."

"That's not unusual. A lot of undercover agents grow close to the people they're with. It's called 'traumatic binding,' sort of like Stockholm Syndrome. You know what that is?"

"Yes, but I'm so confused."

"Okay ... that's not unusual either. Some agents go over to the other side, you know, the Dark Side, like Darth Vader. Just remember this, Daniel: if you don't do your job or if you tell those fat mobster bastards what you're doing, if they don't cut your throat, we will not hesitate to burn you. Remember that. You're ours until we say you're not."

"I understand. What do I do now?"

"You wait. For all you know, De Luca may just close the books on you, figuring you're no threat and you're not a candidate for his criminal enterprise, in which case, you'll never hear from them again."

"Do you think I should have a gun?"

"I think you should have your head examined for even asking that question. What do you think would have happened if you had walked in there with a gun? Tell me. What would have happened?"

"I would have told them I was armed as soon as I walked in because I knew they were going to frisk me."

"Don't you think that would make them suspicious? Why would you have a gun? Maybe, if you had gone in there armed, that would have convinced De Luca that you killed Jimmy. Listen ... if De Luca has any interest in you, it's not as a *button*, as a *soldier*. He has plenty of those. From what you told me a few minutes ago, which jives with what we've heard, his organization is in disarray. The reason why Dominic Savarino and Michael Morici are skimming money, besides their drug abuse problems, is because they expect an eruption, a changing of the guard. De Luca's son or some others may want to take control. De Luca is a smart man ... well educated ... a thinker. He knows he can hold his family together only by being successful and coming up with new ways of making money. The old ways are gone. The Justice Department has decimated the old families. We've put away just about all of the old bosses."

"How come you haven't done that to De Luca?"

"He's old school ... very careful, but that's also his Achilles heel. If he doesn't adapt, he won't survive. Meanwhile, he's still causing great harm."

When Maria walked into the apartment that afternoon, she kissed Daniel and said that a friend had told her that Kingsborough Community College needed instructors for its Remedial Reading and Writing Lab; she gave him the contact information. He took the paper and promised to call about the job. Then he led her to the bedroom.

"You know," she said, "I've decided that you're a big boy, so I'm sure you're going to do the right thing. Let's not fight anymore. Okay?"

In response, he put his arms around her and kissed her. She pushed him down onto the bed. As they made love, first gently, then with ever-growing ferocity and ardor, Daniel knew that she was the center of his life and his reason for living. He promised himself that he would never hurt her again.

They enjoyed a quiet, comforting weekend, catching up on sleep and making up for their months apart. For at least some of the time, Daniel's dreams were free of the usual jarring, sharp-edged violence.

Monday morning, shortly after Maria left for work, Daniel drove the 20 minutes to Kingsborough Community College, where he filled out an application for the instructor job. Since he had no place to be and nothing else to do, he wandered through the frigid, windswept campus. During this second week in January, very few students were there. He walked to the easternmost edge of the campus, which sits at the far end of the quasi-peninsula that contains Coney Island, Brighton Beach, and Manhattan Beach. Then, huddling in his coat against the cold, he walked south and climbed to the top floor of the lighthouse that sits on the southernmost tip of the campus. To the south, across the Rockaway Inlet, he could see Breezy Point and the rest of the Rockaways ... still part of the city, but so distant, so isolated, so vulnerable. That made him think of the beach he had been taken to that night to be killed. He vividly remembered, could almost feel, the claustrophobic suffocation of that coarse, malodorous hood that had been shoved over his head; at times, he could still taste the filth of that foul rag they had stuffed into his mouth. It had been too dark that night and he had been too disoriented to recognize where those men had taken him; he had kept his head down in the back seat of the car driven by the two agents who had rescued him as they drove to the FBI office in Manhattan. He shuddered at the thought of that near-death experience.

As he stood, with Sheepshead Bay less than a mile to his left, the Rockaways across the choppy water to his right, and the rest of Brooklyn and the city and the world all around him, he once again felt alone, lost, adrift, desolate. He had to wait to hear whether he had landed the instructor job at the college. He knew that he should inquire into his teaching status and how to go about securing another high school position, but he also had to wait for a phone call from *them*. When he thought about that, he felt apprehensive, but also animated. He was looking forward to the challenge.

Later in the day, after Daniel had called Lincoln High School to ask about the status of his leave and find out whether his teaching position was still open, to which he was told someone at the school would get back to him later in the week, Dominic called to ask how the car was working out for him.

"I love it, Dom. It's a cream puff. Thanks, man."

"You're welcome. I can hook you up with anything else you need. Just let me know. Never a problem for you, my old friend."

"I know. You're the *go-to* guy."

After a pause, Dominic asked, "Did I hear right? The ol' man, he sat you down in his house the other night?"

"You know, it was strange, Dom. It was an honor too."

"So, you gonna tell me what happened?" Dominic asked.

"Let's be square with each other, Dom. Somebody had to tell you, so you know what happened," Daniel replied.

"Of course. I mean, did anything else happen?"

"Nope. Nothing. Should something have happened?"

"I don't know. The ol' man, he never had me over for a card game or a meal or anything like that. I just wondered."

"Well, I'm wondering too. What do you make of it?"

"I guess it's just what it is ... a nice evening with Mr. D."

After Dominic hung up, Daniel began to believe that Carmine De Luca had plans for him. An hour or so later, when Daniel answered his phone, he could not help but think, "When it rains, it pours" because the voice on the other end said, "Daniel, this is Joe Fish. How ya doin'?"

"I'm fine, Joe. I'm living and breathing and, the last time I looked, I wasn't being chased by low-life hit men."

"Ha. That's funny, kid. That's why I called. It would seem you were a big hit with Mr. De Luca when you went to his house last week."

"He's a very nice man and very smart."

"Yeah. He's happy you're okay and the misunderstanding's been cleared up. He wants to meet with you ... tomorrow for lunch at his house."

Once again, Daniel felt that peculiar combination of fear and exhilaration. He knew this was what he had been waiting for, but he was wary.

When he did not say anything, Joe Fish said, "It's an honor, kid. You don't say no to this kinda thing. It would be an unbelievable insult. I'll tell him you'll be there, right? Tomorrow at noon ... his house."

Daniel said yes, and Joe Fish hung up. Daniel met Maria at work. As they drove home, he felt as sure about her as he was uncertain about what tomorrow would bring. All he knew was that his life was about to change again.

12
His Most Honorable Achievements

Big Al Caselli led Daniel to the living room, offered him a drink, and then left, saying that Mr. De Luca would be with him soon. He did not frisk him. To be polite, Daniel had said yes to a whiskey. He took a sip and then lowered his body into the same deep plush chair in which he had sat last week. After another sip, he placed the glass on a coaster on a mahogany table next to the chair. As he looked around the room, he spotted a group of framed photographs on the mantel of the large fireplace. When he examined them, he saw that they were pictures of Carmine De Luca and a woman he assumed was Mrs. De Luca, children, grandchildren, and others, all in silver frames. One photo in particular caught his eye: Carmine De Luca dressed in a summer outfit, sitting on a lounge chair next to a lake, an open book on his lap, staring off into the distance.

"What do you think of my greatest and most honorable achievements?"

Startled, Daniel turned around to see Carmine De Luca, wearing a loose-fitting sweater, slacks, and slippers.

"Your family ... they're wonderful," Daniel replied.

"Thank you," De Luca said as he slowly approached Daniel. "That's Sophia, my wife, and that's Antonio, who you've met, and his wife and children. They have three daughters. Those pictures are of Victoria, our daughter. She is not married. Such a beautiful girl, but she is a professional, a clinical psychiatrist. She insists she has no intention of ever becoming a wife and mother. Such a shame. And ... that is our other son, Giovanni. He lives in San Francisco. We have not seen him in ... a while."

"Is this his wife and their children?" Daniel asked.

A shadow passed over De Luca's face as he said, "Yes." Then, after a few seconds, during which he mumbled to himself, De Luca brightened and said, "Come. Let us have a nice lunch together."

They sat in a sunny window nook overlooking De Luca's manicured backyard, now in the midst of its long winter rest. Al served them lentil soup, followed by broiled salmon with baked potatoes and asparagus. Daniel sipped Pinot Grigio. De Luca drank hot tea. They talked about families and sports and politics. Much to Daniel's surprise, De Luca expressed the views of a liberal Democrat, saying that Franklin Delano Roosevelt had done more good for the country than all of the other presidents combined, with the exception of George Washington and Abraham Lincoln.

Then they talked about art, about which De Luca was expert, especially in

167

reference to the Renaissance masters. He asked Daniel to name some of his favorite books; then he asked whether he planned on returning to teaching.

"I don't know. I don't have any other field of expertise. I liked teaching, but during the short time I was in a classroom, I knew I wanted more. I thought I wanted to earn a master's degree in literature and then try to find a position in a college, but now I'm not sure."

"Yes, lies and misunderstandings caused your life to jump off the tracks," De Luca said sadly.

"That's true, but during that time when I was running I learned that I have other skills—survival skills—I don't know how those skills will serve me, but I don't think I want to spend the next couple of decades in a classroom. I haven't decided. I might want to go into business. I'll try to decide soon."

De Luca said, "You remind me of someone. Maybe that is one of the reasons why I am honoring you with lunch in my home. Only the few men who hold positions of importance in our organization have ever had lunch with me."

"Thank you for the honor, Don De Luca."

Smiling, De Luca said, "And your sense of courtesy and your intelligence. One of the curses of my life is that I am surrounded by men of no education and no desire to learn ... men who are one step above the level of beasts. I don't blame them for their lack of education; not every family can afford to send their sons, or their daughters, for that matter, to university. I understand. What I do not understand is their contempt for matters of the mind."

"I know. Growing up around here, very few of my friends were good students. Most of them couldn't wait to finish high school so they could work. I was always kind of an outsider."

"One of those is your good friend Dominic, is it not?"

Daniel knew he was being tested, so he said, "Yes."

"And have you repaired your relationship with Dominic?"

"I suppose so. It's hard to know what's in someone's heart," Daniel said.

"That is true. I know that you are not of my world, as you so eloquently said last week, but you are intelligent and I believe you are honest. Also, you are *coraggioso*, courageous. You have overcome adversity."

Daniel frowned at that.

"I believe you have something to say. Go ahead. I will listen."

"Pardon me for being blunt, but, that day at the library in Jamestown, when we concluded our conversation, you told me to go home ... and you said I was off the hook. Then two men followed me and tried to kill me and ended up killing two innocent people. I was blamed for that and—"

De Luca held up his hand and then he said, "Let me tell you a story that I heard when I was a child. My father came from the old country; he told me many tales that had been passed down from generation to generation. You know, they were not literate. They had to rely on oral history. Did you know that?"

Daniel shook his head to indicate that he knew.

"So, the ministers of a young king came to him with a man, a simple man, a farmer, and said that the man had spoken against the king. The ministers said that the man should be executed. The king asked the man whether he had done what the ministers had said. The man replied that he had spoken against the king because his children were hungry and he had no money, but he swore that he would never harm the king. The king instructed the ministers to give the man a gold coin and then release him. The ministers said, 'My lord, your father, who reigned for 65 years, would not have done that. He would have ordered the man to be executed.' The king smiled and said that God Almighty had not put him on the throne to kill starving farmers who spoke out of turn.

"The following day, the ministers brought a soldier who had conspired to kill the king, saying that he should be executed. The king asked the soldier whether the charges against him were true. The soldier said it was true that he had complained because, after 20 years of loyal service, he had not been allowed to advance to the rank of officer, but he swore that he had never conspired to kill the king. The king told the ministers to make the man an officer and release him. Again, the ministers told the king that his father, who had ruled for 65 years, would not have done that. The king said that he was not his father.

"The next day, the ministers brought a young boy who had been caught opening containers of food in the king's kitchen. They said that they found a bag of poison hanging from his belt. They advised that the boy be executed. The king asked the boy whether the charges against him were true. The boy said that he wanted to work in the king's kitchen and had been looking for rats; he explained that the poison would be used to kill them. The king told the ministers to give the boy a job as a rat killer in his kitchen. The ministers stated that the old king, who had reigned for 65 years, would have had the boy executed. The young king said that he could not execute an innocent child.

"The following morning, when his ministers came to the young king's chamber because he was late for his daily ride, they found him sitting up in his bed, dead, a few remains of his breakfast on a tray in front of him. When they went to the kitchen, they found that the rat killer was gone, having left behind the bag that had contained the poison. It was empty.

"The young king had reigned for only 65 days."

169

Daniel had listened attentively as De Luca had told the story.

"Life can be complicated," De Luca said with a sigh. "It is easy to kill and to be killed. It is very difficult to make the right decision, especially during trying times. It is impossible to make the right decision all of the time. I am old. I am not as smart as I once was. I sometimes pay heed to bad advice. I also make my own mistakes. I will do so until my soul departs from this rotting body."

"I understand. I have made many mistakes in my life," Daniel said.

"Yours are the errors of youth. Mine are generally due to the *exalted* position which I have held for so long; not 65 years, I may add," De Luca said with an impish twinkle in his eyes. Daniel took note of how De Luca had enunciated the word "exalted" with a sardonic twist.

Daniel thought of the Mel Brooks line "It's good to be the king."

"Men envy me. Some want to topple me from my perch. Some want to cut my throat. Others despise me for who I am. Life is filled with choices and consequences, with triumphs and disappointments. Permit me to ask you a personal question: Are you a good son?"

"I used to be. I've been kind of a disappointment lately."

"There is nothing more important than family. It is even more to be cherished than health. Do you know how much I have sacrificed to be where I am?" De Luca squeezed shut his eyes for a second, and then he continued: "Those pictures you were admiring ... I referred to my children and my grandchildren as my greatest and most honorable achievements. That is true, but my older son, Antonio, is impatient with me. I imagine he wants to sit in my chair. I hope, when his time comes, he is able to be half the man I have been. My daughter, Victoria, lives far from here. We see her twice a year, on Christmas day and on her mother's birthday. If my Sophia dies before I do, I will see Victoria only once a year. And Giovanni, the one who lives in San Francisco, we never see him. You remind me of him when he was a young man. He does not approve of my life. We have never met his wife. I have never seen his children. The pictures of them, they are copies that Antonio makes for us."

All Daniel could think of saying was, "I feel your grief, Don De Luca," and then he stood up and kissed the old man's cheek.

As Daniel was about to leave Carmine De Luca's house, Al Caselli asked him to wait. He walked to the dining room, returning a few seconds later. He wrote on a small sheet of note paper and then handed it to Daniel, saying, "Call this number. Ask for Mr. Ferris. I'll call him now to tell him to expect your call. He'll give you a good job. This is what Mr. De Luca wants you should do."

Daniel sat in his car. He knew that he was at a crossroads; he could throw the paper away and perhaps, in a short while, be able to get on with his life without any connection to the De Luca family. Would Harris and Canciello find out? Possibly. The FBI was tapping the phones at the social club and at Carmine De Luca's house, so, if somebody talked about how Daniel had not called Mr. Ferris, they would know. Joe Fish might hear about it, and tell Canciello. At that point, Harris and Canciello would throw Daniel to the wolves in upstate New York, and he would spend years in a miserable prison far from home.

Before today's lunch with De Luca, Daniel would have been willing to walk on glass barefoot if that had been necessary for him to maintain a connection to the family so as to obtain information that would help to put all of them in jail. Now, after hearing the old man's sad story and seeing his sorrowful eyes, Daniel did not know what to do. He felt the man's pain. De Luca could not possibly be part of any plans to sell arms to terrorists. Of course, others in the organization might be the ones involved in those deals.

Then Daniel wondered: Had De Luca opened up about his family problems for the express purpose of disarming him? Was the man really estranged from his daughter and his son Giovanni, or was that a fiction that he had created to be able to reach in and grab Daniel's heart? Did Daniel really remind the old man of how Giovanni looked when he was a young man?

Did any of this matter? De Luca, regardless of his many personal attributes, was still the boss of a crime family. With or without De Luca's knowledge, according to the FBI, his family was selling armaments to terrorists.

Daniel knew he did not have to make a decision just yet, but he also knew that the longer he thought about his choices, the more difficult it would be for him to decide. Of course, just calling the number and speaking to the person about a job would not commit him. He sat for another few minutes before dialing the number given to him by Al Caselli.

A female voice said, "Coastal Properties ... How may I direct your call?"

Daniel asked for Mr. Ferris. The woman asked his name and then put him on hold, saying that Mr. Ferris would be with him shortly. Almost immediately, a man came on the line and said that he had been told to expect the call. He asked Daniel when he wanted to come in for the job.

"What kind of job would it be for?"

"Oh, the usual..you'll be happy with it," Ferris brusquely explained.

"What kind of business is this?"

"We're a major commercial property management group. We're on Graham Avenue in Williamsburg."

Daniel scheduled an appointment for the next morning. He understood

171

that he had to take this job, but what kind of experience did he have? One month as a high school English teacher; two months working for a landscaping company in West Virginia; four years as a kind of all-around busboy/waiter/courier for a mob-run social club. Well, he thought, if this management firm is in bed with De Luca's organization, the last job might be the right kind of background.

Maria was delighted to hear that Daniel had an interview with a real estate management company, adding, "You know, Brooklyn is hot right now. This might be the right time to get into that kind of career, as long as you're sure you don't want to return to teaching."

Daniel said he was not sure about teaching, but this kind of job might work out for him. Then, to reassure her, he said, "Dominic has nothing to do with this. I haven't spoken to him since that day we had lunch, so don't worry."

He wore a white shirt, tie, slacks, and sport coat for the interview, which seemed to impress Mr. Ferris. Examining Daniel's résumé, Ferris said, "Most of the men who Mr. La Salle sends to us are not college graduates and they don't come in with résumés."

"I would like to learn about this job; I'm prepared to work," Daniel said.

Ferris smiled uncomfortably. Daniel was surprised by the reference to "Mr. La Salle," but then he remembered that De Luca was not openly associated with any of the dealings of his organization. He thought about what he had read in the book about the Gambino organization on the day he was waiting to return to the social club and what Canciello and Harris had told him about buffers.

"We can offer you the usual $850 a week for starters. Jane will help you fill out papers and she'll explain the payroll process to you."

"Thank you very much," Daniel said as he walked out of Ferris's office.

Jane helped Daniel to fill out several forms. Then she told him that paychecks would be mailed to his address twice each month. When Daniel remained seated, she told him that was all.

"But when do I start? What do I do?"

"What do you mean?" Jane asked.

"The job. What kind of job is it? Where do I work?"

After looking confused for a moment, Jane excused herself and knocked on Mr. Ferris's door. She went in, returning a few minutes later carrying a box, which she placed on her desk in front of Daniel. She explained that the box contained the files for more than 100 properties which required review. She said that each file provided all of the information for a particular office building, warehouse, store, factory, or apartment complex. After she had gone through all of the details of one file, she explained to Daniel that if there was a problem at any of his sites, he would have to visit it and resolve the issues.

"What will I do the rest of the time?" Daniel asked.

"That's up to you. Most of the men they send to us are happy to just collect their paychecks. They don't do anything or ask what they should do."

Shortly after he left Coastal Properties, Daniel pulled the special cell phone from its hiding place under the driver-side seat of his car and called his FBI contacts. Harris said, "Well, lunch with De Luca. That's impressive. As far as the job goes, it sounds like a *no-show* or a *no-work*, like what they do with the unions. Do you know what that is? Have you ever heard of that?"

Daniel said, "It's where they have influence over a union or an industry and they collect pay for fictitious workers. Right?"

"More or less. De Luca owns a lot of real estate. That's one of the legitimate parts of his empire, although it probably also involves payoffs to building inspectors and other crimes that we can't prove. All of these guys have jobs on paper for IRS purposes; otherwise, the government would investigate them to find out how they're able to buy houses and cars and other things."

"That's why Tommy La Salle owns or is part owner of this property management group."

"Yes. You know, it's possible that De Luca's testing you. Maybe he wants to see whether you just collect a paycheck for no work, as the others do when they're set up in one of these jobs, or actually work for your money."

"Could be. He seems to like me ... as if he wishes I were his son or his grandson, but I could be wrong," Daniel said. He did not mention kissing the old man's cheek. In fact, now, he could not imagine what had possessed him to do that. "On the other hand, he may feel guilty about what happened to me, you know, having to run away and hide."

"I doubt he feels guilty about anything he does, but you never know."

"I still feel bad over my part in what happened to Jimmy Tripelli. I have nightmares about it and about the shootings in Jamestown."

"Let's not get into that, Daniel. We still don't totally believe you about those homicides. Don't try to convince me now," Harris said.

"I'm not. I understand the arrangement. Something I wonder about is what De Luca thinks of Dominic. I mean, I told him how he killed Jimmy Tripelli. I guess he's unsure about that the same way you're unsure about me."

"Maybe. What you told me about De Luca's children is interesting. The part about Tony fits in with what we've heard. We have phone transcriptions of people in the organization spreading gossip about him and his father. They talk about tension between them, sort of like the old king versus the young prince who can't wait to inherit the throne. However, we've never heard anything about De Luca's daughter or other son," Harris explained.

"He showed me pictures. They both seem to have rejected him and his way of life. I think, now that he's old—in fact, maybe he's sick; he mumbles to himself—he's thinking about succession, and he's not happy with Tony."

"Well, within the hierarchy, it would seem that Mike Morici is first in line, ahead of De Luca's son, but that's always a tough thing. When there's a son who's in the business, he always expects to be the next boss. To make it more complicated, Morici's only a few years younger than De Luca; in addition, De Luca may now suspect him of being the one skimming the money. Jimmy Tripelli may have been a candidate as boss, but, of course, he's gone."

"So, what do I do now?"

"Do this job. Really work at it, and see where it leads. Maybe, if De Luca gets word of how hard you're working, he may sit down with you again or invite you to the social club."

"So, you think I should stay away from the club for now?"

"Absolutely. De Luca has given you a job, but he hasn't brought you into the family. Don't trust anything that any of them, including De Luca, say to you. These people often speak in metaphors ... complicated metaphors. Don't take anything they say at face value."

"I'll call again in a few days."

"Right," Harris said. "By the way, at the end of the month, you can come in to collect your pay from us ... you know, the $400 per week. Call first. Meanwhile, be careful all the time. No slip-ups. If they suspect you're working with law enforcement, they ... I think you know what they'll do to you."

13

The Warehouse on India Street

By the end of January, Daniel had visited all of the building sites that had been assigned to him. He had introduced himself to building managers, lease holders, superintendents, shop foremen, workers, and whoever else was around. Mr. Ferris had been surprised when Daniel asked for business cards, but he complied with that request. Daniel became a fixture in the cramped, busy offices of Coastal Properties, making sure to spend a few hours each day sitting at a desk in an alcove making phone calls, writing notes in files, and completing forms having to do with rent and lease payments, fire inspections, building code violations, renovations, permits, evictions, and repairs. On one occasion, when a renter indicated that he wanted to move his business, Daniel found a new location for the man, made the arrangements with the building owner and the movers, and handled all of the paperwork.

He became so engrossed in the job that he sometimes forgot the real reason why he was there. He was pleased with his $850 per week salary, which was comparable to what he had been earning during his short stint as a teacher. When he went to the FBI office in Manhattan at the end of January to pick up his $400 weekly cash stipend, he was even more pleased to learn that it totaled $2,000 because January had five weeks. He handed the full amount in cash to Ralphie, the used car dealer from whom he had purchased the Park Avenue, promising to give him a similar amount the next month.

No one from Lincoln High School had returned his call about whether his teaching position was available. Since he did not expect to return to the classroom, he did not call the school again. According to a letter from the New York City Department of Education that had arrived at his parents' house, he was still on a leave without pay, which was fine with him. He seemed to have a world of choices for the future.

Maria was pleased with Daniel's situation because she believed he had cut off all ties with his "mobster buddies." He gave her enough money to cover half of the rent. Since he always paid when they went out to eat or to the movies or the theater, she paid for groceries.

She was not upset when Daniel told her that he had turned down an offer for an instructor position at the Kingsborough Community College Remedial Reading and Writing Lab. She understood that he had moved from the world of academics to that of business, saying, "As long as we have each other, it's all sunny skies and sweet nights filled with love."

His parents were not as pleased with Daniel's career move. "Why did you give up teaching?" his mother asked. "Do you realize you could lose your job at that management company in a flash? It might be they have to cut back or the boss wants to put a friend or relative in your place," she said.

"That's not going to happen," Daniel explained with a grin.

"Oh, you're so sure? And what about health? You don't have health benefits, do you? Teachers have good benefits. Sure, you don't earn very much, but you have security and you're doing a job that involves thinking."

"I know, ma. It's fine. I like it. There's room for advancement, and I might not stay all that long. Who knows?"

"Your mother's right. You should apply for a teaching position for next September. Fill out the paperwork to get back into it before it's too late."

"It is too late, dad. I don't think I would be happy back in a classroom. This is an interesting job. It involves all sorts of skills I never knew I had. Trust me. It's all going to be fine."

Neither Ruth nor Raymond said anything in response, but Daniel was quite sure he knew what they were thinking.

One day, when Daniel was at Coastal, Jane handed a note to him, saying, "Call that number. Mr. La Salle." He dialed. Tommy La Salle answered the phone and told Daniel to meet him at an address in Greenpoint at 2 p.m.

Daniel waited in front of a three-story brick building on India Street, a block from the East River, that had the look of a late nineteenth century factory or warehouse. At 3:45, Tommy, with another man driving, parked behind Daniel's car. Without an apology for being late or a greeting, neither of which Daniel had expected, Tommy walked to the entrance of the building; Daniel followed. When the other man joined them, Tommy pointed to his car; the man walked back to it. Then, pulling a ring of keys from a coat pocket, Tommy turned the rusty lock, forced open the heavy metal door, and led Daniel into the cold, dark, musty interior of the decaying building. Daniel became instantly chilled and felt very anxious in the tomb-like atmosphere.

As they walked over broken glass and what appeared to be decades-old debris, Daniel looked around him. Weak winter sunlight filtered through the filthy windows, many of which were boarded over with water-stained blackened sheets of plywood. There were broken remnants of partially dismantled machines; the rancid odor of fuel oil hung in the stale air. Along one wall there was an old freight elevator and a set of large double-doors leading to what Daniel assumed was a loading dock. He heard the unsettling sound of mice or rats scurrying along the perimeter of the interior.

Tommy led Daniel to a wooden staircase and told him to inspect the second and third floors. As he ascended, Daniel understood why Tommy had stayed on the first floor. Each and every step creaked, groaned, and cracked beneath his slow, careful tread. He held tightly to the grimy banister, preparing to hang from it if the stairs were to disintegrate beneath his feet.

The second floor seemed to be a storage area; it was littered with hundreds of broken, crushed, and shattered wooden crates and cardboard boxes. Fewer of the windows here were boarded up, so more weak sunlight entered, making it slightly less gloomy than the first floor.

Daniel was astonished by what he saw on the third floor: fully intact windows allowed sufficient sunshine in to what looked like, except for the layer of dust, a fully functional nineteenth century business office setting. The room was split down the middle by a wall. On one side, there was a large receptionist's desk and chair and a dozen or so other desks and chairs. Ancient typewriters sat on some of the desks. On the other side of the wall there were a half dozen doors, each of which led to a private office. In some offices, paintings and photographs still hung on the walls. Daniel opened one office door. The stale, dusty air was difficult to breathe, so he quickly closed it and moved back, but he was intrigued by what had seemed to be photographs of men, women, and children on the walls. He thought of Carmine De Luca's comment about his greatest and most honorable achievements. How long had those photographs hung on the walls of those old offices? How long since another person had seen them? Why had the occupants of the offices left? What had happened to them?

When Daniel got down to the first floor, he saw that Tommy La Salle was not there. Daniel walked over to Tommy's car. Tommy asked his driver to get out and he gestured for Daniel to get in and sit next to him.

"So, tell me. What did you see?"

Daniel told about the poor condition of the steps, the debris on the second floor, and the desk areas and offices on the third floor.

Tommy thought for a few seconds before asking, "So, whadda ya think about it? I mean the building as a whole."

"I'm no engineer, but if the floors are structurally sound and a person wants to put money into cleaning it up and modernizing it, I guess it could be turned into something. The steps have to be torn out, of course."

"So, you want it?" Tommy asked.

"Want it? I don't have money to buy something like that."

"No. I don't mean for you to buy it. I mean you wanna be my site man,

177

my supervisor for it? I got big plans."

"Oh. Thanks for the offer, but I'm not a general contractor or a builder. What ... What do I know about that sort of thing?"

"I been hearing good things about you at Coastal. You done more work and done it better than any of their real workers there. I guess you didn't know all you hadda do was to show up to collect your paycheck."

"I wasn't raised that way, Tommy. My dad's a hard worker and so's my mom. I've never taken what wasn't mine."

"That's good ... and you're smart. How's this? I'll pay you the same $850 a week you get at Coastal to be my site man, and you can keep the $850 a week from them. They can afford it."

"I'll keep working that job too. Thanks. I'll do my best."

"I know you will. I'll call ya when we're ready to start the work. I got this building for a song ... a guy was overextended. I'll show ya the plans and get you in touch with the contractors and all that. You do the permits, arrange the inspections, check up on the work, and break a few heads if you have to. By the way, speakin' of that, you visit your friend Dominic?"

"Visit? Where? What do you mean?" Daniel asked.

"Oh. You ain't heard? He caught a beating coupla nights ago. Fractured skull, lots of broken teeth, punctured lung. They did a job on him."

"Who did it?"

"He says he got jumped comin' outta a club in Queens. He's in Lutheran. First coupla days, he was in ICU. Now he's in a room."

Daniel was shocked and distressed when he walked into the hospital room. The purple-colored skin and swollen lips made the person in the bed look like an older, weaker, diminished version of the Dominic he knew. The man was breathing on his own, but it was clear that each inhalation was painful.

Daniel said hello. Dominic stared blankly, not seeming to recognize Daniel. Then he attempted to talk, moaned, grimaced, and then he held up a hand in a kind of anemic wave or as a signal for Daniel to give him a chance to harness his strength so that he could reply. After a long period of silence, during which Dominic swallowed and painfully cleared his throat, he whispered something.

"What'd you say, Dom?"

"You took your fuckin' time gettin' here," he whispered.

"I just found out ... today ... a half hour ago, Dom."

"Oh. Sure. I ... Wait ... I know. Nobody else found out either."

"What do you mean? Nobody's come to visit you?"

"Yeah ... sure ... my family. Listen ... If they keep me here, you're gonna have to get something for me. You understand?"

"I'm sure you'll be out in a day or two, Dom."

"I dunno if I can wait that long," Dominic whined.

"Who did this to you?"

"Don't know. They ... clocked me from behind. I'm finished. Nobody wants nothin' to do with me no more."

Daniel was stunned. The family had abandoned Dominic.

Daniel began to worry. Had he walked into a trap? Had this been a test? Had Tommy La Salle told Daniel about Dominic to see what he would do? Was it right or wrong that he had visited Dominic? Did it show that Daniel was loyal to a friend, which those men would respect, or might it convince them that he was too close to someone who was no longer in the good graces of the family? Well, it was too late now. He would try to comfort Dominic, but that was it. Daniel certainly would not get cocaine for him, if that was what he was hinting.

In truth, Daniel had been pleased—he knew he should not—but, driving to the hospital, he had been pleased that Dominic had been the victim of violence. Who better to be on the receiving end of someone's fists or clubs or whatever than this so-called friend who had done what he had done? Now, though, he could not help but see Dominic as a pathetic fool who was being abandoned by men who were supposed to be part of his larger "family." Had De Luca given the order or granted permission for the attack on Dominic? If so, was it because of what Daniel had said to him about how Jimmy had died? Why now? Maybe they had finally decided that Dominic was the one skimming money. If so, why was he still alive? Daniel knew that he had to be smarter than he had been up to that point; he had to think one move ahead before he acted.

He did not tell Maria about Dominic. Neither did he mention his site supervisor job, deciding to wait to see whether it actually moved from plans to reality. If it did happen, he would not reveal Tommy La Salle's connection to it. He had to always be one move ahead of Maria too.

*****

Tommy La Salle smiled broadly as he leaned over the blueprints. He invited Daniel to take a look. The overhead light in Tommy's office at the rear of an insurance business on Kings Highway flickered as Daniel examined the plans for the old warehouse in Greenpoint.

"It looks nice, Tommy. Looks like it's going be a distribution center of some kind."

"Yeah. That's it. You don't need to know the details. Your job is gonna be to get it off the ground and moving, you know, from blueprint to finished product. These are maximum figures. Try to keep the numbers under that."

"I understand, but I have to repeat that I've never done anything like this. I hope you haven't picked the wrong man for this job."

"You better not be!" Tommy warned, and then he smiled. "I know. Look, the most important things are, one, that you be there to see what's goin' on so nobody steals from me, and, two, that you're honest, which I believe you are."

"I am, Tommy ... and, if I weren't, I'm not such a fool as to try to screw you. I spent enough time running away because of something I didn't do."

"I believe you. I trust you. I know you know how to keep a secret. Right? You know how to keep your mouth shut and protect those around you."

"Of course."

Tommy smiled again, and then he said, "Listen, I'll tell you about a big deal. Two nights from now, Wednesday, very very late, a big shipment of goods ... I can't tell you what, but it's a big shipment of goods that is gonna make good money for me and the whole family—or it could put me away for a few years— is gonna be brought to that place. Then the shipment is gonna head north. Stay away. If I get nabbed by the authorities, I don't want you to go down too because I can see that you're a good guy."

"Sure. I wish you well."

"Yeah. *Madonne!* This one deal should give me all the upfront money I need to pay for this renovation. I'm talking a pile of money ... and it's not just for me. That's not how we do things. Everybody *gets a taste*. Of course, if things *go south*, it will all go up in smoke! You get my drift?"

"I have an idea."

"Okay. That's it. Remember, I don't want you anywhere near that place Wednesday night. Stay home or take your girl out for the night."

Daniel waited until he was miles away to make a call to the FBI agents. When Canciello heard what he started to say, he asked Daniel to wait. Then he told Daniel that he had put his phone on speaker so that Harris could hear too. Once Daniel had finished talking, Harris asked, "What's your gut instinct on this? I don't mean what you want it to mean. What do you really think?"

"I guess I was too keyed up to give it any thought. I was surprised whenTommy told it to me, and I took it at face value, but now I'm beginning to think it's something else. Is that what you think?"

Canciello and Harris talked quietly for a few seconds. Then Harris said, "We're split. Canciello thinks it may be gangster bravado, but he wants to follow up on it. I have a different take on it. Why would a captain in De Luca's family give you this kind of information? Was he bragging? Could be, but I doubt it. Was he bullshitting because he wants to sound bigger than he is? Maybe. Of course, there's one other possibility: it's another test. If there's even a hint of cops being around, he'll know the information came from you."

Daniel was upset because, once again, he had not remembered to stay one step ahead of the men in the family. Luckily, Harris and Canciello were thinking it through. He wanted them to forget what he had just said. If they set up a surveillance operation, and Tommy found out, regardless of whether or not his story was true, Daniel would have to go into hiding again. He had understood that as he was dialing the agents, but now, the reality of it began to sicken him. If he ran, would Maria go with him or would she hate him for lying to her and for destroying their life together, permanently, this time?

Canciello told Daniel not to worry about it, explaining that they would conduct only a deep-distance surveillance operation. If the shipment contained any kind of dangerous goods—they thought Tommy might be hinting about weapons—they would wait until it had left the warehouse and reached its final destination before taking action so they would not blow Daniel's cover.

Even so, Daniel was on edge for the next two days. On Thursday afternoon, Tommy called Daniel; during the short conversation, Daniel attempted to sound confident and relaxed.

"Meet me at the building site now," Tommy said.

"I have to call a guy back about a violation. I'll leave in five minutes."

"No. Meet me now."

Again, Daniel had to wait for Tommy. He looked at the building, wondering what, if anything had occurred the night before. Had there been a big shipment of something illegal? Had the FBI conducted surveillance, as Harris and Canciello said they would? Had Tommy or any of his men caught wind of it? He wished he had thought to call the agents to ask what had happened. Then, in a panic, he reached under his seat and pulled out the FBI cell phone to make sure it was off and would not ring in case Tommy were to sit in his car with him. Then he pushed it back into the leather case he had attached to the underside of the seat. He waited.

Daniel stepped out of his car onto the cold sidewalk as Tommy drove up, alone this time. As Tommy approached, he wrapped his arms around Daniel, kissed his cheek, and patted his back.

"What's a matter? You don't know how to greet a *paisano*? Or is that your cold Jewish half? Give me a hug and a kiss," Tommy cheerfully teased.

Daniel responded in kind and then said, "I guess I didn't expect that kind

181

of greeting from you. After all, who am I?"

"That's very humble of you, but no worries. You're my man. Everything went off without a hitch last night. Come on inside. I'll show ya what we got."

Tommy unlocked the rusty door. As they walked into the cavernous ruin, Daniel saw a veritable mountain of neatly arranged cardboard boxes, from which emanated the strong odor of tobacco.

"Untaxed cigarettes. What do ya think it's worth?" Tommy asked.

"Millions, I guess."

"You can do better than that. How much?"

Trying to think like a gangster, Daniel said, "On the street, five million."

"Man, you're good. I figure just about that. After I kick up my share to Mike for Carmine, I'm looking at, not a pile of smokes, but a mountain of gold. A lot, I'm gonna use to fix up this place, but some, I'm usin' for fun."

"Glad to hear it all worked out for you last night," Daniel said, figuring that would be a reasonable comment to make.

"Yeah. The first shipment, those building supplies in the corner, was my decoy. I know the Feds keep an eye on me," Tommy said as he stared into Daniel's eyes. "Nobody bothered us, so, a few hours later, I gave the okay for this shipment. I was sorta hopin' the law would've made a move on the first one. I woulda laughed my ass off when they saw lumber, tiles, windows, and the like comin' outta the truck, all of it from a big supplier who's strictly *legit*."

Daniel laughed. Then he said, "I thought part of my job was to order supplies and be in charge of deliveries and everything else for this project."

"Yeah. You're right. I had my reasons for ordering this small part of the supplies. Now it's all up to you. You can apply for the permits. Make sure you send the applications to the guy whose name is in that file I gave you. He's easy to work with as long as we give him gifts. Once that's set up, start callin' them contractors to begin the work, and order ... whatever. I'll stay out of the picture."

"What about the boxes of cig ... the boxes of *smokes*? When are they going out?" Daniel asked.

"Well, how would you feel about tryin' to move some of 'em yourself? You know, contact convenience stores, bodegas, whatever. Come up with a price. You can keep 15% of what you sell 'em for. Sound fair to you?"

"That's fair. Thanks, Tommy, but what about the rest of them? Should I leave them in place? I wouldn't want the contractors to see them."

"Always one step ahead. They'll be moving out within a week. I'm still makin' arrangements for them. You just figure how many you can move on your own. Whatever you don't sell, I'll send up north to a big wholesaler I know."

"Sounds good."

"I can see you're gonna be a valuable man in the family," Tommy said.

Daniel suddenly realized that he was about to embark on his first criminal enterprise, albeit a relatively minor one. Later, when he told Harris and Canciello about the stolen cigarettes and how Tommy wanted him to sell some of them on the street, they told him to do it. They said they had known about the cigarette shipment because a different FBI team had been following that truck using satellite surveillance equipment from the time it had left South Carolina. They explained that, normally, once the remaining cigarettes were on the move again, they would alert law enforcement authorities along the route of the truck to stop it for minor traffic violations, at which point they would confiscate the cargo. However, since they feared La Salle might suspect that Daniel had something to do with that, they would let the truck travel unmolested. They were disappointed when Daniel told them that the first truck, which they had seen via closed circuit cameras set up on electrical poles near the warehouse, had contained only building equipment and supplies. They had hoped it was what they had been waiting for—a shipment of weapons that, hopefully, they would be able to link to Carmine De Luca. They told Daniel to keep his eyes open.

*****

"You better talk to your friend," Tommy instructed Daniel one day when he dropped by the warehouse to check on the progress of the renovation.

Daniel, who was on his phone arguing with the electrical contractor, said, "One sec, Tommy." He ended the phone conversation by saying, "Listen, Campbell, if your guys don't finish the rough wiring no later than this week, I can't set up an inspection, and that's lost time, and it will cost you money because you'll pay for the delay. Good-bye."

"Good way to straighten out a hard head," Tommy said with a smile. "Reason why I came here, besides checking things out, which I see are progressin' nicely, is to tell you to talk to your friend before he goes too far and ends up having an unfortunate fatal accident."

Since Tommy and the other men in the family used the word "friend" in so many arcane and hidden ways, Daniel was not sure to whom Tommy was referring in this case. When he saw that Daniel appeared to be confused, Tommy said, "Dominic ... he's been doin' things that are gonna get him killed. Personally, I don't give a shit, but Mike knows Dominic's father from back in the day, so he wants to stop the kid before ... before it's too late."

"I need more information than that, Tommy, like where he is, what he's done, who's pissed off at him."

183

"What? I gotta draw a map for you? He's been knockin' off businesses under our protection and eatin' meals and borrowin' money and not payin' as if he's still part of the family. Besides, he's a junkie. Can't have somebody like him around. It's a liability. Find him and convince him to stop or move away or go for treatment or *eat a gun* or whatever. If it wasn't for Mike, I'd say get him outta the picture. I know you never done nothin' like that, so I wouldn't ask you, but you gotta find him and straighten him out. It's your job. Handle it."

Daniel started by calling Dominic's old phone number and leaving voice mail messages. Dominic did not return the calls. Then Daniel went to the apartment where he assumed Dominic still lived. When no one answered his knock, he looked for the building super to ask when he had last seen Dominic. The old man said it had been a while; he added that the landlord said Dominic was behind in his rent. Daniel held up a twenty-dollar bill and asked the man to let him into the apartment. A quick search of the unkempt one-bedroom apartment and its empty refrigerator convinced Daniel that Dominic had moved.

Later, when Daniel knocked on the door of Dominic's parents' apartment, Lou Savarino invited him in and offered him a glass of wine, which Daniel accepted. After they exchanged small talk, Daniel asked how he could get in touch with Dominic.

"If you figure that one out, please let me know," Lou said with an attempt at a smile which did a poor job of hiding his grief and anxiety.

"I'll find him, Lou, and I'll make sure he gets help ... treatment or whatever else he needs," Daniel promised.

A few of the people in the neighborhood to whom Daniel spoke said that they had seen Dominic during the past few days; a couple of them complained about the strong-arm tactics he had used and the hold-ups he had committed, but none of them knew where he was. Daniel asked them to pass on the word that Dominic should call him as soon as possible.

When he arrived home that night, Maria complained, "You ask me not to call you unless it's an emergency, so I don't. I would think you would call me at some point when you plan on coming home this late. It's almost midnight."

"Sorry. You're right. It was a—"

"I know—a tough day. You say that every night. If it's too much for you, quit one of the jobs ... either one ... the property management or the building renovation ... or both. Maybe it's time to think about going back to teaching. I know you didn't love it, but at least you'd be home at a decent hour."

"Okay, Maria. I get your point!" he shouted.

"You don't have to yell at me!"

"Well, you don't have to yell at me either. I did have a rough day."

"Sorry. It's just ... I worry when you're out late and you don't call. I still don't understand why I can't call you to just ask when you're coming home. You don't have to change your plans ... just let me know."

"You can call me, but there's no point. I've told you ... I never know when I'm coming home until I'm actually home."

"I know you've told me, but I don't understand why that is."

"I've told you, I may think I'm done for the day at a particular time, but then someone calls me to say that a contractor can't make his delivery tomorrow or something went wrong at the warehouse or ... something else. Please don't give me a hard time. I deal with enough pressure all day. I don't need it from you too."

"I'll leave you alone. I might as well. I'm alone in this apartment almost all the time when I'm home from work anyway. I'm going to bed. I have a headache. I've had one all night. If you want to eat, find something in the refrigerator. Please think about what I said."

He sat at the kitchen table for a few minutes. Then he reached into a cabinet and pulled out a bottle of Jameson. As he sipped the whiskey, he tried to imagine where Dominic might be. He hoped he would be able to convince Dominic to ... what? Go for drug treatment? Not likely. To leave the area? If he gave Dominic enough money, he might leave, but he would almost certainly return at some point. He wondered whether he would be able to kill Dominic if Tommy had said that was what Mike Morici had ordered. Why was he even thinking in those terms? He reminded himself that he was a government informant, not a mobster, but the lines had become blurred lately. In his present position, he had to pay off building and fire inspectors; he facilitated the purchase of stolen equipment; he took payoffs from contractors, all of which he handed to Tommy La Salle, knowing that Tommy would give a portion of that money back to him; and he gave gifts to union people so he could hire non-union workers.

Daniel knew that, as time went on, he would not be able to avoid committing progressively more serious criminal acts. Harris and Canciello told him over and over again that he had to do whatever he had to, short of killing *innocent* people, so as not to endanger his position as Tommy La Salle's site manager and, lately, his confidant. When Daniel asked them, point blank, whether they had meant to emphasize the word "innocent," Canciello said, "This is bigger than you or the life of a mobster. We have never had anyone this close to the operations of any of De Luca's captains before. Do whatever you have to do to maintain your position ... other than killing a civilian."

Am I a government mole or am I a criminal? Daniel asked himself, concluding that maybe there was not much difference between the two. He sipped the whiskey, something that he had begun to enjoy at the end of the day, and thought about what he had to do the next day. Then he finished his drink, rinsed the glass, and left it in the sink. He started writing a list of people he had to call or speak to in person the next day, but he was too tired to concentrate, so he got up and began walking toward the bedroom. Then he stopped and returned to the kitchen to put away the whiskey bottle. He made sure to brush his teeth and use mouthwash before he got into bed.

As he slipped under the covers and settled onto his side of the bed, Maria said, "You know what they say about people who drink alone."

He turned away from her and closed his eyes.

14

Branching Out

Daniel's phone rang. It was Dominic.

"So, you're a big man now," Dominic croaked.

"Dom ... glad you called. Let's get together. I made my last car payment yesterday. I want to take you out to lunch. What do you say?"

"That was pretty quick. I guess you're doin' real good for yourself."

"Can't complain. How about you?"

"Oh, I think you know. That's why you wanna find me. Right?"

"I won't lie to you, Dom. They want you off the streets. I want to help you. Meet me for a nice lunch. We'll talk ... no pressure. You won't be any worse off than you are now. Maybe I can do you a good turn."

"Okay, but not in the old neighborhood."

"Sure. How about Amici's?"

"Yeah. That place is good. See ya at noon?"

"Yeah. See you."

Except for the fact that his lips were not swollen, Dominic looked just about as bad as when Daniel had last seen him in the hospital after the assault. He was sitting at a table in the rear of the little restaurant, smoking a cigarette and guzzling a glass of red wine.

"You're lookin' like a real *wise guy*, Danny ... sharp suit, nice shoes, and a real swagger in your walk. I'm proud of you," Dominic said amid a cloud of cigarette smoke. Then he coughed, loudly cleared his throat, and wiped his mouth with the back of his hand.

"I can't say the same of you, Dom. You still look bad."

"Yeah. I had a little scrape. You should see the other guy," he said with a smile that exposed big gaps where teeth used to be.

"Well, you have to take care of yourself. You know, you're kind of pissing off a lot of people. It's not good for you," Daniel said.

"They got their nerve! They close me out, and then they want me to starve. Screw them! I'll do what I gotta do until I can't do it no more."

"That day may come sooner than you think. I'm here to help you. If you don't want my help, they're going to send other guys to deal with you."

"And you think I'm scared of that?"

"No, Dom. I don't think you're scared. Of course not."

The waiter approached and asked whether they were ready to order. Daniel said yes, took a fast look at the menu, and ordered grilled salmon. The

187

waiter looked at Dominic, who asked, "You payin' for this here meal?" When Daniel shook his head, Dominic ordered Minestrone, sirloin steak, and a bowl of Spaghetti Carbonara, explaining with a smile that he had skipped breakfast.

They had very little to say to each other. Daniel picked at his meal and thought about what else he had to do that day. Dominic ate everything quickly and ordered another bottle of wine.

When Dominic had finished eating, Daniel said, "Okay, Dom, here are your choices: I'll arrange for rehab for you or you can move far away ... I'll give you enough money to last you a month or so. That's it. No other options."

"Who the hell are you to tell me what to do? I brought you into this life. I was closer to becoming a *made-man* than you'll ever be, half-Jew that you are, not that I hold it against you."

"Keep your voice down, Dominic."

"Why? Worried you're gonna offend somebody?"

"Listen, Dom, this is a very nice place. Let's not disturb people." Then Daniel continued by saying, "This is not coming from me. I work for people. Tommy said that Mike wants you to stop *jamming up* people. It's bad for business and bad for the image of the family. You need to go to rehab. I'll pay for it. It will save your life. Be smart."

"Screw you! I don't need rehab. If you think I have a drug problem, you're way off base. And Mike ... he's got his nerve tellin' me what to do."

"Okay, so I'm wrong about rehab. Good. Glad to hear it, but you can't be robbing and strong-arming people in the neighborhood. They're not going to stand for it anymore. They won't send me out to find you next time ... and what do you mean about Mike? He's a captain. He's De Luca's *consigliere*."

Dominic's eyes were dark and angry. "Forget Mike. I don't give a damn what any of those bastards say. You think I'm worried?"

"You should be. I would be if I was in your shoes."

"Interesting that you say that. How'd you get in so good?"

"I've worked ... I work and I obey the rules. Let me ask you a question: How did *you* fall down so far?"

Dominic's scowl melted in an instant, to be replaced by a sorrowful, defeated look. He wiped his eyes, and then he said, "I had a coke problem. I don't have it now, but I did stupid things. You think it's too late?"

"Dom, you're lucky to be alive. They know you killed Jimmy. They think you were skimming money from the family. Now you do these stick-ups. They want you gone, or else they're going to make you gone. *Capisce?*"

"Me. Just me! Okay. How much can you give me to disappear?"

188

"How much do you need ... and where will you go?"

"I'd like to go to Florida. Start fresh in a warm climate. Gimme, let's say, ten thousand. That should set me up fine."

"I don't have that kind of money, Dom, and I know they won't give me any. I can give you what I can spare, which is $2,000 and a ticket to any city in Florida you want. How's that?"

"Is that the best you can do?"

"That's it. I'll sell your car for you and send the money to wherever you are. It should be worth at least $20,000, unless you messed it up."

"I don't got that car no more. I traded it in."

"Okay. I'll sell whatever you're driving now."

Dominic wiped his eyes again. Daniel could not look at him.

"Okay ... no car. I get it. No problem. I'll drive you to the airport right now. Anything else you have to take care of before you go?"

After a few seconds of thought, Dominic said, "No, but, before we go, are you gonna finish eating that fish? I'm still kinda hungry."

When they arrived at Kennedy Airport, Daniel handed $2,000 in fifties and hundreds to Dominic and then another $500 in smaller bills. Before Dominic stepped out of the car, Daniel said, "Aren't you forgetting something? Something you can't bring on a plane unless you want to end up in jail?"

After hesitating for a moment, Dominic reached into his jacket and withdrew a revolver, which he handed to Daniel. Then he unfastened a small, flat holster and handed that to him.

"You gonna pay me for that?" Dominic asked.

"That's what the $500 is for. Besides, you should be thanking me. If I wasn't doing this for you, you would probably be dead by the end of the week. Don't come back, Dom. Call your parents and tell them where you are. No one is going to come after you. You're safe. Just don't come back."

After Dominic had exited the car, Daniel slipped the pistol into the holster and placed it in his glove box.

*****

By the middle of the summer, the renovation of the warehouse was almost complete. Even though Daniel no longer did any work for Coastal Properties, he still received his paychecks. He also traveled into Manhattan to pick up his cash allotments from the FBI and to talk with Canciello and Harris, if they were around.

As Daniel slipped deeper and deeper into Tommy La Salle's business—and into his confidence—and as he participated in increasingly more serious criminal activities, he began to feel reluctant to reveal to the agents what he was doing. One day, the agents brought Daniel's file into their office and showed him that one of the forms he had signed months before granted him complete immunity from prosecution for any criminal offenses he might commit as part of his undercover work.

"It's sort of like a 007 license to kill kind of clause," Daniel joked.

"As we said, it doesn't cover killing civilians," Harris said without a hint of a smile, "but yes. Now, we know you're holding back on information."

"No. I'm not. You know, it's kind of amazing that I have your permission to do this. Is it a usual arrangement for people in my position?"

"We don't know. You're kind of a first. All of the undercover people we've ever heard of are either agents or people in organized crime who flipped. Just don't let this go to your head. You're doing good work. Don't get confused and start thinking you're on their side. Remember, De Luca, despite the fact that he acts like a gentleman, is a dangerous, predatory criminal."

"I know. I'm not one of them."

In truth, Daniel no longer saw a clear demarcation between who and what he was and the men in De Luca's family. He was totally at ease and at his best in the company of Tommy La Salle, Mike Morici, and the others. When they talked about "takin' down a big haul" from a warehouse or directly from a truck on the road, he thought of it as business as usual. He had moved up, or down, depending on how he wanted to look at it—from expecting free meals at restaurants, dealing in stolen cigarettes, which Tommy referred to as *butt-legging*, receiving and paying bribes, and accepting shipments of what he knew were hijacked building supplies—to more serious offenses.

At one point, after he had been unsuccessful in his attempts to convince a worker at the warehouse renovation project to stop "borrowing" tools and building supplies, he fired the man and told him to return what he had taken. Not only did the man not bring back the stolen goods, but he was caught on surveillance camera breaking into the job site one night and stealing a big load of copper wire. When Daniel told Tommy about it, he said, "It's your responsibility. Get the equipment back and teach the bastard a lesson. Take two of the guys from my crew ... and I shouldn't have to be telling you shit like this. You gotta take care of your things ... don't involve me. I'm the kinda guy the Feds are always lookin' at. Keep me outta things. Handle 'em yourself." Daniel felt a combination of revulsion and exhilaration as, three nights later, after two of Tommy's *soldiers* had taken the stolen equipment from the man's garage and loaded it onto the back of his pickup truck, they beat him on the front lawn of his tiny house on Staten Island. Then, leaving the man bloody and unconscious, Daniel and the men returned to Brooklyn. One of them drove the man's truck.

Tommy began asking Daniel to "introduce" himself to merchants who opened up businesses in his territory. After the first couple of times, Daniel no longer felt awkward or guilty when he walked into a restaurant, clothing store, or other business to explain the value of his services. On only one occasion did he have to tell Tommy that a merchant needed an additional, more energetic sales pitch, which called for the expertise of a very big man named Sal.

The line between what was right and what he had to do became blurred. As he spent more and more hours each day with Tommy and the other men at restaurants, bars, the social club, and taking care of business, Daniel found that he talked, dressed, walked, and even thought like them. He also kept their hours; he was rarely home before 2 a.m. and generally not out of bed before 11 a.m.

Maria usually did not ask Daniel where he had been when he walked into the apartment at all hours of the night and she rarely commented on the aroma of whiskey and the stench of second-hand tobacco smoke that generally oozed from him as he slipped into bed. They slept in the same bed, but they rarely made love or kissed or even looked at each other now.

One Saturday morning, when Daniel awakened at noon and after using the bathroom began to get dressed, Maria sat up in bed and asked, "So this is what I gave up my virginity for?"

"What do you mean 'this'?"

"I mean we hardly see each other all week. I know you're working and I know who you're working for. I try to keep my mouth shut because you seem to like what you're doing and I love you, but ... today ... this morning ... I mean ... "

After waiting for her to continue, Daniel asked, "What? What do you mean? What do you want to say?"

"Do I have to say it? I'm embarrassed."

"Why are you embarrassed? We can say anything to each other."

"I mean ... I waited in bed ... hours longer than I wanted to ... I could have gotten up, but I waited for you, and you just get out of bed and walk past me."

"I'm sorry. I just didn't think."

"Think? Since when do you have to think? I know you love me. I'm right here ... right next to you every night. All you have to do is reach over."

"I ... have a lot on my mind, Maria. My head is filled to bursting."

"I understand, but you spend so many hours at your ... job. Can't we make weekends for us? I try not to complain when you walk in so late every night, often smelling of liquor. Can't you get home early one night?"

191

"I can't. As it is, I leave before any of the others. When I leave, they're first going out for the evening."

"Where are they going? Let me guess ... to ethical culture lectures. No ... that can't be right. I know ... to strip clubs and high-class saloons. They probably can't understand why you don't go with them and enjoy the women."

"Maria, it's not like that."

"No? I thought all of those guys go from their girlfriends to their wives."

"Some of them do. I don't want that."

"I'm glad because, even though I'm pretending you don't work with gangsters, I won't close my eyes and pretend if I know you're being unfaithful to me. I won't stand for it."

"You know me. I will never do that."

"I used to know you. Now, I'm not so sure."

He sat on the bed, put his arms around her and kissed her gently on her lips. He slipped out of his clothes and then he undressed her. Their embrace was warm and affectionate, but lacking in the fevered passion that used to come so naturally to them. Later, after holding Maria for what he considered to be a reasonable length of time, he got dressed and walked to the kitchen to make coffee. He drank it alone.

*****

Daniel realized he was losing control of his life. Even though he loved Maria as much as he ever had and enjoyed being with her, that part of his life seemed dull and unimportant now. Even in the midst of making love to her—which, after that conversation, he made sure to initiate at least twice a week now—his mind was so crammed with lists of chores he had to complete at the building site, people he had to call, small businesses from which he had to collect protection money, and dozens of other tasks, big and small, that he sometimes had to force himself to focus on what he was doing in order to maintain an erection.

It pained him that Maria was not happy. There were times when he thought about not returning to the apartment in the early hours of the morning because he could not stand to see her reddened eyes and tear-stained face. They spoke gently, lovingly to each other, but he knew that she was just barely holding it together. He understood why the other men chose women from their little world as wives and lovers. Those women complained to and consoled each other. They made sure to look their best when their men came home, and they never asked questions. They all had known what they were getting into before they entered into those relationships.

One day at lunch at the social club, a minor figure in the family, Richie La Rocca, who went by the name "the Rock," made a point of telling how he had to "straighten out my wife and my *goumada* all on the same night because both of 'em was breakin' my balls about how they don't see me enough."

Daniel did not want another woman; he just wanted Maria to be more like the wives and girlfriends of his friends—he thought of them in that way—friends. Even though he did not think about sex very much, at times, when he was with Tommy and the men from his crew, the ones with whom he spent most of his time, he flirted with the women who sat at the bar at which they often ended their evenings. Then he would think of Maria, and go back to his drink.

The first couple of times he sat at a table at Coco's Place he could not help but laugh because all of the women there looked like girls he had known in high school; in fact, he thought, a few of them were the same ones. They wore their poofed-up hair, short, tight skirts, partly unbuttoned blouses, spike heels, and edgy make-up as if it were all part of a uniform.

One time, to stop the other men from mercilessly teasing him about his sexuality—as they said, they had never seen his phantom girlfriend—he close-danced with a full-figured blonde beauty named Bianca. She sat next to him for the rest of the evening and was surprised when, at 1:30, he stood up to say good night. When he saw her look of astonishment and embarrassment, he told her that he had to meet somebody for business, but he would see her again another night and they would spend more time together.

A few minutes later, driving home, he tried, once again, to decide whether he was a government informant who had infiltrated a lower rung of a crime family or a member of a crime family who was acting as an informant. Even though he was very close to Tommy La Salle and knew of his involvement in numerous criminal activities, he had not obtained any hard evidence that linked any of it to Carmine De Luca, for which he was grateful. Neither had he heard of any arms shipments or dealings with terrorists. When he watched the news coming out of Afghanistan on television or skimmed through newspapers, his heart thumped loudly in his chest and he was overcome with a combination of anger and pride. Daniel knew that he would take any risk and search in every dangerous corner to unearth information that would link members of the family to that kind of trade. He hoped he would not find out that Carmine De Luca was involved in that traitorous activity, but, if that was the case, he would do whatever was necessary to see the old man burn in the lowest, hottest pit of hell.

At the same time, he was pleased that Harris and Canciello were not perturbed by his reports of his criminal activities. They always said something like, "That's the price we all have to pay to keep you in there with those bastards." In fact, now that the warehouse project was a week from completion and Tommy was assigning more and more additional jobs to Daniel, he was so busy that he stopped reporting regularly to his FBI contacts. At first, he just assumed they would not be interested in hearing that he was now collecting loan payments and helping to hide stolen goods. Then, as his weekly cash *take* grew exponentially and as he increasingly enjoyed the "high" of being involved in the life, he just stopped calling them.

Now, figuring out what to do with the cash, averaging $2,000 a week, became a perplexing problem. Obviously, with a reportable income of just over $44,000 from Coastal Properties, he could not deposit into his checking or savings account much of the cash he earned, so he spent freely on himself and on gifts and clothes for Maria and kept the rest in a safe deposit box. He realized that was not the best place for it, but he could not think of an alternative. At the beginning, Maria, understanding that the cash that Daniel carried in his wallet, generally around $1,000, did not come from his job as a property manager, refused his gifts of rings, wristwatches, and diamond bracelets. That led to arguments and mutual recriminations. When Maria saw how hurt Daniel seemed to be by her refusals, she relented, but each time she wore one of those gifts she felt soiled and could not wait to take it off and hide it away.

One evening, when Daniel proudly handed to her a beautifully wrapped velvet box containing a necklace made of emeralds and diamonds, which Joe Fontella of Fontella's Fine Jewelry had sold to him at cost (because he knew he did not have a choice), Maria gasped at the beauty of the sparkling gems and then said, "Enough is enough. No." He coaxed; she said no. He tried to convince her that she had nothing to feel guilty about; she said no. Then she said, "This is it, Daniel. You've gotten in too deep. I don't want to live this life. You're going to have to find a way out. This is not working. Figure out how to get out of it."

He walked out of the apartment and drove to Coco's Place. When he walked in, Bianca smiled and said, "I was hoping I'd see you tonight." He stayed away from the apartment for two days.

When he returned, he threw his coat on a chair and went to Maria. She kissed him and asked whether he was okay. He returned her kiss and said he was fine, pleased that she seemed to have finally accepted his way of life.

Then she said, "Daniel, you know I love you and I believe you love me. I think I've been patient, but, as I said the other night, this is the end. I'm not asking where you spent the last two nights. I don't want to know, but I can't live like this for another day."

"Maria," he said with the hint of a smile, "Nothing happened. I won't disappear again. I'm sorry. I should have called. In fact, when you didn't call me, I figured you were upset, so—"

"Daniel, don't."

Her calm, resolute expression deflated him.

"This is it. We've argued about this before. I can't be the girlfriend or wife of a man who makes his living as you do. You're not going to leave them. I understand that. I'm surprised you want money so badly that you do ... whatever you do, but I guess you've changed. I can't adapt to this life and I won't."

"It's not like that, Maria. I'm with them ... you're right, but it's not the money ... well, it didn't start out that way. Now I like the money, but there's another part of this, but I can't tell you."

"You're working for the government as an informant."

In response, he almost said, "Yes." Instead, he said, "No, but I'm not a bad guy. I have a deeper reason for working with them."

"You don't have to explain or justify it to me. You're happy. I'm glad."

"So? What do I have to do to make this right?"

"Now, that sounds like mob talk. Next, you'll be making me an offer I can't refuse. Well, sad to say, I am refusing. This is the end. I want you to move out. If you don't want to take your things now, that's fine. You can take them tomorrow or another day. If they're still here by the weekend, I'll donate them."

"Maria, no. We don't want that."

"We don't, but I'm suffocating. I feel sick. Each morning, I have to concentrate not to throw up—"

"You're not pregnant ... I mean, that would be fine—"

"God forbid! No! If I was, I would not tell you. I've never wanted babies, and now, as much as I love you, I would rather be dead than have your baby. I would never be able to handle that."

"How can you say that, Maria?"

"I say it because it's the sad truth."

"What do you mean?"

"Our life together is like sand in my throat. It chokes me all day; it's suffocating me. Please, Daniel, please leave now and don't come back when you know I'll be here. Be happy. I want you to be happy. Give me a chance to be happy too in another life in another place."

After a few seconds of thought, Daniel said, "Okay, Maria. I'll tell you the truth. I'm not supposed to because it could put us both in danger, but I have to because I don't think either one of us will ever be happy if we're apart."

195

He told her about how he had been boxed into a corner by Harris and Canciello and how, in exchange for his cooperation, they were making sure he would not be prosecuted for the murders in Jamestown or for any crimes he might commit while working with the De Luca family.

Maria thought for a few seconds before she said, "How do I know that's the truth? You've lied to me so much the past few months, how do I know this isn't just another one? You're becoming more and more like them."

"It's the truth," he said, not sure whether he was more upset that she did not believe him or the fact that he had revealed the truth to her. Now that he had said out loud what he had never told anyone else, he felt empty, as if what he had grown to like more and more each day as the center of his life was a sham.

"I don't know, Daniel, and I don't know whether it matters."

"What do you mean?"

"Well, if it's the truth, then, even though you're doing a good thing by helping the government, you're still spending your days and your evenings with them and you're in even more danger than I thought. But, I have to tell you, I can see that you like this life. You were so nervous when you first came out of hiding ... hell, anybody would be. But now, you have a spring in your step when you come home, even when you're half drunk."

"It's a coping mechanism. I've trained myself to think like them so I don't stand out as a nervous guy who's afraid to be caught with his pants down."

"That's the other thing. Please don't lower yourself in terms of my view of you by lying. Don't tell me you were with a friend the past couple of nights. In fact, when you walked in before, you had that grin on your face you used to have at the beginning of our time together after we had screwed our brains out."

Then he thought of Richie the Rock La Rocca.

"Maria, this won't last forever. Once I collect the *intel* that connects De Luca to a very serious crime, I'll be able to get out of it."

"Will you really? Or will you always be in it?"

"I'm not going to argue with you. If you want, I'll leave, but I'm not taking my things. I love you. I will always love you. Call me any time you want. When you do, and I know you will, I'll come back."

"And here I thought I had made a good choice—a smart, good looking guy who was on the straight and narrow. Well, you never know."

"You thought about that? Why?"

"You want to know why? I'll tell you. Remember when I said there were gangs in my neighborhood when I was growing up and how only the smart guys stayed out of them? Well, when I met you, I thought about boys I grew up with who had been killed or arrested or had gotten hooked on drugs, and I looked at you and said to myself, 'He looks like a good one. He's going to love me and have a regular job and I'll never have to worry about whether he's coming home to me or I'm going to have to go to a hospital to identify his body.'"

"You were right. That will never happen."

"It happened. All those months you were on the run after Dominic killed that guy and you helped to bury the body and when those guys grabbed you and threw you into a car to be murdered on the beach ... and now, night after night, I don't know whether you're hurting people or being hurt or screwing another girl. This is no way to live. If we stay together, I'll shrivel up and die."

"Maria—"

"Please go. If you don't, I will."

He sighed. Then he turned around and walked out the door.

*****

Daniel stayed at his parents' basement apartment for the next few days, all the while expecting a phone call from Maria. He did not call her and he stayed away from their apartment. He told his mother and father that it was only a matter of time before she reached out to him They were upset that he and Maria were not together, but now that he was living in their apartment, they were even more distressed when they saw the hours that he kept.

"You don't have to be at work at any particular time?" his mother asked.

"No, ma. I'm in a kind of management position at Coastal. I take care of a lot of my business over the phone. I go to the office or job sites only when there's a problem for me to solve," he explained.

Neither Ruth nor Raymond believed him, but they did not have the heart to dig any deeper for fear that they would not be able to handle the truth.

The warehouse renovation was completed ahead of schedule and below budget, a fact that made Tommy so happy he gave Daniel a $5,000 cash gift. Daniel spent most of his time now driving Tommy around for appointments and taking care of the ever-increasing number of tasks that had been assigned to him. He made sure to stop at the social club at some point each day.

He was a regular at Coco's and a few other watering holes in Brooklyn, along with the Tropicana in Atlantic City and several of the fine restaurants in Manhattan and New Jersey. He was so busy and so deeply immersed in Tommy's end of the De Luca family's business that he never even thought about checking in with Harris and Canciello, who could not reach him at the special cell phone because he had not turned it on in weeks and they would never visit him in person for fear that someone would see them.

A week after he had moved out of the apartment he had shared with Maria, he drove to the FBI office to pick up his last two months of payments. Neither Harris nor Canciello was there. The clerk who normally asked him to sign a form before handing the cash to him asked Daniel to wait. A few months before, he would have been worried; now he was just annoyed, but figuring it was a typical bureaucratic foul up, he waited. Then the clerk handed a telephone to him. Surprised, he took it and said hello.

"Daniel, this is Canciello. Where the hell have you been?"

"Hey, man ... take it easy," he replied. Then, moving away from the clerk and into the empty hallway, he said, "Nothing new has happened ... nothing to report. I figured why waste your time with unnecessary phone calls."

"We'll decide if they're unnecessary. What do you think? We're going to let you pick up a wad of cash each month just for breathing?"

"No. Of course not. I understand. What do you want me to say? You want me to say I'm sorry? Okay. I'm sorry. I won't let it happen again. I'll call. Jeez. You sound like my mother."

"Listen, Daniel ... we have an agreement. You do your job, you call us at least twice each week, and you collect your cash. We can't go to you because we never know who's watching. You have to call us."

"Right. I understand that, but nothing new has happened."

"Nothing? Is that renovation project complete?"

"Yes."

"Well, then that's something. What's La Salle going to do with it?"

"I don't know. He hasn't told me," he said, but that was a lie. Daniel knew it was going to be used to store stolen goods and possibly to manufacture something, but he did not know what it would be.

"Try to find out. I don't suppose you've heard anything about buying or selling weapons. Right?"

"No. Of course not. That's what I'm there for. I know that."

"How much time do you spend at the social club these days?"

"An hour or two each day."

"Any chance you could spend more time there or at De Luca's house? That is what we really want."

"I'm at the club only when it's appropriate. If I hung out there more, it would look suspicious and, as far as De Luca goes, I'm a really small part of their operation. Only the captains are invited there."

"But you were there twice at the beginning."

"That was just to size me up to see whether I was a threat."

"Are you ever at the club alone?"

"No. Why?"

"Could you ever be there alone?"

"I don't know. Maybe. Why?"

"If you think you can ever be there alone, even just for five minutes, you could plant a bug. One of our tech guys would teach you how. We never wanted to do that because they probably sweep for bugs, but that may be our only chance of ever hearing anything we can use in court."

Daniel's sense of danger, which was much stronger and more sensitive now than it had ever been, told him to refuse to do that, so he said, "And who do you think they'd suspect if they found one of those things? No. I won't do it."

"You will if we tell you to."

"Screw you! I won't. Send me back to Jamestown to face the music for two murders I didn't commit. You damned Feds! You're worse than any of those guys in the family. I'd pick them over you any day."

"Oh. Is that how it is?"

"Yeah ... if you would put me in that kind of hot water."

"Okay, Daniel. We understand. We won't put you in danger, but remember that you're still ours. Take care of yourself and call us at least twice a week. Let me talk to Rose, that clerk. I'll tell her to give your money to you."

Daniel brought the phone back to the clerk. She listened, said something, hung up, and handed the envelope to Daniel. He thought about how much he loved the envelopes, both these and the ones he collected for Tommy. He folded this one in half and placed it in a pocket. Then he patted it through his pants.

When, one week later, Daniel had not heard from Maria, he went to Gold's Real Estate and asked Meyer Gold to find a three-bedroom luxury apartment in the neighborhood for him. After flipping through his listings, Gold drove him to a new building on Shore Road in Bay Ridge, which was just a few blocks from where his father's parents lived, where his father had lived before he was married. The spacious, sunny rooms faced the bay; there was a large terrace, a doorman, and a parking garage.

Back at Gold's office, Daniel filled out a credit report, signed the lease agreement, handed over the first month's rent and a security deposit in cash, and took the keys from Gold. Then he drove to Paris Interior Design, where he handed the keys to Lenny Walsh, the owner, telling him to check the place out and then do whatever needed to be done: order furniture, bedding, towels, rugs, pictures, and everything else he would need to fully decorate it.

"Tell whoever you go to that it's for me and that I expect them to charge me based on the fact that it's me. Understand? I'll pay all the bills the same day they arrive ... no quibbling. Make it nice ... modern, sleek, luxurious, young executive ... something that will knock my socks off. It's that kind of place. You'll see what I mean once you're there. I want you to take care of everything I'll need, short of food. I'm too busy to do any of the decorating. I trust you completely. I want to be able to move in when it's ready. And don't worry about your commission. I'll pay you whatever you think is fair."

Just about every store and supplier with whom Lenny dealt knew Daniel or had heard of him, so they charged only a little above cost. They all paid protection money to Tommy La Salle. He was a business partner in several of the businesses, having loaned money to the owners at exorbitant rates and then saying that he would become a partner instead of forcing them to repay the loans by going out of business and selling their assets.

One week later, the apartment was ready. Daniel was delighted with what he saw. Lenny had indeed thought of everything, including a wide-screen television, a state-of-the-art sound system, built-in bookshelves, sleek window treatments, kitchen appliances, and tasteful paintings. That same day, Daniel handed an envelope of cash to Lenny to cover all of the expenditures; then he gave him five one hundred-dollar bills as a bonus above his modest commission.

The following weekend, he invited Tommy, Mike, and a few of the other men from the family to his apartment for a lavish catered dinner; the caterer and his two daughters served the food and cleaned up. After they left, Daniel winked at the men and made a phone call. Ten minutes later, the doorman rang his bell. Daniel opened the door and invited in the entertainment: six scantily dressed women and a DJ with equipment. The DJ played music and sang along as the women danced alone and with the men. A little after midnight, Daniel paid the DJ and asked him to leave. The women stayed. When the men departed the next day at a little past noon, they told Daniel it was the second-best party they had ever attended, the best being a week-long event that De Luca had held on his yacht many years before, when he had been vigorous and a lot less serious.

After the men left, Daniel returned to bed, where a very pretty redhead whose name he could not quite remember, except that it was something like Lorraine or Lorena or Laurieann, waited for him. He did not show up at the social club until 5 p.m. Only the boy who did the clean-up job that Daniel had done years before was there. His name was Vinnie. Daniel asked him for a Seven-Up; he had drunk enough whiskey and wine during the party to keep him at least slightly buzzed for the next couple of days.

Looking at the ancient *Brooklyn Dodgers* clock that hung on a wall, he called Vinnie over, handed a twenty-dollar bill to him, and told him to pick up a plain pizza from Angelo's. Once Vinnie had left, Daniel stood up and looked around. Then he walked to the back of the bar, reached into a pants pocket, withdrew his hand, and held it under the bar for a few seconds as if he was planting a listening device; then he walked to a floor lamp in a corner, reached into his pocket again, pulled out his hand, and placed it at the top of the lamp. He did the same thing five more times in different parts of the room, each time holding his hand on a piece of furniture. Then he sat, looked up at the clock, and smiled. Vinnie did not return for close to 30 minutes.

When he called the FBI the next day, he told Harris that he had moved. Harris assured him that they would never visit him.

"Have you heard anything of importance?" Harris asked.

"Nope. All the usual."

"Have you had a chance to scope out the social club to see if you would ever have a chance to plant bugs, as Canciello suggested?"

"No. There's always somebody else there. It can't be done. Sorry."

*****

Daniel invited his parents and grandparents to his new apartment for dinner the following weekend. He sent a chauffeured limousine to pick up his mother's mother because she did not drive anymore.

They dined on food from the catering service that he had used the week before. He invited Bianca, the woman from Coco's, to join them. His parents and grandparents were impressed with the apartment and were happy for him, but his mother was upset to see Bianca. She had been hoping that Daniel and Maria would have patched up their disagreement by then. Ruth and Bianca did not talk to each other very much. Bianca's only real interests were shopping and dancing. She complained about how difficult it was to deal with customers all day in the hair salon where she worked as a manager, saying, "You just can't please them."

As Daniel and his father drank and ate and drank, they became progressively sillier and happier, at one point, doing the *Who's on first?* routine that they had always enjoyed when Daniel was a child. They laughed so hard that they choked. After they had gone through the entire skit twice, Daniel began to cry. Everyone looked at him. He *stopped on a dime* and said, "Fooled you all," but it took all of his inner strength for him to smile.

At the end of the evening, as his parents were on their way out, his mother pulled Daniel into the hallway outside of the apartment and whispered, "She's not for you. Yes, she's very pretty and sexy, but not up to your caliber. If you stick with this one, you'll never be happy. Call Maria and do what you have to do to make it work. She's a gem and you two are perfect together."

Once the caterer and his daughters had put away the leftover food, packed up their equipment, and departed, Daniel walked to his bedroom, where he undressed, dropped his clothes to the floor, and sprawled out on the bed.

When Bianca walked in a minute later, she said, "Oh, I didn't know we were going to bed already. Do you wanna watch TV or go out for a drink?"

Daniel said no, and told her to undress.

"Do *you* want to do it? I mean take off my clothes?"

"No. Stand there. Undress right there."

"Okay," she said as she disrobed. Then she said, "I had fun tonight. Your family is nice. Can I get in bed with you now?"

"No. Stand there. Turn around slowly. Nice. Do it again. Stand there."

"Daniel, this is ... I don't know ... it's *not* nice. Can I come into bed now?"

"Not yet. Stand there a bit longer. Now walk to the door. Now come back slowly, like a runway model. Okay. Come into bed."

He assured himself that Bianca was certainly not lacking in pleasing physical attributes. She was very different from Maria, but that was good. Where Maria was short and very nicely shaped and enigmatic, Bianca was tall and extravagantly voluptuous and direct; where Maria's silky smooth brown skin tasted like honey and vanilla, Bianca was an alabaster beauty who brought to mind flowers and sugary fruit.

Minutes later, they were in the throes of unrestrained, fevered, coupling, holding each other tightly and writhing in unison. He repeatedly kissed her and pushed his fingers through her smooth, luxurious hair as he thrust into her warm, compliant body.

Then, when they had finished, he got up, walked to the living room, and poured a glass of wine. As he stood by the large sliding glass doors that opened onto the terrace, he understood that Bianca was a substitute, a weak replacement for Maria, who possessed his very soul.

15
Last Judgment

During dinner at Peter Luger Steak House, Tommy told Daniel that the first major delivery to the warehouse was going to take place the next day, and he wanted Daniel there to supervise and to take charge.

"Just make sure there's 48 boxes ... big mothers. Wooden crates. They're kind of delicate, so make sure the delivery guys are careful. That's all you need to know. I'll pick it up from there. I'm depending on you."

The next morning, as two oversized tractor trailers drove into the freight yard, Daniel opened the doors to the delivery bays. He watched as the truckers, using forklifts, moved the huge wooden crates into the warehouse. Even though the truckers were careful, as they lowered each heavy crate, the concrete floor vibrated and a harsh slamming sound echoed throughout the otherwise empty space of the warehouse.

When the truckers had completed their task, they nodded to Daniel and drove off without giving him any kind of paperwork. Each crate was about eight by eight by six. Did these boxes contain armaments that would be sold to terrorists? If they did and Daniel kept the information to himself, he would be endangering the lives of large numbers of people. But, what if the crates contained something else? What if they held slot machines or air conditioners or something else that would not endanger national security or people's lives? Why would he tell Harris and Canciello about that? Other than the issue of weapons being sold to terrorists, his first, his only loyalty was to Tommy and the family.

Was it? Was this his life now?

Yes. He was a member of Tommy La Salle's crew, a minor member of Carmine De Luca's family, and he was proud of that.

He grabbed an oversized crowbar, a heavy hammer, and a box of large nails from the equipment closet. Then, climbing a stepstool, he grasped the top of one of the crates. As he struggled to loosen one edge of the top piece, Daniel tried to think of how he would explain what he was doing if Tommy decided to visit the warehouse. Daniel jumped down and reset the alarm, figuring if Tommy entered the warehouse, he would almost certainly stop to turn it off, giving Daniel a few extra seconds to jump down from the box.

With a mighty effort of his arms and shoulders, he loosened the spikes that held one corner in place. Then he dug the crowbar into an adjoining section and pried up that part of the cover. When he could no longer reach any new sections, he jumped off the stepstool, moved it over a few feet, climbed back up and resumed his work. After several minutes of prying, moving the stool, and prying again, Daniel was, with great effort, able to slide the heavy wooden cover a few inches so that he could peer inside. It was too dark in the crate for him to see what it held. He reached in and moved his hand around until he gripped something hard, smooth, and cold. It felt like iron or steel.

He climbed down once again, took a flashlight from the equipment closet, and mounted the stepstool. His heart raced as he flicked on the flashlight and pushed it into the small opening so that he would be able to see.

Motorcycles! The crate held two shiny red and black motorcycles. Daniel sighed with relief. Then he felt ashamed.

As he knew it would be, sliding the rough, weighty cover back in place and securing it so that it looked as if it had never been moved was as difficult as removing it had been. Luckily, he was able to use the original spikes.

When Daniel dialed his FBI contacts later that day to report on the motorcycles, he felt dirty, lowdown, and worthless. If it were not for the fact that the building was under surveillance, he would not have called. He swore to himself that he would find a way to break free of his connection to the government. He had to be his own man.

"We heard about a shipment of motorcycles. That La Salle will steal anything! We won't touch this one. Don't want to make him suspicious of you."

"Good."

"Before you go, we've made a decision ... no fault of yours, but since you say you can't plant those bugs for us in the social club, we're going to do it ourselves. A couple of our guys will break in and plant them," Canciello said.

Daniel was speechless with indignation.

"A few questions," Canciello said. "First, when would be the safest time in terms of day of the week and hour for us to do this?"

"I don't think it's a good idea. The first thing they'd do would be to look for bugs. There's no point," Daniel said.

"It's not your call. When would be the best time, when nobody would be there? Our guys will need five minutes."

"I guess any time after about 4 a.m. The latest anyone ever stays is maybe 3 a.m." Then he had a thought: "But there's always the chance one of the guys could fall asleep there if he's drinking alone. You never know."

"There's two ways of dealing with that. One is you make sure you're the last one there one night, and you call us immediately; we'll have a team ready nearby to go right in."

"Not a good plan."

"Okay. Then, our guys will be prepared to take out whoever might be there. We don't want to do that, but the men above us want that place bugged now ... immediately. We can't hold off."

"Why?" Daniel asked.

"Because we're at war with Islamic fundamentalists who want to strike at the homeland again and again. We can't take a chance that there's talk of arms smuggling and we're not hearing it."

"How likely is it that any of the men at the club talk about that? I've never heard. I mean, really."

"You're right ... it's not likely, but you're not a captain. Perhaps Morici or De Luca's son or any of the other top guys discuss that kind of stuff when you're not around. Anyway, as I said," Canciello repeated, "the guys above us have decided this is the plan. So, which day of the week?"

"I guess any time after 4 a.m. We ... I mean they ... we hang out and talk and party the same every night, so the day of the week doesn't matter."

"Okay ... next thing ... Which six spots in the club would be best for planting a bug? Check the place out today and get back to us later."

"I don't know if I—"

"Don't! You're being paid. You're our man. Do your job. Get in there today, and call us back later. Three spots up front and three in the back. Next question: Are we better off breaking in through the front or the back?"

"I guess the back," Daniel answered, feeling sick to his stomach.

"Is there an alarm system?"

"No."

"Where should our guys search while they're there for papers or anything that might help us to link the dealings in the club to De Luca?"

"There's nothing."

"Nothing? Tripelli used to write notes on legal pads. Does anyone else write any notes or use a computer there?"

"No."

"Okay. Call us back. Let us know where to plant the bugs. We'll make it look like kids. We'll steal some liquor and cause some property damage so it looks like an unprofessional job. And, Daniel, remember who we are and what we can do to you. We don't want to, but, if you push us, you'll spend the next couple of decades of your life in a prison upstate."

After he hung up his phone, Daniel cursed himself for ever agreeing to work with the FBI to betray the family. Each time after he spoke to Canciello or Harris, he felt dirty and remorseful. Then he called Tommy to let him know that the delivery had gone off without a hitch.

Later that day, as he had been instructed, Daniel conducted a careful survey. As usual, Mike Morici was there drinking whiskey, making phone calls, and holding meetings. At this point, Mike and the other high-ranking members of the club allowed Daniel to listen to most of those conversations, most of which involved who owed money and how well the various family businesses were functioning. On occasion, Mike or one of the other captains would politely ask Daniel to "give us a minute" or "go and take care of other business" when they had sensitive topics to discuss.

"I hear Tommy's warehouse is in full operation today," Mike said.

"Yes. First big shipment this morning," Daniel replied.

"Oh, yeah. And what might that be?"

"Don't know, Mike ... 48 big, heavy wooden crates."

"Interesting. Maybe it's bathtubs," Mike joked.

Daniel smiled. As he looked around the club, he spotted three places where microphones could be placed; then, as he walked to the tiny bathroom that was off a narrow hallway at the back, he made a mental note of three places in the kitchen and storeroom areas. He looked at the reproduction of Michelangelo's "Last Judgment" from the ceiling of the Sistine Chapel that he knew covered a small steel safe built into a wall of the social club. On two or three occasions over the years, he had seen Mike take down the painting, open the safe, and place into it or remove from it white envelopes. Those white envelopes were the be-all and end-all of the family business. Daniel thought about how the organization was an extreme example of American capitalism.

After pretending to use the bathroom, he walked into the hallway and stared long and hard at the steel door with its sturdy dead bolt that led to an alleyway at the back of the building. He talked to Mike and the others for a while and finished off two cups of espresso before departing. Once he was a few blocks away, he called Harris and Canciello to tell them of the six locations he had chosen for the electronic eavesdropping equipment.

He had to talk to the owners of Ambrosino's Bakery and the manager of a local gym, both of whom had been late with their weekly payments. Lou Ambrosino apologized and explained that he had fallen behind in his payments to a supplier, and so he had used some of the money for Tommy to catch up with the man. After all, he explained, if the supplier stopped delivering flour, eggs, flavorings, and sugar, he would not be able to make his cakes and bread, and then he would have to go out of business.

"Why did you fall behind?" Daniel asked.

"Two reasons, Mr. Montello," Ambrosino said, "One is I had a baker who was drinking on the job and not putting out his quota. I fired him and I had to do the work of two men, but I couldn't keep up. Luckily, I have another guy now. The other reason is the Key Food down the street opened up a fancy bakery section. They sell a lot of the cakes and breads we make for less than us."

Daniel's next stop, before the gym, was to Key Food, where he congratulated the manager on the success of the new bakery section. He told the man how much he and Mr. La Salle enjoyed the sleek, modern display. "This is what the neighborhood needs ... new ideas, a new business model. My guess is it brings in at least an additional three or four thousand a week for the store."

"Not that much, Mr. Montello," Russell Tompkins, the manager, said.

"Okay. I'm sure you're right, but I'm also sure I'm close. We'll talk it over when I return at the end of the week. Have a good day."

The manager of the gym, Susanne Berger, greeted Daniel with a bright smile and then said that she did not see any reason to continue making payments to him. Daniel explained to her that, even though she was in a good neighborhood, there were plenty of teenage boys with very little to do at night, especially during the summer. "If, by chance, one of those boys—it only takes one—decides to throw a brick through a window or spray-paint the exterior of the building or, worse, figures he'll break in and steal or damage some gym equipment, do you honestly believe the police will be able to find him? In my experience, although they do their best, they never solve those kinds of crimes. That's why we're here. We would find the kid and make sure his parents make restitution so you don't have to file an insurance claim. You know what happens when you file a claim? The company raises your rates or they insist you put in extra security, or both."

"Sure, but," Susanne explained, "we've never had a problem with vandalism or break-ins or anything all the time we've been here."

"Of course not," Daniel countered. "That's because we're looking out for you. Besides that, you know that Mr. La Salle steers lots of business your way. He thinks of this place as his club. We all work out here—and we appreciate the modest fee that you charge us. If Mr. La Salle were to stop honoring you with his patronage, I don't think you would last a month."

Susanne told Daniel that he would have his payment on Friday.

As he drove to his next appointment, Daniel thought about what Tommy had suggested to him recently—that he should consider spreading his wings and initiating his own business enterprises. He suggested credit cards, cell phones, buying into a nightclub or restaurant, and selling stolen cars to exporters.

Smiling proudly, he had said, "You're like a young rock star in our organization. Nobody ever took on so much and done such a good job so fast. We're all glad you never got whacked."

"Well, thank you, Tommy. I'm glad I didn't get whacked too."

However, no matter how much he thought about it, Daniel could not think of a new business in which to become involved. He liked what he did, felt fiercely loyal to Tommy and to the family, and managed to justify all of it to himself. He was making more money than he needed and was proud of his success. Would moving into a new enterprise do anything for him? He doubted it. In fact, he reasoned, doing so might expose him to the threat of failure, so why bother? Tommy had explained to him that the family, just like any other business conglomerate, had to continuously grow; if it failed to do so, it would stagnate, become fleshy and weak, and cease to exist.

Even though he knew that what Tommy said was true, Daniel was reluctant to explore new business avenues. He was satisfied with what he had and saw only sunny skies and rainbows on the horizon.

Then Dominic showed up.

Daniel answered his phone. It was Tommy: "Mike called me first thing this morning! Your buddy Dominic was out there pounding on Mr. De Luca's door real early. Good thing Big Al was there. He just got there right before Dominic. That maniac was demanding a chance to talk to the old man. Of course, Big Al didn't let him in. When Dominic acted really crazy, Al pushed him down the stairs and told him to bring his complaints to Mike or just quietly disappear. Then Al called Mike to tell him what happened and to relay De Luca's message: solve this problem immediately. Then Mike called me."

"Where is he now?" Daniel asked.

"Nobody knows. After Al shoved him down the steps, he went to the club. He and Mike mixed it up—not actually slugging each other, but arguing—and then he ran out, saying something about how he needs to make a livin' and he ain't going back to Florida no matter what anybody tells him."

"I'll find him, Tommy."

Daniel assumed that Dominic had no money, and so he would be unlikely to go far. He drove to the club, parked his car, and began walking along 86th Street, asking shopkeepers whether they had seen Dominic. Morris Weissman, the hardware store owner, said that Dominic had come into his store to buy a pocket knife. Mr. Weissman, seeing Dominic's disheveled appearance and hearing his slurred speech, refused to sell to him. When Dominic reached across the counter to grab Mr. Weissman, the shopkeeper reached for a stout club that he kept there, and slugged Dominic in the head. That stunned him, and he stumbled out the door, cursing and swearing that he was going to kill somebody. "In fact," Weissman said, "his exact words were 'You'll see ... I'm gonna leave a blood trail.'"

When Daniel walked into Reichmann's Deli, the owner said, "He was here ten minutes ago ... Dominic Savarino. He was hungry. I gave him a sandwich and coffee in a bag. He didn't have any money. I told him to go. I didn't want him hanging around here scaring my customers."

When Daniel asked which way Dominic had gone, Reichmann pointed in the direction of the social club, so Daniel retraced his steps. Two hours later, when he had not found Dominic, he got into his car and drove, scanning the sidewalks. He knew that if he did not find Dominic soon, it would be too late. Desperate as Dominic appeared to be, based on what people had told Daniel, he was likely to break into a store or mug someone or kill someone or be killed.

At 9 p.m., Daniel walked into the social club. He had not located Dominic. The usual card games, whiskey drinking, and conversations were in progress. Daniel asked the boy working the bar to bring him a cup of coffee.

"You better find your friend before I do," Mike Morici warned.

"I've looked for him, Mike. He'll turn up, and you know better than anybody else in this room that Dominic Savarino is not my friend."

"Oh, yeah. How would I know better?"

"Never mind, Mike. I'm just in a bad mood. Forget what I said."

"I won't bring it up, but I won't forget it either," Mike said.

When Daniel returned to his apartment at 2 a.m., Bianca, clothed a sheer ivory-hued negligee, greeted him with a deeply affectionate kiss. Then she asked whether he wanted something to eat or drink. He shook his head no.

"Do you wanna watch TV or read a book or take a bath? I'll run a real nice hot one for you," she offered.

"No. I'll just take a shower. Thanks."

In the shower, he decided that once he had settled this business with Dominic he would ask Bianca to move out. He would give her money to find and set up a new apartment or she could move back in with her parents. He knew that she would make a perfect wife. She clearly loved him and always wanted him; she never complained or asked questions, but he wanted more.

When Daniel slipped into bed, before he had a chance to make himself comfortable, she rolled on top of him.

Twenty minutes later, they fell into an exhausted sleep.

*****

Daniel's phone rang at 6 a.m. It was Tommy.

"Some bastard, my guess is Dominic, broke into the club last night. Ruiz, the beat cop, called me to say he heard smashing sounds coming from the place, but he didn't call it in as a personal favor to me. He tried the front door, but it was locked, so he went around the back to investigate. Just as he got there, he saw a guy sprintin' down the back alley going the other way. He didn't get a look at his face."

"Where are you?" Daniel asked.

"I'm going to the club now."

"I'll be there in ten minutes," Daniel said.

As Daniel got out of bed, Bianca sleepily asked, "Do you want me to make breakfast for you?"

"No. Don't have time. Do you need money?" he asked.

"Nope. I'm fine," she answered.

"I'll be back as soon as I can."

Daniel got to the social club before Tommy or anyone else. The front door was locked, so he walked around to the back and entered through the smashed steel door. What he saw astonished and offended him. Furniture had been overturned, bottles of whiskey, beer, soda, and wine, along with glasses, had been smashed and cigarette butts had been stubbed out on the bar. Daniel looked at the places that he had designated as ideal locations for electronic devices, but could not find any. The "Last Judgment" reproduction had not been moved, so he was pretty sure the safe had not been touched.

He heard the front door lock open, and Tommy, followed by Mike Morici and two other men, entered. All of the men looked stunned. Daniel, who, of course, had known the break-in was going to happen, although he had not expected it to be so soon, tried to look as flabbergasted as the other men.

"I know it's that son of a bitch Dominic. I'm gonna fuckin' kill him!" Mike, his face turning beet red, shouted.

"Calm down, Mike," Tommy said. "Our boy Danny is gonna find him. Come here, Danny ... we gotta talk."

As they walked out to the sidewalk, Tommy lit a cigarette. Then he told Daniel what he already knew—that since he had been the one to get Dominic out of the picture a few months earlier, it was his responsibility to find him and make sure he disappeared ... permanently.

"Now. Today. Drop everything else. You tell Carlo and Paulie what they have to do for you. You can have them go with you or they can take care of your business, or both. Do whatever you have to do. *Capisce?*"

210

Daniel said that he understood.

"I know you don't carry a piece. I want you should get one. You gotta get rid of this here Dominic. I know Carlo's got an extra piece. Take his."

"I don't need it. He'll listen to me. I'll make sure he stays away."

"Oh, yeah? Didn't you tell him to stay away before? Huh?"

"Yes, but—"

"No buts. Get a piece and do whatever the hell you have to do."

"I have a piece, Tommy."

"You do? Good. Find him—now. Ruiz, the cop, did us a solid by not filing a report. I been greasing his palm for years, but if that Dominic comes back and does something else, the cops ... some other cops ... are sure to find out and start investigating. We don't want no investigations 'cause that's always very bad for business."

Daniel and Tommy walked back into the club. Tommy attempted to calm Mike. Daniel told Carlo and Paulie what he had on his schedule for the day and asked them to take care of those tasks for him. Then he left the club and walked to Angelo's Pizzeria, where he asked for a paper bag. He got into his car and drove to the garage beneath his building. He pulled Dominic's pistol and holster from the glove compartment, placed them in the paper bag, took the elevator to his floor, and entered his apartment.

The place was empty. Bianca was at work or shopping; he never remembered her schedule. He spread some sheets of newspaper on the kitchen table. Then he took the pistol from the bag, unlocked and opened the cylinder, and dropped the bullets to the table. He peered into the chambers to make sure they were all empty. He closed and locked the cylinder. Then, even though he was sure the gun was not loaded, to play it safe, he pushed the barrel of the pistol against one of the plush pillows on his living room couch, and pulled the trigger. It clicked. A charge of electricity ran from his hand to the center of his body and then up to his brain and down to his genitals. He shivered. He pulled the trigger two more times, feeling similarly electrified with each click.

Then he opened the cylinder again and examined it closely; it looked clean. He looked into the barrel, but could not see clearly, so he cut off a small corner of one of his handkerchiefs. He picked up one of Bianca's knitting needles, poked it through the cloth, and slid the cloth down to the butt end of the needle. Then he sprayed the bit of cloth with 409 and inserted the needle, butt end first, into the barrel. After swishing it around for a few seconds, he pulled it out. It was clean. Either Dominic was more thorough than Daniel imagined him to be or he had never fired the pistol. Daniel repeated the swishing process, this

211

time with a piece of dry cloth. He reloaded the pistol and locked the cylinder.

Although he doubted he would need it or even be willing to use it, he slipped the pistol into the pancake holster and attached it to his belt. Even though the weather was warm, he put on a lightweight jacket to hide the weapon. As he rode down the elevator to the garage, he felt different. It was not just that, for the first time in his life, he was armed; it was that, for the first time in his life, he was not *looking* for someone, but *hunting* for him.

As he started his car, he thought about something he had heard on a Discovery Channel program: to find wild creatures, you have to think like them. Okay, he thought, where would I go if I were Dominic? He was obviously desperate, so he probably would try to rob someone, but who and where? Daniel scanned the neighborhood once again from his car. Then he parked and walked up 86th Street, stopping in each and every store to ask about Dominic.

Three hours later, Daniel stopped at Lamberti's for coffee. He had gotten used to the feel of the holster against his side, but still thought it odd that he was carrying a weapon. He marveled at the twists and turns that his life had taken during the past year: college graduate ... high school English teacher living with Maria ... accessory to murder after the fact ... man on the run ... target of murder and witness to a double homicide ... kidnap victim about to be executed on a beach ... suspect in the custody of the FBI ... to whatever he was now. He closed his eyes and thought and remembered.

Then he saw her face.

Although, on many occasions during the past six months, he had been strong enough to resist calling Maria, now he was overcome with the desperate need to hear her voice. Before he could convince himself not to, he dialed. When Maria answered her phone, the black clouds that had darkened his day lifted; he saw her eyes and breathed in her sweetness.

"Oh, my, how are you?" she asked.

"I'm fine ... busy. How are you doing?"

"Very busy. I got that assistant director job. I still can't believe it."

"I'm not surprised you got the job. You're the smartest one there."

"I don't know about that, but I sure have been working my tail off."

"I miss you so much," he said.

"I know. I miss you too. I think about you all the time."

"So? Can I see you at some point?"

After a few seconds, she said, "No, Daniel. That might make me ... us feel good for an hour or a day, but I can't live that life. It was killing me ... waiting for you ... worrying about you ... feeling sick thinking about where you were and what you might be doing. You were killing me, both when we were together and when we were apart. Besides, I know I was an anchor around your neck."

"No ... not an anchor. I've never been really happy without you."

"I feel the same way, but ... please, you have to understand: I will not put myself through that again ... that life of waiting and being sick to my stomach."

"I *do* understand. Maybe I'll make a change. Don't disappear. I'll call you again in a week or so after I take care of some important business."

"I ... I won't disappear, but I ... I am sort of involved with someone. I don't know how it's going to turn out, but ... "

Neither one spoke for almost a full minute.

"Call me," she said.

"I will."

He called the FBI, reaching Canciello. Daniel told him that Mike and the others thought Dominic had caused the damage in the club. Canciello said that was better cover than they could have hoped for under the best of circumstances.

"We won't shed a tear if one of those guys puts a bullet in your friend."

When Daniel returned to the social club later, he saw that the damaged furniture and broken glass had been removed and the rear door fixed. Other than the empty spaces on the liquor shelves, the place looked as it always did.

Besides the bar boy, only Mike was there, glass of whiskey in hand, telephone to his ear. Daniel sat. He told the boy he did not want anything. He had no reason to stay. He had wanted to conduct a more thorough search for the electronic devices, but, obviously, he could not do that now, so he left.

He called Paulie to ask how things were going.

"We're takin' care of business for you. How's your special work going today? Did you get a lead on him?"

"No. Not yet, but I will," Daniel replied, trying to sound confident.

He went home.

"Wow, you're home early," Bianca said with a rapturous smile. Then, as she kissed him and held him tightly to her, one of her hands brushed against the gun holster under his thin jacket. She did not say anything. As he nuzzled and kissed her neck, inhaling her sweet fragrance, she threw her head back and giggled. Then she pulled him toward the bedroom.

"No. Not now. I have to think about something," he murmured.

"Think later. Let's make love now."

When Daniel awakened, it was dark. The clock on the night table read 9 p.m. He slipped out of bed, washed up, and got dressed.

"Do you want something to eat?" Bianca asked.

213

"No. I have to go out."

It was a pleasantly warm September night. Daniel patrolled the neighborhood, scanning the busy sidewalks. If he did not find Dominic tonight, he would have to assign Paulie and Carlo to help him. He knew they would not hesitate to shoot Dominic on sight. He parked his car and, once again, walked up and down 86th Street. This time, when he entered stores and eateries, the owners and managers, knowing his mission, just shook their heads to indicate that they had not seen Dominic, but they were frightened because they had heard that he was desperate and very dangerous.

He got back in his car and drove along just about every street in Bensonhurst, Gravesend, Bay Ridge, and Dyker Heights, returning, bleary-eyed and disgusted, to the social club at 2 a.m. The door was unlocked, but after he pushed it open a few inches, it stopped, as if it were blocked. He forced it open just enough to be able to step into the dark room. As he reached for the wall switch, he stumbled over a heavy bundle and fell forward to the floor, smacking his forehead against a table leg. He sat up and touched his head. Then he looked in the direction of the door; in the darkness of the room, he was just able to see that a man was lying there. As he stood up, he heard moaning coming from the rear of the room, where he was able to make out, in a corner, two ghostly figures sitting near each other on the floor.

"Don't touch the lights."

"Dom?" Daniel asked.

"Yeah. I guess I forgot to lock the door."

"What's happening? I can't see you too well, but I see a man, a body by the door. Who's that? Looks like Tommy, and who's that with you?" Daniel asked, attempting to mask his anxiety.

"Yeah. It's Tommy. He interrupted Mike and me. We were having a business discussion. Too bad. I didn't wanna hurt Tommy. He's one of the good guys in this bunch."

"I'll check him out," Daniel said.

"No. Don't."

As Daniel walked to the door, Dominic said, "I said no. I guess you can't see. I'm holding a gun. It's pointed at you. Now it's pointed at Mike. Now it's pointed at you. I can see you good enough to shoot you. I can kill you both."

"Okay, Dom. What's happening? I've been looking for you all over."

"I know. They sent you out to kill me."

"No. That's where you're wrong. They wanted me to convince you to go away. I have money for you. If they wanted you dead, they wouldn't have sent me. You know I'm not a killer."

"I heard you changed ... you're like a big man now."

"No. I just take orders. I'm nobody. How are you feeling, Dom?"

"I feel like shit. You know what? Yeah ... go to the door. Lock it. I don't wanna be interrupted again."

Daniel walked to the door and locked it. "You're not going to be interrupted. I don't think anybody's coming here now. It's too late. They're all out somewhere else."

"How come you're here?"

"I didn't know where else to go. I thought there was a chance somebody would still be here. I was hoping to hear that you had agreed to leave town."

"Turn on the light."

Once he got used to the light, Daniel saw that Dominic was sitting on the floor under the wall safe, which was open. He was holding a gun in one hand. It was pointed at Daniel. His other hand was against his abdomen. The "Last Judgment" reproduction was on the floor. Sitting a foot in front of Dominic was a clearly frightened Mike Morici, who was holding both of his hands to the top of his head. Thick snake-like lines of glistening blood streamed down his face.

"I'm gonna sit, Dom. Ok?"

Dominic shook his head. Daniel sat on one of the wooden chairs.

"No," Dominic said. "Not back there. Here. Right in front of Mike. I want to be able to see your every move."

Daniel did as he was told, sitting closer to Dominic and Mike.

"This way, when I shoot this bastard in the back of his fat head, if I aim right, a piece of shrapnel should hit you," Dominic said with a vicious smile.

Trying to sound calm and in control, Daniel asked, "What happened, Dom? I don't mean now. I think I understand. You need money, so you tried to rip off the place. I understand just—"

"You don't understand shit, and I don't have to explain. I just need to rest long enough to figure out which one of you two to shoot first."

"Me? Why me?" Daniel asked.

"That's funny. You know you just basically said, 'Go ahead and shoot Mike, but not me.'"

"That's not what I mean. Why do you have to shoot anybody? Just take the money that I can see is in the safe, and get out of here."

"Too late. This old fuck was giving me my money from the safe. Did you hear me say *my money*? The money he owes me. The money he's been taking all this time. I never shoulda went in with him, but I needed lotsa cash at the time

215

when I had my problem. Then Tommy, he has to open the door. Shit!!"

"That's too bad. I know you didn't mean to shoot Tommy. Take the money. Take my car. Just go."

"Maybe I will. Give me the keys ... toss them to me."

Daniel tossed his car keys to a spot on the floor near Dominic.

"I might just shoot Mike, and not you. I used to like you, Danny, but you just had to go and rat on me and get me in bad."

"What did you expect, Dom? You know you implicated me in what happened to Jimmy. I know you told them where to find his body and you made sure my fingerprints were on the shovel. What would *you* have done?"

"Yeah. That's true, but I was sure you was gonna squeal. I had to protect myself. They were sure to figure I had somethin' to do with Jimmy's disappearance. Mike too. Another guy's involved in the skimming, but I ain't ratting him out. Anyway, that's why *I dropped a dime* on you. I know I shouldn't a done that. Damn it! Jimmy. He just *had* to put his fucking two cents in and try to find out who was skimming the cash! It was Mike's plan the whole time. Jimmy wanted to see if I was involved with it. I was coverin' for him ... for Mike and the other guy 'cause they gave me a little *taste* of the cash and Mike promised to give me a bigger cut. That's why I hadda kill Jimmy." His smile was demonic. Dominic was clearly out of control and at the end of his rope. His expression was so animal-like that Daniel no longer saw him as human.

"You ought to be ashamed of yourself, Mike. Dominic was just a kid."

Mike looked up at Daniel with tears running down his face.

"So," Dominic continued, "this bastard is opening the safe to give me the money he says he's been holding for me—the liar—and then Tommy comes in, and I get startled, and this bastard, Mike, he grabs a gun that's in the safe and he rams it against my stomach and he shoots me. He shoots me! The bitch!" As Dominic said that, he slammed the gun in his hand down on Mike's head, knocking him forward so that he landed a few inches from Daniel. Mike groaned and put his hands to his head. Then, holding one hand to the back of his head, he slowly sat up again and looked at Daniel, mouthing, "Help me."

Focusing on Dominic, Daniel said, "Oh. That was a shitty thing for Mike to do. Are you hurt bad, Dom? Do you want me to get something for you? You want me to take you to a doctor?"

"No. Maybe. Not yet. I'll stand up soon," he said, grimacing in pain.

"You know, Dom. I have ... let me think ... about $150,000 in a safe deposit box. Why don't we both make a run for it? You and me?"

"What about your little bit of brown sugar? Is she gonna go too?"

"No. We split up. I'm between women right now."

"Now, that's a surprise. Maybe you and me ain't so different."

"Maybe, Dom. What do you say?"

"I don't need your money. There's plenty in this here safe. I'm gonna stand up. Don't move. I haven't decided not to kill you yet."

As Daniel watched Dominic slowly, painfully stand up, he saw that the hand that he held against his abdomen was stained red and, beneath it, his shirt and pants were saturated with blood. Dominic wobbled and lurched as he got up, just barely managing to steady himself enough to stand and then lean, breathlessly, against the wall. He grimaced in pain.

"This shoulda never happened. I came in here with a knife I swiped from a store down the street. I told Mike I wouldn't cut him. All he hadda do was give me the money he owed me. That's all. Oh ... this hurts so damned much."

"I want to help you, Dom."

"Yeah. Maybe I'll let ya. Is he dead? Tommy, I mean."

Daniel walked over to Tommy and held his wrist to check his pulse. He put his ear near Tommy's chest. He reached inside Tommy's waistband to see whether there was a gun because Daniel did not think he would be able to pull the revolver from the holster he was wearing under his jacket quickly enough to raise it, point it, and fire without Dominic seeing what he was doing. No gun.

Daniel slowly stood up and then he shook his head to indicate that Tommy was dead.

"Too bad. I didn't think he had a gun. I didn't know for sure. When this bastard shot me, I sliced a piece of his scalp off, and then he dropped the gun he was holding ... and then Tommy—it looked like he was reaching for a gun—so I picked up the gun Mike dropped, and shot him. I never killed nobody before."

"I think Mike's bleeding to death," Daniel said, ignoring Dominic's lie.

"I'll help him." As Dominic said that, he aimed at the back of Mike's head and fired, hitting the floor next to the man. Mike flinched and attempted to stand up. Daniel quickly pulled down the table behind which he had been sitting. Before he was able to duck down behind it, Dominic fired again. Daniel saw an explosion of blood erupt from Mike's face. Mike fell heavily to the floor.

As Daniel squeezed himself into a ball behind the table, he reached for the revolver at his side. Dominic fired at the table. Splinters exploded from it and clattered to the floor near Daniel. Another gunshot sent a stinging geyser of wood fragments against Daniel's face. Remaining behind the table, Daniel reached over and, without looking, fired twice at where he imagined Dominic was standing. Then he rolled to his right and took a fast look from the side of the

217

table. Dominic was not there. Daniel held his breath and, holding the pistol in front of him, slowly, inch by inch, he raised himself up. Dominic was slumped forward against a chair; blood was gushing from his neck. Even so, he pointed the gun at Daniel and fired again. As he threw himself down, Daniel pulled the trigger twice, and then he rolled in the opposite direction—to his left. He waited. His heart was thumping so loudly that it blocked out all other noises.

He heard moaning, crying. In the distance, he heard sirens. If Dominic was still alive, he would shoot again. If Daniel remained where he was and waited, the police would arrive and he would be arrested and, no matter what Harris and Canciello might say, he would certainly be prosecuted.

Gripping the pistol tightly in both hands, remembering that he had fired four times and that he had two more bullets, Daniel jumped up, pointed at Dominic, and fired twice.

Through the filmy haze of gun smoke, Daniel saw that Dominic's eyes were still open. The seat of the chair against which he was slumped held a pool of blood. Dominic still held the gun, pointed at Daniel. As Daniel started to fall to the floor again, Dominic squeezed the trigger.

The gun clicked. It clicked again. And again.

Daniel slowly, hesitantly stood up, edged over to Dominic, and, using his foot, nudged the gun from his hand. The siren sound was closer now. Daniel knew that if he left Dominic alive, he might tell the police who had shot him. Dominic might even blame the other two deaths on Daniel. He thought of the gurgling sound coming from the trunk of the car as Dominic strangled Jimmy to death. He clenched and unclenched his free hand, all the while staring at Dominic's glistening eyes.

Dominic, still bleeding from both of his gunshot wounds, looked up at Daniel. His breathing was shallow; bloody bubbles covered his lips. He smiled weakly. Then his smile drooped and became fixed. His eyes, though directed at Daniel, were immobile. Daniel waited a few more seconds to be sure.

He wiped down his revolver with the tail of his shirt. Then he placed it in Tommy's limp hand. He took the envelopes of cash from the safe and his car keys from the floor and looked around the room. Tommy, Mike, Dominic.

"Last Judgment" lying on the floor between them.

Daniel walked out the back door and went home.

16

The Best and the Worst Days

Still wearing his sweaty, soiled clothing, Daniel collapsed onto the bed. He remained awake for the next three hours, reliving the grisly scene as it flashed through his throbbing brain. As he struggled to gain control, to slow his racing heartbeat and lessen his growing sense of terror and distress, Bianca snuggled against him and slept, her light snoring like the purring of a kitten.

*****

He rang the doorbell at Carmine De Luca's house at 7 a.m. Al Caselli let him in, but said it was too early to awaken the old man, so they sat in the kitchen drinking coffee and talking about baseball.

At 8 a.m., when De Luca had still not come down to the kitchen, Daniel insisted that Al awaken him. Seeing the desperation in Daniel's eyes, Al slowly clumped up the stairs to De Luca's room.

Carmine De Luca, wearing a silk bathrobe and soft slippers, walked into the kitchen. As Daniel stood up, the old man told him to sit. He sat across from Daniel and said, "I see you have bad news for me. Al, please give me a cup of coffee, and then sit with us."

Daniel slowly, dispassionately told De Luca what had happened at the club only a few hours before. When he finished talking, De Luca, who had not touched his coffee, closed his eyes and shook his head in grief.

Then, opening his eyes, he asked, "And so, they are all dead?"

"Yes. I don't know whether my shot to his neck killed Dominic or whether it was the gut shot by Mike. Dominic killed the other two."

De Luca stared directly at Daniel and opened his mouth to speak but said nothing. Daniel reached into a satchel at his feet, pulled out the envelopes, and slid them across the table to De Luca.

"That's all that was in there," he explained.

"You know, young man, Daniel, this money," he said, tapping the envelopes, "this money is what it was all about. It's what it is always about. This is what killed those three and Jimmy and caused you so much misery."

"I know."

"This money ... and not knowing who to trust. I'm sure you remember the story I told you a while back ... the one about the young king."

Daniel shook his head.

"Well, you see, unlike the young king, I took the advice of my minister, my *consigliere*, Mike. That is why you had to run. He told me you were a threat.

219

I trusted him, Mike. I trusted him for so many years. He is the one who arranged for those men to kill you after we had concluded our meeting in that little town upstate. I did not know about that until after. He also arranged for the men to kidnap and kill you when you came back to Brooklyn. I didn't know about that either, but when he told me, afterwards, I approved. I trusted his counsel."

When Daniel did not speak, De Luca continued: "Another man, most men would have kept this money. How would I ever know? I would have believed the police took it. How was I to know you are the one to be trusted?"

"I did think about keeping it. There's enough cash there, along with what I have, to set me up for years. I lay awake the past few hours trying to decide what to do. It was not an easy decision."

"Very few of the big ones are easy. But there's something else. I know you thought about something else ... worried about something else. Right?"

"Yes. I worried you would not believe what I had to tell you ... that you might think I had killed Tommy and Mike. I lay awake thinking about that too. I considered pretending I didn't know anything about the shootings and acting surprised when, later today, one of the other men tells me about it."

"I never would have known the truth if you had lied," De Luca said. "Do any of the others know about the shootings?"

"If they went to the club, they know. I ran out the back right before the police arrived. I heard them pulling up. I'm sure they've closed down the place."

"Is there anything of value ... anything that could implicate us there?"

"I don't believe so, but I don't think we should go back. Who knows? Maybe the police will install listening devices now that they are there."

"Mike was the one who checked for that sort of thing. He has ... had a man who is an expert in those sorts of things."

"Who owns the building?" Daniel asked.

"Mike owned it. You are right. We should not go back there. Al, call my captains right away. Don't tell them what happened. Tell them to stay away from that place. Tell them to call all their men to tell them the same thing. And tell them ... you know, my top men, to come here today ... at noon. We have much to discuss."

"How can I help, Don De Luca?" Daniel asked.

Looking sorrowful and drained, the old man said, "Go home. Come back here tonight. Let's say 6 p.m."

When Daniel got home, he showered. Then he called the FBI.

"Are you okay?" Harris said.

"A bit shaken up, but I'm unhurt."

"We heard the whole thing last night. We made an anonymous 911 call when Savarino shot La Salle. The police notified us of the shootout from the scene. We didn't tell them we had bugged the place, so they thought we didn't know what had happened."

When Daniel did not comment, Harris continued by asking, "So, let me get this straight: Morici gut-shot Savarino, who sliced Morici's head and grabbed the gun and then he shot La Salle. Then you came in ... then Savarino put one in the back of Morici's head. Then you shot Savarino. Is that it?"

"I didn't shoot anyone, Harris."

"Daniel, it's me you're talking to. I heard the tape. I just wanted to confirm what happened. Tell me. You can trust us."

"I didn't shoot anyone. You have it right until the end of the story. After Dominic killed Mike, Tommy La Salle came up with a revolver and shot Dominic. Then I left before the cops got there. End of story."

"That's not what it sounds like on the tape. We distinctly heard Savarino say that La Salle didn't have a gun."

"He was wrong. It must have been on his ankle or something. I don't know. All I know is I didn't shoot anybody."

"If that's the way you want to play it, fine. It doesn't matter. Now, there's going to be a real power scramble. You may be in position to move up to become a captain in the family."

"That's not going to happen. I'm not full Italian. Besides, I want out. Enough is enough. I don't want to do this anymore."

"You can't get out ... not until we connect De Luca to the arms smuggling. That's what we care about. Maybe the bugs will provide us with the information we need to catch him with his hands on the weapons."

"What if I just stop calling you?"

"Daniel, you know what will happen. You signed papers. If you violate our agreement, we make a call, and the murder charges are reinstated against you and, in addition, we use all the information you've given us about your illegal activities with the family to lock you up for more years."

"What if I want a vacation?"

"That's fine, but don't take more than two weeks ... and make sure you return. If you run off, Canciello will tell Joe Fish you've been cooperating with the FBI. Once they hear that, they will scrape through cow shit to find you."

After Daniel hung up, he fell asleep on the living room couch. He dreamed about the icy snow-covered scrub-pine hills of West Virginia and his friend Prior and his dog Shadow. The dog was gently, sweetly licking his face

221

and breathing warmly into his ear.

He awakened. Bianca was tenderly stroking his cheek.

"What time is it?" he asked.

"It's 4:30. Are you okay?"

"Yes ... just tired."

He grasped her warm hand and held it against his face.

"I know something bad happened last night. You don't have to tell me, but are you sure you're okay?" she asked.

"Yes. Something happened, but I'm fine. Everything is fine. How are you today? How was work?"

"It was boring, as usual, but I'm happy to see you. Do you know how much I love you, Daniel? I hope you do. It's okay that you don't feel the same way about me, but I want you to know I think about you all day long."

"I know, and I do care for you, Bianca. It's just ... I'm going through a lot right now. I don't mean to neglect you. I just—"

"It's okay. I understand. I've never really loved a guy before. I sorta thought I did once, but it wasn't like this and he wasn't as good as you. I don't always know how to say things. I'm not smart like you, but you, I know in my heart you are everything I want."

"Are you happy, Bianca?"

"Yeah ... yes. I am. You make me happy. I worry when you're out, but I'm always happy and I feel kind of filled up inside when we're together."

"Good." Sitting up, Daniel looked into Bianca's deep amethyst eyes, and saw something that he had never seen before. Then, it was as if his reflection in her eyes was speaking; he heard himself say to her, "Please be patient. I need time. I don't want you to disappear."

She smiled at him and stroked his face again.

They sat on the couch, holding each other; neither one moved. He found it surprisingly easy to push thoughts of the horrific events of the night before from his consciousness. As Bianca nestled against him, he felt simultaneously aroused and at ease, excited and composed. He did not lead her to the bedroom. She melted into his arms like scented candle wax, warmly sliding into the hollows of his body and fixing herself there.

At 5:30, he gently pushed Bianca away and said he had an appointment. She lay back on the couch and smiled as he walked out the door.

As he was driving to Carmine De Luca's house, Maria called.

"Oh, my God, are you okay?" she asked.

"Yes. I'm fine."

222

"I read in the paper about ... you know ... what happened at that place last night. I just wondered whether ... you know."

"I'm fine. I wasn't there. How are you?"

"Me? Fine ... good. I guess you're busy. Glad to hear you're okay. I just ... oh well. I just wanted to be sure you were okay."

"Thanks, Maria. I'll call you again. We'll talk."

*****

They sat in Carmine De Luca's kitchen. Late afternoon September sunshine brightened the little table.

"Al went to pick up Chinese food. Do you like that?" De Luca asked.

"Of course. In my house, when we weren't eating Italian or Jewish food, we always brought in Chinese."

"Good. Before the food arrives, I want to talk to you about two things." After taking a few seconds to compose his thoughts, De Luca said, "I'm taking a big chance with you, but, as I said, I believe I can trust you."

Daniel shook his head gravely.

"We took a big blow last night. Mike, even though, from what you told me—and I believe you—Mike was cheating me, he was my *consigliere*, my advisor. Tommy was ... Tommy was indispensable. I met him when he was a little boy ... terrible family. My Sophia and I helped to raise him. I thought he would take Mike's place when he got too old and maybe he would even take my place. Now? It's terrible. Who's left? Robert Licardelli, George Salerno, and Joe Galliano, along with Antonio, my son. I have to fill the gaps left by Tommy and Mike. I hate to give him up as my personal bodyguard and right hand man, but I'm moving Al up as a captain. He'll choose another man to take his place. Al will take over Antonio's business. I am moving Antonio up to *consigliere* to take Mike's place. That leaves Tommy's spot. I need someone to run his business interests. Even though you're young, I'm thinking of you. You know his business. It can't be official ... you'd be an *acting* captain. It's not that I'm stuck in the old ways, but we have to move slowly. How would you feel about that? About taking on more responsibility?"

"I'm ... overwhelmed, Don De Luca. I don't know what to say."

"Here's what you say: you say yes."

"Yes. *Grazie.*"

"Now, this means Tommy's businesses are yours. His men take orders from you. They bring the cash to you and you give it to Antonio. We'll take care of the families of Tommy and Mike. You should check in on Tommy's wife and see if she needs anything; be like a brother to her. If you want to branch out to new enterprises, you speak to Antonio for advice. *Capisce?*"

"Yes."

"Okay. The second thing is ... I ... Let me think how to say this. I was not meant for this life. Believe it or not, I wanted to be a teacher ... I think I once told that to you, but things happened. The war ... I was 16 years old on December 7, 1941. Do you know what happened that day?"

"Pearl Harbor ... the sneak attack."

"The Japs attacked us. Worst day of my life until then. I was so mad, I wanted to join up right there and then. My mother made me promise I'd finish high school first. I enlisted in the Navy at the end of 1942."

Daniel shook his head, but remained silent.

"Proudest day of my life was September 2, 1945. Do you know what happened on that day, Daniel?"

"The Japanese surrender."

"Yes. I stood at attention on the deck of the U.S.S. Missouri in Tokyo Bay as they signed the surrender. I felt ten feet tall that day."

"It must have been a wonderful moment."

"Wonderful ... sad ... I smelled the burning oil from a time a year before when a ship I had been on was torpedoed and I floated on a lifesaver ... hundreds of boys died, but, yes, it was a good day for America. I love this country."

"I know."

"Anyway, after the war, I couldn't concentrate in college. I guess I needed time to adjust. I ran wild. My mother, who was from a little village outside of Palermo ... very proper lady ... she was horrified. I stayed out late. I got in trouble. I got into fights. I would have ended up in jail, but one of the priests from our parish ... I'll never forget him ... Father Balducci ... he took me under his wing. I went back to college and I worked at my father's fruit stand, but then some men began demanding money from him; I don't mean a little protection money—they took more and more until he couldn't pay his bills. Then they burned his stand and beat him up so badly he couldn't work again. *Bastardi!* The bastards! I couldn't look at him ... at my father after that."

When Al Caselli arrived with the food, De Luca asked him to put it down and join them at the table, saying, "Picking up food is no job for a captain in my family, Al. This little dinner will be a celebration ... a celebration in the midst of such tragedy. Such is life: sorrow and sweet wine at the same time."

Big Al appeared to be struggling to suppress tears.

"To continue ... to conclude ... I trust the two of you completely. Al, who has served this family for so long and Daniel, who has proven his loyalty. To conclude my little story, I knew some men from a local family who knew some people who knew the Gambinos. They helped my brother Francis and me to avenge our father and they took my brother and me in and gave us work. We had to work. Our father could not anymore. He was broken physically and in other ways ... in his manhood and his reason to live.

"Very few people understand the seed from which those first families in America grew into *this thing of ours* ... it is a subject that should be studied. Very complicated, but I will tell you this. The people of the *Mezzogiorno*, the south of Italy, especially in Naples and Calabria and particularly my people, those in Sicily, were forever conquered and pillaged and raped by other countries. The ones in the rest of Italy, those to the north, always spit on us. My father told me that in the old country, in the old days, the enemy was always the government and sometimes the parish priest. Which government, you may ask? Any government. The old families in Sicily always protected the people. That is why my brother and I went to those men in our neighborhood in our time of need. We had no place else to turn for help.

"Francis eventually moved to San Francisco. I dropped out and did not return to college. Too many things happened to go into now, but that is how I find myself where I am today, which brings me to my second point. I think it is time ... this terrible situation has convinced me. I want to move into more honest businesses so that, some day, before I die, we're 100% legitimate."

De Luca looked at Al and then at Daniel.

"I have thought about that too," Daniel said. "The world is different today. I don't mean because of what happened last September 11th. The big families are gone. The FBI is putting away the leadership. They use listening devices and satellites. They tap telephones. They may know what you talk about. Perhaps this *is* the time to restructure the family. It operates like a corporation already. Why not branch out into legitimate businesses? Take some of the capital, ten percent first, more later, and buy into or create businesses. No more loan sharking, gambling, hijacking, or any other dirty business that could put any of us away."

De Luca smiled, and then he said, "It's as if you saw my dreams. Maybe you transmit *your* dreams to me while I sleep. I have wanted to do that. Two people have held me back for years—Mike Morici, may he rest in peace, and my son Antonio. The two of them, whenever I have brought up this subject, have vehemently opposed me. Sometimes ... I hesitate to say this ... sometimes they have looked as if they would lock me up in a nursing home if I tried to do that."

Daniel and Al looked at each other and frowned.

225

Al said, "We will look out for you. Daniel here is the smart one. I'm sure he'll come up with good ideas for the future of this family. I'll protect you."

"I trust you will," De Luca said to the men. "We all need to plan our future now. It should be one that takes us away from bloodshed and regret."
*****

Two weeks later, as Daniel stood in the elevator, his eyes fixed on the lighted control panel, his heart fluttered as he pictured Bianca's sparkling violet eyes, so like the shimmering water in a tropical lagoon, and her sumptuous hair. More than that, he hungered for her soothing touch and the way her fragrant body vibrated when he held her. He was astonished by how much he wanted her. With Maria, it had always been sweet and loving and fulfilling. With Bianca lately, it was dazzlingly electrifying and ferocious, but warmly loving and very satisfying too.

She was not there. He felt empty, like a cold shell on a wintry beach. Then he heard a door open. Bianca emerged from the bathroom, dressed in a terrycloth bathrobe, drying her hair. She approached him.

"Hi. I took a shower. You okay? You have a funny look on your face."

"Yes. I guess I do. The funny look means I'm happy to see you."

"Oh, you never ... you've never said that before."

He grasped her shoulders, kissed her forehead, cheeks, throat. He held her to his chest, her damp towel against the side of his face. Then, gently pushing her away and looking intently at her, he said, "I'm going to be better."
*****

Daniel met Antonio De Luca for lunch at Ferrara's in Little Italy. Although he had been pleased to have moved up to the number two position in the family, Tony, as everyone other than his father called him, seemed to feel slighted, as if the elder De Luca should have retired and left him in charge. At the age of 48, he had been waiting quite a few years for his father to step down. Tommy had once said that Tony suffered from "Prince Charles syndrome."

At the end of the meal, Tony said, "I have a meeting to go to, so I'm gonna tell you why I invited you to lunch. I want to tell you—it's not that I don't like you—it's that you don't seem to really fit in. I don't know why Tommy liked you so much and why the old man thinks so highly of you, but they do. I mean Tommy did and my father, he does. I can bend. I'm gonna try to see what's so hot about you. Let's toast to a new friendship. *Salut!*"

Daniel held up his wine glass and said, "*Salut!*"
*****

A week later, Daniel called Maria to say that the family business would be moving in the direction of completely legal activities. She said that was good, and then she asked, "How long will this take?"

"We're going to start right away, but it will take years."

"And, during that time, you'll still be involved in ... those other things?"

"Yes. I will. I can't drop out now ... maybe in a few years, maybe in five years or so, I'll be able to make a clean break, or maybe I'll stay after that."

"Oh. So, until all that changes, if it changes, you'll be dealing with things that could put you in jail or hurt you or get you killed? Right?"

"Jail ... no. I told you ... I don't want to talk about it on the phone, but that's not going to happen. The other things ... maybe, but I'm always careful."

"I hope you are, Daniel. I still feel something for you. I think about you, but I'm different now. My life is different. The one thing that has not changed is I know I cannot live that life ... that girlfriend or wife who sits home at night waiting. I'm not built that way. I can't do it. I can't live huddled in a corner."

"I know. That's why I called. Be happy. I'll call you again sometime."

"Daniel, no. Please don't call me again, at least, not until you're out of that life ... if that ever happens. I hope you are very very careful. Don't get hurt."

The thought of calling Harris and Canciello stuck in his throat, so he let two weeks pass before he had to accept the fact that he was treading on thin ice.

"Daniel, you son of a bitch, we warned you about going AWOL!" Canciello yelled into the phone.

"I told you I was going on vacation," Daniel calmly replied.

"You didn't tell me shit!"

"Oh. You're right. I told Harris. He said I should take as long as I want."

"Really? He didn't tell me that. You can't do this. You have to call twice a week, or else you don't get your government cash."

"I don't need it. I haven't picked it up in weeks."

"Well, it's here. Pick it up, or don't ... that's up to you, but you're not out of the arrangement until we say you are. What's been happening?"

"Well, as you surely know, we don't use that storefront anymore. Too many bad memories or something. I don't know who decided that."

"What else? Who's taken Morici's place and La Salle's spot?"

"Al Caselli took Tony's spot. He ... Tony took Morici's place. Tommy's is up in the air right now."

"Do you think they're onto the phone tap at De Luca's house? The only thing we've heard since the shootings—not that we heard much before—is about picking up pizza or visiting the grandchildren. What's going on?"

227

"I wouldn't know, Canciello. I don't deal with the high echelon of the family. You know that. I'm just a small cog in a very big wheel."

Now that, despite what Daniel said to Canciello, he *was* a member of the upper ranks in the family, he had more to do than ever before. Since he liked to keep his hands on his enterprises, unlike Tommy, who always delegated authority, Daniel spent many hours each day talking to people, straightening out problems, and keeping track of money. He was also earning much more than before; his *take* averaged $10,000 per week. That much cash was a problem; he wanted to buy a house in a nice neighborhood in Brooklyn or Queens, but his reportable annual income from Coastal Properties had moved up to only $50,000. He knew he could pay for a house in cash and not miss the money, but that would be a red flag with the IRS that even Harris and Canciello might not be able to squelch. He met with Robert Licardelli, who, besides being a captain, was a CPA. Together, they came up with some safe strategies for the money; Daniel would partner with legitimate businesses that would pay him regular, reportable salaries and he would buy another one, a karate studio, which would produce steady income.

*****

One Sunday morning, a few months after the shooting at the social club, as he and Bianca ate breakfast, Daniel looked at her and, suddenly, a hazy fragment of a dream from a few hours before came back to him. He was overcome by a powerful flood of sweet warmth that penetrated his very soul as he remembered—no, as he *felt* Bianca's gentle touch. When he raised a hand to his forehead, it was as if her smooth, supple fingers were there, tenderly comforting him. As he looked at her across the table, she seemed to shimmer with golden radiance. He realized that when he thought about Bianca—even when images of her simply flitted through his consciousness—he was not tormented by the horrors that he had witnessed. The hideous thoughts that plagued him during the day and as he slept, when he was *able* to sleep, were no longer there. He loved this woman who, over a short, intense period of time, had become an essential part of his life.

But he had to be sure, so he brought to mind images of Maria. As he did so, he realized that he had not thought of her for weeks. Now, as he pictured Maria, he smiled and hoped that she was happy, but her image receded into the background of his consciousness, replaced by the reality of Bianca. He realized that she had taken complete possession of him and all that he hoped to be.

He was sure.

*****

Smiling at the three-carat engagement ring that she knew she would never take off her finger, Bianca said, "Today, tomorrow, whenever you want. I don't care. As long as we're together, we can elope, if that's what you want."

"But don't you want a big wedding?"

"I do, but only if you do," she replied.

"Whatever makes you happy," he replied.

"You know what makes me happy," she said with a giggle.

They decided on June of the following year, 2003. Daniel said that she should make all of the arrangements. They agreed that they should attempt to make both families happy; they hoped to accomplish that by having a priest and a rabbi perform the wedding service.

"How about at the beach?" she asked.

"Sounds great. As I said, you take care of it."

*****

"I think we should find a regular place to meet," Daniel said to Tony. "It's not good for us and the other men to talk in restaurants and in our houses. We need someplace permanent and respectable to conduct business. Listen, there's a new small-office complex on Bay Parkway. They just started leasing spaces. I took a look. Very nice."

"Yeah. Good idea. Tell me how much money we need. Anything else?"

"I don't know how to say this, so I'll just come out with it ... that guy in your crew, Johnny Griselli, is too physical. I'm sure you've heard he's been roughing up people who are a little behind in their payments. Not necessary."

"As you said, Daniel, he's in *my* crew. It's my business."

"I know, Tony. I don't mean to offend you or step on your toes, but, sometimes, you ... I don't mean you ... I mean a person may not see how people close to him are acting. This Johnny thinks it's the 1920s."

"I don't see a problem. People pay. When they don't pay, we convince them to pay. We always do that."

"Right, and sometimes it's necessary, but things are changing. *We're* changing. At some point, when this family is strictly legitimate, we won't be touching anybody anymore. It will all be done through letters from lawyers. We should not be using force anymore unless it's completely necessary."

"Legitimate? That's my old man's crazy idea. What's he think? We're gonna be G.E. or Microsoft and be on the Big Board? He's gettin' soft in the head. If *you're* gettin' soft, you better remember who you are in this here organization. It's all sharks and guppies out here. I hope to God you figure out which one you are."

229

"I know who I am. You know what I'm capable of when it's necessary. Okay. I'll drop the subject ... for now."

"You see, Danny, that's why I can't share certain information with you. You're a good earner and a good administrator and I know we can trust you, but, deep down inside, do you know who you really are?"

"I think I do, Tony, but tell me. I'm all ears."

"You are still that high school English teacher who's looking over his shoulder and runnin' away. You wish you was still back in that classroom, and not out here in the real world makin' tons of money and bein' respected."

"That's where you're very wrong. I like my life. I just think we need to change with the times. Get away from crooked dealing and, by the way, what would be so wrong with being the next Microsoft? A few smart legal investments and picking the brains of guys on Wall Street, and we could be making a lot more money than we ever dreamed of without having to worry about breaking the law or being arrested or spending time in jail. And, yes, it is your father's wish."

"You don't think G.E. breaks the law? Or any of those big companies? None of them make it without cheating on their taxes or paying off somebody or hiding evidence of illegal activities and business practices. Be real."

"You're probably right. For that matter, half the people in Congress should probably be in jail, but I'm talking about us."

"Are you worried about that, Daniel?"

"Well, I don't lie awake at night thinking of it, but neither did Frankie Marconi or Charlie Resputo."

"They were stupid. That's why they got caught."

"They're your guys, Tony. They're your responsibility. You should have counseled them so they would know what to do and what not to do."

"They got lawyers. They should've known better."

"It could happen to you or me."

"Now, that attitude is why I can't let you in on a really big, multi-million dollar deal that I got in the works. It's not ready yet ... lots of pieces to put into play. Too bad ... I'll have to ask one of the other guys to help me."

"What deal is that, Tony?"

"If you don't have the heart, you can't be in on it, and that's a shame because I could use you. It involves people from ... let us say a different part of the world. I dealt with them once before, but I don't speak their language."

"What language is that?"

"I don't mean it that way. This one guy, he talks English okay. I mean they don't think like we do. I have a hard time makin' the best deal."

"Who are they?"

"I'll tell you this much ... then you can think about whether you wanna make some of that money along with me: back home, when these guys take the wife and kiddies out for the weekend, they drive camels."

*****

Daniel drove directly to the FBI office in Manhattan. Harris was there.

"Call Canciello. You both need to hear this," he said.

"He's talking to our boss. He'll be back soon. I'll get you a cup of coffee, or you can pick up your payment for your work for us."

Daniel sat, waiting for Canciello. Harris's use of the word "payment" rankled him. He did not need their payment and he was *not* working *for* them.

Sitting there, he felt conspicuous and uncomfortable and uneasy, as if he were enmeshed in an all-encompassing nightmare of a bureaucratic tangle in a backwater country with a totally alien culture. The little office was quiet, but men and women were busily striding up and down the corridors. He heard doors slamming and phones ringing and the dull drone of muffled conversations.

Daniel had never liked the atmosphere of this place, but now he hated it. He thought back to the first time he had been here ... that morning when, groggy, frightened, disoriented, he had sat waiting for someone to uncuff him or release him or kill him. He had felt all alone in the world, lost and confused. Now, he was a man of substance, of wealth and power. He controlled the daily activities and destinies of a dozen men; he handled tens of thousands of dollars in cash each week, much of which remained with him. He went home every night to a woman who glowed with happiness when he walked in the door, a feeling that he shared when he saw her ... *when* he thought of her.

"So, what do you have for us?" Canciello asked.

"Sit down. I have something to tell you," he said.

"I hope it's good," said Canciello.

"It is. It's what we've been waiting to hear ... what I've been trying to smoke out this whole time. Tony De Luca has an appointment to meet with people; from his cryptic reference to 'camels,' I think it's safe to say they're from a middle eastern country and part of a terrorist group."

"Do you think—"

"It has to be weapons, but I really don't know that for sure. That's all he said, other than the fact that he dealt with these people one previous time and this deal involves millions of dollars in profit."

"We'll talk to our supervisor. Call us in a couple of days or if you hear more. We're finally gonna nail De Luca and put him and his lousy family behind bars ... and for a long time."

"Wait," Daniel said. "Listen to what I said. I was talking to *Tony* De Luca, not his father. In fact, he complains all the time about his father. The old man wants to buy into legitimate businesses, and Tony doesn't like it. He's a hood from way back; his father is a gentleman who got caught up in this ... life. He would never deal with terrorists."

"Well, we don't know that and neither do you," said Canciello.

"I know it. I would trust him with my life," Daniel replied.

"You've been in deep with them for too long. Once we nail them on this arms deal, if that's what it is, you're out."

"Ah, gee ... just when I'm beginning to like what I'm doing," Daniel replied with a wink.

"I mean it ... once this is over, you're out."

"Whatever you say," said Daniel. "Now, let me collect my *payment*."

17
Father and Son

"Hi. How are you?" Maria asked.

"I'm fine." Daniel hesitated for a moment before saying, "I had to call you to say you should move on. Things will probably never be the way you want. I can't explain. My ... situation is different now. It is what it is."

"Oh," was all she said.

"I want you to know I loved you. I still do. I always will, but our lives are different, and that will not change. I'm sorry, but that's how it is."

"Don't be sorry. I feel the same way. There's a little spot in my heart that you occupy. No one else will ever have it, but I understand that we'll never be together again. Thank you for telling me. I have sort of been keeping my life on hold ... not completely, but sort of holding back a little."

"Oh? Is it serious?"

"Yes. He wants to marry me. I told him I had to think about it."

Daniel pulled the phone from his ear and placed it against his chest. He worked to control his thrumming heart. He put the phone back to his ear and, in a choking voice, asked Maria to give him a second. Then he breathed deeply.

"Sorry," he said, "I thought I had to sneeze. So, what's his name?"

"Rafael. He's an attorney. He's very nice."

"Good. I'm glad. You deserve the best. If he ever mistreats you, let me know. I'll send over two big ugly guys to break his legs."

"That's not funny."

"I mean it."

"That's even worse. I'm glad you called. No reason why we can't remain friends and keep in touch with each other. Anybody in your life?"

"Yes. Her name is Bianca. She's a sweetheart. We're ... close, very close. In fact, we're going to get married."

After a few seconds of silence, Maria said, "Good. If she ever mistreats you, call me. I'll personally beat her up. I won't send anyone to do it for me."

*****

On Daniel's way out of the FBI office the day he told them about the possible arms deal, Harris had said, "Become Tony De Luca's best friend in any way you can." Daniel understood Tony. Men like him, the ones who take a back seat to other men, who wait for years to move up, burn with resentment. In Tony's case, his bitterness was all-consuming. He consoled himself by thinking that his father could not last much longer. The old man had already had two

233

heart attacks. Surely, the next one would kill him or debilitate him enough so that he would have to retire. Tony did not feel guilty about those thoughts because he was not actually wishing for his father to become ill or die; he was just thinking logically, realistically. After all, the man was almost 77 years old. Why did he still want to run the family? Why was he still in Brooklyn, and not in some old-fart retirement village with a golf course? Had he ever played golf? Tony did not know. In fact, he could not remember a time when the old man had ever played anything, except games with his grandchildren. It was too bad that Giovanni and Victoria kept their distance. If they had remained close to the old man, he might have retired so he would be able to visit them or even move closer to one of them.

But Tony knew that would never happen. Giovanni, who was four years younger than he was, and Victoria, who was born a year after Giovanni, grew up playing together and never spent much time with their father or their older brother. They had even used a secret language when they were very young that only they understood. Their mother, horrified by Tony's bad behavior in school and on the streets, which she was never able to modify, made sure her two youngest children grew up differently. Where Tony had stickball and fist fights, Giovanni and Victoria had piano and art lessons. When Tony was cutting classes and getting high, his siblings were making the honor roll and creating posters for drug prevention programs. During his years right after high school, when Tony was committing armed robberies and beating up people, Giovanni and Victoria kept their distance from their brother and stopped speaking to their father because they blamed him for Tony's wild, dangerous behavior.

Carmine De Luca had tried to restrain his older son and help him to stay out of trouble, but he had been unable to alter the boy's antisocial ways. Shortly before Tony's 19th birthday, the elder De Luca sent an elegant hand-written dinner invitation to Father O'Connor, the long-time parish priest. Flattered that so great and wealthy a parishioner had invited him, O'Connor sent out his positive response that same day.

During the lavish dinner a few nights later, Father O'Connor said, "Mr. De Luca, I know you do not attend Mass on a regular basis (in truth, De Luca had not stepped foot in any church in decades), but I would like you to consider joining one of our boards. A man of your intellect and insight would be most welcome. We would appreciate your participation in the life of the church."

De Luca carefully wiped his mouth with his napkin and said, "Father O'Connor, I sit on several boards; unfortunately, I do not have time to become involved in another. However, I would like to make a very sizable donation to your church to be used as you wish. We can discuss that after dinner. Please take another slice of cake. My Sophia made it."

When they talked after dinner, De Luca offered to pay $10,000 cash directly to the priest to use as he saw fit. In return, he wanted Father O'Connor to do whatever he had to do ... call in whoever he could find to counsel or perform an exorcism or whatever would be needed to change his son's dangerous, rebellious conduct.

"Have you attempted to guide him, Mr. De Luca?" the priest asked.

"Yes. Until I have wanted to smash his head through a wall."

"Have you done that? I mean a strict regime of discipline?"

"Yes. No matter what harsh words or dire threats or punishments I have implemented, he has stood firm and defied me. He is *una bestia selvaggia*, a wild beast. I love him, but he is out of control. He is as I was when I was a boy, but worse. At least, I listened to my mother and my poor broken father. I had to be that way back then. I had no choice. He does not have to be like this."

"How did you change, Mr. De Luca?"

"I ... I found my way. I was fortunate enough to find men who taught me how to live a civilized life."

Father O'Connor raised a skeptical eyebrow.

"You think you know me and my ways? You do not. I abhor violence and brutishness. It should be used as a last resort, such as in time of war."

"I am not here to judge you, Mr. De Luca. Only our Lord and Savior Jesus Christ can do that. You must live your life according to the dictates of God and the one eternal and legitimate church. Alas, I cannot help you. Cleanse your soul and beg for forgiveness of your sins, and that will lead to the redemption of your son. At that point, I would be happy to speak to Antonio."

"Oh? Then? Not now?"

"No. You are in a state of sin now. You must be as pure as the priests and the Roman Catholic Church, and then I will be able to help you."

"Ah ... as *pure* as the priests and the Church? I understand. I thank you for your time. Have a safe trip home."

"You are welcome. I hope you didn't mind that I spoke so frankly to you. And so, when can I expect that generous donation? Cash, you said?"

"The donation? Ah ... I will give it to you when we meet in hell."

After the priest left, more confused than insulted, De Luca went to his desk, from which he took a clean white envelope. He wrote "See me" on it. Then he placed $500 in twenties in the envelope and sealed it. He walked to his son's room and left it on his bed.

235

When Tony fell onto his bed in the wee hours of the morning, sore and bloody from a drunken fist fight, he felt a lump under his chest. He turned on a lamp and examined the envelope. Then he opened it and fanned out the money, smiled, and slept. When he awakened at noon, he went to his father, who was sitting at his desk, writing. The elder De Luca looked up and said, "That money is your first week's pay. As long as you follow the rules and act with moderation and caution, you will be able to take my place one day."

Now, Tony was almost 49 years old. He was not willing to follow the rules and was tired of waiting to succeed his father. And Daniel was going to become Tony's best friend, maybe play the role of younger brother. Daniel thought long and hard about how to approach Tony in such a way as to change their longstanding stiff and distant relationship.

When Tony asked Daniel how much money he needed to lease an office, Daniel said, "I really could use your advice on this, Tony ... you know, about picking out an office and filling out the papers."

Tony smiled and said that since he was not doing anything important, he would run down to the place with Daniel. In the car, Daniel shared with Tony his tentative wedding plans: "Next July ... on the beach, maybe the Jersey shore."

"Sounds nice. Bianca's a great girl. She came outta nowhere ... from Queens, I think. Before the other guys could get to know her, she latched onto you. I gotta tell you, man, she is a piece of ass ... no offense."

"Sure, Tony. No offense. I love her and she loves me."

"I understand."

They chose a three-room first-floor office with a kitchen and a small storeroom. On the way back to Tony's car, Daniel asked, "Hey, I have an idea. Would you like to come over for dinner at my place one night soon, maybe next week? You and Valerie? Bianca's a great cook, or we could bring in something."

Tony, looking genuinely touched, said he would love it. They set a date.

When Daniel told Bianca about the dinner and how important it would be to make sure Tony felt flattered and happy, she began chirping and fluttering around the apartment, opening and closing cabinets and calling out ideas for what to serve that night. He told her that it would be her call.

The dinner was a success. Bianca, believing that simple food properly prepared and presented was better than elaborate dishes, served salad, roast chicken, vegetables, and homemade bread. For dessert, she brought out a chocolate mousse cheesecake that she made from scratch.

While she and Valerie talked about wedding plans and children and what to look for in a house, Daniel and Tony sat on the breezy terrace. Daniel had bought cigars because he knew that Tony liked them; even though he hated the smell and the taste, when Tony lit up, he smoked one too. They sipped Sambuca and puffed away and looked at ships passing in the bay. Tony talked about an action movie he had seen, saying, "The gunfight scenes were fake looking."

After a while, when Tony did not bring up the subject which was the purpose of the dinner, Daniel led into it by asking, "What do you think I should get into, Tony? This wedding's going to cost a fortune, and, besides that, Bianca wants us to buy a house, a big one. What do you think?"

"What?" Tony said. "Aren't you reeling in the cash?"

"Sure. I've done well over the past couple of years, but I've spent a lot. I'd like to start a real nest egg. Where I've made thousands, I would like to move up to the next income bracket. After all, a guy can't start too soon."

Looking into the apartment to make sure the women could not hear him, Tony said, "Do you remember that really really big business deal I was alludin' to a few days ago?"

"Yes. That was the day I was feeling kind of down. That's why I was talking about being careful. I got over that bad attitude."

"Really? Good. Let me ask you this ... What do you think about politics? You know, this war in Afghanistan and these so-called terrorists and shit?"

"Well, Tony," Daniel began, "How can I put this?"

"This ain't no congressional hearing. What do you think?"

Hoping he was on the right track, Daniel said, "Well, I'm not the patriotic type, if that's what you mean. You're never going to find me slogging through shit in some crappy country fighting for Uncle Sam."

"My sentiments exactly."

Warming to his subject, Daniel said, "When you come right down to it, wars are started by old-fart politicians and the big shots in industry. The guys in politics get to make speeches and act like they're doing something and the men in the boardrooms sell planes and guns and computers, and they all get rich."

"Right. It's all about money."

"Now," Daniel continued, hoping he sounded as if he were in the dark, "if we could get our hands on rifles or something like that, and sell them to some of these so-called terrorist groups, we'd have a chance to make a bundle."

Tony looked behind him again. Valerie and Bianca were laughing. Tony shook his head and said, "Tomorrow ... in the office. Let's say noon."

Later, as they lay in bed, Bianca asked whether the dinner had worked to

Daniel's advantage. He smiled, drew her to him, and kissed her velvety neck.

*****

The plan was simple. It involved three groups of people. The first was a full colonel in the Army with a serious gambling addiction, an unmanageable need for alcohol, and a seemingly unquenchable libido who stayed as far away from his wife as possible. After settling the man's gambling debts and lining up attractive young women for him, Tony made it clear that, if the colonel ever refused to do whatever he asked, he would make sure the man's genteel Protestant wife and grown children, the United States Army, and anyone else who would listen found out about his proclivities and addictions.

The second was a trio of contractors who sold weapons to the military. They eagerly awaited the colonel's phone calls and the money he would pay them to divert some of those armaments to him.

Finally, there were two brothers from Yemen who Tony had hired for some dirty work a while back. At one point, they told Tony that they were in touch with certain men from certain countries who needed high-tech weapons to "fight a glorious fight for political and religious liberty." Tony did not ask for details. He told the brothers to give him a list of what the "freedom fighters" wanted, saying he would come up with a price.

The next day, in their office, Tony explained the deal to Daniel. "Just like the last time with these guys, the devil is in the details and in the negotiations. Once we agree on what I can supply and how much it will cost them, these camel jockeys will nickel and dime me like you won't believe. On that deal with them a year ago, I made $50,000, but it was very risky—I heard part of the shipment got stopped by the Feds, but nobody got caught—and, besides that, I shoulda made a lot more. Don't tell my father. He's got this idea of being a patriot because he fought in the big war against Hitler and the Japs."

"I know. What can I do?" Daniel asked.

Tony locked his eyes onto Daniel as if he was attempting to probe his very soul. When he was younger, Daniel had always found it difficult to outstare people. Now, after all he had been through, he was able to maintain an unremitting laser-like stare which eventually unnerved Tony.

"Here's a list of what these ragheads want. It's pretty big stuff—RPG launchers, 50-caliber machine guns, missiles, mortars, ammunition, explosives, that kind of stuff—my guy can get it all from the manufacturers. With the war on, there's loads of these babies just sitting in warehouses. Nobody can keep track of it all. There's some other stuff down at the bottom of the paper that he probably can't get. That's okay. If this deal works, I'll be able to buy more and more of this stuff. They'll keep playing ball with my colonel and me—although I may cut him loose at some point—because the only color any of these guys respect ain't the red, white, and blue; it's the green, green, and green."

"Powerful weaponry," Daniel said as he examined the list.

"Yeah. And then I have another long-range plan. With the money I make from this enterprise, I can go big into the really steady money stream."

"You mean drugs."

"Yeah. My dad don't know. He's old-fashioned. Don't want us sellin' drugs; he's always been against the hookers too. It took me years to convince him, but drugs ... no. A few of my guys supply some small-time dealers, but with this money, I can buy directly from the big guys and make a fortune."

"You know, Dominic was hooked on cocaine."

"Yeah. I know. I used to supply him, but when he got in too deep, I cut him loose. You never know what a junkie's gonna do. Obviously, nobody else knows about that. Drugs and *our thing* don't usually mix."

"That's true. I understand."

"So, are you in with me? Tomorrow I'm gonna meet with the big shot colonel who can't keep his pants on for more than a minute."

"Okay. Where?"

"Connecticut. We fly out in the morning from La Guardia."
*****

Colonel Thaddeus Bushwell looked nervous and uncomfortable during their meeting at the Crossroads Hotel in Hartford. As he polished off glass after glass of scotch from the bottle that Tony had placed on a table by the window, he perspired and repeatedly looked out to the parking lot below.

"So, whadda ya think? Can you get it all?" Tony asked.

"Yes. I can. With my commission, it will run you $800,000."

"Whoa! Forget your commission. Since I bailed you out of those gambling debts, if anything, you owe me," Tony replied.

"Okay. Right. Look, Mr. De Luca, when we conclude this deal, I'll have to retire. I can't do this anymore. You may get away with it if we're caught, but I'll spend the rest of my life in jail, if I'm lucky."

"You're not out until I say you're out. You're mine ... I treat you good. You don't wanna change that relationship with me, do you? And, nobody's gonna get caught, as long as you talk to the right people, and nobody else ... and you make sure you're sober. *Capisce?*"

"Yes. I ... I understand. Of course. I'll talk to my people now."

While the colonel talked on the phone to his suppliers, Tony and Daniel sipped their drinks and waited. Daniel studied the exceedingly worried man who was a victim of his own cravings, addictions, and weaknesses. After a few minutes, the colonel hung up, put his phone in his pants pocket, and showed the list to Tony, pointing out the items that he had checked off and their prices.

"Good," Tony said. "Now relax. You can keep this room. Why don't you take a shower? While you're doing that I'll arrange for your companion to come up and spend the rest of the day with you ... or would you like two companions? Up to you."

"One would be very nice. I'll hop in right now," Colonel Bushwell said.

Daniel turned on the television and tuned in to a rock music channel. Then, as Tony began dialing his phone, Daniel raised the volume.

"What the hell?" Tony asked.

"I love this song," Daniel replied and began singing.

Tony shook his head and walked out to the hallway to make his phone call. Daniel waited only a few seconds before walking toward the bathroom and putting his ear to the door. When he was sure Bushwell was in the shower, he slowly opened the door and peeked in. He was not able to see the colonel through the heavily patterned shower curtain; that meant that Bushwell was not able to see him. The man's clothes were neatly folded over the sink. Daniel looked at the closed door that led to the hallway and then back at the clothing. He entered the bathroom, leaving the door partially open, and walked to the sink. He reached into the man's pants pocket—wrong one. As he reached into the other pocket, Tony called to him from the bathroom door.

"What the hell are you doing?"

Daniel quickly moved over to the toilet, lifted the seat, and unzipped his fly. The colonel, startled by Tony's outburst, slid back the curtain and looked at Daniel and Tony.

"Sorry, colonel. I couldn't wait until you were out."

"That's okay. We'll all friends here," the colonel said as he pushed the shower curtain back and resumed his pre-orgy ablution.

"What the hell were you doing?" Tony whispered to Daniel when he came out of the bathroom.

"I wanted to see whether he had been wearing a wire or had a recording device in his pocket."

"Never! He's in this deeper than you and me. He's not gonna rat."

"Really? And what if the Army is on to him and offered him a deal?"

"Hmm. Never thought of that. Okay. Good. So, he was clean?"

"I didn't finish checking. You interrupted me."

"Okay ... let me think. I got it. I'll be right back. Stay here," Tony said.

When Bushwell walked back into the room, dressed and looking relaxed, Daniel poured two drinks and offered one to him. They sat and sipped.

"You probably think I'm too old for this sort of thing ... young women, I mean. I'm 63 fucking years old, but when I look in the mirror, I see a young man. I feel like a young man and I have the needs of a young man. My wife, I love her dearly, but she's like an older sister now or like my mother."

"I understand," Daniel said.

"I'll bet you have a beautiful young wife or girlfriend, good looking man like you. How often do you do it, if you don't mind my asking."

"I do mind."

"Oh ... sorry. I didn't mean to embarrass you."

"You didn't embarrass me." Then, looking Bushwell straight in the eye, Daniel said, "I didn't want to embarrass *you*. My fiancé, who is gorgeous, and I *do it* two or three times each night and much more than that on weekends."

Just then, Tony came into the room holding a plastic bag. He held it out to the colonel, saying, "Here. Put this on. It's silk ... from the gift shop. Women love the feel of silk. It makes them hot. Believe me."

Bushwell withdrew a pale blue bathrobe from the bag.

"Go ahead. Put it on. Leave all your clothes in the bathroom. This way, you don't have to wear your stinky underwear. There's some nice cologne in the bag too. That will drive the beautiful young thing crazy."

The colonel smiled and walked back into the bathroom. When he emerged, dressed in the robe, Tony told him that he looked like a young stud.

"Let's have another drink," Tony said. "You want one, Danny?"

"No ... I don't know what's with me, but I have to run to the john again."

"Can't take him nowhere," Tony said.

Daniel closed and locked the bathroom door and went straight to the colonel's pants. He located the man's cell phone and placed it in his pocket. Then he flushed the bowl and waited. Then he flushed it again, washed and dried his hands, and walked out of the bathroom.

"I hope you didn't leave a stink in there," Bushwell said.

"I didn't. I feel better," Daniel said as he shook his head "no" to Tony.

"Time for us to go," Tony said. "I'll call you in a couple of days to come up with a shipment date. Don't drink too much and shoot your mouth off."

"Oh, I'll be shooting all right, but it won't be from my mouth," Bushwell said with a wink.

In the hallway, Daniel told Tony that there were no devices of any kind in

Bushwell's clothes. Then he said, "He's just an old guy who hates his life."

"What are you ... a philosopher now?" Then, as they rode down in the elevator, Tony said, "I think we better get rid of him when this deal is done."

Daniel shook his head in agreement, even as some of the alcohol that he had consumed shot back up to his mouth.

"You wanna stay here a few more hours? I can call a coupla hookers for us. Why not make a little vacation outta this trip?"

"That sounds good, Tony, but I'm already neglecting business. I can't take the time today, but I'll take a rain check."

On the flight back to New York, Tony said, "Once I contact the buyers, you go with me. You don't pack a piece, do ya? Do you have one?"

"No, I don't, but I can get one."

"Get an automatic ... no more revolvers. I heard what you used against crazy Dominic. You're lucky you ain't dead."

"You're right. I'll be better prepared from now on."

When he was back in his car, Daniel thought hard and wrote down as many of the names and descriptions of the weapons on the list as he was able to remember. Then he called Harris and Canciello to say that he would be coming in with important information. He was always careful to choose a secluded spot when he called the FBI and he always made sure the phone was off before he put it back in its hiding spot under his car seat. Before he brought his car in to be serviced, he always removed the phone and hid it at home.

Daniel also knew how to make sure he was not being followed. Before heading into Manhattan, he always drove along familiar streets for a while before parking in a quiet spot, where he would sit for a few minutes, observing cars that passed, before resuming his journey. However, there was no reason for him to be concerned. At this point, he was an unofficial captain in De Luca's family. The only one who might be unsure of his loyalty was Tony, but Daniel was confident that he had won him over and did not need to be concerned.

Nevertheless, he followed his usual routine before taking the Belt Parkway to the Brooklyn-Battery Tunnel to Manhattan and then uptown to the FBI office. Once he was there, as usual, he parked in a garage a few blocks away, took a taxi to some other part of Manhattan, ducked into a store, and then took another taxi, getting off a block from the FBI office.

Daniel gave Harris his copy of the inventory of weapons. Then he handed Bushwell's cell phone to him, saying, "The last outgoing calls were to the arms suppliers. I imagine you can use that information to locate them."

"Good work. The most important thing," explained Canciello, "is to do whatever you must to keep this thing going forward, and keep us in the loop."

"And," added Harris, "at least a couple of days before the meet, we need to know the address of where you're going ... and ... you're probably going to have to wear a wire, so leave time to come in here that day."

"I can probably get the address, but I'm not going to wear a wire."

"Why? Tony trusts you. He's not going to frisk you."

"Of course not, but what if the men we meet frisk me?"

"It will be so tiny they'll never find it."

"I'll think about it," Daniel said, knowing that he would never consent to wearing a listening device.

"Another subject as long as you're here," Harris said. "What's with this new office? Any chance we can put devices in there? We have the phones bugged, but all we hear is nonsense conversations."

"I don't think so," Daniel said.

*****

"You look like you want to tell me something," Bianca said when Daniel walked into the apartment that night.

When he saw the look of apprehension in her eyes, he reassured her by saying, "It's nothing bad. I just want to ask you a question. Sit." He kissed her gently on her forehead. She kissed him on his lips. He pulled away and said, "If we keep that up, we won't get to discuss anything."

"Okay, but make it quick. I need you."

"Of course. You know I think about you all day long."

"Liar. As long as you think about me when you're on your way home."

"I do. Here's my question: How would you feel if I were to get out of this business? Live a life where I'm on the right side of the law?"

"Honest, Daniel, I hope you wanna ... want to do that. I get scared sometimes when I think about your ... you know, your business."

"You never ask, and I'm grateful for that. I don't do what you probably think I do. I'm an administrator. I check on businesses and make sure the men under me are doing their jobs. I collect money and bring it up the chain of command. That night back in the old social club, that was the only time."

"Good. I don't think you were cut out for this kind of life."

"Funny, though ... I've become pretty good at it, and I'm trying to bring the family business up from the Dark Ages, but you're right."

When he did not say anything else, Bianca asked, "So, is this a move you're gonna make? Really?"

"It's a move I would like to make. I might be able to do it. I just wanted to make sure you would be okay with the change."

"Why wouldn't I be?"

"I didn't know. We've never talked about it. When you met me, I was doing this ... this kind of work. I just wondered whether that is part of the appeal."

"It's not. I love you because of who you are, not what you do. You're a smart, good looking man who makes me all fluttery inside because I love you and I know you love me."

"Good. You know, I never expected to be in this life. It just sort of happened to me. Before I knew it, I was in ... and it's been that way for a while now, but I can do a lot of other things with my life.'

"I know. Whatever you do is fine with me, Daniel."

"Good. Is there anything else you want to say?"

"Yeah. If you're done talking, let's get to bed."

18

What Happened in the Little Room

It was a balmy Sunday afternoon with a luminous sky. Daniel and Bianca took in the dazzling scenery as they drove out to Long Island for Carmine and Sophia De Luca's 50th wedding anniversary celebration. Tony had organized it and invited dozens of relatives, the captains and a few others in the De Luca organization, scores of business partners, associates, and members of other local crime families, along with area politicians to share in the festivities at an exclusive country club at which he was a member.

As Daniel pulled up to the ornate front entrance, a valet opened his door and another opened Bianca's and held out a gloved hand to her. Daniel stepped out and handed a twenty-dollar bill to the valet, asking him to be especially careful with his car, saying it was only a month old.

"It's beautiful, sir. We see lots of BMWs and Mercedes, but not many Bentleys. I think this may be the only one."

"How do I look?" Bianca asked as she straightened out her dress.

"How do you look? Like a work of art; like a modern-day Venus."

She glowed as Daniel accompanied her into the building and to the reception hall, where they were greeted by Carmine De Luca and his wife. They chatted about the weather, how lovely all of the women looked, and how beautifully decorated the room was. De Luca told Daniel and Bianca to go out to the veranda for the cocktail hour. After Daniel introduced Bianca to some of the wives, he walked over to Robert Licardelli, George Salerno, and Joe Galliano, who were sipping whiskey and admiring the expansive golf course.

"Danny, I know we're not supposed to talk about any business here today, but I heard ... we heard you and Tony, you're working on a big deal. How's that coming along? Is it working out?" Joe Galliano asked.

"Yes, Joe," Daniel said. "We shouldn't be talking about business."

The others laughed nervously. Joe frowned, and then he smiled, saying, "Fuckin' college boy ... always with the smart mouth."

"Can't help who I am, Joe," Daniel replied.

After a couple of minutes of labored conversation, Daniel excused himself and walked over to Dante Testoro and Mike Ciffarello, who, as lower-ranking members of the family, often found themselves excluded from conversations with the upper echelon. Daniel felt comfortable with them.

Tony De Luca joined them; after a minute of small talk, he told the two men to give him and Daniel a minute. Then he said, "Did those fat galoots ask you about our special business proposition?"

"These guys? No."

"Any of the others?"

"Like who, Tony?"

"I'm not gonna do anything. It's just, Joe overheard me on my cell phone the other day. He looked like he wanted to ask, but he didn't."

As Tony was talking, Daniel turned toward the three captains he had walked away from earlier. Joe Galliano looked nervously in Daniel's direction.

"No. Nobody asked."

"Good. I set up a meeting for tomorrow ... up in Newark. I'll give you the details tomorrow on the way there. If all goes well, by next week, you and me should be looking at least a coupla million bucks."

"Where's it going to be, Tony?"

Tony's eyes narrowed. "Like I said, up in Newark."

When Tony introduced his brother and sister to Daniel and Bianca, his siblings smiled politely and then almost immediately walked away.

Tony said, "Don't feel bad. They don't have much to say to me either. At least they showed up for our mom."

The food was delicious and beautifully presented, the music was delightful, and the temperature was so comfortable that much of the party played out on the terrace far into the night. It would have been a perfect occasion except for the fact that Giovanni and Victoria snubbed their father and Tony had too much to drink. Toward the end of the evening, he climbed up to the bandstand, grabbed the microphone from the singer, and began what turned out to be a long, rambling, almost incoherent, and very slurred speech about his parents' 50th wedding anniversary. Even though it started out amusing, it quickly turned into an inappropriate and angry discourse about the unfairness of life. The guests, all of whom stared uncomfortably at Tony with their champagne glasses held high, almost immediately became embarrassed as he complained in what he thought was a light-hearted manner that his father was still living and "runnin' the fuckin' family business as if it was 1952."

As he thrust his champagne glass into the air, spilling most of its contents and splashing a few members of the band, he said, "Yeah, this is a great occasion. My mom's a peach, a beautiful woman, and my dad's okay too, but he shoulda retired years ago. I'm fuckin' 49 years old and I'm still waitin' to take over the business. He's just hangin' in there for dear life ... you know, a kinda death grip. Who knows? You might be attendin' my funeral before his."

As the laughter and smiles turned to frowns, people started to examine their shoes. Sophia De Luca, although she tried to look amused, was clearly horrified; Carmine De Luca's face turned so fiery red that it looked like he might be having the heart attack that Tony had, on more than one occasion, secretly hoped for; Giovanni, who had come without his family, and his sister, Victoria, stood, champagne glasses in hand, like exhibits at a wax museum.

Daniel, who felt sorry for Tony and mortified for the couple being honored, moved toward the stage. He stood in front of Tony and smiled up at him. Then he held up his phone and gestured that a call had come in for Tony. He ignored Daniel and continued to ramble and then look around the room, waiting for laughs. Finally, Daniel motioned for the band leader to pull the plug on Tony's microphone, but the man did not comply, so Daniel climbed up to the stage and, reaching over Tony, grabbed the microphone and said, "Great speech, Tony. Everyone, let's give Tony a big round of applause."

As people began clapping, Daniel handed the microphone to the band leader and helped Tony down from the stage, all the while, telling him how amusing and insightful his toast had been. When he got Tony back to his table, he instructed a waiter to bring black coffee. Then he told Tony that he had to drink some water. When Tony refused, Daniel turned to Valerie, who tried to convince him to drink. Then, holding his mouth with both hands, Tony ducked his head down and vomited over and over again.

Everyone nearby scattered. Only Valerie and Daniel stayed with Tony. Finally, Tony lifted his head. Valerie wiped his face with a damp dinner napkin and held a glass of water to his mouth. After a few minutes, Daniel and Valerie led Tony to a bridal chamber, where they gently pushed him to a couch and helped him off with his jacket, tie, and shoes. Once Daniel saw that Tony had dozed off, he left him there with Valerie and rejoined the party.

Carmine De Luca walked over to Daniel with his hands extended. They hugged, and then De Luca said, "Such an embarrassment ... such a fool he made of himself. His mother, my Sophia. What am I going to do?"

"You do nothing, Don De Luca. Tony is not usually like this. Maybe he drank too much because he got caught up in the moment. Don't let it worry you. People will forget. What they will remember is this wonderful party."

Then, looking at Daniel thoughtfully, De Luca said, "And maybe the alcohol loosened his tongue, and he said what he really feels. Ah, maybe he's right. Maybe I should step down, but I have a big problem. Do you know what it is? My insurmountable problem?"

Feigning ignorance, Daniel shook his head.

"Yes, you know. I have alluded to it. Antonio is not the one to lead this family. He talks about me being mired in the 1950s. That is wrong! I am old fashioned ... Yes. I believe in honor and courtesy and respect. He is only a little better than he was way back when he was engaging in fights and stick-ups every night. He is still a troubled little boy inside. Very insecure and untamed."

Daniel remained silent.

"If he succeeds me, this family and everyone who depends on it will be ruined or in jail or ... dead. I have no one else."

"That was awful," Daniel said to Bianca when he returned to their table.

"I know. You did the right thing ... taking him away, I mean."

"Somebody had to do it."

As they danced, he held her close to him. Then he asked, "Are you sure about our wedding plans? I mean, the beach. If you want to have it in a place like this, we can still make a change."

"No. I love the idea of the Jersey shore, and besides, we ... I started making all of the arrangements. You know that."

"We can always make changes. I want you to be happy."

"As long as we're together, it doesn't matter to me where we get married, but, like I said, I'm happy with what we planned."

At 11 p.m., as people started to leave, Daniel said, "Let's start saying good night. Then I'll check on Tony."

When they approached the elder De Luca, he smiled unconvincingly.

"Still upset about Tony?" Daniel asked.

"Yes, and ... I don't know. My other children ... I don't see them for so long, and they come ... Giovanni without his family and Victoria like I'm poison to her. I know they disapprove of my life and they still blame me for Antonio, but they should make an effort to show some warmth to me."

Daniel was embarrassed by this confession.

On the way home, he asked Bianca whether she was sure she wanted to have children once they were married.

"Of course. I want lots ... well, not lots ... four or five. Don't you?"

"I've always thought so, but you never know how they're going to turn out. And, with kids, you're tied down."

"You won't be tied down, and I won't either. We'll have a nanny. And, besides, our kids will have your brains and your ... I don't know the word ... you know, like you're always sure of yourself and always do the right thing."

Daniel looked sadly at her and said, "No. I don't know, Bianca. There *is* no word for that; it doesn't exist."

*****

Driving through Staten Island on their way to the New Jersey Turnpike, Tony, who had been quiet from the time they met at the office that night, asked Daniel, "So, what'd you get? I mean what kinda piece?"

"A Walther ... P99."

"How come?"

"It's small and I was able to get my hands on a new one."

"You fire it yet?"

"No."

A short while later, once they had crossed the Goethals Bridge, instead of heading north on the Turnpike, Tony turned off and drove to a deserted park on the Arthur Kill. He parked and got out; Daniel followed. After he had looked around to make sure they were alone, Tony pulled a semi-automatic from his waistband. He aimed at a buoy that was bobbing up and down in the dark, swirling water, and fired three times. Daniel could just make out small geysers erupting from the water a few feet from the target.

"Not bad," Tony said. "Now you."

Daniel looked around and listened. The only sound was the clanking of chains on swings as the wind pushed them back and forth. He pulled back and released the slide, disengaged the safety, aimed at the buoy, and fired three times. He was wide of the target, so he aimed more carefully and fired three more shots, coming closer this time.

"Okay," Tony said, "If we have to defend ourselves, which I doubt, we're gonna be a lot closer to our targets than this ... more like two feet away. In fact, if you never been to this part of Newark, I gotta tell ya, some nights, all ya hear is gunshots. You drive. I wanna think about some things before we get there."

After they exited the Turnpike, they drove down quiet streets. Tony pulled a scrap of paper from his pocket and examined it, saying, "It's gotta be coming up. You ready for this?"

"I'm ready. How do we know these guys aren't cops or federal agents?"

"They're the same guys I dealt with before. If they were Feds, they woulda arrested me a long time ago. I really need this deal to come through tonight." After a few seconds of thought, Tony asked, "On another topic, how bad was I last night? I mean at my old man's party?"

"You started out fine. In fact, you were funny, but then ... Are you sure you want to know, Tony?"

"Yeah."

"You started carrying on about how your father has kept you waiting too long and how he's living in the past."

"I know. That's what I thought. I don't usually drink like that, but, all of a sudden, I got so fuckin' mad. I mean, my old man's sittin' there like he's gonna be the boss forever ... and he mumbles to himself ... and he's holding me back from ways of makin' a lot of money, and there's my stinkin' sister and brother ... they just say hello with sour pusses, and then they ignore me like they're better than me. I don't get it."

"I know. You're right about one thing ... your father would never go along with a deal like this. He would never understand."

"Don't I know that! Here it is."

Daniel parked the car. They surveyed the street and sidewalk. Then they entered an unlit derelict building, walked up two flights of dark stairs, and, after flicking on a cigarette lighter to see the numbers, knocked on a door. Daniel heard the scraping sound of the peephole being slid back. Then the door opened and Tony and Daniel walked into an uncomfortably warm apartment that smelled of cigarette smoke and garbage. Daniel, who had called Canciello and Harris after the party the night before to tell them what he knew—that the meeting was going to be in Newark and that he and Tony would start out from their office in Brooklyn the following evening at midnight—hoped the FBI or police had followed them. When the agents had insisted that Daniel come in immediately to be fitted with a wire, he refused, saying he was taking enough of a chance as it was.

A man about Daniel's age who was holding a flashlight led them to a dim bedroom in the rear of the apartment, where two men sat at a small card table smoking cigarettes and writing. The only light in the room came from a large candle sitting on a dish in the center of the table. Three mattresses were propped up against a wall; there were two additional chairs around the table. That was it. No other furniture. The wooden floor was stained and broken up and creaky. Cigarette smoke hung in the heavy, still air of the small room.

The man with the flashlight walked out of the room, closing the door behind him. Tony and Daniel stood near the two seated men, neither of whom looked up at them. One of the men, around Tony's age, large, heavy, and dark-skinned with a thick beard and unkempt black hair, held up a finger as if to signal them to be patient. Then the other one, who appeared to be a younger, slimmer version of the first man, stopped writing and slid a sheet of paper to the first man, who compared the two lists, smiled, and said something in what sounded to Daniel like Arabic.

"Welcome, Tony," the older man said with just a trace of an accent.

The other man looked up and silently acknowledged the visitors.

Gazing at Daniel and gesturing with a hand, the older man said, "I am Faruq, and this is my brother, Mahir. You may sit."

"This is my associate. His name is Daniel," Tony said.

"Ah. A novice gangster. So much the better. Are you Italian also?"

"Yes," Daniel replied, and then because he did not like the man's superior attitude and because when he looked at him he could not help but think of the September 11th attacks, he added, "but my mother is Jewish."

"Oh, but that is not your fault."

"No, but I'm grateful for it every day."

First the man scowled, and then he grinned. "Very good answer, my friend. After all, we are cousins. You know the story of Abraham?"

"Yes," Daniel replied. "He kept his real son, Isaac, and threw the bastard son, Ishmael, into the desert. He became the father of the Arab people."

"Oh, a scholar, I see, but like all of your people, instead of sitting down to talk, you try to take advantage. That is okay. We will prevail. *Allāhu Akbar.*"

"Enough of that bullshit. We're here for business, not to have a chat about religion or politics or any of that crap," Tony said, sounding nervous.

"Of course, you and your Jew friend are here to give us what we want."

"We got what you want as long as you pay. Here's the list you gave me. Next to each item is the cost. We can give you a ten percent discount if you buy large quantities. We can horse trade about what constitutes large quantities."

"Of course. Leave the list with us. We will get back to you at a future date to let you know whether or not we are interested."

"What? I thought this was gonna be a deal. I can get the goods within a day or two after you give me a down payment. I expected it to be tonight."

"We are going to entertain other offers. We are not dependent on your pork-eating *mafia* brothers or your Jew suppliers."

Daniel bit his lip, and then he smiled.

"Don't your skinny brother have an opinion?" Tony asked.

"He does, but, as you must remember from the last time, he listens and remains quiet. Besides, you would not understand him. Unlike the way in which you speak, his English is impeccable. He was educated in the U.K., but he does not like to speak your gutter language. He talks only the holy Arabic tongue. I, on the other hand, am a practical man; I know that to achieve our lofty goals we must deal with infidels and even Jews."

"Oh, good for him! You know, when you guys talk that camel jockey lingo, it sounds like when I'm choked up with a cold," Tony said with a smile.

"Boys, boys," Daniel said, "Let's get back to business. Faruq, why don't you examine our prices? Then tell us what you would like to pay. Surely, we can reach a deal tonight. We can supply you in a few days with what you want."

Faruq smiled grimly. Then he and Mahir examined the list and talked to each other in Arabic, occasionally looking at Tony and Daniel.

"For all of it, we are willing to pay one million dollars," Faruq said.

"What? It's worth at least triple that!" Tony exclaimed.

"If that is what you think, then you have wasted your trip. You may as well leave and return to your *mafia*-Jew heaven in Brooklyn."

"Oh, yeah? Well, any part of the old US of A is better than the best part of your shit-stinkin' country. If you're not careful, you're likely to find yourselves in a six-by-six cell in Guantanamo Bay."

Faruq's eyes widened. Then he glared at Tony and asked, "What did you mean by that, my loyal American friend? Are you going to report us to your government? Is that what you plan on doing?"

Daniel said, "He didn't mean anything."

"Yeah. I didn't mean anything by it. I just have to tell you: our guys are kicking your asses in Afghanistan. I'm glad we're not selling this stuff to you, you raghead assholes. Go see if Allah is gonna protect you. Mark my words, you and your brother and the rest of you bastards will end up dead or in jail."

Daniel tensed. When Faruq and Mahir stood up, Tony and Daniel did also. With Faruq and Mahir in the lead, the four men walked to the door. Faruq opened it and walked into the other room. Mahir and Tony followed, but Daniel, sensing something ominous in the way that Faruq held himself, hesitated at the doorway. Faruq turned and put a hand on Tony's chest to halt him. The other man pointed the flashlight at the men. Then Faruq said something in Arabic. He, Mahir, and the other man drew guns from their waistbands, released the safeties, and pointed them at Daniel and Tony. Faruq took Tony's gun from him.

Tony stared angrily at the men and asked, "You gonna shoot us now?"

"We have not decided yet. We do not trust you. We are going to walk you down to make sure you go on your way."

Then, as he spoke in Arabic again, his two companions nodded gravely.

"Did you come here alone, or are others of your kind waiting for you?"

"What? Sure, we came here alone. Oh, no. I'm wrong. Your asshole prophet Muhammad chauffeured us, you candy-assed raghead."

Faruq smacked Tony on the forehead with the barrel of his gun, causing him to stagger and collapse against the man with the flashlight, who fell to the floor. Daniel, who was still in the doorway, quickly stepped back, kicked the door shut, and pulled his pistol from its holster. Just as the door began opening,

Daniel fired into it four times. Then he ducked down and crawled along the floor to the window at the opposite end of the bedroom. He tried to open it, but it was jammed. Turning his face away, he smashed it with his elbow; then, using his gun, he knocked away the jagged shards of glass that remained, and, as bullets tore through the door from the other room, shooting out an eruption of wooden fragments, Daniel scrambled out, falling onto the fire escape.

He looked below him and thought about climbing down to the street. Then he lifted his head and stared at the door through the shattered window frame. All was still and dark. He looked down to the sidewalk again.

Then the bedroom door swung open and two figures burst into the room shooting wildly. Daniel ducked down. He heard creaking footsteps on the wooden floor approaching the window. He looked down again at the sidewalk below. Then, holding the gun in both hands, he reached over his head and fired repeatedly into the room. He heard a groan. There was no return fire. Still crouching, Daniel waddled a few feet to the left of the window along the fire escape. He hugged the outside wall of the building, sure that one of the men would reach through the window and try to shoot him. He expected to hear police sirens soon. If the men in the room did not kill him, he would be arrested.

Then, a head and torso burst through the shattered window frame, firing down at the spot on the fire escape where Daniel had crouched a few seconds earlier. In the darkness, flames shot from the gun and sparks and bullets and shards of metal from the fire escape ricocheted from the railing to the wall and to Daniel, grazing his face and chest. Then, as the man pivoted toward Daniel's new spot on the fire escape, Daniel lunged at him and fired twice. Then his pistol clicked. The man, Faruq, looking surprised, collapsed on the window sill. Daniel backed away, almost falling down the fire escape ladder shaft.

Faruq's pistol lay on the fire escape. Daniel stared at the man for a few seconds before he inched over to the gun and picked it up. He pushed his own pistol back into its holster. Then, slowly, carefully, he lifted his head and, holding Faruq's pistol, he looked into the bedroom. It was empty and dark. The table was on its side, the candle probably lying on the floor. The door to the other room was open. He stood up and inspected the room again. Seeing no one there and no one in the part of the other room that was visible through the open doorway, he pushed Faruq through the window and into the bedroom. His body fell to the floor with a dull thud.

Daniel climbed over the window sill and into the bedroom. He removed his shoes and made his way to the opposite wall. Then, holding his body against the wall, he inched toward the doorway of the room.

Although a fresh breeze wafted into the room, Daniel was bathed in sweat. He dried one hand and then the other on his slacks. Then, holding the gun in both hands, he swung into the doorway and scanned the murky outer room. He saw Mahir on the floor, the flashlight a few feet away, shining onto his shoulder and face. Daniel picked up the flashlight and pointed it and the gun at Mahir. Blood spurted from a gaping wound on his thigh. The man looked at Daniel through half-closed eyes and then at a spot on the floor. When Daniel shined the flashlight in that direction, he saw a pistol. Daniel figured it must have skittered away from Mahir when he was hit by Daniel's gunshots through the closed door. He picked up the pistol and put it in a pocket of his windbreaker. The flashlight revealed glistening globs of blood on the floor of this room all the way to the outer door, which was open. Daniel turned the flashlight toward the bedroom. Under Faruq's body there was a pool of blood. A trail of blood led from a spot in the middle of the bedroom to the room where Daniel was standing.

He walked back into the bedroom. As he put his shoes on, he was suddenly aware of the fact that his socks felt slimy-sticky and wet. He exited the bedroom and shined the flashlight onto Mahir's face again. The man's eyes were still open, but they were unfocused. Then, after turning the flashlight into the dark hallway for a few seconds, where the trail of blood continued, he moved into it, down the stairs, and to the lobby.

He shut the flashlight, wiped it down, and threw it to the floor of the lobby. Then he warily peeked through the lobby door to the sidewalk. Breathing slowly and deeply, he waited; he listened. After what seemed to be an eternity, during which time no one walked by the building and no cars passed by on the street, Daniel carefully opened the door and looked, first to his right, and then to his left. He placed Faruq's pistol in the other pocket of his windbreaker and stepped down to the deserted sidewalk.

Tony's car was where he had parked it. After standing uncertainly for a few seconds, Daniel walked along the sidewalk and then across the street. He ducked into the lobby of another building, and waited.

He dialed Tony's cell phone. The call went directly to voicemail.

He looked at his watch; it was 2:00. He had checked the time when he and Tony had arrived at the building. It had been 1:25. The gunplay could not have lasted more than two or three minutes. One man, Faruq, dead; another one, Mahir, grievously wounded, bleeding to death. Daniel assumed that the young man who had held the flashlight was wounded too; the trail of blood from the middle of the bedroom to the outside hallway had probably come from him.

254

Tony was nowhere in sight.

After all he had done during his time in the De Luca family, even though he was no longer squeamish about violence in general and had, at times, given orders for it, Daniel still found the thought of killing someone sickening. He had shot Dominic, but he did not know whether any of his bullets had killed him or whether Mike Morici's shot to his abdomen had done it. He sometimes thought about the violence of that evening as he lay in bed at night, but he rarely dreamed of it now. He had just shot two ... possibly three more people. Standing in that building lobby, keeping watch over Tony's car, he assured himself that there had been no choice because those men had planned on killing Tony and him. Besides, he reasoned, they were enemies of his country.

He crossed the deserted street and, unlocking Tony's car, opened the door and sat in the driver's seat. He called Tony's phone again; once more, it went to voicemail. His watch read 2:45. Holding Faruq's pistol in his hand under his jacket, he ducked down in the seat and kept watch.

He waited. After calling Tony's number again and hearing the phone go to voicemail, Daniel started the car and slowly drove down the street, stopping every so often to scan the sidewalk. Then he drove back to the office, where he parked Tony's car. He sat in his car and, after checking his phone, he closed his eyes. He tasted metal ... blood ... Tony was there ... As he awakened, he saw that the sky was lightening. He drove home.

In the parking garage, Daniel stashed all three guns under his seat and took the elevator to his apartment. On the short ride up, he closed his eyes, breathed deeply, and attempted to compose himself.

In answer to her question, he told Bianca that he was fine. He showered and changed his clothes, placing his bloody socks in the bathroom garbage pail. Then, as he drank the coffee that Bianca had made for him, he saw that her eyes were red and that she was sniffling.

"It was a very bad night. Things happened. I'm not hurt ... except for these little cuts and bruises on my face. Don't worry. I'll be able to get out of this business, all of it, pretty soon, as soon as I can, but not before our wedding."

"I was so scared. I was going crazy. I thought you were hurt, and then I thought ... I mean, I know a lot of the men ... they have other women—"

"That is never going to happen. It was business ... bad business. I don't know where Tony is. He might be dead. I can't tell you anything else."

"Oh, no. Be careful. No matter what you do, always come home to me."
*****

A couple of hours later, Daniel faced the fact that he could no longer put off telling Carmine De Luca what had happened, so he drove to the man's house. The new bodyguard/personal assistant, a man about Daniel's age named Enzo, let him in and said, "Can't bother Mr. De Luca. The old man's layin' down. He didn't come down to breakfast. He don't feel so good today. Somethin's botherin' him. He says I can't disturb him."

"Get him up now. We have important business to discuss. He'll want to talk to me." Daniel waited in the living room. He examined the photographs on the fireplace mantel. There was a new one: Carmine and Sophia De Luca, Tony, Valerie, and their children, and Giovanni and Victoria. No one was smiling.

"I imagine you have bad news to tell me," De Luca said as he entered the room. He looked unkempt.

Daniel looked down. De Luca headed toward the staircase to the basement. As Daniel followed, he thought of the first time he had been in this grand house. At the time, he had been in danger and he had been frightened. Now, he was as used to perilous situations as one can be. He was not concerned about his own safety, but that of De Luca because he was sure that, upon hearing what had happened to Tony, the man would suffer a heart attack.

De Luca, looking pale and weak, sat on a comfortable chair and pointed to the bar. Daniel declined the drink and sat opposite him. "Something happened last night. Tony is in danger ... he may be a captive of some very dangerous people or he may be dead."

"I know. Give me a moment to prepare for the details."

Daniel looked at the man. Then he looked down at his hands. He waited for De Luca to be ready. After De Luca sat a little deeper into his chair and wiped his eyes, he asked Daniel for a brandy. Daniel poured two and sat across from the man again. Then he told what had happened.

When Daniel finished talking, De Luca said, "Please don't say anymore. Let me think." De Luca closed his eyes. After a few seconds, he opened them and said, "When I was a boy, before the war, people on Elizabeth Street in Manhattan, where we lived, where we all lived, people used to refer to *La Mala Vita*. That's a term they used in Sicily. It refers to the way of life of the bad men who lived among us. My parents told me to stay away from them because knowing them would lead to tragedy. I chose this life, not because I wanted to be a criminal and not because I wanted great wealth or power. I told you what happened to my father. However, we thought the bad men we knew were better than the police, who were Irish, or the government or any of the others around us because they were our people. We understood them and we knew what they wanted. I have done a lot of good. I never let my men—when I was actually in charge—terrify or take advantage of poor people. I thought I was doing a good thing because I knew another man in my position may not have had my scruples. I guess my thinking was 'If I don't do it, another man worse than me will.'" He sipped his brandy. Then he pulled a handkerchief from his pocket and blew his nose. He looked at Daniel and then down to his drink. "Life is not black and white, you know. It is like this brandy. On a bright day, it shimmers and reflects the golden sunlight; in the shadows of afternoon, it appears to be darker than it really is; at night, it is bleak and inky. And now, I have lost my last child, the only one who speaks to me; worse than lost ... he is in the clutches of savages."

"We don't know that for sure."

"And you—you were in agreement with this scheme to make blood money by selling weapons to monsters who want to bring this country down?"

"No. I hated every second of it. I ... was ... I agreed to join Tony because, with or without me, he was going to do it."

"So, you thought as I did: 'If I don't do it, someone else who is worse than me will be willing.' Is that what you thought?"

"Yes, and I had other reasons, but I cannot say."

"I think I know," De Luca said.

The man's eyes drilled into Daniel. At that moment, Daniel was sure De Luca suspected that he was involved with the government."

"You want to get out of the business, so you thought this scheme, this evil plan would provide you with the money you need."

"No. That's not it. I think I am ready to move on, if that's possible, but that was not my reason. It has to do with a dark secret in my life."

"I don't want to know your secrets or your private grief. I have enough of my own. In the old days, once you had sworn the oath ... you know, *omertà*, you were committed for life, but now ... ah ... I must tell my wife about Antonio."

"Why don't you wait for another day?"

"No. Antonio's wife has called us three times. The last time, she was hysterical. She knew he was going to a dangerous meeting. She suspects he is dead. So does his mother. Women have that gift, that curse. Men rely on facts, and think they are in control of their fates. Women understand that we are all powerless in the face of destiny, and they have the ability to read the signs."

Daniel followed De Luca up the stairs.

At the door, the old man said, "Just stay with me long enough to mourn my son and to do what I should have done years ago."

"I will be here to help you for as long as you need me," Daniel said.

"I know. I should have always known that."

De Luca put a hand on Daniel's shoulder. It felt as light and insubstantial as a feather. Then the old man trained his wet, red-rimmed eyes on Daniel and said, "If I had pursued my dream of leaving behind all of this ... criminality and replacing those enterprises with legitimate ones, I would not have lost my children, my most, my *only* honorable achievements."

Daniel made his final trip to the FBI office in Manhattan to tell Canciello and Harris that it was over. A day before the bloody meeting in Newark, a private investigator Daniel had hired, Hyman Shaw, had reported to him that, months ago, the man in the sweat suit who had tried to kill him at that farm in upstate New York, Manny Friedman, had been arrested in the Bronx as he fled from a bank robbery in which a guard had been killed. Friedman had agreed to plead guilty to that crime and to others he had committed, including the murder of Mrs. Van Eyck, and to talk about the killing of Mr. Van Eyck in exchange for a lighter sentence. Since the FBI always investigated bank robberies, Daniel was sure that Canciello and Harris had known for a while about Friedman's testimony, but they had never said anything to Daniel about it. Instead, they had continued to hold over his head the possibility that he could still be prosecuted for the murders of the Van Eycks.

Daniel told Canciello and Harris about the botched deal and the shootings. He gave them the address of the building in Newark. He said that he hoped the FBI would be able to prosecute Colonel Bushwell and the weapons manufacturers involved in the arms deal without him because he did not want to testify. The agents, believing they had enough evidence to use against the conspirators, told Daniel that they doubted they would need him. They said that if they did, they would protect his identity, but Daniel did not trust them. He knew that, while they were allies of his, they were not concerned about his welfare. That was fine because he was not interested in them. He understood to whom he owed his allegiance and he clearly saw the direction in which his life was headed. He sighed with satisfaction because he believed he had finally achieved the sense of balance that had evaded him all of his life.

If Harris and Canciello were to need Daniel for a court appearance, they would have a difficult time reaching him because, shortly after he left their office, he went out on the fishing boat owned by one of his men, Benny Martelli. They sailed five miles out from Gerritsen Beach, where, without dropping anchor, Daniel tossed a plastic bag over the side. It contained the three pistols from the night of the arms deal and the special cell phone that he had used when he had to contact the agents. Then they took the long way back to the dock.

19

Beginnings and Endings

Daniel called Maria.

"Oh. On the beach. How nice," Maria said. "I hope you didn't call to invite me. I don't think I'd be able to handle it ... to watch you walk down the aisle with another woman, but I'm sure you'll be happy."

"No. I don't think I'd be able to handle it either. How are things going for you and ... Rafael? That's his name, right?"

"Yes. Well, I fin ... I said yes to Rafael. It's going to be a small wedding with just immediate family."

"That sounds nice. Bianca wants a big wedding. I really don't care."

"Good luck. Be happy, Daniel."

"You too."

*****

Daniel attempted to comfort Carmine De Luca during those first weeks after the disappearance of his son. Since no body had been found, they could not be sure of Tony's fate. Daniel lay awake for hours on many nights, picturing Tony being tortured in a dismal cellar or garage.

Months later, at the beginning of 2003, Carmine De Luca called for a meeting of the captains at his house. He did not offer food or drink. He told the men that, as of that day, Daniel Montello would be the unofficial "administrator" of the family's business. Daniel would make all of the decisions about which aspects of the family's operations would be retained and which would be phased out, to be replaced by legitimate businesses and investments. He assured the men that they would continue to earn good money, even if he had to pay them from his own substantial resources. The men grumbled, but they respected De Luca and accepted his decision.

Daniel put into action the metamorphosis of the family's enterprises, first by purchasing property throughout Brooklyn, Queens, and Manhattan because he believed that real estate in those parts of the city was guaranteed to appreciate in value. Then, at about the same time that United States military forces were searching Iraq for weapons of mass destruction, which were not there, and for Saddam Hussein, who was found hiding in a burrow, Daniel realized that the stock market was headed for the sky, so he invested millions of De Luca family money. He also bought into small businesses and encouraged their owners to expand. Within a few years, almost all of the investments of what became De Luca Assets had grown exponentially in value.

259

*****

The weather on the afternoon of Daniel and Bianca's wedding was threatening, but then, as the couple, the priest, the rabbi, and the guests made their way along the sand in Long Branch, stopping just a few yards from the pounding surf, the sky miraculously cleared. As Daniel stomped on the ceremonial glass and guests shouted "Mazel Tov!" the couple found themselves bathed in sparkling summer sunlight.

*****

As the years passed, despite the upward trajectory of the family's fortunes, a few of the captains continued to pursue criminal activities. Daniel persuaded the ones running gambling parlors to close them down and he told the men who continued to be involved in prostitution, narcotics, extortion, hijacking, and other more serious crimes that they were no longer part of De Luca Assets and could have no further contact with Carmine De Luca.

One of those men was Joe Galliano. In a previous era, he would have been referred to as a "Moustache Pete." At this point, 2007, he was a dinosaur.

"You know, this ain't right," Galliano told Daniel one day as they sat over coffee. "I went along with the boss when he wanted to go *legit*. I understand that idea. It's good to diversify, but I don't see how it makes sense to give up drugs and hookers and other money-makers. If we don't supply those things, then somebody else will: colored guys or Colombians or Chinese."

"That's true, Joe, but De Luca Assets is no longer involved in those activities, and we cannot maintain an association with people who are. It's as simple as that. I hope you can understand."

"I understand, but I don't like it. I was with the old man before you were born, and now, *you* are cutting me out? I don't think so!"

"Don't take it personally, Joe. Mr. De Luca values you and respects you, and I certainly do too, but I have been instructed by him to cut off all association with criminal activities. You will no longer be protected by his good name or his political or police contacts. It's the way he wants it. Not personal, just business."

"Yeah, and it's gonna be just business when you slip and fall and your skull gets cracked open some night. And I ain't gonna cry."

"I assume you're speaking hypothetically, Joe, because, you see, even though the business is 100% legitimate, the men who operate it, including me, are pretty careful and able to take care of themselves. We don't usually slip and fall, but when we do, we always find out the cause and we always do whatever we have to do to make sure it never happens again."

That conversation sparked a dusty, years-old memory. Perhaps because

Daniel had not felt threatened in a long time, he suddenly recalled the days after Jimmy's death, when he had felt guilty and vulnerable and imperiled. He remembered how difficult the everyday tasks of life had been and how he had not known how to come to terms with what had happened. He thought of Maria and their first few weeks together and the long black months of running and hiding and feeling abandoned and utterly alone.

It had been ... he could not remember how long it had been since he had spoken to Maria. Then their last conversation came to mind; it had been at some point before his wedding, more than four years ago.

Daniel dialed her number. When a little girl answered the phone, he assumed she was Maria's child. He asked to speak to Maria. He heard the phone clunk down. When a woman whose voice he did not recognize came on the line, he asked for Maria. The woman told him that he had the wrong number.

"I see. I want Maria Reyes. That's not her married name. I don't know what it is. Is this Maria's phone?"

"No. You called my number. I've had this number for about a year."

He called Maria's parents' number, but their phone was disconnected. When he called Pratt Institute, the woman with whom he spoke said that no one by that name was employed by the college. He persuaded her to check into whether anyone named Maria was on the faculty. After a few minutes, the woman said that she had not come up with anyone with that name on the college faculty or staff.

His next call was to Hyman Shaw, the private investigator. He told Shaw all that he knew about Maria: her maiden name, her birth date, her old address and phone number, her parents' information, and the fact that she had worked at the Pratt Institute library.

Daniel felt dejected. He thought about how odd it was to be upset and forlorn because he was unable to speak to someone he had not bothered to contact in years, someone who had not attempted to reach him in that length of time, a woman about whom he knew so little but understood so much. He felt that she was the lens through which he would be able to examine his life to determine how well or how poorly he had lived it to that point. He had an overwhelming need to connect with Maria so that he (and she) would understand what had happened. He wanted to talk with her about what they used to have and what they had lost and what they had gained in each other's absence.

As Daniel drove to his home in Brooklyn Heights that night, he wanted to tell Bianca that he had tried to reach out to Maria. He thought she would understand and not feel the least bit threatened. He loved Bianca as much as he

261

ever had and he knew that she loved him, but it was married love, which is a world apart from young love and first love and being madly in love. Unlike many of the men with whom he spent much of his time, both in and outside of De Luca Assets, Daniel had never felt the least temptation to stray. He and Bianca had a *safe*, loving, *safe*, happy, *safe* marriage and two children, Morton, two, who was named after Daniel's mother's father, and Angela, seven months old, who was named in honor of his father's mother, who had died a year after he and Bianca had gotten married. Since Bianca said she wanted at least two more children, she did not mind naming the first two after members of Daniel's family, as long as she could choose names for the next offspring.

Daniel finally decided not to tell Bianca about his attempts to reach Maria. Hyman Shaw, the investigator, called a couple of days later to say that he had located Maria; she was living in Manhattan. Her married name was Rosato and she had two children. Daniel called her immediately.

"Oh, my God! I can't believe it's you!" she screamed into the phone.

They talked for close to an hour. He said he would call again, promising that they would set up a time and place to meet for lunch or dinner. He told her that he wanted it to be without their spouses so that they could talk freely about their time together and what had happened over the years since then. However, although they talked again after that, they did not arrange to meet.

*****

It happened just as Joe Galliano had said it would. One night, as Daniel reached for the door handle of his car in the parking lot, the lights began to go out. In the second during which he felt the crushing blow to the back of his head, before he crashed to the ground, he knew that someone had clubbed him. Somehow, he had the strength to roll under his car before he fell into unconsciousness.

Two police officers who were riding past the parking lot said that when they saw two men reach under the car, they assumed they were trying to break into it. As the police car turned quickly into the parking lot with its lights flashing, the attackers fled on foot.

Daniel spent two days in the hospital. When Carmine De Luca, who was a frail 82 years old, visited Daniel, he said that when he heard about the attack, he felt almost as sick as when Tony disappeared, intoning, "may God bless and protect him and his everlasting soul."

"Do you know who did this terrible thing?" De Luca asked.

"No idea. Probably some kids who wanted to steal my car. Don't worry, Don De Luca. I'm fine. Thank you for visiting."

"The police said there was only one other car in the office parking lot that night. One of Joe Galliano's men. A man named Richie Merada. Was he in the office with you? I told Captain Butcher I would ask you."

Despite the pain radiating through his head, Daniel smiled.

Two months passed. Then, one night, Daniel and six men walked into the clothing shop that Joe Galliano used as his headquarters. As Galliano and the members of his crew, who were sitting at a table, looked in astonishment at the intruders, Daniel brought a chair over to them. He stared at Joe and his lieutenant, Arthur Mazzara, until they made room for him. Once he was seated, Daniel looked at each of the men at the table in turn before turning back to Joe.

Then he said, "A while back, when you predicted that I might slip and fall down some day, I told you, if that happened, we would find the cause and make sure it never happens again. Do you remember?"

When Joe remained silent, Daniel repeated the question. When Joe still did not answer, Daniel said, "If you're a man, you will answer. Maybe you'll deny we ever had the conversation. Maybe you'll spit in my face, but a real man would not sit and fail to respond to such a question."

Finally, Joe said, "Yeah. I remember. So what? If you think I had anything to do with that unfortunate situation of yours, you're wrong."

"That's all I wanted to know. I'm pleased to hear you say that."

Then Daniel stood up, put the chair back where he had found it, and began walking to the door. He reached for the door handle; then he stopped, turned around, and returned, saying, "Oh. Right. I should speak to Richard Merada before I go. You're Merada. Right?" Daniel said to one of the men.

"Yeah," said a heavily-built man. "So what."

"Oh, I guess your friends call you Richie. We've never talked and I'm not your friend, so I guess calling you Richie is out."

"I don't think we got anything to say to each other."

"We do. Had your car been stolen that night? The night I was clubbed? Or did you lend it to a friend? Or did you park it in my parking lot and then go for a walk and forget to pick it up for a couple of days?"

"Drop dead," the man said as he turned from Daniel.

Daniel smacked the back of Merada's head. The man stood up and faced Daniel. They stood toe to toe, Merada, angry and confused, Daniel, composed and calculating, his fists tight, his shoulders ready.

"So, Merada, what's it going to be? I'll move back so you can swing freely at me, or is it too hard for you to hit a man who's looking at you?"

When Merada did not move, Daniel turned to the other men at the table, and asked, "Which one of you slimy bastards was in the parking lot with Richie Merada that night? I may as well smack both of you around at the same time. You see, since Mr. Galliano denies he had anything to do with it, I'll have to teach little Richie here and his partner a lesson."

"You're nuts, Montello," Galliano said. "Nobody here wants to hurt you. Go home before we end up smacking *you* around."

"Well, we know *you're* not going to get hurt, Joe. You're good at giving orders, and then you hide out like a weak little girl."

Just then, one of the men at the table reached into his jacket. Daniel zeroed in on him, saying, "You're betting my men aren't armed, right?" The other men sitting at the table kept their hands in sight. The one who had reached into his jacket put his hands on the table. Richard Merada looked worried. Joe Galliano, who was attempting to appear to be unconcerned, was perspiring.

"Let me explain," Daniel said. "This little criminal crew is finished. Carmine De Luca no longer protects you. The only reason you men are still walking the streets is that I haven't used my contacts with the police to put you out of business and in jail. Tomorrow, I will do that." Then, turning to the man in front of him, who had backed up a few steps, Daniel said, "Okay. Last time, Little Richie, who is the other piece of crap who was with you that night? The truth will set you free ... in fact, if you open up, *I* will set you free."

"I was there," said another man. "I didn't want to do it. Joe forced me."

"Well, I guess that happens. You're ... Mario Vitelli. Right?"

"Yeah. I am."

"Okay, Mario, you get to go home. Go! Now!"

The man walked quickly to the door and out to the street.

"Now, Little Richie Merada, time is money. Take a swing at me. Nobody's going to interfere. It's now or never."

"I ain't gonna swing. I'm sorry. I was just following orders."

"If you were a student of history, you would know what a pathetic, inadequate excuse that is. However, since you're clearly an idiot, I accept your apology. Go! Now. Get the hell out of here."

Merada walked out of the shop.

"The rest of you, go. If I see any of you anywhere near me at any time without my permission, I will kick your asses until you're not able to sit for a week, and then I will make a phone call to Captain Butcher in the precinct here. You'll all be in jail the same day."

As the men stood up to leave, Daniel said to one of them, "Not you." When the man sat down, Daniel said, "Well, Joe Fish, we have a long history together, beginning with when you were attempting to track me down and get me killed. Funny that we haven't talked much to each other all these years."

When Joe Fish remained silent, Daniel said, "I guess you haven't learned anything tonight, so let me spell it out for you: if you refuse to talk, you will stay here until my men and I are done with you, and then I'll make sure you spend time in jail. When you tell me the truth, you can go on with your life."

"Right. I understand. It's just business. I was told to track you down. You know that. It wasn't personal. Nothing happened to you. Right?"

"A great deal happened to me. Let's say that your phone calls and your wrong information changed my life. Now you have a chance to change yours."

"What do you want to know?" Joe Fish asked.

"Who told you I had killed Jimmy?"

Joe Fish looked at Daniel and then at Joe Galliano and then at the men standing behind Daniel. Finally, he said, "It was Dominic Savarino."

"And who else? Time for the truth now."

"And Mike Morici."

"And? I don't want to ask you again."

"And Joe here. Joe Galliano. They told me to tell Mr. De Luca."

"You see how easy that was? Now, go home. Don't come back here."

After Joe Fish made a hurried exit from the room, Daniel sat down next to Joe Galliano again and focused on the man's face with laser-like intensity. First, Galliano tried to outstare Daniel, then he turned away, looked down, and busied himself adjusting his tie and smoothing down his shirt, leaving wet spots on both. Then he smiled nervously at Daniel.

Turning around, Daniel said, "Okay, boys, you may as well go home. Joe and I have to conduct some important business. By the way, this is never going to happen again. We're not gangsters. We're businessmen. This was a one-time operation." Then, as the men started to leave, Daniel said, "One more thing ... show Mr. Galliano here what you have under your coats. Show him."

As Joe Galliano gripped the arms of his chair, the men held open their jackets to show that they were unarmed.

Once they were alone, Daniel asked Joe, "How much money do you have? I mean in savings ... liquid assets?"

"You're not gonna shake me down. I won't allow it," Joe replied.

"No, Joe. I don't need your money and I don't want your money. While you've been earning thousands on drugs and prostitution and all that, the rest of us have been making millions ... legally. You've been too busy with your head up your ass to notice. I am asking how much money you have because that's your retirement package. You are retired as of tonight. Now."

"Yeah? How's that gonna happen?"

"Simple ... if any of my men or I see you—I'll give you, let's say two days—any time after that, I will personally pick you up, put a bullet in your brain, or at least where your brain should be, and drop you off on that beach where those guys you hired were going to kill me all those years ago."

Joe was clearly astonished.

"Joe, Joe, do you think I'm blind? I know you and Mike Morici were tight as thieves. That's funny because, at the time, every man in the family was a thief. In any case, I know you and Mike, with Carmine's grudging approval *after the fact*, were the ones who arranged for me to be grabbed that night. And you're probably the one who met with those two contract killers who ended up killing that old farm couple. And you're the one who called me when I was on the run to tell me that you saw a story about me on the news about that double murder. You see how controlled I am? I could have gone after you years ago, but I figured it was over. All's well that ends well ... at least that's how it's going to be for us, Joe."

"Oh, yeah? What are you going to do? I still have my men."

"No. You won't as of tomorrow. I'm going to contact each one of them and offer legal jobs in our organization. If they try to stay out on the street, as I said, I'll contact my friends in the police department and make sure those men end up in jail. That's how I knew it was Richie Merada's car. You see, the precinct captain is our friend because we donate to all the police charities. I can call him whenever I need help."

*****

Over the next few years, De Luca Assets continued to prosper and grow. Carmine De Luca, who never fully recovered from the loss of his son, died from a heart attack, as Tony had predicted he would one day. Carmine's final words to Sophia were, "I should have been a better boy." She dabbed at her eyes and told people that he had confused the last word, that he had meant to say "man," but Daniel understood what he had meant, thinking, *after all, that's when it all begins ... when we're boys*. Daniel wished he had been there to comfort the old man during his last moments by telling him about how well the company was doing and how many people it employed.

When the economy began losing steam in the middle of 2008, Daniel sold his vacation home in Key Biscayne, his townhouse in Manhattan, and his brand new Bentley. He began selling company-owned stock and real estate, cutting executive salaries, including his own, and finding ways for the still healthy conglomerate that he operated to economize. De Luca Assets weathered the storm without laying off a single employee.

Near the end of 2012, when Daniel finally got around to calling Maria again, he heard a message saying that her phone number was no longer in use. A Google search led him to a site that listed a Maria Reyes Rosato of the right age living in Ship Bottom, New Jersey. The woman who answered the phone sounded like a much older, sadder version of the Maria he had known; the frail, whispered voice seemed to come from a cold, dismal, distant place. He cursed himself for allowing so much time to pass.

"How did you get my number?"

"Google is amazing. You can find out anything. How are you?"

"I'm a mess. My life is a mess. I don't want to talk about it. In fact, I took comfort in the fact that nobody would ever be able to find me here."

"What happened, Maria? Please tell me."

After a bit of hesitation, she told him that her marriage had been a mistake from the beginning and that it was over now ... had been for a couple of years. When Daniel heard those words, his stomach dropped. Why had he waited so long to reach out to her?

"He was ... is a controlling, self-centered, evil bastard," Maria said. "He ruined my life. I don't know what I was thinking when I married him. All the signs were there. I just didn't want to see them."

"That's awful," Daniel said.

"How's Bianca?"

"She's fine. We're fine."

"And your children? You have two, right?" she asked.

"Actually, four now. They're great. How are yours?" Daniel said.

Maria hesitated before she answered. "I have ... had ... have two. It's a long story. I can't get into it now."

"Let's meet. Let's set it up now, Maria. I really want to see you. I want to hear ... you sound so sad. I want to talk to you ... help you, if I can."

"You can't. I don't want to see you ... anybody from my old life."

Then let's talk. I have plenty of time. Do you have time now?"

"Sure. I have more time than I know what to do with." She told Daniel that when she and Rafael were engaged and she told him she was quite sure she did not want children, he made it clear that he did. She fooled herself into thinking it was a problem that they would be able to amicably resolve once they were married. She also believed she would be able to smooth down all of his rough edges as easily as she would be able to decorate whatever apartment or house in which they decided to live.

The first year was good. She admired Rafael for all of his good qualities and ignored his flaws; she believed he loved her, although he rarely said it. She never said that she loved him ... she just could not get the words out of her mouth. However, he worked hard, brought home a good salary, treated her with respect, and took her on nice vacations. Their sex life was troubling because he wanted her every night. She complied, but rarely enjoyed it.

By the beginning of their second year of marriage, Rafael began pressuring her to become pregnant. When she told him that she still thought she did not want children, he became insistent, repeatedly asking, "If you're not going to bear my children, why the hell did I marry you?"

That summer, he gave her an ultimatum: she either agreed to have his children or they should separate. She was so upset that she was ready to move out of the house, but then he told her that they should stop talking about it and "let nature take its course." He said he had arranged for them to cruise the Caribbean on a yacht that he would pilot—he was an expert sailor.

They both took time off from work and flew down to Key West, where they boarded the yacht and set sail. The first day was wonderful. That evening, under a balmy, star-studded sky, he dropped anchor near a small island and they ate a light meal accompanied by two bottles of wine. When they retired to the stateroom, he began kissing and fondling her. She asked him to wait while she prepared. She searched her suitcase, becoming more and more frantic when she was not able to find her diaphragm—she had stopped using birth control pills because of a skin reaction. She was sure she had packed it. Rather than saying what she thought, she returned to bed and told Rafael they would have to dock at the island the next day to purchase condoms or, if she could find a gynecologist, she would obtain a prescription for a new diaphragm.

Rafael, who was tipsy—or pretending to be—resumed his ardent kissing and touching, which she attempted to control. Then he pulled down her panties and forced himself into her. Even though he promised that he would not, he ejaculated into her. Then, after Maria had extricated herself, Rafael threw an arm over her and would not allow her to move for hours. Each time she attempted to get out of bed so that she could shower in what she knew would be a futile attempt to wash his semen out of her, he awakened and held her tight.

Neither one spoke of the incident the next morning. When she asked Rafael to sail to a port, he told her that he had just the place in mind. Hours later, as evening fell, he dropped anchor a mile from another island, saying he was not sure where the dock was. He asked her to prepare dinner, promising that he would look for it in the morning.

That night, when he attempted to have sex with her, she struggled. He held her wrists and ejaculated into her again. He did that several more times— Maria could not remember how many—during the next four days before he docked the yacht at Kingston, Jamaica. At one point that day, while they were shopping for supplies, she bolted out of the store they were in and ran for several blocks before, exhausted and hysterical, she stopped. She had only a few dollars and a credit card. She used the cash to pay for a taxi to the airport, where she bought a ticket with the card, and flew home.

"When he arrived a week later, tanned and rested, I was pretty sure I was pregnant. I told him to find another place to stay, but he told me he owned the apartment and he was staying. Then he apologized and said that he loved me. I was tired and depressed and confused, so I just gave in to him."

"I'm so sorry, Maria," Daniel said.

"I am too. Do you want to hear the rest of this pathetic story?"

"Only if you want to tell me."

"Who else would I tell? No one, except for Rafael, knows."

She gave birth to a beautiful girl who they named Regina. Even though Maria loved her baby, each time she held her she thought of how Regina had been conceived, and she felt violated all over again.

Rafael convinced her to quit her job. She became an unenthusiastic full-time mother. Her parents and siblings loved Regina. That made Maria happy.

Then, when Regina was 18 months old, Rafael, who had repeatedly apologized for what he had done during their Caribbean "vacation," began pressuring her to become pregnant again. When she refused, he told her that he would give her time to think it over, saying that Regina should have at least one brother or sister so that she would not have to grow up alone.

One night a couple of months later, he straddled her and, without one word of discussion, he pulled down her underwear, entered her, and ejaculated. Maria said he must have known her cycle because he hit the nail on the head— she was pregnant again. This time, she had a boy. They named him Roberto.

"I tried really hard to be a good mother, but I guess it's not in my DNA. I was very depressed and so tired that I used to doze off during the middle of the day when the kids were up and around. Nothing ever happened to them, but Rafael knew that I was not a super mom. We had a cleaning woman, but, even so, I couldn't keep up. He told me that being a mother and housewife was my full-time job. He also said that he wanted at least two more children. More than once, I thought about leaving him, but I didn't have the strength or the will to do it. I used to cry ... a lot and I began taking Prozac and a couple of other medications just to be able to cope.

"The next summer, we rented a house in East Hampton. We went to the beach every day. Rafael was there most of the time, but one day, he had to return to the city for work. As the kids played near me, I read ... it was my third romance novel of the week ... reading them had become a kind of obsession. I dozed off. When I woke up, the kids were gone. I searched for them everywhere, but they were gone. I was frantic. I found a police officer, and he called it in. Then he told me they were at the hospital. When we got there, Regina was sitting with a social worker. Roberto was in a room under observation. He had gone into the water. A big wave caught him and threw him down on his head. Somebody pulled him out and called for help. He suffered a minor concussion. No permanent injury. After a night at the hospital, I brought them back to the beach house the next day."

Maria said that when she arrived at the house with the children, Rafael was there. He had been panic-stricken trying to find out where they had been all night. Maria had turned off her phone when she arrived at the hospital and had not turned it back on. She had been afraid to tell Rafael what had happened, so, thinking he was in the city, she had not called him. He became furious when she told him about the accident. He said Maria had wanted Roberto—and maybe Regina too—to be killed because she wanted to drown their marriage. She said he looked as if he was going to hit her, but he did not. Instead, he went into another room and made some phone calls. Then he told Maria that he was going back to the city with the children and that she should stay at the beach house for a couple of days. That afternoon, after drinking an entire bottle of wine, Maria was awakened from a nap by the doorbell. A detective was there. He asked whether he could come into the house to question her about the accident. An hour later, before he left, he told Maria that she should hire an attorney.

"I was frantic ... I wasn't drunk or anything, but that detective smelled the wine ... that came up later. I'll get back to that in a second ... Anyway, I called Rafael, but he didn't answer his phone. He had driven the car back to Manhattan, so I had to take a taxi to the train and go back to the city that way.

"When I walked into our apartment, Rafael asked me what I was doing there. We argued. I cried. He told me I couldn't stay and I couldn't see our children. He said I was an unfit mother." After she said that, Maria sobbed and took some time catching her breath. Then she continued: "I told him that since we were married the apartment was also mine and the children were certainly mine as much as his. Then he put his hands on my throat and said some crazy things about how I had wanted to kill Roberto so that the family line wouldn't continue. Honestly, if it had been Regina who had gotten hurt, he wouldn't have been as upset. You know ... these old-world men and their sons."

"I don't know what to say."

"You know, it's ironic ... I've read about you several times. You're a very up-and-coming entrepreneur; you're no longer involved in that other business. I'm glad for you. I just wish you had done that sooner ... when we were together."

"Don't think that way. It took years, and some very bad things happened during that time. You would have been miserable. I didn't deserve you."

"Don't. Please don't say that, Daniel. Who the hell knows who deserves who and why these things happen in people's lives?" Then Maria started to cry. After a few seconds, she said she had to go.

"No. Don't go. My heart is breaking. I want to see you. I want to give you a hug and help you. Sounds like you need a friend."

"I need more than a friend, Daniel. I need to rewind my life. I need to ... I don't know. It all seems so pointless."

"Don't say that. I'll visit you. I'll take you out for lunch. We'll talk. Are you working? Are you working as a librarian?"

"Yes. I work here. It's not much of a job, but I don't need much money, so it's okay. It's the times off from work that are hard. Now, that's pretty ironic too ... remember how upset I used to be because you were out so much and I was alone in that little apartment in Brooklyn? What I wouldn't give to be back to that time and place now, but that's not how life works, is it?"

"No. When it comes to the past, all you can do is be happy for the good things and regret the bad ones, but you can't ... I can't go back."

"Right. I feel better. Thanks for calling, Daniel. You'll always be very special to me. You're my best ... actually, my only friend."

"I'll call you again. We'll really get together this time."

"No. I enjoyed talking to you. Call me again, if you want, but I don't want to see you ... at least, not now. I need to be alone for a while longer."

"Don't hesitate to call if ... when you need to speak to me."

"Okay. I will."

Daniel mourned what he and Maria had lost.

20
Looking to the Future

Captain Butcher from the 62nd police precinct in Bensonhurst called Daniel to ask him to drop by the station in reference to a man named Joe Galliano. When Daniel asked what had happened, the captain said, "I'd rather not discuss it on the phone, but it's important. Can you make it in here today?"

Daniel, who had recently moved the headquarters of De Luca Assets to Manhattan, left his office immediately and drove to the police station. He was annoyed because now, years after the family had become totally legitimate and had pumped hundreds of millions of dollars into New York City's economy as a whole and several million specifically into businesses in Bensonhurst, he was still thought of as a "former *mafia* associate." However, as he drove through the old neighborhood, which he had not visited in years—at the same time that he and Bianca had sold their Brooklyn Heights brownstone and moved to a townhouse in Manhattan he had purchased a house for his parents in Howard Beach, Queens—he was overwhelmed with nostalgia. Most of the stores—many still operated by the same people from when he had been a child—were unchanged; the smells—mostly tomato sauce, garlic, and fresh bread—were unchanged; the sounds—music, the screeching and scraping of train wheels on elevated tracks, the honking of horns—were unchanged. However, the people looked different; although plenty of Italian-Americans and Jews still lived there, the neighborhood was now home to thriving, upwardly mobile Chinese and Hispanic populations. He had heard about that, but had been too busy to visit and see it for himself.

When he entered the police station, several officers glared at him. The desk sergeant, a ruddy-faced man named Leary, asked him to wait because the captain was at a meeting. Daniel looked at his watch. Then, forcing himself to relax, he smiled as he remembered.

When he was nine years old, he and a friend had bicycled to the New Utrecht branch of the library, which was several blocks from his home, to do some after-school research. When they emerged, Daniel's bicycle was gone. His friend—he could not remember who it had been—rode home on his bike, leaving Daniel, so he walked to this precinct to report the robbery, only to be told that it was unlikely he would ever see his bicycle again. However, a few days later, a police officer called his house to say that they had found a bicycle in the street and had brought it to the station. After Daniel had run the distance to the police station and told the desk sergeant why he was there, the man asked him to describe the bicycle. Daniel had shot out a detailed description, down to the rust spot on the rear wheel frame. When the police officer handed the bicycle over to Daniel, he had said, "Buy a chain and a lock."

Daniel had said, "Thank you, sir. Now I know why they call you New York's Finest."

"Well, not many people around here smile like that."

Daniel looked up to see that the voice interrupting his recollection belonged to Captain Butcher. They walked to his office, where he offered Daniel a cup of coffee. Then he closed the door and sat at his desk.

"You know, Joe Galliano, right?"

Daniel said that he did, although he had not seen him in years.

"Did you see the news today?" the captain asked.

"No. I've been busy. Why? What happened?"

"Two of our men were found shot to death in a storefront that we believe this Joe Galliano has been using to conduct his business."

"Oh. I'm sorry. As I said, I haven't seen or talked to him in years."

"Be that as it may, perhaps you can help us locate him for questioning."

Daniel said he would like to do so, but did not know where to look.

"Friends? Associates? Relatives? Anybody would help."

Daniel wrote down the names of the men who, at one time, had been in Galliano's crew. After the confrontation in the store that night, Galliano had disappeared. Daniel had sent men into the wider neighborhood on a weekly basis for a couple of months in an attempt to make sure Galliano had actually left. Only two of Galliano's men had taken jobs with De Luca Assets, but they ended up quitting a short time later. The others had melted into the background.

"That's it," Daniel said, handing the list of names to Captain Butcher.

The captain said, "You have my number. Call me day or night. We really want this guy, *whatever* it takes."

When he was back in his car, Daniel called George Salerno, who was a vice president at De Luca Assets, and asked, "Do you have any idea where Joe Galliano is? He may have killed a couple of cops."

"That's bad. I don't know. Don't know ... and I don't know who would know. I think I remember hearing he moved to California someplace. That was a while ago. Sorry. You coming back to the office today?"

"I don't know. How about Joe Fish?"

"Him? No. Don't know. I never liked that guy. But why are you getting involved in this? Let the cops find Galliano."

"No, George. This is something I have to do."

"Why?"

"It's because I didn't do what I should have done years ago. I trusted that snake to slither away. Besides, even if the cops find him, which I doubt, they probably won't be able to bring him in or make a case against him. I'm sure he's covered his tracks. I know this guy. I have to take care of this. It's the final part of closing out the books on the old family so that the new family is safe."

After Daniel hung up, he drove to Manhattan, but instead of returning to his office in the Financial District, he headed to midtown, parked in a garage, and walked to the FBI building to talk to Agents Harris and Canciello. Harris was there, in a new office. He recognized Daniel immediately and greeted him like a long-lost friend.

"Looks like you've moved up in the world, Harris. Nice office."

"Yeah. I'm a supervisor now. So, what can I do for you?"

"I need a phone number or a location," Daniel said.

"Of?"

"Joe Galliano. He's a former member of the family, the De Luca family, from when we ... it was in crime."

"I thought you were out of that business. I've seen your picture in the paper at society gatherings and things like that. In fact, didn't they write an article about you in *Forbes* a while back?"

"Yes. Things have worked out well. I'm on a few boards and my wife and I go to those boring cocktail parties every so often."

"You still live in Brooklyn?"

"No. We live here in Manhattan."

"I'm sure it's in the best part of town. So, why do you want Galliano?"

"He may have killed a couple of cops. I want to help the cops find him, but I don't know where to look," Daniel replied.

"You should let them do it. They'll probably find him before you do."

"I doubt it. Besides, I can't sit this one out. I have to find him."

"Don't tell me anything else. I don't want to know. I'll check the database," Harris said as he turned to his computer and began typing. As Daniel waited, he remembered sitting for hours, in handcuffs, in a barren office similar to this one. Finally, Harris read off, "Joseph Anthony Galliano, age 68; last known address: Blue Moon Motel, Los Angeles, California. Want the address?"

"No. How about Joe Fish?"

"Oh. That was Canciello's man on the inside. Right?"

"Yes. How is Canciello?"

"He's down there in DC. I haven't spoken to him in ... more than a year."

"Can you give me Joe Fish's information?"

"I'll do better than that. I'll call Canciello right now."

After Harris exchanged pleasantries with Canciello, he passed the phone to Daniel, who got right to the point.

"Why do you want to contact Joe Fish?" Canciello asked.

Daniel explained the situation. Canciello said, "You know, Harris probably didn't say anything to you about it—he's too nice—but we almost pulled you in again. We know you kept working for the De Luca family after we cut you loose. We thought we'd hear from you."

Annoyed by what Canciello had said, Daniel replied, "That was to turn around the family. I'm not in that life anymore. You know that, and if you don't, ask Harris. He reads about me in the society pages. This is to catch a cop killer."

Canciello said that he would email to Harris all of the information he had on Joe Fish, explaining that he had not spoken to him in a long time.

Rather than returning to his office, Daniel headed straight to the address Canciello had sent, the VA nursing home in Lyons, New Jersey.

Daniel gasped when he approached Joe Fish, not so much because of his flaccid gray skin, but because of the strong, offensive odor emanating from him as he sat in a wheelchair in a small, dimly lit recreation room. The several days of gray stubble on Joe's face did not enhance his appearance.

Daniel brought a chair to Joe and sat next to him. When Joe looked at Daniel, at first, he did not recognize him. Then he smiled, revealing the fact that he was mostly toothless. He coughed. Then he held up a hand and coughed again. After catching his breath, he wiped his mouth with a tissue.

"I remember you," Joe managed to blurt out before he was overcome with a spasm of moist-sounding coughs. Then he loudly cleared his throat, spit into a tissue, and said, "Once I do that—cough and clear out my lungs—I'm okay ... at least for a while."

"Joe ... I ... I'm glad to see you." Then, handing a package to him, Daniel said, "Look what I brought for you. Go ahead. Open it."

It was a navy blue fleece robe and matching slippers. Joe rubbed his palms over the soft fabric and then he wiped his eyes with a hand.

"You know ... I been here a year, and you're my first visitor."

"That's too bad, Joe."

"I'm lucky to be in this place. As crappy as it is, it beats livin' on the street, and I'm a veteran ... Vietnam. I was a good soldier. They take good care of me here, unlike other people who will remain nameless."

"I called you and offered you a job, Joe ... back then."

"I know. I didn't want that. I didn't know anything besides hijacking and extortion and all that crap. I knew I wouldn't fit in a nine-to-five job."

"What about your specialty? You know, *Joe Fish, go fish?*"

"Yeah. I was good at that."

"I'll bet you still are, Joe."

"Naw. I can't get around so good. Besides the breathing problems, my legs ain't so good anymore. That's why I'm in this chair."

"You still have it where it matters," Daniel said, tapping Joe's head.

"Maybe, but who needs me now?"

"I do. I want to hire you to help me to find someone. Here. Take this."

Joe's eyes widened as he stared at the crisp bills. After looking around to make sure no one else had seen the money, he took it from Daniel and pushed it into a pocket in his pajamas. Then he patted the pocket.

When Daniel said, "I need to find Joe Galliano," Joe Fish broke into a smile. He sat back in his chair and started to laugh, only to be interrupted by another paroxysm of heavy coughing that turned his face fiery red.

Once the coughing stopped, he said, "I woulda helped you find that son of a bitch without the money, but a deal's a deal, so I'm keeping the *moolah.*"

"Of course, Joe. This is business. Where is he?"

"That bastard turned his back on me. I told him I'd stick with him— mostly because he owed me a lot of money—but, as I said, I ... Wait! I gotta cough again." He coughed, cleared his throat, and then resumed talking, sounding a bit out of breath. "As I said, I didn't know no other life, but, after I talked to Galliano, he left town. Gone. But I wanted my money, so I found him in L.A. Then he came back to the city ... Flushing ... in Queens. If you give me a second, I'll go into my card catalogue to retrieve the address."

Daniel stood up and pushed his chair aside so that Joe would be able to move, but he did not budge. Instead, he closed his eyes so tightly that all Daniel saw were slits; then he pressed his fingertips to his temples. Then he smiled.

"Accessed! You got paper? Wait. I got my pad." He reached into a pocket and pulled out a creased, torn red memo pad of the type Daniel remembered using in school to write down homework assignments. Using a broken pencil stub, Joe wrote down an address, saying, "This is it. Don't remember the phone number."

After looking at what Joe had written, Daniel put the scrap of paper in a pocket. Then he thanked Joe, stood up, and walked to the door of the little room.

"You gonna come back to visit me again?"

"Yes. I will," Daniel said, telling himself that he would.

It was dark by the time Daniel reached Flushing. He stopped at a pizzeria and ordered a mushroom pie. Then he stopped at a liquor store and bought a cold six-pack of Bud. He drove to the address that Joe had given to him. It was a six-story apartment building. He parked, entered the building, and took the elevator to the sixth floor. After looking at the name tag on a nearby apartment door, he knocked on Joe Galliano's door. He held the pizza box and six-pack up so that they hid his face. He heard the sound of someone leaning against the door and sliding the cover to the peephole.

"Who's there. Whadda ya want?"

"Pizza delivery ... and beer for ... let me see ... Bukowski. It's all paid for. My boss told me to just deliver it to ... ah ... Bukowski. Are you Bukowski?" Daniel asked in what he hoped was a convincing delivery man voice.

As the door opened, Daniel pushed the pizza and beer into Galliano's outstretched arms; then he shoved the man into the apartment and closed the door behind them. Then he pushed Joe again, causing the man to lose his balance. The six-pack clunked to the floor.

"Hey! What the hell? Get outta here! I got a gun," Joe bellowed.

"And I have the drop on you, Joe," Daniel said in a calm voice. "Sit down. We have to talk. No violence. I'm not here to hurt you."

"You! You son of a bitch, get the hell outta here!"

"I will when I'm done. Nice little place you have here," Daniel said as he took in the squalid, messy apartment. "Although, it could use a cleaning."

"Okay. No small talk. Say what you gotta say, and then go."

"I will. Why don't we sit at that table and eat together? I haven't eaten since breakfast, I think. I've been on the go all day, Joe."

"Naw. Take the pizza and beer and get the hell—"

"No, Joe. This is how it's going to be: we're going to talk. You don't want to eat the pizza or drink the beer, that's up to you. We're going to talk, and then I'll leave ... and if I have to slap you around first, I'll do that."

Within seconds, the expression on Joe's face transformed in such a way as to remind Daniel of a game he used to play with his father when he was a child: his father would cover his face with his hands, and then take them away to reveal a funny expression, and then cover his face again and remove his hands to expose a different face, and so on. Joe's face changed from angry to offended to confused to resigned before Daniel's eyes. Then he brought the pizza to the kitchen table. Daniel picked up the six-pack and placed it next to the pizza box.

"I don't got no napkins or clean dishes," Joe said as he sat, opened the box, grabbed a slice, smiled, and ravenously bit off a huge mouthful. Then he

277

put the slice down on the filthy table, yanked a can of beer from the plastic holder, popped it open, and, without waiting for it to stop fizzing, inhaled half of it. Then he put it down and attacked the pizza again.

Daniel took a beer and slowly sipped. He waited until Joe had polished off three slices of pizza before he said, "You always liked mushroom."

After wiping his mouth with the back of his hand and licking sauce from his fingers, Joe said, "Yeah. I'm touched you remember. How come you ain't eating? You didn't put somethin' in the friggin' pizza, did ya?"

"No, Joe. I bought it down the street."

"Lemme see you eat a slice."

"Sure, Joe, but if I had put something it in, you'd be dead by now."

Daniel slowly nibbled a slice of pizza. That encouraged Joe to quickly gobble down another slice and gulp down two more beers. Daniel waited. He knew that he held the higher ground. The longer he kept Joe waiting, the stronger his position would be when he began questioning the man.

When Joe had satisfied his hunger and thirst, he belched, looked at Daniel, and said, "You've been doin' all right for yourself."

"Yes I have, Joe. Can't say the same for you. This place is a sty."

"Yeah. I know. I can't seem to keep a cleaning girl. They do a good job and then I screw them and they all wanna move in with me."

"I don't believe any of that. It's obvious you've hit the end of the road."

"Oh, yeah? That's how much you know."

"How much do you have in your wallet, Joe?"

"Plenty!"

"More than me?" Daniel asked.

"Guaranteed."

"Okay. Here's a bet. Are you still a betting man?"

"I am if I like the odds."

"Okay, Joe. You're sure you have more cash than I do. I'll give you what's in my wallet if you have more than me. And, to sweeten the pot, I'll give you this Rolex. It's not my best one, but it's very nice."

"Naw. I don't wanna take your money."

"Now, you see, Joe ... you just lied. You're the kind of man who will take anything at any time and never think twice about it."

"You don't know me, Mr. Big Shot."

"Oh, but I do, Joe. Do you need to use the bathroom?"

"What're you mean? Do I smell like I need to use the bathroom?"

"You do smell ... or maybe it's just this apartment. Whatever. If you don't need to use the bathroom, let's go."

"Go? Where?"

"For a ride in my car."

As Daniel said that, Joe shot a glance to the sofa in the adjoining room.

"Come on, Joe. We'll talk in the car," Daniel said as he stood up.

After waiting a second, Joe stood up and said, "I do have to go to the bathroom after all. Give me a second." Then he walked toward the sofa.

"On the sofa, Joe? That's disgusting. Isn't the bathroom down there?"

"Yeah. I have to get something."

As Joe reached under the sofa cushion, coming up with a pistol, Daniel quickly moved to the man and punched him hard on the side of his head, knocking him down. The pistol fell and skittered along the parquet floor.

"What're you doin'? Get outta here!" Joe yelled from the floor.

"Sorry, Joe. I hope I didn't hurt you. Stand up. I won't hit you again."

Joe slowly got to his feet, keeping his eyes on the gun the entire time.

"I'll put my hands behind my back. I really have to learn how to control my temper. I wouldn't blame you if you wanted to take a swing at me."

"Naw. You're younger and stronger than me. You'd just end up breaking my jaw. In fact, if you do that, I'll make sure you're charged for it."

"Have it your way. We're going to the police. We'll leave the gun here for them to pick up later," Daniel said as he reached for Joe's shoulders.

"Yeah? I know a thing about the law," Joe said as he backed away from Daniel. "That would holding me against my will. You ain't no cop. You can't do that. I'm staying right here."

"Maybe you're right, Joe. I'll just call 911 right now."

"Then we'll see who's in more trouble ... me or you."

"You're right. We'll just have to see, but, you know what? I want to be fair. As I said, I'll keep my hands behind my back. Take a swing at me. Maybe you'll knock me down. Then you can make your getaway. Go ahead. This is your one and only chance. If you don't, I'll make that call. Take a shot, Joe, if you're man enough. Swing away!"

"You're nuts, Montello." Then Galliano lashed out, connecting with Daniel's jaw. Daniel, who had kept his hands down, quickly brought them up; he shook his head and then he threw a hard right to Joe's jaw. Joe went down, landing a foot from the pistol. Daniel quickly kicked the gun into a corner of the room. Then, smiling, he dialed his phone.

A few minutes later, when Joe was able to speak, he said, "You didn't have to do that. Let me go. I'll make it worth your while."

"This *is* worth my while. I hope that snub-nosed 38 on the floor is the one you used to kill those cops."

"It ain't mine. Honest. I found it under the couch when I moved in," Joe bawled from the floor.

"We'll let the police decide whose gun it is. Oh, by the way, if you even try to move or get up, I will kick the living shit out of you."

A few minutes later, Daniel let two police officers with guns drawn and two EMTs into the apartment. Joe was still on the floor. Daniel told the EMTs to take care of Joe first, saying that he was only bruised. They knelt down next to Galliano and evaluated his injuries. While they were doing that, Daniel explained to the police officers that the man on the floor had assaulted him and then pulled a pistol from under the sofa, at which point, he had punched the man. He also told them that he had called Captain Butcher from the 62nd precinct, and that he would be arriving shortly. One of the police officers told Daniel to sit and not talk. Then he put on a pair of search gloves and picked up the pistol while the other officer called in a report to their precinct.

When Captain Butcher, two of his officers, and two detectives from the local precinct walked in, Joe Galliano said, "This is illegal. You can't do nothin' to me. You can't use that gun. I don't even know how it got here."

"I'm sure we can, Galliano," Captain Butcher said. "I would imagine Mr. Montello here, who seems to have been injured, will be willing to testify as to what happened here. In any case, I have a warrant for your arrest."

"That's it? That's bullshit. All of it's bullshit!"

"That's all life is sometimes," Captain Butcher said.
*****

"I want to see you ... I mean I guess you can come see me, if you want," Maria said when Daniel picked up the phone.

"I can't this week. I have an important conference in Chicago. I have to be there. I was supposed to have left yesterday, but we can talk now, on my way to the airport. When I get back, I'll drive down to you. I'll stay with you for the day. If you want, I'll get a hotel room and stay a couple of days."

"Okay, but I don't want to bother you now. You can call this number some other time. It's a new number. I didn't want anyone else to call me."

"Stay on the line. I want to talk to you."

He saw the look of surprise on Bianca's face as she heard bits and pieces of his end of the conversation, but he continued talking.

"I'm having a very hard time ... with ... everything. That's why I called you. That's why I want to see you. I'll never see my kids again. Rafael is gone. I don't know where. I think maybe Venezuela. He has family there. I thought I had a shot, but he beat me in court. He lied about me. He got other people to lie about me. He made that detective who questioned me back on Long Island say that I was drinking while he was there. I told you I had drunk a bottle of wine and then I fell asleep and then he rang the doorbell. Oh, God!"

"Do you have anyone else you can talk to?"

"No."

"Your parents? The rest of your family? The people you work with?"

"I told you I don't talk to anybody, including my family. They blame me for losing my children. They believe what that bastard said about me being an unfit mother and drinking and taking pills. And my job? I quit last week. I get such headaches. I can't concentrate. What's the point of anything? I'm a throwaway woman. I've served my purpose; now I'm ready for the trash heap."

"Don't think that way. You are valuable and ... there's always a point."

"Really? Who needs me? Who cares about me? My family is disgusted with me. My children are going to forget I ever existed, or worse. He'll probably tell them I didn't love them. You have your life ... your wife and kids. Are you going to take care of me? That's a big responsibility. I don't want you to do that. I didn't want to be an anchor back then, and I'm not going to be one now."

"That's not going to happen. Listen: I'll leave the conference early. I'll stay there only two days. That's all I really need. Are you still in Jersey? I'll go straight from ... I'll fly down to Atlantic City. I'll be at your house two days from now. I'll do anything I can to help you. I want to see you ... to talk to you. Okay?"

"Thank you for saying that, but I think this will probably be our last conversation. I don't see the point anymore, but I want you to know you always made me happy. I'm glad things are working out for you."

"You always made me happy." Then, looking at Bianca, who was sitting frozen on the seat of the limousine next to him, he said, "You never know what's going to happen. Don't tell me it's going to be our last conversation. That sounds very bad. Things can look grim, and then they get better. Be hopeful."

"There is no hope because I have no life."

"Don't say that. You're young ... like me ... we're both young. You have so many years ahead of you to ... for your life to improve."

"That's part of the problem: too many years left to live. Each minute I'm awake is torture. I sleep a lot, but even then ... my dreams are ... terrible."

"I understand. I *will* be there. Things will improve."

"You don't know that. I'm glad I have a way out. Good-bye, Daniel."

The line went dead. After looking at Bianca for a few seconds, Daniel dialed the number again, but it rang and rang ...

Bianca said she was not jealous, but she was upset that Daniel had not told her that he had been speaking to Maria over the years. He told her that he felt a connection to Maria, but not *that* kind of connection. She was a link, a vital tie to whom he had once been and to whom he might have become. At this point in his life, Maria was like a childhood friend, but more than that. As he held Bianca's hand, grateful that she was a loving, understanding wife and companion and a wonderful mother to their four children, he attempted to find the words to reassure her. She said she did not need reassurance ... that she trusted him and that she would not mind his visiting Maria, but she wondered why he had not told her about his conversations with his former girlfriend.

"It's ... I guess I was projecting. I would have been upset if I knew you were talking to a former boyfriend. It's not that I think you would be unfaithful to me. I know you wouldn't. It's just ... when a person thinks about someone from the past, it's natural, I think, to picture how things were back then. Younger, full of hope, so many great plans. I guess I would worry whether you'd feel your life could have been better with someone else."

"Is that what you think?" she asked. "We've had ten great years together. We have four terrific kids. You work hard. You're always there for us ... I still love you as much as you ... you know ... as at the time we first fell in love. Do you wish your life was different? That you had stayed with her?"

"Different? Yes ... sometimes. With her? I'll tell you this: if I had not gotten involved ... had not been pulled into that life, she and I would have stayed together and I would not have met you. I imagine I would have been happy with Maria, but that doesn't mean I regret one second of my life with you."

"So, it's sort of like which door you open? In your case, both choices would've been good? It just worked out that you opened the door with me behind it? Is that it?"

After he thought for a few seconds, Daniel said, "Yes, but that's what happens in everybody's life. It's not as if you or I or anyone can see the future or that you and I were destined to be together. That's not real life. My life was one way when I was with Maria ... one ... rendition of it. Your life was one way ... one version before you knew me. I chose you ... you chose me. We're lucky because we've had a good life together. I love you. I'm grateful that I opened your door."

"I understand, but I don't see it that way. Before I met you, I didn't have a life. I mean I *had* a life, of course, but I wasn't happy. I was never complete. I know we *were* destined to be together and that we'll be together for life. You're my own true love, just like from the song."

Daniel put his arms around Bianca and kissed her as he had when he first knew that he loved her. Then he held her close to him and kissed her neck. When he pulled away, she said, "If this dress didn't wrinkle so easy I'd say let's do it right now on the back seat of this car."

*****

Daniel kept his promise. Two days later, he and Bianca separated, she to board her flight to Newark, he to fly to Atlantic City Airport. When he had called Maria from the hotel in Chicago during the conference, after she had given him her address, she said she was feeling "wretched." He called her a dozen more times, but her phone rang and rang and did not go to voicemail.

When he arrived at Maria's bungalow near the sea, he jumped out, paid the taxi driver, and knocked on the door. Nothing. He looked in the windows. The interior of the house was dark. The street was deserted except for an old, dented black Volkswagen parked in front of the house. He walked to the back and sat on a split wooden chair, gazing at the chilly, choppy water. The pounding surf reminded him of summer days at Brighton Beach when he was a boy. He thought about swimming and the sound of seagulls.

An hour later, as afternoon turned into cold early evening, he walked to the front and knocked again. No answer. The house was dark. He called Maria's phone. Again, it rang and rang. He called the cab company that he had used on the ride from the airport. The driver took him to a nearby hotel. He spoke to Bianca from the hotel restaurant, telling her he did not know what to do.

"Oh, Daniel, you always know what to do. Do what you think."

"I'll try again tomorrow."

The next morning, after calling Maria's phone several more times and then knocking on her door, he turned the doorknob. The door was unlocked. The tiny bungalow was neat, but several empty medicine containers littered the floor. He used his phone to Google the nearest hospital. It was Long Beach Island Medical Center. He called to ask whether a Maria Reyes or Maria Rosato was a patient. He was told no. He asked whether there were any other hospitals nearby to which an emergency patient might be taken. The receptionist said that the next nearest one was 25 miles away, too far to be taken for an emergency.

He called for a taxi and asked to be taken to that nearby hospital. It took close to an hour to find someone at the hospital who would help him. When he said that he was Maria's cousin, a man in the hospital records department agreed to check. Sitting at his desk and looking into a computer monitor, the man told

Daniel that a Maria Reyes, age 34, had been treated and released. Then, looking concerned, the man turned to Daniel and said, "You know, without the patient's permission, I can't release any medical information to you. I'll be right back. Stay here." As he stood up, he nudged the monitor so that it partially faced Daniel. Then he exited the room, closing the door behind him. Daniel scanned the screen. Then he left the room and took a taxi back to Maria's bungalow.

The doors of the old Volkswagen parked in front of the bungalow were unlocked. He searched, checking the floor, the glove box, under the seats. According to the hospital report, a passer-by had found Maria here, unconscious. Daniel found only an open half-filled bottle of water.

In the house, Daniel searched her medicine cabinet, under her bed, and her garbage pail, coming up empty in each place he looked. He knew it did not matter. He had seen the medical report. Then he removed his shoes and lay down on her bed. He sobbed and took a deep breath as he wondered where he had been and what he had had been doing when she did what she had done. Then he thought about one of their last times together; it had been a week or so before their argument about the diamond and emerald necklace. He had been sipping coffee, lost in thought, when he realized that Maria had said something.

"I asked you whether you ever think about when we were first together, when we were happy and didn't have a care in the world."

"I do. Not all the time, but I do. Does it matter?"

Now, as he lay on Maria's bed in the cottage, Daniel thought about what they had lost. So much in his life had changed. His path had been so different from what he had once imagined it would be. He took comfort in the fact that, no matter how hard one may plan, life, like a river, changes course according to outside events and accidents that can be neither predicted nor prevented.

He concentrated and remembered more of that conversation with Maria in the apartment so many years before. After he had asked, "Does it matter?" he had slowly stood up, shuffled to the sink, and poured out the remains of his coffee. Then, looking into the cup as if he had hoped to find answers there, he had washed and rinsed it and placed it on the drain board. Then he had looked at Maria, waiting for her to resume.

"Of course it matters. I matter ... you matter. I don't ... I don't understand what happened. We were happy. I thought you were happy. Everything changed. Can't it change back? Doesn't our relationship matter?"

"It matters, but things happen," he had whispered.

"What are you doing? Are you going? Come back here, please."

"I don't have answers for you, Maria, or for myself ... not now."

"But, what's going to happen?" she asked.

"I can't tell you now. Please be patient."

"There have to be answers."

"I ... I don't know, Maria. I'm sorry."

"Please, Daniel ... Do something before it's too late for us."

Her words had been rasping background noises as he had walked out of the apartment that day.

*****

When Daniel returned home, Bianca did not ask.

Each time during the next week that he called Maria's phone, it rang and rang. He tried to imagine where she was and what she was doing. Was she ignoring the ringing? Was she in a hospital? He wondered whether she had acted a second time on what Daniel now knew she had been implying when she had said, "I don't see the point anymore. This will probably be our last conversation." He felt powerless and angry that he had not been with her then.

Hyman Shaw, the private investigator, reported that the trail was cold, dead, saying, "That Volkswagen is registered to her. I went down there and checked it out. It's still there. The house is still empty. She owes back rent. I'm sorry. I can't find her. It's as if she stopped existing ... as if she's been erased."

Daniel mourned. He tried to imagine Maria's unhappiness, her sense of hopelessness, the cold, dead world that she seemed to have inhabited for ... he did not know how many years. He felt her loneliness and despair. He brought to mind a picture of her, an image of how she had looked the last time he had seen her. When had that been? How many years? Ten? Eleven? She had been a vibrant, beautiful, intelligent woman and a loving soul. He knew she would be happy and glowing now if he had done as she wished—lived a normal life with her. Maria had paid the price for his disastrous choices. What had happened to her was the consequence of his actions, starting from the day he asked Dominic to arrange for him to work at the social club. She had warned him, but, by that time, he had begun to enjoy the atmosphere of that place and believed that he fit in there. Everything that he had done during those years to consolidate his connection to those men and enhance his position in the organization and then to enrich himself had set in motion the series of consequences that led to Maria's eventual empty, lonely, abject existence. Daniel knew that, more than anyone else, he had caused Maria to become what she had called a throwaway woman.

Drowning in remorse and mourning the lost opportunities, he asked himself, *If she no longer exists, does that mean that our time together has also been erased? That none of it happened?*

285

His own good fortune in life weighed heavily on him. All that had been joyful and pleasurable now oppressed him. When he looked at Bianca and his happy children and his lovely home with its view of Central Park and his bright, cheery office, he was assailed by guilt. He remembered when Maria had said, "Nobody should ever die alone."

One day, Bianca said to him, "Daniel, I love you. I'm alive ... I'm right here. She's not."

He thought, *But where am I?*

He found it odd, incongruous, unbelievable that he was engaged in the tasks of his life as if nothing had changed. Even though everything looked the same as it always had, the world, life, even the way food tasted was different. It had to be different—otherwise, what was the point? If it did not matter that a life had crumbled, ended, evaporated, did that mean it had served no purpose?

One day, when Daniel called Maria's phone, instead of it ringing over and over again, he heard a message saying that the number was no longer in use. At that point, he forced his grief far into the recesses of his mind and attempted to enjoy Bianca and his children and his work as he once had.

Months later, when he was leaving the apartment to meet with a business group in the old neighborhood, Bianca asked him to bring home some loaves of freshly baked bread from Ambrosino's. They often said that nobody could make bread, cookies, cakes, and Italian "sweets" that smelled as good and tasted as delicious as the ones made by Lou Ambrosino. "It must be the Brooklyn water," they would say with a smile.

Later that day, after he had concluded his business, he drove to the apartment building on whose roof he and Dominic had played so many years before, the one on which Dominic had intended to ambush Jimmy Tripelli. As he walked to the building, he avoided looking at or peering into the adjacent alleyway which was the bloody birthplace of the nightmares and agonizing thoughts that had haunted him for so many years. It was also the starting point of his long, tortuous journey from what had been a congenial, uneventful life of conventional ups and downs to ... how he had lived since then.

As he unhurriedly walked up the stairway to the roof, he ran his hands along the smooth, painted cinderblock walls. At the top of the stairs, he opened the door and made his way to the edge of the roof, where he had a clear view of the neighborhood and, a short distance away, the Verrazano Bridge. He turned toward 86th Street, where the Huntington Social Club had been located. Then he looked in the direction where, in the distance, he imagined Lincoln High School was, and then, to the left a few miles further from there, Ocean Avenue and the apartment that he had shared with Maria. He closed his eyes and remembered and, again, he wondered where she was and *whether* she still was. If, as he feared, as he knew, she had taken her life, who had found her and who had arranged for her funeral? Then he became anxious at the thought that, perhaps, no one had found her because she had no one, because no one missed her. After a while, he pushed away the crushing waves of anguish and regret that threatened to overpower him. Then, as he recited his version of a silent prayer of supplication to whatever power might be listening, he asked forgiveness for ... for more transgressions and poor choices and missed opportunities than he could verbalize. He sobbed. Then he wiped his eyes.

He turned again and looked to the north, past Brooklyn, beyond the East River to the shimmering towers of Manhattan, where his office was and the home that he shared with his wife and children.

He looked up and gazed with wonder at the cold inky-black star-studded sky. Again, as he had on his first night in the encampment in the woods in West Virginia, he hoped against hope that Maria was looking at the same glimmering sky. He shook his head and rubbed his eyes.

It was late. He had to leave. Bianca and his children were waiting for him. But first, he had to go to Ambrosino's to buy bread.

The End

Please review this book on amazon.com

Made in the USA
Columbia, SC
16 June 2017